A NORN IN BLOOM

JENNIFER ANGLADE DAHLBERG

A Norn in Bloom
Jennifer Anglade Dahlberg
ISBN 978-1-77342-129-2

Editing: Larissa Melo Pientowski
Cover Design & Interior Layout:
    Saul Bottcher, *IndieBookLauncher.com*

Also Available
Ebook, ISBN 978-1-77342-128-5

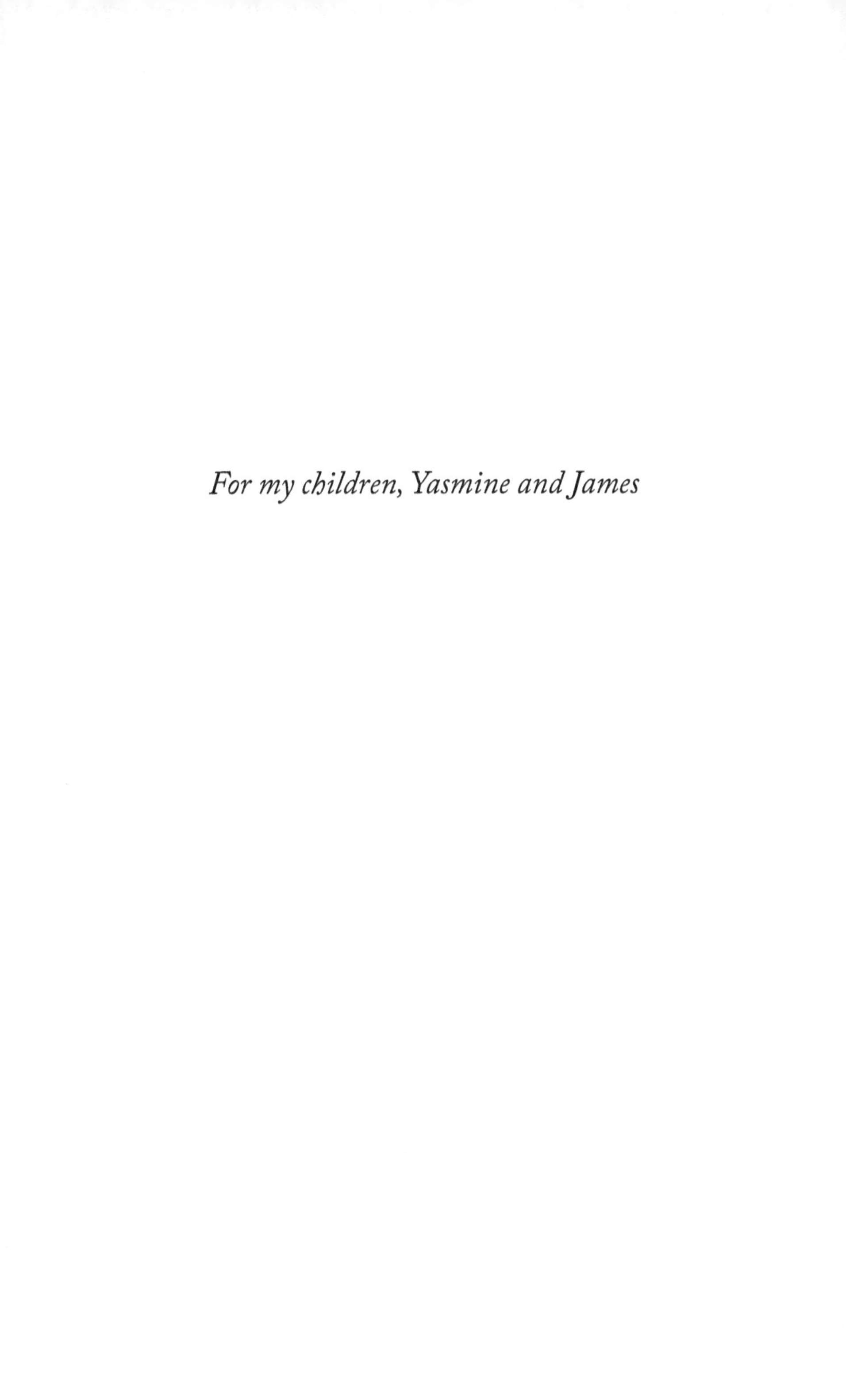

For my children, Yasmine and James

There stands an ash called Yggdrasil
A mighty tree showered in white hail
From there come the dews that fall in the valleys
It stands evergreen above Urd's Well

From there come maidens, very wise
Three from the lake that lies beneath the pole
One is called Urd, she's the weaver of faith
Another, Verdandi, who is forever present
Skuld is the third, the future lives within her
Together they carve into the tree
The lives and destinies of children, men and gods

—"The Prophecy of the Seeress," *Poetic Edda*

1

ZOË

"I don't understand why she would put that giant chess set on her front lawn," Ulla remarked.

"As if that big white house didn't stand out enough already!" Britta said.

"It's such an eyesore!" Ulla added.

"And *so* American . . ." Britta sneered, nailing the ultimate put-down.

They prattled on and on, impervious to the line snaking around the checkout counter at Holmgren's, the only supermarket on the tiny island of Nornö that had been in my family for generations. Nevertheless, I had a soft spot for Britta. She was a local like my maternal grandmother, Mormor Agnes, and hearing her gossip about the newly built house—a jaw-dropping, New England-style villa that looked more like a country club than a home—was an encouraging sign. Widowed since the previous winter, Britta finally seemed to be emerging from her grief. Hope was welcome in these parts, since Nornö often felt like an island of forlorn women—women whose men had died, disappeared, or never been around to begin with, as was the case with my father.

After scanning Britta's items—jars of herring, potatoes, smoked salmon, and cartons of strawberries—I watched her bend to pack the groceries into a faded red-and-black rolling bag. She'd been using that same carrier for as long as I could remember.

"Can I help you load?" I asked.

"No, *lilla gumman.* Finish taking care of these people"—she looked up and gestured to the pack of customers— "so you can close up and enjoy *Midsommarafton.*"

Bless Britta and her wishful thinking, but there'd be no partying for me on Midsummer's Eve. The big holiday celebrating the longest day of the year was the start of peak tourist season and our busiest day at Holmgren's. In other words, I would work hard so other people could relax and enjoy themselves. Ferryboats from Stockholm and the closest mainland harbor in Stavsnäs had been dropping off visitors to Nornö all morning. Young women wore flowy dresses and flower crowns; guys donned linen button-downs, Ray-Bans, and Panama hats. The summer people renting homes or opening their own cottages had also begun to arrive for their four, five, or six-week breaks, transforming Nornö from an island of ninety-four year-round residents to a summer sanctuary of five hundred. They would all gather in Nornö's open meadow to dance and sing in a few hours, flanked by the island's best-known relics.

For years, I had done the reverse journey in much gloomier conditions: to attend school on the mainland, since Nornö had no educational facilities beyond elementary school. Since I was a precocious only child, Mormor Agnes had enrolled me at the village primary school a year early, making me the youngest in my class and an easy target for teasing, especially from Douglas Bohlander, the only other kid in Nornö in my grade. We had ridden the boat back and forth to Stavnäs Harbor from junior high until we graduated from Djurö Gymnasium a few weeks ago. Despite being on the mainland, Djurö needed extra funding and tougher teachers, given that my classmates were more interested in cigarettes and cutting class than studying. I felt little connection to anyone, but one upside to my pathetic social life was that I graduated at the top of my class and could have easily gained a spot at a prominent university in Uppsala or Lund. Still, I told anyone who bothered to ask that I was undecided about my future. But that was a lie. Usually so honest and straitlaced, I felt this weird satisfaction at keeping something to myself. It was empowering, the secret knowledge that once summer was over, I would finally embark on the mission that had consumed me for the past year.

However, I still had to get through this overhyped holiday. Midsummer was notorious for its overflowing light and fleeting warmth. Sometimes it was only ten degrees warmer than Christmas Eve, but a deep-rooted Swedish proverb proclaimed there was no such thing as bad weather, only bad clothes. I had spent too many Midsummers swathed in layers, preparing for every meteorological possibility: a white linen dress paired with leggings, a down jacket, and rubber boots. Although the forecast predicted warmth and sun this year, I still couldn't find the merriment Midsummer sparked in others, no matter how hard I tried. Maybe it was because I inhabited that fuzzy, in-between spot, the overlapping genes in my DNA at odds with each other. For all the fun and games, once Midsummer was over, the cycle shifted and nightfall came earlier, day-by-day, minute-by-minute, until the visitors dwindled and Nornö was submerged in darkness again.

My mother, Linn, usually moody and unpredictable, was always euphoric on Midsummer. She would typically wake me up first thing in the morning, the blazing sunlight piercing through my window, and bribe me with breakfast in bed. Then, after tea and toast, we would spend a few hours making crowns with the flowers Linn had collected around the island. Cornflower, lady's-mantle, bluebonnet, Galium, cow parsley, poppy, and daisies lined Mormor's dining table. Linn's crown was always perfect, a circle of evenly spaced, color-coordinated petals, while mine was always a little cockeyed—too much wire and greenery, not enough blooms—with bits and pieces lost while hopping around the maypole.

"Now, you have to solve something once and for all. Who looks better—him or me?"

The sudden, non-store-related question pulled me from my thoughts. A guy dressed in a cloak, fake gray beard, and platinum-blond wig pointed to his friend, another oddball covered in a bloody and bruised zombie mask.

"Okay, how about you both look scary?" I said, chuckling. It wasn't the first time people had shown up in Holmgren's in bizarre Middle-earth costumes. They belonged to a fandom that had grown after Netflix recorded a fantasy series on Nornö a few years ago.

"Oh no. You have to decide," Platinum Wig insisted.

"Seriously, it's a tie! Besides, I was an extra in *Between the Seas,* so I know what I'm talking about."

"Are you kidding?"

"Nope."

"Which episode?"

"Season three, episode four. But I was so done up, I'm unrecognizable," I said, ringing up their two cans of General *snus.*

"So, I guess your costume was better than ours," Platinum Wig laughed.

I smiled. "Pretty much."

The Netflix film crew had only stayed two weeks, but their presence had been the most exciting thing in Nornö in all my eighteen years. The island, which was tucked away in the outer banks of the Stockholm archipelago, was only about one mile long and half a mile wide. It probably would have gotten lost amidst the other thirty thousand islands, skerries, and rocks dotting the seascape, if not for one spectacular piece of history from the Viking Age: runestones. Three towering columns stood in the middle of a dry patch near the lush, green meadow where Midsummer celebrations took place. Like gray ghosts rising from the depths of the earth, the runestones stood over twelve feet tall, inscribed with characters from the runic alphabet. Runestones were usually memorials to dead men or people who had committed good deeds and were raised by their villages or clans as tributes. But the seventh-century runestones on our little island honored the goddesses of fate in Norse mythology, collectively known as the *Nornir*, hence the area's name: *Norn ö*. The Island of the Norns.

The three runestones had certainly saved Nornö from obscurity—not to mention total decline—since people first started coming to see them in the 1800s. In the beginning, a tavern opened, and then a small bed-and-breakfast. Stalls selling food delivered every other day from Stockholm also cropped up. Mormor Agnes's paternal grandfather, Nils, had been one of those stallkeepers, and he started Holmgren's in 1925 by putting up stakes in the same stucco building across the harbor where I now stood. Since Holmgren's was the only store in the village of its kind, Nils had relished his status as a big fish in a small pond. I learned early on that whatever material trappings we possessed today were thanks to Nils. Aside from working in his passed-down store, I was the fourth-generation Holmgren to live in the comfortable, yellow-and-white gingerbread house he built.

What would our patriarch think if he could see what

remained of the Holmgrens today, the lopsided trio of Agnes, Linn, and me? Judging from the solemn, black-and-white family photos that showed Nils's slicked-back hair and stern expression, he would have turned in his grave when Linn got pregnant at nineteen and gave birth to a half Black child. It was the type of skeleton in the closet a pious Lutheran like Nils could never imagine. Mormor said that Nornö had been the foundation of his life, and that he'd disapproved of anything that upset its long-established social order.

Well, Linn's surprise pregnancy and my arrival had shattered that social order completely, opening the door for everyone to gossip about how hard the mighty Holmgrens had fallen.

2

LINN

Thinking back to how self-involved I'd been at eighteen, I shouldn't have been too surprised when Zoë refused, for the first time, to get up early and make the flower crowns with me. I entered her room at five o'clock in the morning and stood beside her bed, staring down as though she were a newborn in a crib again, when I couldn't believe the little lump lying on her back had sprouted from my body. Now, Zoë was sprawled on her stomach, mouth open, left cheek on the pillow, hand cradling the iPhone she had fallen asleep with like a stuffed animal.

I placed a hand on her shoulder and gently rocked her. "Zoë," I whispered in a singsong voice. "It's *Midsommarafton.* Time to get up for our special tradition."

She moaned faintly, a hopeful sign she was returning to the land of the living.

"The weather's supposed to be warm and sunny today," I continued. "We can have breakfast outside. I prepared your favorite: fresh bread and Nutella." I usually discouraged such sweet, empty calories first thing in the morning, but one was allowed to indulge on Midsummer.

But that didn't tempt her. She turned toward the wall, giving me a view of her back (in an old Justin Bieber concert T-shirt), and hugged her knees.

Maybe she hadn't heard correctly, so I tried again. "I know it's early, but this is the only time we have to make the crowns.

I got some pretty purple bellflowers but no baby's breath. I know you think they look tacky."

Zoë jerked up from her pillow suddenly and barked, "Please just leave me alone! I'm tired and want to sleep!"

Caught off guard, I froze, preparing a snippy comeback. *Don't speak to me like that. Stop acting like a spoiled brat.* Instead, I took a deep breath and tiptoed out of her room. I suppose this was what payback looked like. At least she had said *please*.

I should have anticipated Zoë would grow bored of our little tradition. Most Midsummer crowns were created at a more decent hour of the day, in a festive setting with family and friends, alongside a glass of champagne or Aperol Spritz. But our ritual of capturing the Midsummer spirit was invented out of necessity to coordinate with the 8:00 a.m. ferry arriving from Stockholm. We would delude ourselves for a few hours, pretending to be free and easy, and it was precisely when we started to get comfortable that we'd have to put everything away because Duty Called. We worked when our customers were off—they counted on us for those last-minute buys, and Holmgren's needed the business.

Although I couldn't blame Zoë for finally bailing on me, I was still disappointed by her rejection. For years, wreath making had been our special mother-daughter tradition, one of the few activities we could do together without arguing. But perhaps the time had come to move on.

I let Zoë sleep in and stayed out of her way at the store later. I couldn't deal with her sour demeanor, especially since I didn't feel I had done anything to provoke it. It was ironic: when Zoë was a child and I barely an adult, I had silently wished for the day when she would be older and less clingy. Becoming a mom a few months shy of my twentieth birthday had upended all my plans, and I'd been impatient for the next phase. Each of her developmental milestones—walking, talking, reading, riding a bike—would make her more independent and bring me closer to the beginning of my own life, the one I had fantasized about before Zoë. My mother, Agnes, who was fond of using idioms to explain life's mysteries, often said, "The days are long, but the years are short." I was an accidental mother; my days with a fussy baby were time-consuming and tedious. But nowadays, with an eighteen-year-old who had changed—seemingly overnight—from good-natured and willing to sullen and difficult, I finally understood Agnes's message. Before, I had been so full of conflicting emotions and been scarcely more than a child myself, unable to see the magic within the monotony. I'd never predicted Zoë would grow up and be sassy enough to give me a taste of my own medicine.

I suppose you could say I had been rebellious my whole life, so what right did I have to complain? Agnes told me I had been that nosy kid who went up to customers at Holmgren's, grilling them about items in their cart or what they were making for dinner. She said no matter how annoying or pushy I came across, I was difficult to resist. People paid me compliments as a toddler, commenting on my big blue eyes and skin that turned slightly olive in the summer, but my hair was what really set me apart. Unlike most Swedish babies, who were usually born with imperceptible strands of white fluff, I arrived with tufts of flaxen curls circling my head, as though a beautician had readied me in the womb.

More experienced mothers told Agnes I would shed my mane as the months went by, but the growth continued, and by the time I was three, it was wavy and past my shoulders. In pictures from those days, I looked like I was wearing a wig, since my thick head of hair was inconsistent with my button nose and thin lips. One Sunday, I skipped into the kitchen, where Agnes and my father, Thomas, were enjoying a *fika*, clutching what, according to my mother, appeared to be a Barbie doll's head. However, when her eyes traveled from my tiny fist to my face, she realized I had cut off a chunk of hair. The strands weren't even; some were by my chin and others were closer to my ear, but it didn't matter. To fix the disaster, Agnes would have to give me bangs, a mullet, or a short bob. Bangs won out, but when she asked me why I had done it— were the other girls jealous of my thick tresses?—I shook my head and replied, "No. The boys said I couldn't play with them because my hair was so long. I really wanted to be in their crew, so I cut it." I can't recall the physical act of inserting my little fingers into the scissors and chopping off fistfuls of hair, but I do remember feeling victorious after doing something thrilling and unexpected.

Now, back at home, I slipped into my Midsummer dress, a yellow crochet number I had purchased online. As I palmed the intricate threading, I congratulated myself for buying it early; it was sold out now. Looking in the mirror of my childhood bedroom, I admired how the neckline dipped into a *V*, showcasing my tanned chest and a little cleavage. The hem stopped below the knee, giving it a naughty but nice effect. The practical clothes I had worn to Holmgren's that morning were piled in front of my bed, and I stepped over them to grab a pair of nude wedges. Or would sneakers be more fun with the dress? Sneakers were the sensible choice, but I wore boots or sneakers all year long; Midsummer's Eve was a day to look pretty. I put on the wedges, careful not to buckle them too tightly around the ankles, and grabbed a straw bag from a row of hooks on my wall. After packing my wallet, makeup case, denim jacket, and scarf, I threw in a pair of threadbare

Superga sneakers. Old habits die hard when you've spent your entire life on a rugged island in the archipelago.

I tottered down the stairs to the veranda, using the railing for support. My father had installed a glass enclosure with sliding doors, so we would never have to worry about the weather. Agnes had objected, afraid it would feel claustrophobic, but when the heaters allowed us to extend the outdoor season, she stopped protesting. It had become my favorite part of the whole house, especially during the winter months. I liked to sit back in one of the wicker chairs late at night, under a sheepskin throw, with a glass of red wine and scented candles, staring into the darkness and tuning everything out.

My great-grandfather Nils had secured a desirable spot for the Holmgrens on almost an acre of land. Our plot was flat, enabling us to follow the lawn to the sea. As a safety precaution, I—and then Zoë—had run around wearing life vests until we were five and learned to swim properly. Two boats could be docked on either side of our narrow pier, but my father's Bertram had long been sold, and we only kept a small motorboat for trips to Stavsnäs. The boathouse stored fenders, lines, fishing rods, and an assortment of flotation devices from the fifties to the present day. The sauna was also in the boathouse, but we rarely used it and I wondered if it was still functional.

Despite the ravages of time, we received phone calls every summer, inquiring if we wanted to sell. Postcards from realtors inundated our mailbox, promising a record price for our home. Agnes merely snickered and chucked them in the garbage. If she moved, where on Earth would she go? Plus, we all knew whoever bought our old house would tear it down. It hadn't been renovated in decades and needed a total overhaul to be habitable. We shared a lifetime of knowledge of all its kinks and glitches, but a newcomer would think it was in shambles. One only had to look at Karin Eklund for proof.

Speculators had circled like vultures when the eighty-nine-year-old woman died in her sleep two years ago, leaving no husband or children. Her property was also in a prized location, on a bluff overlooking the bay, and everyone had wondered to whom she'd bequeathed the house in her will. I had been as surprised as everyone else to learn Karin had left it to a distant cousin half her age who lived in New York City. And if that weren't enough, this new "heiress" was a former model who hadn't lived in Sweden since she was eighteen. The outrage that followed was astounding, with the gossipmongers implying Karin Eklund didn't have the right to leave her home to whomever she wished. Things went from bad to worse when this model relative demolished Karin's traditional red cottage and laid the foundation for an abode four times its size. Having already been on the receiving end of their vicious chatter, I had firsthand experience with how meddlesome Nornö locals could be. Whenever they grumbled about it, I bit my tongue, refusing to partake in the character assassination of someone I had never met. Eighteen months later, the grand house was finally complete, and the Nornö rumor mill was in overdrive with guesses as to when the new owner would grace us with her presence.

As I stared out through the veranda's glass panels to the vastness of the Baltic Sea, which had transformed from its usual pewter gray to a glistening denim blue, it wasn't difficult to guess why Karin Eklund's long-lost cousin had succumbed to the sublime beauty of the archipelago. Small islands and boulders in the distance. Sailboats drifting by. The Waxholmsbolaget ferries cruising in both directions. Stopping to savor the natural beauty I usually took for granted always made me nostalgic. Memories of a simpler era, when I knew nothing besides the dimensions of Nornö, became more vivid: the nooks and crannies unearthed on scavenger hunts or by playing hide-and-seek, my whole world consisting of running in and out of neighbors' houses and building sandcastles on the beach. When I'd blissfully dove into the water, I'd been immune to the cold sea.

If I squinted, I could almost see my father puttering away at his Bertram. He suffered a heart attack nine summers ago while taking his morning swim and drowned. When he didn't return to the house for breakfast, Agnes came down to the dock and found his mottled terry bathrobe and clogs abandoned. She made out something floating in the distance and knew it was too late. We buried my father in Nornö's little cemetery, next to all the other Holmgrens, even though his last name at birth was Gustafsson. But my father had been an evolved, enlightened man, and Agnes was a proud bearer of her family legacy. She'd never wanted to change her name, so my father had adopted it and passed it down to me. His final resting place on the island gave me solace, as though I could feel his love and support from the grave.

I exhaled, erasing the memory, and picked up one of the flower crowns from the dining table. I had created them earlier that morning, determined not to let Zoë's tantrum spoil my day, even though her Nutella sandwich had sat untouched across the table, a reminder of her brush-off. My flower-foraging duties had gotten much easier once I convinced Agnes to stock ready-made bouquets at the store. Nornö's climate wasn't suited to growing anything besides wildflowers. The cultivated flowers blooming in people's yards were the product of meticulous care; it ached to pluck them from the ground. This year, I had chosen a pastel color scheme, diffused purples, pinks, and yellows interlaced with white waxflowers and small eucalyptus leaves.

I walked to the antique mirror above the chalky-white, Gustavian sideboard where Agnes usually laid out the Christmas Eve buffet and placed the Midsummer crown on my head, straightening the angle of the blooms so that the ripest, plumpest flowers had pride of place. Next, I fluffed up my hair; it was still full but had lost some of its luster from too much dyeing and sun damage. My current hue was a buttery yellow, and I thought it set off the bubblegum colors of the flowers rather well. Finally, I rummaged through the drawer for a plastic bag and placed the other wreath inside, tying the two handles in a knot to keep the petals fresh and secure. I put it carefully inside my straw tote—just in case Zoë might want to wear it later.

3

ZOË

I reached the Midsummer clearing just as the procession wormed its way toward the center of the field, led by marchers in traditional folk costumes. Kurt Bohlander, Nornö's resident carpenter, solemnly stood front and center as he held the Swedish flag. Kurt had traded his standard, multipocketed work pants for yellow breeches, tights, a white linen shirt, and a black vest trimmed with red. He was followed by two men clad in similar garments, pressing melodies in and out of squeaky accordions. Ladies in long, colorful skirts and embellished bodices rounded out the ensemble, gliding their arms, sleeves billowing, across violins in a classic rendition of "Rättvikarnas Gånglåt." There were dozens of local and visiting participants behind this little orchestra, balancing the massive maypole on their shoulders. It was a group effort; many had been at it since nine in the morning, gathering in the old schoolyard to decorate the wooden beams with leaves, branches, and wildflowers. They marched to the middle of the field at an unhurried but well-coordinated pace. Kurt and the musicians fanned to the sides, but the maypole bearers stopped in front of a hole dug in the ground. They lowered the pole into the opening, using ropes and forked wooden rods to keep it steady. Once the maypole was straight and secure, rising in the sky like a sacred tree—or a creepy phallic symbol—the crowd rejoiced and applauded.

I leaned against a fence, breathing in the air awash with the candied fragrance of Red Pixie lilacs and watching the old-timers waltz in pairs around the maypole. It was a dance I used to perform with Morfar Thomas, standing on my tiptoes as we flitted across the grass. Morfar had always called me *lillgammal,* an "old soul," since I preferred the elegance of traditional folk dances to the silliness of hopping around to "The Little Frogs." When Kurt asked the crowd to give three cheers for *sommartiden,* I mouthed the hip-hip-hoorays, checking the faces of the public for my mother. Mormor had a backache and skipped the raising of the maypole, choosing to go home and prepare an early dinner. A good idea, considering the circus this holiday had become. More and more people traveled to the archipelago every year, turning Stockholm into a ghost town on Midsummer weekend. The popular islands and boat transportation companies had succeeded in marketing the archipelago as a foolproof way to usher in the sunny season, especially if you didn't have a place of your own. It was a catch-22: Nornö depended on the traffic, but I knew the mess the partying would bring. Bottles of rosé and cans of beer on the beaches. Cigarette buds and dried-up packets of tobacco along the paths. Flammable, disposable barbecue kits in the forest. And last but not least: used-up condoms on the ground. A hot hookup spot was behind the runes, but I thought it sacrilegious to have sex in the presence of the three Norns and downright nasty to leave evidence of it behind.

If the partiers knew the full history of the Norns, they wouldn't be so cavalier. Sagas about the deities Odin, Thor, and Freya abounded, but the Norns, female beings who ruled the destiny of humans and gods, were even more powerful. Legend had it that the Norns were present at the birth of every child to determine the newborn's fate. They were capable of good and evil, and their ruling could not be changed. According to myth, Norns originated from several races; some came from the gods and others from the elves or dwarfs, but not all Norns were created equal. There was a hierarchy, and three Norns soared above the rest, literally and figuratively: the giantesses, Urd, Verdandi, and Skuld, who sat at the root of Yggdrasil, the Tree of Life. They became known as the Greater Norns, watching over the Well of Fate and watering Yggdrasil to make sure its branches did not rot. The three Norns worked together, spinning the threads of life and weaving an intricate cloth for mortals and gods alike. Urd was said to represent the past, Verdandi the present, and Skuld the future. The runestones on Nornö were also said to be cursed. A message at the base of Skuld warned that catastrophe would fall on whoever disturbed or destroyed the stones.

"Hallo, hallo!" Kurt Bohlander hollered, megaphone in hand. He was reserved for most of the year but loved giving orders and directing hundreds of people on Midsummer's Eve. After a few words of welcome in Swedish and English, he invited everyone to sing "Räven raskar över isen." "And if you can't sing, just dance!" he urged.

I loved this number but had trouble listening to it on Midsummer's Eve, since we also sang it at Christmastime. Someone passing by would think I was the ultimate party pooper, hanging back at the fringes of the festivities, refusing to participate in any of the songs or games. I would've rather been lounging on the dock, feeling the sun's rays on my skin, but I needed to see my mother and measure her mood after my blowup that morning. I put a hand to my forehead and looked in both directions. Still no sign of her. It was difficult to find anyone specific in the mayhem of the Fox Dance. At least five separate rings surrounded the maypole. Tourists stopped halfway to take pictures with their phones, disrupting the line flow. People spun in different directions when everyone was supposed to clap and turn in place, knocking over several toddlers.

I was struck by how unabashedly Swedish the entire thing was—centuries-old costumes and floral garlands, popular folk songs, and the cultish maypole worship—which I knew sounded ridiculous. We lived in Sweden, and there was nothing inherently unpleasant about the tradition. Weather permitting, *Midsommarafton* could be the most wonderful day of the year. But as I looked at all the native Swedes prancing around, with their fair skin and varying shades of straight, silky hair, I was reminded of my otherness. How many times had strangers asked me in this exact same field, *Where are you from?* I could only reply with what I had known my entire life: *Here. Nornö. Sweden.*

Then the skepticism on their faces before the inevitable *But where are you* really *from?* Initially, I persisted with the Sweden response but eventually added that my father was American. Black American. *Aha!* That extra morsel of information solved it all.

I had pieced together the clues early on, by looking at myself in the mirror and acknowledging that I didn't look like my mother, Mormor, or other people in Nornö. I rarely saw girls who looked like me in children's books or television shows. I was an exception, an anomaly, a separate breed who knew very little about the duality of my origins. My mother never wanted to talk about my father, other than to say they'd fallen in love when he'd visited Sweden. He was an American soldier who'd died tragically in Afghanistan during the Global War on Terror and never had the chance to meet me. As a kid, I had believed that story. It was a brave, noble explanation that shut nosy people up.

Until the day I fed it to the wrong audience.

Douglas Bohlander and I had all our classes together at the small school in Nornö. As Kurt the Carpenter's son, his family had been on the island for less time than mine, but long enough to have known my grandparents and Linn. Douglas and I were ten years old when we first learned about the Great Migration from Sweden to the U.S., when hundreds of thousands of Swedes fled crop failures and class snobbery in the nineteenth century to find better lives in places like Minneapolis and Chicago. A new teacher, Johanna, had come to the school—the district rotated them every couple of years, since few were willing to stay in Nornö for too long—and she asked my class if any of us had been to the U.S. No one raised their hand. The furthest we had ever traveled was Skåne in the South of Sweden. I felt sorry for Johanna; she was only trying to personalize the lesson, but we were simple island kids who never went anywhere exciting. Still, I was determined not to appear uninteresting and blurted out, "I've never been to America, but my father was American. He came from New York but died fighting in Afghanistan." I made up the New York bit. My mother had never told me where my father came from, but New York and California were the two states every Swede talked about, and I wanted to sound cool. Johanna's eyes lit up, and she asked where in New York. The best I could come up with was, "The city." To that, she responded there was a Swedish Church in Midtown. Midtown meant nothing to me. I only hoped Johanna was impressed enough to stop asking questions for which we had no answers.

I might have gone home and asked my mother for more details about my father regardless of what happened later, but Douglas's childish snooping turned everything upside down, both muddying and clarifying my existence.

"Zoe, hang on!" he cried as I walked home from school.

I turned and saw him running uphill. Douglas was shorter than I was at ten; his camouflage cargo pants and Levi's sweatshirt hung loosely over his skinny frame. He kept his sandy hair in a neat buzz cut, touched up every two weeks by his dad. We were always paired together for group projects and gym exercises. On his own, he was nice enough. But in the presence of other boys, he could be a pain in the neck and found every opportunity to tease me about being the youngest person in our grade.

"What's up?" I asked.

"I'm sorry to hear about your dad," he said, matching my stride.

"Oh, that's okay. Thanks."

"I didn't know he died."

"You didn't?"

"No. It's pretty cool that your father was in the military, though."

"Yeah. I guess." Douglas looked like a toy soldier. I understood why he would have found my dad's military service impressive.

He rubbed his chin. "Must've been a hero. Maybe he even got a medal or something."

"Do they give medals when you're dead?" I asked.

"Yeah, I think so. If he died in action."

"Hmmm." I had never considered that and would ask my mother to investigate.

"Anyway, you should be proud. My parents just say he was

a 'one-night stand,'" he said, copying the snooty accent of adults.

"What?" I asked. "What's a one-night stand?"

Douglas shrugged. "I don't know. That's just what they said."

Linn and Mormor were still at the store when I got home, so I waited until dinner to ask them what a "one-night stand" was. My mother's cheeks became flushed and Mormor stopped cutting the meat on her plate.

"Where did you hear that word?" Mormor asked.

"From Douglas," I replied. "He told me my father was a 'one-night stand.'"

Linn covered her face and began to sniffle.

"Mamma, what's wrong?" I asked. "Are you sad because he's dead?"

Mormor set down her utensils and caressed my mother's shoulder. "Maybe it's time for you to tell Zoë the truth."

I looked from one woman to the other, confused. "The truth? I don't get it. Mamma, what's Mormor talking about?"

Linn took her napkin and blew her nose. I had never seen my mother so shaken. Angry, yes. Sad, often. But this seemed primal, the heavy breathing and manic blinking.

She took my hand and said, "I'm sorry, baby, but I barely knew your father."

"B-b-but you were in love," I stammered. I may have been ten, but I knew what love was. It happened when two people cared so much about each other that they wanted to spend the rest of their lives together. Mormor and Morfar had it until he died. Even Douglas's parents were married. If my father hadn't gotten killed in Afghanistan, he and my mother would have been together. All three of us would've lived under one roof, like a real family.

"It's complicated. I'm so sorry I haven't been honest with you. I was only trying to protect you because you're so young. But I don't want Douglas Bohlander or his stupid parents—"

"Linn!" Mormor scolded. "There's no need to criticize them."

"Why not?" Linn shot back. "That kid is going around spreading stories about our family. He has no right!"

I could see the fire and fury returning to my mother's personality. There was a risk she would fixate on the Bohlanders, and the truth about my father would fall to the wayside. I tried to bring the conversation back to its original topic. "Mamma, please tell me what happened with my father."

She took a sip of red wine. "Remember when we talked about where babies come from?"

I nodded. Linn had explained it to me over the summer when we'd watched an ant colony build a dirt hill. I'd commented on how bugs and babies appeared out of nowhere, which inspired my mother to give a rambling speech about the birds and the bees.

"And I told you it happens when a man and a woman have sex and the man's sperm finds the woman's egg to create a baby."

"Yes," I replied.

"Linn!" Mormor scolded.

She released my hand and her head jerked back to Mormor. "What else am I supposed to say? You told me to be up-front."

"Mamma, please go on!" I pleaded.

"Well, that's what happened with the man who's your father," she said.

"Is that it?" I cried. It sounded so scientific and

unromantic—the opposite of the warm and fuzzy fairy tales and rom-coms I saw in movies.

"Linn, you're making things worse," Mormor said. "Zoë has a right to know as much as you do about her father."

My mother exhaled. "Eleven years ago, I met a guy at a music festival in Hultsfred. He was very interesting and nice, and we just bonded." She shrugged. "I don't know, sometimes you meet someone you connect with, even if you're different and come from two different places. We liked each other and got close one night—"

"Dear God!" Mormor shrieked. "I didn't mean that kind of detail!"

"I don't want Zoë to feel ashamed," Linn said, retaking my hand. "It was just a thing that happened, but we never made plans to keep in touch. He lived in the U.S. I lived in Sweden. We had different ideas about where we wanted to go in our lives. I wanted to see the world. He was joining the military, as I've told you. That was the truth. But I didn't know his last name. When I found out I was pregnant, I had no way of finding or telling him."

"So . . . he's alive?" I asked.

"I don't know," she admitted. "We never saw each other again. He was joining the Army. I'm sure he was sent out after 9/11. Anything could have happened."

I pulled my hand away in anger. "Why did you tell me my father was dead?"

"Oh, baby. He might as well be dead. Even if he were alive, I don't know his full name or where he lives. I made a mistake." Her eyes went distant. "It happened so long ago."

I could scarcely wrap my ten-year-old mind around this monumental news. My world, everything I had been taught and believed to be true, was turned upside down. I had so many questions but lacked the vocabulary to formulate them.

"Was I a mistake?" I asked, confused.

Linn shook her head vehemently, as though discarding the past. "I meant I made a mistake by not telling you the truth."

"Were you happy I was born?"

"Such a silly question!" Mormor exclaimed.

When Linn glanced at Mormor, she seemed childlike and weak, frightening me.

"Mamma," I insisted, "were you happy I was born?"

"You were unexpected, but you've always been loved. Never forget that. You've always been loved."

It was Mormor who broke the silence. But this time, my ten-year-old mind wasn't too young to understand that my mother hadn't answered the question.

"There you are!"

Hearing Linn's voice zapped me back to the present. She pulled me in for a hug, and I responded woodenly at first, arms at my sides, but then I relented and clapped her on the back.

"I've been looking for you too," I said.

"Did you just get here?" I nodded. She tilted her head, scanning my appearance. "Why aren't you dressed up?" she asked, raising an eyebrow.

I looked down at my polo, which was embroidered with the Holmgren's script to the right and the Pripps beer logo on the left. "I came from the store."

"You could have gone home to change like I did."

"That's because you left early. Mormor and I had to close up."

"I appreciate you covering for me, but that's no excuse.

You're a beautiful girl, Zoë. It bothers me when you hide behind those baggy clothes. I bought you that pretty dress from Zara—"

Scoffing, I glanced at my mother's bright yellow dress, which was embarrassingly low-cut. If she shifted with a little too much enthusiasm, a nipple might pop out. "The fabric itched."

"But the weather is so nice. It would have been perfect, especially with . . ." Linn put down her straw tote and reached for something inside a plastic bag. She planted a floral wreath on my head. "This!"

I squirmed as soon as the crown touched my scalp. "I told you I didn't want one."

"Why are you being so negative?" she asked, scrunching up her face.

It was a common refrain, and as usual, I was stunned by the question and her persistence in playing the victim. How could I be anything but negative when my mother constantly criticized my appearance? She assumed something was wrong with me because I didn't crave attention by wearing skimpy clothes. My refusal to primp and preen had become a personal insult to her. My mother put enormous time and energy into her appearance—the hair dye, facials, manicures, online shopping at Zara and H&M—and for what? There was no one in Nornö to impress. She tried desperately to coax me into these frivolous pursuits, even bribing me with extra allowance money if I stopped biting my nails, but to no avail. As a kid, I'd been proud my mother was so young and pretty, but that attention only fed her narcissism. She refused to get her hands dirty at community events like the annual Valborg bonfire, which turned the rest of the island off. She probably hadn't helped decorate the Midsummer pole either, yet she had no problem showing up, looking like a princess and enjoying the spectacle.

"I'm not even staying, so I won't need it." I yanked off the crown and bent to put it back inside her straw bag. As I moved a beige-patterned scarf out of the way, my fingers brushed against a hard surface. A bottle of rosé. Lifting it out of the bag, I said, "You promised you wouldn't get carried away today."

"And I won't!" she responded, her tone mild and no longer accusatory. "That bottle is a gift for Erik. He's having a little get-together on his boat when this ceremony ends."

Erik Lindström owned the Nornö Hotel. Originally from Stockholm, he'd made a lot of money starting a betting website and burned out because of all the pressure, at which point he'd cashed in, escaping to Nornö for a summer to regroup. When the hotel went up for sale five years ago, he bought it. The original owners were elderly, the place had fallen into disrepair, and bookings were low. Erik got it for a song but invested all his savings on renovating and remodeling the decor from dark, ocean liner-inspired lodgings into a light, homey nautical resort. He brought cover bands for the after-sail cocktail hour and arranged a nightclub with Stockholm DJs on Friday and Saturday nights. The old-timers hated it, but the redesigned hotel brought visitors to Nornö in droves. Erik also liked to party, and it hadn't taken long for him and my mother to find each other. Once, I chanced upon her at an after-sail, shimmying on a table with a bottle of rosé in hand. She sashayed, occasionally taking swigs from the flask, while a crowd of bloated, sunburned men and women cheered her on. Near the end of her show, Erik climbed on the tabletop and began gyrating on her. The following day, I'd caught him sneaking out of our guest cottage. I didn't know how often they hooked up, but the odds were higher if alcohol was involved.

"You know what happens when you go down there." I paused, giving my mother time to let the words sink in. "It's like you can't help yourself."

She snatched the wine bottle away. "Zoë, I understand I may have given you reasons to be concerned in the past, but you have nothing to worry about. I promise. I want to have a little fun today. It's so beautiful outside! And who knows how the rest of the summer will turn out? It might rain for weeks, and I'll have to live on today for the rest of the year."

I shook my head and sighed, wondering if other people had conversations like this with their parents. But how many only had a twenty-year age gap with their mother? Most adults had kids after thirty. My mother wasn't even forty and she had an adult daughter. Frankly, the older I got, the more I felt like her peer. Save for the difference in skin color, we had begun to look more alike. After years of baby fat, I had finally shed the fullness on my face, leaving me with the same upturned nose and sculpted cheekbones as her. I could pass for her sister if I dyed my hair blonde and wore tighter clothes.

As much as it pained me to admit, my mother, with her ripped jeans, salty humor, and terrifying knowledge of pop culture, was much cooler than I was. I often felt our mother-daughter roles were reversed. I watched out for Linn to ensure she didn't lose control. It had become instinctual, a hawk-eyed vigilance that often had me on edge. But who could blame me? I never forgot when she picked me up from daycare late and drunk. Even though I'd been only five years old, I still remembered how she'd wobbled into the playroom with glassy eyes and jumbled speech. Thankfully, the other kids had gone home, and I was the last one left with my teacher, coloring at one of the tiny desks. For the first time, I couldn't connect the person in front of me with the woman I called Mamma.

When the teacher had asked if she was all right, my mother had raised her voice, chewing out the innocent woman who had been babysitting me after hours. I'd been taught that talking back to the teacher was strictly forbidden, yet my mother had no qualms about doing so. Shouting with a strange stench on her breath, she reminded me of a dragon. Eventually, the teacher called Mormor to escort us home, and Mamma was sent to Stockholm for a few weeks to "get better."

When she returned, her drinking never got that bad again, at least not in my presence. But that didn't mean it stopped. It simply took on another quality—a slow burn kindled by a glass or two or three of red wine on a winter's day, when her shift at Holmgren's ended. When she fell "asleep" on the couch, I would cuddle up next to her warm body and sniff the peculiar scent wafting from her lips. She would hug me back, saying how much she loved me. Ironically, my mother was her most touchy-feely during those bleary moments.

Now, I considered her earnest expression, the plea in her voice. Maybe this time, things would be different. Maybe she had changed for good. "I can't stop you, but you know how I feel. So please take it easy."

"Why don't you join me? Go home, get changed, and let's meet by the main harbor in half an hour. That way, you can keep an eye on me," she suggested, chuckling.

Was my mother seriously asking me to *party* with her? She still didn't get it. The thought of watching her in action was nauseating. But Linn's unsuspecting smile—her expectant, perfectly made-up face—fractured my protective shell. I was probably overreacting. I may have felt like the Grinch on

Midsummer's Eve, but I didn't have to force it upon everybody else.

"I can't. I have to take Simba out for his walk," I said, using my nine-year-old golden retriever as an excuse. "But if you promise to behave, you can go."

She nodded and hugged me again. This time, I opened my arms and returned her embrace properly.

4

LINN

A week after Midsummer, I rushed out of our gingerbread house onto the path that would take me down to the pier and *Aurora,* the 3:00 p.m. express ferry from Nornö to Stockholm. Today, I had chosen function over fashion and wore running shoes to keep the dirt and pebbles from staining my feet. My wedges were stashed in the Louis Vuitton Neverfull tote I used whenever I visited the capital, as were my makeup bag, toothbrush, underwear, and an extra dress. I was heading to a girls' night out with Alicia Lejonstierna, my best friend from Sigtuna Humanistiska Läroverket—the boarding school my parents had shipped me off to in tenth grade—and I planned to sleep over at Alicia's beautiful apartment in Östermalm.

Alicia was the daughter of a Swedish diplomat. She lived in Kenya, Singapore, and Washington, DC, before her parents decided she needed to experience her country of birth. Auburn-haired, hazel-eyed Alicia once confessed she was drawn to my classically Swedish traits and was fascinated by my life on quaint, rustic Nornö. Alicia's idyllic impressions of small-town Sweden were the product of her favorite Astrid Lindgren book, *The Children of Noisy Village,* a copy of which she'd brought wherever her father was stationed in the world. After spending most of her life abroad, Alicia had hoped I would help her become more Swedish, but little did she know I was determined to become the opposite of my provincial upbringing. Unlike the other girls in our grade, Alicia and I had shown little interest or talent for tennis and soccer, so we bonded over our shared infatuation with fashion, celebrities, and gossip, poring over issues of *VeckoRevyn* and *Se & Hör* magazines. We wanted to experience firsthand every trend we read about, so clubbing in Stockholm and letting loose on ski trips had been our main objectives.

Motherhood hadn't dimmed our enthusiasm, and for the past few days, I'd felt that familiar restlessness coming on—cabin fever from staying on Nornö too long. Archipelago life was suffocating me, and I needed to escape. I longed to surround myself with attractive, well-dressed people in hip restaurants and maybe smoke a pack of cigarettes. I wanted to be waited on for a change, instead of catering to others hand and foot.

I took a shortcut through the meadow, where the Midsummer pole was still standing strong, though the leaves and flowers had begun to brown—casualties of the unusual heatwave. It hadn't rained in over a week, and everyone on Nornö worried about the dry grass. But I would shamelessly trade in a verdant lawn for the hot weather; we earned it after the long, dark winter. As a kid, it had snowed like clockwork on the appropriate months; the crystals reflected light from the sky, making the days brighter. But climate change made the snow-covered landscape I'd grown up with rarer. Instead, brown slush made the ground look like a swamp, splattering everything in its wake. Leaden fog hovered over Nornö, receding into an onyx, starless sky and an unbearable sense of loneliness and isolation. Colorless days bled into each other, and I lacked the will or motivation to do anything besides drag myself down to the village. The winter season was slow, and Holmgren's had the cheerless air of a funeral parlor. Some days, only a handful of people—mostly locals—came in, and I questioned why we bothered opening when closing would have saved us the electricity costs.

But Summertime Linn was different. I was upbeat and full of life, determined to enjoy the hell out of every waking, light-filled moment.

When I passed the runestones, I rubbed the palm of my hand against Skuld, the Norn representing the future, and made a wish. The ritual was supposed to bring good luck, but I'd been paying tribute to Skuld for the last twenty years and was still waiting to find out what the future had in store. My dreams had been on standby since Zoë's arrival eighteen years ago, and I sometimes had difficulty remembering what they even were. World travel? A job and co-op in Stockholm? F-you money in the bank? Had I ever been ambitious to begin with? Or had I expected my good looks and spicy charm to compensate for my lack of direction? Pondering these questions terrified me. There was a chance that I might have been just as lost, even without Zoë.

The main dock teemed with day visitors returning to Stockholm, but the ticket operator recognized me and let me slink to the beginning of the line. People were too polite or distracted to protest, and I found a window seat by the boat's bow. The sun blazed against the glass pane, prompting me to draw the curtains. I put a scarf on the headrest and leaned back in thought.

I had been so good on Midsummer's Eve, heeding Zoë's advice not to get too tipsy. I mingled on Erik's boat, sipping rosé and sangria, chitchatting about this and that. But when the schnapps and vodka came out, I strategically placed myself next to a mother who was still nursing and drank only a few glasses of Chablis. The guys and the younger, bolder girls got more and more animated, bellowing out *snapsvisor* before each shot and banging their empty glasses on the table. They were showing off, obviously stoked to prove how much they could gulp down. Although I sat back, observing them from a distance, I knew I could match them, drink for drink, and I contemplated breaking my promise to Zoë and joining in. After all, it was a high holiday, and overindulging was acceptable. But something about being comfortably buzzed and lucid, watching them get loud and raunchy, stopped me. I fast-forwarded to the next day and could almost feel the pounding headache, churning stomach, and racing heartbeat that would grip my body. Would it be worth it? A few hours of fun and debauchery for days of nausea and regret? Erik wouldn't second-guess his behavior; he made no apologies for his drinking. It also helped that he was over six feet tall and weighed about two hundred pounds. He would wake up the following day and make the rounds at the Nornö Hotel, a little worse for wear but still present. As for me, a Friday binge meant I wouldn't recover until Monday. My weekend would be lost; I would stay in bed until noon and then sleepwalk through my responsibilities. It had been easier when my father was alive and my mother was more mobile. They would take over Zoë's morning routine and never interrogate me about the night before. Even when a monster hangover slowed my thinking, I was perceptive enough to know they did it to avoid conflict and protect Zoë.

The counselors at the program I had been to all those years ago advised me to change my environment and circle of friends to resist the alcohol cravings and temptation. Aside from Alicia, my crowd had dwindled after becoming a single mother, and I hadn't been willing to cut off the few people who were still left. But I did find ways to pretend I was in the thick of it all when, in fact, I wasn't. So preoccupied with their own pleasure, no one ever questioned why I disappeared to the bathroom whenever rounds of shots appeared. They failed to pick up on how much water I crammed in between sips of cocktails. Even though I had still gone astray more times than I cared to remember, at least I was painfully aware of my blind spots and tried to exercise more self-control.

On Midsummer's Eve, when Erik uncorked another bottle of champagne, I sat with the new mom, watching the sun dip below the horizon, the sky marbling with violet, pink, and orange. Midsummer didn't have to mean getting smashed. Dusk turning to dawn in one fell swoop was a spiritual experience, and I decided to honor it by showing restraint. The only sticky moment was when the new mom asked about my birthing experience. Eighteen years later, it was still a touchy subject, and that's when I knew it was time to go. After excusing myself, I walked back home just as the birds were chirping. I crawled into my bed, alone but aware, holding on to a small victory.

Now, two hours later, *Aurora* docked in its designated spot on Nybrokajen, across the wide boulevard that bordered Strandvägen. With its tree-lined blocks and ornate architecture, it was hard to believe Strandvägen originally housed sheds and was once deemed a slum. Still, shrewd developers had understood its waterfront value, and gentrification took place just in time for the Stockholm World's Fair in 1897. The surrounding streets were valued real estate, prized for their peace, quiet, and, if you got lucky, a view of the water from up high. Alicia lived nearby on Grev Magnigatan, a short distance from Djurgården, the green oasis in the middle of the city. I hoped we would wake up tomorrow with enough energy for a power walk, stopping for coffee and sandwiches afterward at KMK. Maybe we could squeeze in lunch at one of the trendy restaurants on the avenue, Strandvägen 1 or Milles, and then browse the iconic Svenskt Tenn design boutique.

The boat's gentle rocking had lulled me to sleep; my mouth felt dry and bitter. Since the quay faced Diplomat Hotel, I could sneak inside and freshen up in one of their public bathrooms before meeting Alicia. I walked across the street and entered the hotel as though I were a paying guest; I'd learned that if one moved with purpose, no one would stop you.

After passing around the reception desk to the bathrooms in the back, I slipped into one with the door ajar and grunted when I surveyed my reflection in the mirror. My catnap had flattened the right side of my hair and smudged my eyeliner. I squeezed a dab of Colgate Fresh Mint onto my toothbrush and buffed the sleep from my teeth, thinking about how this outing was becoming increasingly complicated: Taking a two-hour boat ride. Spending the night. I should've been living in town at this point in my life. Going out for drinks at a Stockholm bar with a friend should've been part of my weekly schedule, not a one-off special occasion.

After spitting out the toothpaste, I rinsed my mouth and face. I drove a brush through the matted sections of my hair and redid my makeup. Once I switched out my sneakers for wedges, I straightened my posture and felt more confident. I practiced smiling in the mirror and couldn't resist pouting seductively. I looked better than average—pretty good for a woman pushing forty—and would have fun tonight, come hell or high water.

I had suggested Grand Hotel, about a mile away, for cocktails and dinner. It was close enough to walk, but I didn't want to get sweaty and sore feet in my heels. The taxi dropped me off a block from The Terrace, the hotel's outdoor bar and restaurant in the heart of Stockholm, which offered panoramic views of Gamla Stan and the Royal Palace.

For all my rebellious tendencies, I was an unabashed royalist. Crown Princess Victoria was only a couple of years older than me, and I had followed her gilded youth, daring marriage to her personal trainer, and the birth of their two children with great interest. I even took Zoë to Stockholm to watch Victoria's wedding celebration festivities nearly a decade ago. Even though my life often played out like a chaotic episode of *Teen Mom,* I was far from unsusceptible to the charms of a royal love story.

Grand Hotel was a favorite among celebrities, diplomats, Nobel laureates, and upscale Swedes. The imposing building exuded over a century's worth of history and tradition. The elegant interior emanated five-star luxury, the Scandinavian kind, meaning it wasn't archaic, vulgar, or loud but rather modern, reserved, and discreet. Money in Sweden reflected the climate (cool) and people (collected). In adherence to the Law of Jante, people didn't brag about their wealth. *Do not think you are anything special.* My years at Sigtuna had taught me that. A hundred-acre estate was referred to as a "farm." Kids performed verbal gymnastics to downplay their vacation plans and prying personal details out of them had been like pulling teeth. In Sweden, being wealthy enabled you to buy a nice apartment, a summer home, a German-made car, and vacations to Thailand or the Maldives. These were all preapproved indulgences, and you could sleep well at night if you didn't deviate from that well-constructed road map.

While being a Holmgren afforded us a certain status and advantages on Nornö, I had also understood, even as a kid, the varying tiers of privilege, the taken-for-granted freedom others got to choose and explore. My parents, sensing my internal struggles within the limited confines of my environment, had tried to expand my world: They splurged and took me to stay at Grand Hotel twice, visiting at Christmastime so I could attend a performance of *The Nutcracker* at the Royal Opera. Afterward, we'd delight in the spectacular holiday windows at NK, where I'd been allowed to choose one toy and one item of clothing. Walking around—awestruck by the gleaming streetlamps and tinseled shop windows, gawking at the monied style and mannerisms of sophisticated Stockholmers—had given me a taste for what was possible, for what I was missing in Nornö. I had naively assumed a place in this dazzling environment could be mine for the taking.

Maybe that was why I loved having cocktails at hotel bars. The cosmopolitan, international clientele made me feel like I was on vacation. I loved imagining what they did for a living or what had brought them to Stockholm. Most importantly, I never met anyone from my previous life—or current circumstances—in hotel bars, and I could pretend to be someone else. Midweek, The Terrace was the ideal after-work haunt, as it overlooked the water and ferries docked at Strömkajen. A superyacht was also moored on Skeppsbron, adding glamour to the atmosphere. The Terrace only offered drop-in seats, so I couldn't make a reservation. As I looked around for an empty wrought-iron table or one of the long built-in benches with teal cushions and mosaic-patterned throw pillows, I saw only chic patrons, drinking without a care in the world and showing no signs of leaving their hard-won spots anytime soon. After a second sweep of the crowd, I finally saw Alicia's profile, partially obscured by the tall citrus and olive trees that evoked a Scandi-Mediterranean vibe. The maître d' escorted me to Alicia's table, where she was staring into space, twirling her bright orange drink with a straw.

"Alicia!" I said, waving to catch her attention.

She lurched forward upon hearing her name but smiled wider than normal, deepening the lines in her cheeks. "Linn!" she replied, leaning over to give me a double kiss. "*Älskling!* How are you?"

"I'm good, thanks, but how about you?" I asked, pointing to the glasses on the table.

"Fine," she said quickly.

I squeezed between the tables and settled next to her, both of us facing out into the colorful, boisterous crowd. "Well, at least you got us a good seat."

"I've been here since three o'clock, so there were plenty of them."

"Have you been drinking alone since then?" I asked, examining Alicia's demeanor for signs of intoxication. As old friends, we possessed weird, intimate knowledge of each other's loopy, drunken antics. In addition to spending countless hours rehashing the previous night's bender, we always looked out for one another, holding back each other's hair whenever one of us needed to vomit or making sure we went to bed lying sideways.

The glassy film was missing from Alicia's hazel eyes, but her face was splotchy, shoulders slumped. "No, I've just been ordering refills so we wouldn't lose this seat."

Something was amiss. Alicia's flat tone didn't sound like the self-assured, happy-go-lucky girl who would've otherwise been able to sweet-talk her way into the best spot. "What's the matter, *gumman*? Is everything all right?"

Alicia looked at me with quivering lips. "Jonas wants a divorce."

"No!" I shrieked. "That can't be—"

"He told me last night."

"What? Have you guys been having problems?"

"We've been married for ten years. Things change. You have problems here and there."

"Anything specific?"

"You know, the usual stuff—who would get up early with the girls on weekends, the crap he would feed them when I wasn't around, how late he'd come home after a guys' dinner . . . but I never imagined it would come to this."

I was struck silent at Alicia's news. I immediately began questioning what I'd always taken at face value. She seemed to have the ideal life: marriage, a mother with two girls, ages six and eight; a desirable apartment in an exclusive part of town; and a beach house on the West Coast. Jonas was a financial adviser twelve years her senior and had inundated her with phone calls, flowers, and weekend getaways when they were dating. I'd found his intensity disconcerting, but Alicia had fallen for his urbane ways (remember, she *was* the daughter of a diplomat) and mature confidence. She had willingly relinquished her free-wheeling life for a man who bragged about having a diamond frequent flyer card.

I had never clicked with Jonas. He spoke to me as though I were an annoying child to be tolerated, not a grown woman with opinions worthy of attention. I think he looked down on me because I was a single mom. I had no clout, nothing that could help him advance his agenda. But he was my best friend's husband, so I'd swallowed my irritation and played nice out of my love and respect for her. If anything, I'd thought that warm, positive, open Alicia would eventually get tired of Jonas's stuffy pretentiousness and leave *him.*

"I'm so sorry, Alicia. What happened?"

"He met someone else."

"Met someone else?!" I exclaimed. "How could he—"

"Because he's older, a little overweight, and stiff, you didn't think someone else would find him attractive?"

Ouch. Apparently, Alicia had always known my true opinion about Jonas. "I didn't mean it that way."

"I know you didn't, but believe me, I've been asking myself that same question. Jonas may be a wrinkly, out-of-shape smartass, but he was *my* smartass. My girls' father." She paused. "Turns out there's no shortage of women—younger women—who find that type of man attractive, especially if he has money."

Alicia's bluntness highlighted how cliché her situation was. Not for the first time, I considered it a blessing I didn't have a man in my life. I heard so many horror stories of men who had morphed from princes to monsters, leaving their wives broke, depressed, and displaced. At least my problems were my own, not caused by someone else's whims or desires.

"Who is she?" I asked.

"Our art adviser at Auktionshuset."

"What the fuck?" I shrieked and then covered my mouth in disbelief.

"She'd been helping us set up our collection," Alicia continued. "I guess she was doing more than showing Jonas the latest pieces at auction . . ."

"But you used to go with him too!"

"I know. I don't think they began an affair right away. But after a while, I didn't have the energy to look at more art we didn't need or have the space for." She shrugged. "And when I wasn't around, he found other ways to amuse himself."

"*Herregud!* I'm completely floored."

Alicia lowered her gaze, staring intently at the ice cubes

melting in her glass. "I gave up so much for him. He wanted me to stop working and stay home with the girls, so I did. I missed my job in PR like hell, but I did it for the family. He wanted me to be available for travel and client events. I did that too. In the end, it still wasn't enough."

"You did more than he deserved."

"But where has that gotten me? We signed a prenup, so I'll get the bare minimum. My marriage is over. I don't have a career. I won't get to see my girls every day—"

"Do you think Jonas will want shared custody? I can't see him caring for the girls on his own for a week at a time. You do everything!"

Alicia was a *lyxhemmafru* with an instinctive talent for managing her children and household. She had been a natural with Zoë, much better at playing peekaboo and doing arts and crafts than I ever was. When Zoë was ten and asked Alicia to be her godmother, my best friend hadn't wavered for a moment. Children and family were a natural extension of who she was. Though I teased Alicia about her over-the-top children's parties and elaborate table settings, she put her heart and soul into family life. In my eyes, Alicia was the perfect wife and mother. Maybe too perfect.

"But he'll have her to help him," Alicia said. "It wouldn't surprise me if they have a kid together."

"You can't leave your girls with her," I blurted out and instantly regretted it. Alicia's face shriveled in despair, and she draped herself on my shoulder to hide it, but her body heaved.

When people glanced in our direction, I wished we were someplace more private. Alicia's hot tears seeped through my new silk dress, and I felt guilty for worrying if they would leave a permanent stain. Why hadn't Alicia canceled our get-together? I would have understood. But I had texted her in the morning to say how much I was looking forward to our night out, and Alicia, the ever-loyal friend, hadn't wanted to disappoint me. She constantly looked out for everyone else's happiness, prioritizing their needs over her own. And what good had that done her? Alicia's self-centered, unappreciative husband had replaced her with a newer edition.

Enraged by Jonas's betrayal, I tightened my arms around her. "It'll be okay. Just let it out. Jonas is an asshole. You were too young and too pretty and too good for him anyway. Let that art adviser have him. You had Jonas in his prime. She'll have to take care of him in his stinky old age!"

Alicia looked up. "If she doesn't leave him before then."

"Exactly!"

Suddenly, a waiter appeared, holding a tray with two fluted glasses.

"We didn't order those," I told him.

He gave us a sly wink. "Bellinis—compliments of the two gentlemen over there," he explained, tilting his head toward the middle of the seating area.

I craned my neck but had difficulty seeing who the waiter was referring to among the sea of faces. I normally never accepted drinks from strangers, especially when they were offered in such a cheesy way, but Alicia was sniffling, and our night out had taken on a melancholy tone. The Bellinis were a pale peachy color, and I could almost taste the sugary, cold nectar.

Sitting up straighter, I said, "That's very kind. We'd love to have them."

The waiter placed the champagne flutes down on the table, removing Alicia's old cocktail glasses and replacing them with small bowls of olives, almonds, and chips.

"Enjoy," he said, leaving as stealthily as he had arrived.

"Alicia," I said, patting her on the back. "Some guys just sent us two Bellinis. We can't let them go to waste. I know you'll get through this. You're a strong woman and it's Jonas's loss. You're finally free of that jerk!"

Alicia snapped to attention and cleared her throat. "You're right. I should stop wasting tears on someone who doesn't want me anymore."

"Cheers to that!"

We tapped our glasses together American-style, but before tasting my drink, I scanned the restaurant again for the mystery men who had gifted us the Bellinis. I finally made eye contact with a dark-haired hottie drinking a beer. It was as though he had been waiting for me to find him, since he didn't hesitate to salute me with his bottle. I raised my glass and held his gaze for a beat. Then I smiled and took a generous sip.

Two hours later, Alicia and I had bolstered the Bellinis with other pretty cocktails: a strawberry-puree Rossini and an elderflower Hugo. We also shared a bottle of Minuty with our *pasta vongole.* Eventually, my eyelids grew heavy and people began to sway in front of me, so I ordered a triple espresso to regain my balance. But Alicia had been hit by a second wind and was blathering about everything she couldn't stand about Jonas.

"He would leave his sweaty workout clothes on the bathroom floor," she said, wrinkling her nose. "Disgusting! I practically needed a pair of tongs to pick them up."

I nodded, savoring the bitter, scalding espresso on my tongue. The burning sensation would get me back on track. The Terrace had thinned out, and more people were sitting than standing, making it easier to inspect the crowd. The two Bellini guys were still there, but they hadn't offered us more drinks. Maybe they expected us to come by their table and express our thanks. I had secretly hoped the dark-haired hottie would make an overture, but the drinks and depressing conversation had made me a little less cheeky. Alicia and I probably looked like two middle-aged lushes, long past our sell-by dates. This swanky cocktail outing was a mirage, and reality would bite us in the ass tomorrow. It was smarter to leave now, get a good night's sleep, and face the aftermath head-on.

"I think it's time for us to go," I said.

Alicia checked the time on the gold Cartier watch Jonas had given her as a wedding gift. It was oversized, with a circle of diamonds surrounding the face. Big and bold, it was supposed to symbolize Jonas's love and commitment, but it was just another toy he had lavished upon Alicia, rich in gems but hollow in meaning. I would advise her to sell it.

"But it's only ten and super bright outside!" Alicia said.

"We can go back to your place and rest." I signaled the waiter for the bill. Jonas had already moved out, and Alicia's daughters were in Falsterbo with her parents, so we would be able to sober up uninterrupted.

"Okay, fine," she huffed.

We gathered our belongings, and I led the way out of the restaurant. Impulsively, I walked past the table with the Bellini guys. I hadn't yet worked out what I would say but hoped a clever comment would spontaneously spill from my lips. The dark-haired hottie spared me further deliberation by touching my arm.

"Leaving so soon?" he asked.

His accent was American, which I hadn't expected, but it explained his audacity. Swedish men didn't usually treat random women to pricey drinks, and Swedish women rarely accepted such chauvinistic gestures from strangers. I had only acquiesced in my desperation to pep Alicia up.

"Afraid so," I replied. "But thank you so much for the Bellinis. They got us off to a good start."

"Then let's keep the party going! The night's still young." Glancing upward, he added, "I can't get over this light!" He turned to his companion. "What do you say, Martin? Up for another round?"

Martin nodded. "Yeah, man, for sure." Martin spoke with a Swedish accent. His bobbed, middle-parted hair and buttoned-up style reminded me of my preppy male classmates at Sigtuna. It wouldn't have surprised me if he graduated from the Stockholm School of Economics.

"Ladies, why don't you have a seat and join us?" the American asked, directing his cobalt-blue eyes at me. The dark pupils were the same ebony shade as his hair, giving them a piercing, commanding quality. He had the air of someone used to getting his way.

Still, I responded, "It's been a long day. We should really call it a night."

"Martin and I have had a long day too. Sit, and we'll compare war stories."

Alicia, who was standing still and seemed to have lost her voice, suddenly exclaimed, "My husband just left me!"

"Whoa! You win," the American said. "You need to sit"—he pulled out a chair for Alicia—"and you definitely need another drink."

Martin moved over and motioned for me to take a seat. Alicia and I made eye contact—*Should we?*—a throwback to our party days, when we could almost read each other's minds. The thrill of the unknown had always tempted us, so we sat.

The American snapped his fingers—another brash move most Swedes wouldn't attempt—but the same waiter who had served the Bellinis appeared instantly. He was probably banking on a large tip. Americans didn't understand the modest tipping rules we had in Sweden and left much more than was customary.

"I think it's about time we introduced ourselves. I'm Wes," the American said, extending his hand.

"*Hej, Martin heter jag,*" his friend said, reverting to Swedish.

Alicia introduced herself, offering her hand in greeting. When it was my turn, a surge of mischief overtook me. It had been so long since I'd played this game, and tonight was as good a time as any to resurrect it. Alicia was miserable—why else would she have announced her divorce to these strangers? —and needed a good distraction. Most of all, it would be fun to fool these macho strivers. Wes and Martin seemed so cocky. They needed to be taken down a notch or two.

"I'm Inga," I replied, offering the obligatory handshakes. "Inga" was an inside joke, the ultimate parody of a Scandinavian name in American films. I was sure Martin would comment, but both guys repeated it without any trace of irony. I heard Alicia emit a *pfft* sound, which she tried to cover up by coughing. What mattered was she had caught on to the prank, despite the not-so-subtle theatrics, and would be my willing accomplice.

Wes rubbed his hands together. "What should we order? What are you ladies in the mood for?" He looked at Alicia. "What would make *you* feel better?"

Alicia furrowed her brows in thought. "A shot. A shot of something would make me feel better."

A shot was the worst suggestion. Now I wondered if Alicia had proposed it to get back at me, but judging from the greedy smile on her lips, she was in her own world, thirsty to put her problems on the back burner.

"Vodka? Jäger? Your call," Wes said.

"Have you ever had a hot shot, Wes?" I asked.

"No, what's that?"

"Galliano, coffee, and whipped cream," Martin piped in.

"It's so yummy," I raved. *And not that strong.*

Alicia smacked her lips together. "Yes! You have to try it!"

"Then hot shots it is!" Wes said, ordering them from his trusty waiter. He gazed at me again. "Where are you from, Inga?" He pronounced it *In-GA,* with a hard emphasis on the last syllable. The ruse was so absurd and contrived; I couldn't believe he hadn't already seen right through it. Frankly, I wasn't sure I could continue without cracking up.

"Uppsala. It's about forty-five minutes from Stockholm." Uppsala was my standard game-face response. Although it wasn't Stockholm, it still sounded more exciting than Nornö. My boarding school, Sigtuna, was in the county of Uppsala, and after spending three years there, I knew the region well enough to handle any specific questions. "Where are you from in the States?"

"I'm originally from New Jersey."

"Mmm. Didn't think people owned up to that."

He laughed. "Been trying to beat the negative Jersey rap my whole life. So, what do you do?"

"I'm a massage therapist and esthetician." At least that was the truth. It was impossible to keep a slew of lies straight. "And you?"

"I'm in real estate and make private investments on the side."

"Is that what brought you to Stockholm?"

Wes nodded. "A friend of mine recommended Martin's start-up. You Swedes are good entrepreneurs, and who knows?

Martin's idea may be the next Spotify." Wes nudged Martin with his elbow. "Right?"

Martin smiled shyly and shook his head. "It's nowhere as sexy as Spotify. It's actually a fintech start-up—"

At that moment, the waiter materialized, presenting us with a tray of four mocha hot shots. "Let's not talk business now," Wes said. "These look delicious!"

The waiter set down the shot glasses, and Wes picked his up expectantly. "Should we drink it at the same time? Or is there a special custom?"

"I think we should sing 'Helan Går.' What do my fellow Swedes think?" I asked, eyeing Alicia and Martin.

"Oh yes," Martin agreed. "You can't come to Sweden without a proper intro to 'Helan Går'!"

Alicia, Martin, and I raised our glasses, signaling Wes to do the same. Martin took a deep breath and began singing in a deep baritone. After the first few verses, Alicia and I chimed in, jacking up our voices until the whole restaurant stopped to stare.

At the song's end, I shouted, "*Ett, två, tre!*" We downed the hot shots in unison.

Martin finished with another, "*Sjung hopp faderallan lej!*"

Everyone around us clapped and cheered. Giddy, we doubled over in laughter.

"I don't know what the hell you guys said, but that was great. Aggressive, but great," Wes said enthusiastically.

"All our drinking songs are a little brutal and barbaric. Like Vikings on the warpath," I said, licking whipped cream from my top lip.

"But Swedes are so civilized and unthreatening these days," Wes said.

"That's because we've learned from our plundering ways,"

Alicia said.

"And don't be fooled by us," I added. "On the outside, we're like vodka, plain and simple, maybe a little boring, but once you get a taste—all bets are off!"

Wes grinned. "I think that's the best advertisement I've ever heard for ordering a round of Absolut."

My pulse raced. Vodka straight was my nightmare, the exact opposite of what I wanted. How could I get out of it? Why did I agree to sit? I had only wanted to toy with Wes for a little while, to bring the Bellini episode to an amusing, satisfying ending, and then leave the restaurant. But these guys were on a mission to get hammered—and Alicia, too, seemed determined to drown her sorrows in alcohol.

I was in a tough spot myself since I didn't wholly hate the idea of having a round of Absolut and getting drunk. The moral dilemma made me anxious—the realization that I *shouldn't* get drunk, not with my history.

But then I reminded myself that tonight was better than usual. I was staying over at Alicia's place, and we could help each other sober up in the morning.

By the second round of vodka shots, Martin announced he had to go home. "I'm n-n-not on vacat-t-tion," he slurred. "I have to work tomorrow." He said his goodbyes and wobbled over to the harbor side of the street bordering the ferryboats.

"I hope he doesn't fall into the water," I said, mildly concerned.

"I don't think he lives that far from here," Wes said. "Walking home will sober him up."

"I have to use the bathroom," Alicia announced, flushed and bug-eyed.

I pushed back my chair. "Wait, let me go with you."

"No! Might be a while." Rising, she shuffled out of the

seating area toward the hotel, where the bathrooms were located.

After Martin and Alicia's abrupt departure, an awkward silence fell over the table. It was as though our sloshed antics had run their course. Funnily enough, I felt better than expected after all that hard liquor. Of course, it helped that we had ordered truffle pizza and parmesan French fries between shots; I'd stuffed my stomach with starchy carbs to absorb the alcohol.

Smiling gingerly at Wes, I racked my brain for conversation starters. "Tell me," I said finally, "why'd you send those drinks over to us?"

He leaned closer, tilting his head and offering me a close-up of his face. His top lip was a little thinner than the bottom, but the asymmetry was alluring, enhancing his cleft chin and square jaw. I imagined those lips on mine for a split second and felt heat prickle my cheeks.

"Because . . ." Wes drew out the word. "You looked really uncomfortable when Alicia started crying on your shoulder, and I wanted to give you a reason to stay."

"I was this close"—I held my thumb and index finger a centimeter apart for emphasis—"from taking Alicia home."

Wes looked into my eyes, unblinking. God, he was a good flirt.

"I'm glad you didn't," he said.

Suddenly, my phone, which was facedown on the table, vibrated. It could've been Zoë, so I picked it up immediately, shielding the message's contents from Wes's view.

But the text wasn't from Zoë. It was from Alicia, and I sighed after reading it.

"What is it?" Wes asked.

"Alicia. She felt sick and took a cab back to her apartment."

"Oh, that's too bad. I hope she feels better." His eyes twinkled. "I guess it's just the two of us now."

Several hours later, my eyes flew open, my body rigid under the weight of Wes's arm over my shoulder. After blinking to adjust my cloudy vision, the red digital numbers on the nightstand came into focus: 6:00. It felt later, the plush hotel bed clashing with the rough landscape I had left fifteen hours earlier. My evening in Stockholm should've followed a tried-and-true playbook, but it had taken strange detours, like garbled acts in a play. Alicia's divorce announcement. Drinking and flirting with two random guys. Steamy sex with one of them.

And now, the postcoital angst.

By waking up first, it was my move, and I knew the unspoken rules. There was no need to overstay my welcome by ordering room service or engaging in a repeat performance. Small talk under the pretense of "getting to know each other" was also unnecessary. Every clever word had been a prelude to sex; more dialogue would only be a disappointment. Wiser to leave on a high note, with vague, pleasant recollections of the sex that had briefly united us.

I wriggled from Wes's arm, grabbed my tote bag, and padded to the bathroom. When I turned on the lights, I didn't recoil at my appearance: bedraggled, sticky, haggard. I stepped into the shower, setting the hot water at one hundred degrees. Steam engulfed the room, and I mentally retraced my steps from the restaurant to Wes's hotel room.

He had primarily talked about himself—his work and favorite European summer spots. Capri topped the list; he'd bragged about a "wonderful beachside restaurant that made the best zucchini pasta." I typically would've found his self-absorption annoying, but it saved me from answering questions about myself. Listening to him granted me a reprieve from telling more lies about fictional Inga. Once Wes paid the bill, he'd raised an eyebrow, and I'd turned up the corners of my mouth knowingly. Then, without saying a word, we'd gotten up, made a half loop through Grand Hotel's revolving doors, walked past the concierge desk, and taken an elevator to the twelfth floor.

Chest heaving, I'd followed him down the hall to his room (which turned out to be a suite), only exhaling when the door swung shut. *Clunk.* That sound was our cue. We'd reached for each other simultaneously, bodies satiny and liquified, mouths parting and exploring. Soaring on an elixir of arousal and alcohol, this state of being always emboldened me. Forgetting reality, I could be whoever I wanted—Linn, Inga, nameless, it didn't matter. Wes had jacked up my dress and his firm hands had squeezed my bottom, sending a thrill up my spine. I'd clawed at his waistband, untucking his shirt, unbuttoning it from the bottom up, and reached inside to caress his broad shoulders. Heat and hunger had comingled as we fell onto the king-size bed. Clothes vanished. Wes had put on a condom, and after a few thrusts, mission accomplished.

Huffing and puffing, he'd rolled over, and I'd finally submitted to the boozed-up fatigue I'd been fighting most of the night.

But I'd woken in the morning, unable to keep sleeping, and felt jittery as daylight filtered through the slits in the blackout shades. Not because I regretted sleeping with Wes; that had been a possibility almost from the moment I'd sat at his table. He was a handsome, successful American, and in all honesty,

I'd slept with much worse. But—unsavory as it sounded—I had gone through with the whole thing to see if I could. I'd been bored with trying to behave like a respectable, self-controlled, mature woman for the last few months. No drunken binges. No trifling flirtations. No casual sex. Last night had been a belated exercise to see if I still had it in me.

Yet as my alcoholic bliss fizzled, I was no longer convinced I found the experience as titillating and empowering as before. Worse, I had broken a silent pledge to Zoë—not that I would ever say a word about this to her. Still, it was gut-wrenching to know my daughter would be ashamed of me.

I stepped out of the shower and dropped two Treo tablets—the best hangover cure—from my makeup bag into a glass of water. Waiting for the disks to dissolve, I brushed my teeth and changed into the clean underwear and striped cotton dress I had packed. My phone pinged with a text message from Alicia.

> Hello! So sorry I ran out on you last night, but I threw up in the bathroom and made a total mess. I had to go home and pull myself together. Believe me, I did you guys a favor! How did it go with Wes? Since you didn't make it back to my place, I can only assume...

I chugged the Treo mixture, grimacing at the sour, sudsy taste. Using a gold-beaded hair tie, I gathered my wet locks into a low ponytail, arranged my possessions in the tote, and crept to Wes's side of the bed. He was snoring lightly, an air pocket between his attractively uneven lips. A splattering of freckles dusted his nose, and pinpricks of stubble darkened his cheeks. He looked defenseless, like a teenage boy who had slept with a sex worker for the first time. Perhaps I was being too hard on myself and projecting my insecurities. Wes was no amateur; his tactics had been well-rehearsed from the get-go.

I spotted a small diagonal scar across one of his eyebrows where the hair had stopped growing. I wished I'd seen it earlier; it could have been my conversation starter after the table cleared out and it was just the two of us. But who was I kidding? It would have been filler conversation, delaying the sexual tension that had been building all night. I stepped back and aimed my phone above his face to take a picture. His eyelids fluttered, but apart from that, he didn't react. I was astonished he was so knocked out. Maybe it was jet lag. Or maybe he couldn't hold his liquor.

The thought made me a little smug. Wes's aggressive posturing was still no match for my tolerance. I brought my face down next to his and took a selfie. He still didn't react, but it would be a silly souvenir, the latest installment of Linn and Alicia's Aimless Adventures. I sent both photos to Alicia and wrote:

> Oops—I did it again😖! I'm leaving Grand
> now and heading over to your place. Don't
> fall asleep!

Grabbing my wedges, I tiptoed out of the room. Once outside, I walked the cobblestone streets of Blasieholmstorg back to Strandvägen, turning east toward Alicia's place on Grev Magnigatan. A running club jogged by with military precision. I watched their backs dart past me, envying their wholesomeness and early morning vigor.

Deep down, I felt messy and guilt-ridden—not because of Wes, but because of Alicia. Although Alicia hadn't sounded upset in her text message, it would've been justified if she was. I shouldn't have let her spend the night alone in such a precarious condition. It was rule number one of our friendship: Never abandon each other. Despite Alicia's protests, I should've followed her to the bathroom and accompanied her home. She had just announced her divorce, but rather than being fully present to provide comfort and support, I had responded by sleeping with a stranger.

Had the alcohol made me do it? Or was there a fundamental flaw in my personality? A defect where I was missing a sensitivity chip?

We'd been friends for twenty-three years, but our ties ran far deeper than friendship. It was a sisterhood, an unspoken pact that Alicia honored to protect whatever was left of my reputation and spare Zoë unnecessary pain. Alicia was the only friend who hadn't abandoned me after my unplanned pregnancy. The others—classmates and acquaintances I had considered part of my social network—avoided me once my stomach swelled, as though my new condition was an infectious disease.

Only Alicia knew the real story about the weekend that changed my life.

Alicia was the sole person who had met Zoë's father.

Interlude

Linn

June 15, 2000

"Alicia, I think we messed up," I said, plodding through the patchy lawn that was the main camping site for the Hultsfred Festival. It was one in the afternoon, and I was exhausted after the four-hour train ride from Stockholm Central Station, which had included a transfer in Linköping. I was also weighed down by a twenty-pound backpack and a blue IKEA shopping bag containing miscellaneous items that couldn't fit in the backpack. Although Alicia and I had been up since six in the morning to catch the first train of our journey, savvier festivalgoers had been a step ahead of us. The lawn was dotted with hundreds of colorful, dome-shaped tents.

Alicia was hauling her backpack and the storage case holding our tent. Surveying the scene, she groaned. "When the hell did these people get here? A week ago? The festival starts today. I thought most people were coming today."

"Rookie mistake," I replied, taking stock of the empty beer bottles and cardboard food containers littering the lawn. "They've been here for at least a day or two."

It had become evident on the train ride that Alicia and I were festival virgins. Everybody who hopped on in Linköping seemed to know everybody else. They were a rowdy, older crowd in their early twenties, and a few were so loose-limbed, they must have been drinking since breakfast. The guys carried cartons of beer and boom boxes while the girls lugged plastic grocery bags loaded with bread and canned food. We sat quietly, our backpacks sandwiched between our legs, trying to decipher the pregaming rituals of a music festival we had dreamed of since 1997. Back then, the Wu-Tang Clan ruled the charts in England and Sweden, and at Hultsfred, they brought down the house with their throbbing beats and irreverent attitude. After that triumphant performance, Wu-Tang had abandoned the rest of their European tour, and it became one of many legendary stories that created the Hultsfred mystique.

Alicia and I had graduated from Sigtuna two weeks earlier. Tickets to Hultsfred had been on our bucket list, and I felt like I'd earned the reward. As a new Sigtuna graduate—albeit one at the bottom of the class—I had a diploma from one of Sweden's most prestigious high schools. I'd been waiting my whole life to finish my studies. Sure, turning eighteen the previous year had been an important milestone, but I was still at the mercy of my parents and the state's educational requirements. A high school diploma was my ticket to freedom. I'd also silenced my parents; there were no more accusations of being lazy or unmotivated. A Sigtuna diploma validated Agnes and Thomas's decision to send me there in the first place, so now they were bending over backward to give me whatever I wanted. The festival ticket had cost 880 kronor, but there was much more to budget for: a hiker's backpack, tent, train ticket, and money for food. I had paid for my clothes and nonessential items with monetary gifts, supplemented by savings from working at Holmgren's last summer. I had felt well-prepared for Hultsfred, but then I wasn't so sure on the train, as I watched the festival veterans mix and mingle. Their laid-back, tuned-in attitude couldn't be bought. It had to be experienced.

Alicia stopped and dropped the case to the ground. Yanking off her backpack, she exhaled heavily. "I need to take a break."

I was scoping out the tent grounds for a decent spot and didn't want to break our momentum. "Alicia, we can't stop now. It's too crowded. We'll end up with the leftovers."

"I don't care. I just want to rest. And it's friggin' cold!"

We'd worn denim shorts, Doc Martens, and Gore-Tex jackets from Peak Performance, but the weather was wet and raw; goosebumps ran up our bare legs. I'd recently recovered from a bacterial infection, a side effect of the nonstop graduation parties, and been on antibiotics for a week. Luckily, I felt better now—just in time for Hultsfred—but I worried the soggy conditions would weaken my immune system further.

"The sooner we pitch our tent, the sooner we'll be able to warm up. *Kom igen!*" I said. "We can do this!"

"Ugh!" Alicia moaned, but she picked up her gear and lumbered off behind me.

We finally found an empty plot at the edge of the lawn near the trees. The ground sloped downward, but we didn't have the energy to look further. Alicia kicked the garbage away while I weeded through the various parts needed to assemble our tent. One of the few advantages of growing up on Nornö was that I knew how to pitch a tent. My father had taken me camping on nearby islands and taught me tricks to optimize the experience. For example, tents were more cramped than advertised, so Thomas had advised Alicia and me to buy a four-person tent, even though it would only be the two of us. He'd also suggested getting extra guylines, stakes, and a tarp in case of rain. Yes to the first two, but we had vetoed the tarp—too bulky to carry. I regretted it now, as raindrops flecked our equipment.

A half hour later, the tent was up. We placed our bags

inside, securing our valuables with a lock on the door zipper. Someone could slash the fabric and steal everything, but it was still worth trying.

"What should we do now?" Alicia asked, uncapping the wand to her pink, iridescent lip gloss and sliding it across her mouth.

I lengthened the straps of my black fanny pack to wear it cross-body over my jacket. "I actually have to go to the bathroom."

Alicia shrugged and pointed to the woods.

"It's number two," I clarified.

"We packed toilet paper. You are a country girl, after all."

"I'm not pooping in the woods on the first day! Come on, let's go exploring. We'll look for the bathroom and then get something to eat."

"More like a porta-potty," Alicia muttered.

It had since stopped drizzling. We traversed the maze of tents, fascinated by the whimsical, uninhibited atmosphere that had transformed the camping site into a mad carnival. Subvillages formed by arranging smaller tents around one big party tent. Each cluster blasted its own music, becoming a battle of the airwaves. The latest songs from Eminem and Savage Garden clashed with Swedish summertime classics from Ted Gärdestad and Gyllene Tider. Beat-up sofas, card tables, and minibars created makeshift outdoor living rooms. A posse of punks had scrawled slogans like FUCK DA POLICE! and PROPERTY IS THEFT! in thick black marker over their tents. Some sprayed each other with water guns, accidentally squirting another group parading around in crazy hats. A dapper dude marched by in a marine-blue sailor suit, but he was no competition for the screwball in a furry Pink Panther costume. I had deliberated for months over my clothes for the weekend (sexy-grunge: crop tops, loose denim, flannel shirts, floral dresses, a moto jacket), but now I wondered if I had played it too safe. Hultsfred would have been the perfect venue to reinvent myself, style-wise. Maybe with a sparkly headpiece and cowboy boots. I clocked my impressions, storing them for inspiration next year.

Alicia and I reached the gravel footpath where throngs of people had queued to enter the festival grounds and the six performance stages. VÄLKOMMEN TILL HULTSFRED, hailed an elevated sign in big, welcoming letters. We waited patiently, listening in on conversations:

"Where are you staying?"

"Which band do you want to see the most?"

"Who's having the after party?"

"Do you have any hash?"

No one paid attention to us, and we were too shy to initiate conversation, so we moseyed along, ears alert, cataloging all the comments we wanted to discuss later. At the entrance, we presented our tickets and were given wristbands, officially becoming part of Hultsfred 2000. Many people had rows of colorful wristbands from previous festivals encircling their wrists, proving they were Hultsfred regulars. Some bragged about having attended the very first one in 1986. I decided then and there that I wouldn't take off my wristband when I returned to Nornö.

"Food or bathroom first?" Alicia asked.

"Bathroom, please!"

"Where are they?"

I had bought the festival program, a glossy pamphlet with a beaming, brown-skinned girl wearing twists and a canary-yellow muscle tee on the cover, for ten kronor. Flipping to the pages with maps, I said, "There are a couple of bathrooms about five hundred meters ahead. Let's get going because I don't know how much longer I can hold it in!"

We turned right, hurrying until two greenish-blue porta-potties came into view. Unfortunately, another person had beaten us to it. We took our place behind a guy who stood with his hands shoved in the pockets of his baggy jeans. Trying to focus on something other than my stomach, I stared at the back of his black hoodie and yellow mesh trucker hat.

Minutes passed with no movement from the bathrooms. I began gritting my teeth, jiggling from side to side. Finally, one of the doors burst open, and a hefty guy stumbled out, wiping his mouth with the palm of his hand.

Snickering, Alicia elbowed me, but I could only think about how badly I needed to use the toilet. The guy ahead of me entered the porta-potty and then screeched, staggering backward.

"Damn! Hell no!" he shrieked in English and turned around. "*Hell* no!" He strode back to the line, pinching his nose. "You don't wanna go in there," he warned. "It's lethal!"

"Can I go ahead of you?" I asked.

"Are you serious?" he said, scrunching his face incredulously.

"Dead serious. If you're not going in, I will," I said.

"Okay, girl, but enter at your own risk."

"Thanks!" I shouted, running to the porta-potty. I locked the door, hovered above the seat, and did my business. To be safe, I tried not to inhale the foul odor contaminating the cubicle. When I came out ten minutes later, the guy was still chatting away with Alicia.

"Feeling better?" he asked, looking me straight in the eye.

Mortified, I felt my cheeks grow hot. I attempted to mask my embarrassment with a snotty, "Like a rock star."

"Linn, this is J.G.," Alicia said, patching over the awkwardness. "He's part of the road crew for Kelis."

Alicia pronounced it *Kuh-lees,* so I corrected her by saying *Ke-less* in the way I had heard it pronounced on Swedish radio stations.

"No, it's actually *Kuh-lees,*" J.G. said. "A combination of her parents' names: Kelly and Everliss."

"Oh. That's so cool," I responded, feeling stupid. Everything about this encounter had started on the wrong foot, and I longed to make a quick getaway.

"What's it like being a roadie for *Kuh-lees?*" Alicia asked.

"I'm not gonna front—it's dope."

"Cool," I said again. Although Sigtuna was an IB school and most of my classes had been in English, the hip-hop vernacular dotting J.G.'s speech was simultaneously familiar and unfamiliar. From watching movies and music videos, I knew what he alluded to, but I would never respond in kind for fear of sounding corny and using expressions out of context.

"Are you busy now?" Alicia asked him. "Do you want to come with us and get something to eat?"

J.G. took off his trucker hat, which was stamped with a human brain graphic and the letters *N.E.R.D,* and ran one hand over his hair. He sported a close-cropped Afro, bringing his features into full effect: smooth complexion; dark, straight eyebrows above almond-shaped eyes; and high cheekbones. He smiled. "Sure. I'd be down with that." Pausing, he added, "But I gotta use the facilities first."

J.G. jogged to the other available bathroom, and I turned to Alicia, seething.

"What are you doing?" I hissed.

"What do you mean?"

"Why are you asking him to have lunch with us?"

"Why not?" Alicia asked. "He's hot!"

I rolled my eyes.

"C'mon, fess up," Alicia teased. "He's cute—and funny!"

"It doesn't matter. We don't even know him!"

"While you were taking a ten-minute shit, I got to know him. He's from North Carolina and wants to be a doctor. So there."

"Are you interested in him or something?" I asked her.

"Not like that! But think about it—if he's a roadie for Kelis, he might be able to get us special access passes, so we should be friendly instead of acting like stuck-up bitches. Why are you suddenly being so lame?"

"Easy for you to say. You're not the one who couldn't control her bowels! I wish we hadn't met him in front of the porta-potties."

"That's what makes it so hilarious!" Alicia crowed. "Besides, this is our first Hultsfred. Let's make it one for the ages!"

5

ZOË

Simba refused to stay with Mormor inside Holmgren's back cubicle, where we stored the wine and spirits orders from Systembolaget. He kept sneaking out, tail wagging, to join me behind the register.

Looking down at him, I whispered, "Simba, you know you shouldn't even be here. I'm only being nice because you were so whiney this morning."

He whimpered, staring back at me with chocolate-brown eyes. I sighed, defenseless whenever my grown-up dog behaved like a puppy. Simba pulled this trick now and again, howling and barking when I left the house and sending me on a fool's errand trying to figure out what ailed him, only to realize he was acting out a form of separation anxiety. Simba had been a surprise present from Morfar a few months before his tragic death. It always felt like the big, gentle animal was my guardian angel, somehow—Morfar reincarnated. Simba usually didn't mind staying at the house by himself, but he often needed to reassert his position in our family lest we believe he was less important than the store. I'd bring him to work sometimes to make up for it, but not everyone took kindly to having a hulking dog inside a grocery store, especially since Holmgren's had a strict no-pet policy for our customers. Luckily, it was late afternoon by the time the midday rush ended, and the predinner pandemonium had yet to begin.

I stooped to murmur, "You can stay here with me, but don't move." He tried to lick my chin when I scratched behind his ear, but I backed off, giggling.

When I stood again, I noticed a woman had quietly entered the store, someone I had never seen before. She composed her face into a closed-mouth smile, turning her head from left to right, apparently uncertain about where to begin. After countless hours of observing people who came in and out of Holmgren's, I could gauge when someone was a little more interesting than your average shopper. For one thing, this woman was slim and statuesque; her head nearly reached the top shelf, which was stacked with cereals and crackers. She wore white jeans, cropped and flared at just the right point by the ankle; a fitted striped shirt, untucked and ruffled at the cuffs; and a pair of beige T-strap sandals. Big tortoiseshell sunglasses perched above her forehead, binding a chestnut mane that tapered into lighter, honey-colored strands at the ends. An orange monogrammed bag with blue-and-white bands down the middle was slung over her shoulder. Still, this woman's timid body language didn't fit her polished beauty.

"Hi, can I help you?" I called out, speaking English rather than Swedish for some strange reason—maybe it was the woman's worldly aura, indicating she could be from anywhere.

She walked up to the register. "*Hej!*" she said, flashing perfect white teeth and a spattering of crow's feet by the corners of her eyes.

"*Nej men—hej! Förlåt! Visste inte att du pratade svenska!*" Sorry, I didn't realize you spoke Swedish.

"*Det är lugnt!*" she responded in Swedish again, laughing. "*Min svenska är ändå så rostig. Jag tar alla chanser jag kan få att träna upp mig.*" No worries. My Swedish is so rusty anyway. I'll take any chance I can get to practice.

That rustiness cropped up in the last sentence; she drew out the vowels and spoke at a slower clip than native Swedes.

"And I need to practice my English," I said, switching back.

"Perfect for my son, who barely knows Swedish," she replied in kind, ending our bumbling language duet. "And your English is excellent."

"Well, we start in second grade, but most of us pick it up from watching TV." I couldn't reveal that my goal had always been more personal. Mastering English would bring me closer to finding and communicating with my father.

"I remember all too well. Although I was born and raised in Sweden, I've spent most of my life abroad, speaking English," she explained.

"Aha! Are you the one who—" I stopped midsentence. Saying what I was thinking would be rude. *Are you the one who inherited Karin Eklund's house and built that villa on the cliff? The one with the ginormous chess set?*

"Yes, I'm Karin Eklund's cousin!" she said, catching on. "Well, technically, her third cousin once removed. I guess we were *bryllingar* in Swedish? I always get confused with the terminology. We got here last night." She extended her hand. "Camilla Easton."

Once she introduced herself, it all made sense—the long-lost relative to whom Karin had inexplicably left her house. This former model, an expat Swede Manhattanite, had thrown Nornö into further confusion by tearing down the house and building a villa that rivaled the Nornö Hotel. Camilla Easton was shrouded in mystery, and speculation about her character had blown up epically. We'd assumed this distant relative would be aloof and snooty, but the cheery person offering her hand to me seemed nervous and eager to please.

"Nice to meet you," I said, returning her handshake. "I'm Zoë Holmgren. My family owns this store, so please let us know if you need anything."

Camilla loosened the straps of her tote bag and searched inside, eventually producing a stack of cards secured by a rubber band. "Actually, there is. My family and I would be so pleased if you could join us for a housewarming party this Saturday," she said, peeling off one of the cards and handing it to me.

I glanced at the invitation, admiring the casually elegant style. Party details were printed in navy-blue ink, superimposed against a whitewashed picture of the new house. "Thank you. I'll talk about it with Mormor and my mother. We usually work on Saturdays."

"It starts at 1:00 p.m., but stop by whenever you can."

"We'll try." Camilla had piqued my curiosity in just a few words, and suddenly, I wanted to attend the Eastons' party very badly. The prospect of brand-new faces and impressions would break up the monotony of my summer.

"Can I ask you another question?"

"Sure."

"I want to invite the other island locals, but I don't know where everyone lives. What's the best way to get an invitation to them?"

"The easiest way would be the post office. Ask the clerk to put an invitation in each of their mailboxes," I suggested.

"That's a great idea!" Camilla exclaimed. "Why didn't I think of that earlier?"

"But they're closed now," I informed her. "They'll open for an hour tomorrow. Between eleven and twelve."

"I'll make sure to get there on time."

"Holmgren's is close to the post office, and I'll be here tomorrow morning—I can drop them off for you, if you'd like?"

Camilla looked pensive. "Are you sure? I don't want to take advantage of your time at work."

"No problem at all."

"Maybe I should stop by there anyway and introduce myself?"

I shrugged. "The clerk doesn't even live in Nornö, so it's not a big deal."

Camilla laughed. "Okay, I get it. Lord knows I have enough to do before Saturday—"

"I'm happy to help," I assured her.

"In that case, you have to come!"

I smiled. "Hopefully we can."

Camilla gave me the invitations and said, "Thank you again. Just call me if anything comes up. My number is at the bottom of the card."

Our warm, friendly chatter heightened my need to know more. I wasn't ready for Camilla to leave the store. "Since you just got here, do you need anything? Bread? Milk?"

"No, thank you, we're good. Our property manager stocked up the house before we arrived."

Property manager? In Nornö? Maybe a handyman or jack-of-all-trades, but not a property manager.

"Oh, that's so convenient," I fibbed. "Who's your property manager?"

"They're a couple. Kurt and Evalina Bohlander."

Douglas's sneaky parents! They had been cozying up to the Eastons without telling anyone else in Nornö about it.

I smiled neutrally. "Where'd your property managers recommend you buy groceries?"

"Mm . . . someplace online."

"FoodDirekt?" I asked. FoodDirekt, an online grocery shopping and delivery service, was Holmgren's archenemy. The company owned several slick, modern inflatable boats, and it was impossible to miss them zooming up and down the archipelago. They also employed hunky, sailorly guys who brought sacks of goods to customers' docks. I had stalked their website and could not understand how they turned a profit with all the special deals they offered. They had cornered the market for bulk shopping in the archipelago in only a few years, making it difficult for stores like ours to compete.

Thinking about FoodDirekt put me in a foul mood. The company had put nearly one hundred years of my family's blood, sweat, and tears at risk. It felt like we were in the middle of a losing battle, further underscored whenever I caught Nornö's snooty vacationers picking up their FoodDirekt orders from the main dock. They didn't bother hiding those beige-and-green paper bags either, shamelessly reusing them "in the name of the environment" to pack their purchases from Holmgren's—right in front of my face! But Mormor had taught me to be professional, so I smiled and bit my tongue, suppressing the urge to give those ungrateful customers a piece of my mind.

Camilla shrugged slightly. "I don't remember what it was called."

I doubted she didn't remember but gave her credit for being tactful.

"I certainly didn't know there was such a well-stocked supermarket on the island," Camilla continued, "and I firmly believe in supporting local businesses."

It was a good answer, so I said, "Holmgren's can get you anything you want. Email us your shopping list or special requests, and we'll take care of it."

I had never been this accommodating to a customer before. The shifty Bohlanders were probably charging the Eastons a pretty penny for placing those FoodDirekt orders, fleecing newcomers who didn't understand the ways of the island. I couldn't pass up an opportunity to put a wrench in their plans and simultaneously stick it to FoodDirekt.

"I'll definitely take you up on that."

I finally stopped grilling Camilla, and she left with a polite wave of her hand. The store was empty again, and I snuck into the storage cubicle to talk with Mormor. Simba, who had obediently sat still behind the register, hurried after me.

"Mormor! Guess what?"

Mormor Agnes looked up from the pile of papers on her desk and removed her reading glasses. "I don't know, *sötnos*. What's got you so excited?"

"Camilla Easton, Karin Eklund's long-lost cousin, just came into the store!"

A bemused smile lit up Agnes's face—a solid, pink-toned grin—but I couldn't tell if she was genuinely intrigued or simply humoring me.

Mormor's baby-blue eyes had always given me their undivided attention. She had the softest skin of anyone I knew, warm and comforting like fresh laundry. Her silver hair was still thick, styled in a side-parted bob that gave her a casual elegance. Mormor wore her age with an ease I preferred to Linn's studied attempts at looking young. Besides, Mormor had both feet on the ground and never considered herself too precious for anything—pounding a hammer, chopping wood, or mowing the lawn. A lifetime in Nornö was inscribed in every line on her face. Mormor was a proud product of the sea, wind, and cold, embodying the resilience bred in her family for generations.

"About time," she said. "I was beginning to wonder if Karin was playing a joke on us."

"It's no joke—and Camilla invited us to a housewarming party on Saturday," I said, reaching over the bags and boxes of alcohol to show Mormor the invitation.

She put her reading glasses back on and examined the card. "Pretty paper. That house is something!"

"I know. I'm dying to see it up close. Can we go? I know it's during business hours, but Simon and Ebba can manage on their own for half a day."

Mormor handed the invitation back to me and limped to the filing cabinet a few feet away. It was a small space to negotiate, and I noticed how she was dragging her left foot. The effort she exuded worried me. Mormor's wit, positive attitude, and strong work ethic made it easy to forget she had chronic arthritis.

Two years ago, Mormor had mentioned (because she never complained) feeling stiffness in her left knee and how difficult it had become to bend down. Linn and I had told her to see a doctor, but she'd scoffed at the idea. Instead, she took an anti-inflammatory pill whenever the pain flared up. One morning, she woke up to find her knee had swollen like a grapefruit, and Linn had insisted on taking her to a hospital on the mainland. After a physical exam and MRI, the doctor discovered Mormor's knee cartilage had deteriorated and the bones were rubbing against each other, causing irritation. He recommended more pain relievers, icing, and bandaging to alleviate the pain. He also told her to scale back on the physical activities aggravating her condition—namely, the heavy labor at Holmgren's. Unsurprisingly, Mormor refused to slow down, gradually losing more agility in her left leg. Her morning walks and swims dwindled. After much cajoling, she relied on a walker for long distances and finally bought a mobility scooter to get around the island.

Watching Mormor struggle with those few steps threw me into an internal panic. We had always been so close, yet she hadn't the faintest knowledge of what I had been contemplating. Would I have the heart to leave her and Holmgren's? Who would do the extra work if her arthritis became more debilitating?

Mormor opened a drawer and took out a thick folder. "You go with your mother," she said, focusing on the documents. "I'll stay here and hold down the fort."

"Is it your knee, Mormor? Does it feel worse? Is that why you don't want to go?"

"Honey, Saturday's our busiest day. I'd rather be here than mingle with a bunch of people."

"But we can't go without you. You're, like, the pillar of our community. You know everything about Nornö—the stories, the families, the history. The party won't be as interesting if you're not there."

"If Camilla Easton wants to know more about her new home away from home, she's welcome to come here for a *fika*. And boy, do I have some good stories about Karin Eklund," she said, chuckling.

Mormor never suffered from FOMO, so I knew she wouldn't have a change of heart. But of course, Linn was enthusiastic when I told her about the Eastons' party, and we agreed to go together.

After dinner, I excused myself and ran up the stairs to the attic, my private wing of the house. As a kid, I'd loved spending time in the cluttered, unfinished space, reading books by flashlight or camping out with my sleeping bag. The low ceilings made it feel like a bunker, my secret refuge from Linn's mood swings and the jumbled mess of Mormor's odds and ends. For my sixteenth birthday, the two of them surprised me with a book on attic-decorating ideas and gave me a blank check to transform it into the bedroom of my dreams. Linn and I had combed Pinterest for inspiration, creating a mood board that was remarkably free of our standard mother-daughter bickering. The hardest part had been going through a century's worth of family memorabilia that chronicled the Holmgren footprint in Nornö: old photographs, handcrafted porcelain, and watercolors of the runestones. Linn wanted to burn everything. Mormor swore she could find a place for them downstairs.

Once the objects had been cleared out, the area became open and inviting, purged from the ghosts and grievances of the past. We painted the walls and slanted ceiling white but preserved the dark beams. A newly installed skylight brightened the space, and we changed the irregular alcoves into built in bookcases for shelving and storage. I compromised by keeping a few antiques: a reproduction rococo desk from my great-great-grandmother's side of the family, a peach velvet sofa from Mormor's childhood bedroom, and a curved wooden table Morfar had purchased in the seventies. I positioned my queen-sized bed against one of the sloping walls and called it my cozy corner, since I loved snuggling under a fluffy duvet, surrounded by pillows, my laptop, and *The Real Housewives* for company.

I took my laptop from the desk and settled back in bed. Right now, I had no intention of binge-watching a reality show. Instead, I was preparing to go down the Google rabbit hole.

I was much more fascinated by the Eastons than I'd let on.

My encounter with Camilla may have been brief, but her presence in Nornö had loomed long before her arrival. Talk about Camilla's plans for Karin's house had been rampant, but I'd ignored the petty gossip—frankly, I didn't get why people cared so much about an old house, and Camilla sounded like another middle-aged prima donna, my mother on steroids. Douglas Bohlander had been obsessed with the building project, inspecting the site and reporting on the expensive materials. I'd assumed he was being his usual nosy self, but now I knew he had a direct interest in it, since Kurt and Evalina had been courting a business relationship with the Eastons. Ever since Douglas had repeated his parents' rumor about my mother's "one-night stand," I'd been suspicious of the Bohlanders. They behaved appropriately in public but plotted and planned behind closed doors, determined to assert themselves at everyone else's expense.

I googled "Camilla Easton," but more matches than anticipated appeared. Logistics Manager. Rug Importer. Once I clicked on "All Images" and scrolled past a series of Moroccan rugs, I finally found photos of the woman who had entered Holmgren's.

There were snapshots of Camilla Easton in a black satin ball gown, chairing a gala to raise money for cancer research. Camilla Easton in riding pants at a horse competition in the Hamptons. Camilla Easton in a fur vest at a Michael Kors fashion show. Camilla Easton at an extravagant hat lunch in Central Park. Her tuxedo-clad husband appeared in a few photos, but he looked like a typical handsome partner from central casting. Despite standing next to other well-groomed, wealthy-looking women, Camilla stood out, with her natural good looks and effortless style. While the other ladies appeared overeager and overdone, Camilla was Scandi-cool, preferring blazers, jeans, and flats to suits, shifts, and heels. In my favorite photo, she pulled off a daring white dress with cutout sides at a museum benefit without looking trashy. Amid all the boring evening attire, she was the epitome of cutting-edge chic.

Scrolling further, I came upon a 2009 blog post about "Swedish Models of the Nineties" and an entry on someone named Kami Gunnarsson. I pressed the link, and a black-and-white cover from French *Elle* popped up. Four faces filled the screen: a classic blonde, a swan-necked Black beauty, a doe-eyed Asian model, and a brunette bombshell with thick eyebrows and large, lush lips. Her sultry features overpowered the others, almost like she'd sat for an entirely different photo shoot. It was difficult not to focus only on her, but I tore my eyes away to read the caption underneath, which identified the stunner as Kami Gunnarsson.

I zoomed in on the photo. Was Kami Camilla? I supposed "Kami" was a plausible nickname, but she bore little resemblance to the person I'd met earlier today. Her hair was much lighter now, her brows and lips less extreme. Still, the picture was almost twenty-five years old, and lighting and makeup did wonders to transform facial features. I scrolled down, and more photos of Kami frolicking on the beach and posing against a Harley-Davidson motorcycle appeared, immortalizing her online as a beautiful face who had achieved some recognition. A few sentences at the end described how Kami Gunnarsson married an American and lived in New York City. She now went by her given name, Camilla, and her husband's surname, Easton. They had one child, Gunnar, and the accompanying picture was the polar opposite of her modeling days—Camilla holding hands with a cute little boy at a charity Easter egg hunt in Palm Beach.

My curiosity was insatiable. I couldn't help myself and googled "Gunnar Easton," but the only photos available were school-related. He played lacrosse, was on the wrestling team, and wrote newspaper articles for Putnam Preparatory Academy in Manhattan, class of 2019—he must have just graduated from high school. Gunnar looked so American, sporty and confident with tousled hair and a toothy smile. I went on Instagram to check if Gunnar Easton had a public account, but he was private. He didn't seem to be seeking attention, either, having chosen a snow-capped photo of the Matterhorn as his profile picture. There were no descriptive emojis or pithy quotes, only his name, eleven posts, and 394 followers versus the 506 accounts he followed.

Gunnar had turned out to be as enigmatic as his mother. For the umpteenth time since I'd met Camilla, I wondered how the hell little Nornö would satisfy a family like the Eastons.

6

LINN

"Mamma, how do I look?"

I stopped emptying the dishwasher and tried to disguise my surprise. Zoë never asked my opinion about anything, but now she stood with arms akimbo, posing in the printed paisley minidress I bought her for Midsummer's Eve. *Didn't the fabric itch?* I thought. But Zoë seemed nervous, sucking in her cheeks and averting my gaze, so there was no need for sarcasm.

She shouldn't have felt so insecure. The halter-neck dress boasted a coral, off-white pattern with a lace band around the waist. Freshly showered after a morning at Holmgren's, Zoë's skin glistened with the jasmine-infused sheen of her moisturizer, reminding me of the sand at Brunnsbad Beach or the shiny interior of a seashell. She was lovely but too self-conscious to see it.

Walking over to her, I said, "You look beautiful! And I love what you did with your hair."

Zoë twisted a few corkscrews around her fingers. "It was a little puffy, so I have to wear it half up, half down."

"Your hair is not puffy. It's thick and healthy, like all the Holmgrens'. We have many problems, but hair has never been one of them." Caring for Zoë's hair had been a challenge for me when she was growing up. I hadn't understood that Zoë's curly texture required specific products and had mistakenly used the standard Barnängen two-in-one shampoo and conditioner until toddlerhood. Zoë's dense hair would break whenever I tried combing through it, and sometimes looked unkempt. One day, a Kenyan woman at a café in Stockholm approached us when Zoë's hair was sticking out in all directions and recommended a leave-in conditioner for extra moisture and a detangling spray to prevent breakage. More embarrassed than offended, I'd gone to an Afro-Swedish beauty supply store on Olof Palmes gata as instructed and purchased the shea butter products. Finally, I could comb out Zoë's hair without hurting her. Zoë eventually devised a personal hair care system from watching video tutorials and kept her ringlets in their natural state, avoiding straightening techniques like relaxers or blowouts.

Today's styled look departed from her usual carefree curls—not a strand out of place—but I resisted asking why. Our afternoon together was beginning on an encouraging note. I didn't want to spoil it by dwelling on her appearance.

"Yeah, well, I hope the weather holds out, or else my hair—and the Eastons—are in trouble."

I looked outside the veranda window. "It's a little overcast, but I think we'll be in good shape."

"Can we go now? It's already two thirty, and I don't want to get there too late."

"Race you to the bikes!" I teased and bolted out the door.

"That's not fair!" Zoë called out from behind me.

It took us fifteen minutes to bicycle to the other end of Nornö, a part of the island not easily accessible to the general public, since the area contained a dense thicket of pine trees, deadwood, and blueberry bushes. When we reached the narrow footpath, which was a scraggy trail overlapped with brittle branches and exposed tree roots, we got off our bikes and walked uphill to the white shingle house. As I parked next to an array of other two-wheelers, I heard the gaggle of voices, laughter, and music reverberating from the property. After removing our housewarming gift for the Eastons—a set of three scented candles named after the Greater Norns—from the basket, Zoë and I walked in comfortable silence to the back of the house.

"Should we walk inside to get to the front? Or is it better to go around?" I asked.

Zoë widened her eyes and shrugged, reflecting my own apprehension at the scale and perfection of Karin Eklund's old homestead. It was now unrecognizable, as though Karin and her little red cottage had never existed. What was once pebble-and-sand terrain was a landscaped turf of grass and flower beds. Where Karin's rotting furniture and rusty appliances had piled up, the Eastons had created an outdoor lounge area with seating, a fire pit, and a ping-pong table. I was burning with curiosity, but I had to play it cool. The Eastons were unknown, and I didn't want to appear overly impressed.

"Let's go inside," I finally decided, opening the screen door.

But once Zoë and I stepped over the threshold into the kitchen, we couldn't help but gasp in astonishment. We had entered a culinary version of Santa's workshop. The room was bathed in white, from the cabinetry to the tiles, anchored by a long black granite island in the center, where caterers assembled bite-sized Skagen toasts and salmon rounds. Next to the industrial-sized refrigerator, one person hammered away at a block of ice, transferring the smaller chunks into wine buckets. Waitstaff balanced trays with glasses, barely registering our presence.

We disappeared through the open archway into the living room but were stopped in our tracks when a woman's voice called out Zoë's name. She advanced toward us, arms outstretched, in a chevron-striped maxi dress—a Missoni, I noted. The metallic rainbow threads shimmered in the sunlit room, making my pink linen jumpsuit look dull in comparison.

"You made it!" the woman said, pulling Zoë in for a hug. She released her and then looked at me. "And this must be your lovely mother. She gets a hug too."

I was suddenly drawn into her embrace. Assuming she was our hostess, Camilla Easton, I had to return the gesture. I felt Camilla's dangly earrings brush against my cheek. I wasn't accustomed to this physical display of warmth from a stranger. It was very un-Swedish, but Camilla had lived abroad for more than half her life. Although it was difficult to assess the sincerity of her greeting, it reassured me in the intimidating environment, especially since we had come in through the back door.

After we formally introduced ourselves, I struggled to recall Camilla's face. She had the grace and style of a former model, but the patina of age, experience, and wealth complemented her beauty. I estimated Camilla was eight or ten years older than me—though she could easily pass for younger—but I didn't remember her face from fashion magazines. The models Alicia and I had idolized growing up were nineties icons Cindy Crawford, Naomi Campbell, and Kate Moss. We'd also followed the international success of Swedes Emma S. and Vendela, but Camilla seemed like just another tall, pretty Swedish girl who had caught the eye of modeling agents. Many of them had built successful careers, even if they weren't well-known.

But whether I recognized her was irrelevant. Modeling seemed to have springboarded Camilla to a new life.

"Thank you so much for having us," I said.

"My pleasure," Camilla replied.

"Your place is amazing," Zoë added, eyes traveling from one end of the open-plan living room to the other.

Her youth allowed her to get away with outright staring, but I had to be more discreet about checking out the interior. The house was simultaneously serene and dramatic; a neutral color palette of sand, cream, and ivory didn't detract from the spellbinding views of the sea and sky from the floor-to-ceiling windows. Even the giant lawn chess set, eye-catching behind the glass, was carved in teak and blended in with the natural environment's greens and browns. A long walnut dining table with serrated edges dominated one end of the room, providing alternate views of the seascape. Camilla had introduced texture by layering a sisal rug on the wooden plank floor and adding decorative accents like pillows, also in muted shades of blue and gray. There were none of the nautical elements prevalent in many archipelago homes. Instead, the most powerful statement was a large-scale, black-and-white photograph of the Nornir runestones.

I angled my body to examine the image better. "This is stunning! I've never seen anything like it before."

"It was a special commission by Mikael Jansson. We worked together way back when. Glad I have a seal of approval from a local."

"What's not to like? Everything you've done here is fantastic," I said, abandoning my vow to maintain my composure.

Camilla touched her heart with the palm of her hand. "Thank you so much. Karin left me a wonderful surprise, and I'm so grateful to her for giving me a chance to create a family home in Sweden."

"I'm impressed you could get it done in eighteen months," I said.

Camilla chuckled. "It wasn't easy, but I've done other renovation projects in New York, so I knew what I wanted. My builder and decorator—also here today—were geniuses, and we made every decision via email with drawings and pictures. It helps when everyone's on the same page."

And when you have an unlimited budget, I couldn't help thinking. Instead, I asked, "Did you do all of this sight unseen?"

"I came to Nornö twice, in secret. Once after Karin's funeral in Ljusdal, when I found out she had left the house to me, and then again when the construction was complete."

"How'd you manage that without anyone seeing you?" Zoë asked.

"I took a private ferry directly to the dock here."

"Smart," Zoë remarked.

"It may sound excessive, but I know people were suspicious of me and this project. 'Karin Eklund leaves prime property to some cousin no one has ever heard of,'" she imitated a disgruntled voice. "But I also come from a small town. I know how sensitive things can get with the neighbors. People don't realize that Karin was very close to my grandmother—they were first cousins—and since she never had any children, she took an interest in me, like an aunt. When I became a model and moved to Paris, Milan, and finally New York, Karin always sent me beautiful letters and little care packages with Swedish candy." Camilla gave something of a wistful smile. "I always took Bilar and Marabou chocolate with me on shoots. When the builders cleared out the house, they found a stack of magazines with pictures of me inside. Karin had saved everything she could get her hands on."

"Wow, I had no idea," I said, touched by the memory.

"That is so sweet!" Zoë added.

"I know, which is why—" Camilla stopped. "Follow me. I want to show you something." We followed her to the front door, and Camilla pointed to a brass plaque beneath the knocker that read: KARINTORP. "My tribute to her. This house will be a new chapter for my family and me."

There was a respectful moment of silence as we remembered Karin. Finally, I said, "We all need a clean slate from time to time."

"With some peace and quiet," Camilla added. "I've never slept better."

"How do you usually spend the summers?" Zoë asked.

"In Water Mill, for the last twenty years," she answered, taking for granted we knew where that was. "But it never felt like a vacation—all the running around and schmoozing. And the traffic is terrible! We spent more time in the car than at the beach."

"Cars won't be a problem in Nornö," Zoë quipped.

"Exactly." Camilla chuckled. "It's been a crazy year, and I've been dying to come out here and just . . . be. And then aside from the house project, our son, Gunnar, was applying to colleges, which was so stressful. I want the three of us to spend quality time together before he goes to school. I also want to reconnect with my Swedish roots, so Karin's gift couldn't have come at a better time." She paused. "My apologies for talking your ear off! Please make yourself at home. Get a drink and mingle!"

"She seems very nice," Zoë whispered when Camilla was out of earshot.

And maybe even a little vulnerable, I thought, parsing Camilla's words.

Zoë and I pivoted to the spacious front lawn, which was laid out with tables draped in white, matching bamboo chairs, an oyster station, and a three-piece band serenading guests with breezy summer ballads. A soaring pole with bunting flew both the Swedish and American flags. Every detail was meticulously thought-out, and I had to commend Camilla, a newcomer, for organizing a party of this caliber in the far-flung reaches of the archipelago. All the supplies, rentals, and staff had had to be imported from the mainland. The environment made it clear that our hostess had high standards, and the vendors and staff had brought their A-game. No sour Swedish faces or indifference—they refilled drinks and passed out canapés with aplomb. Although Camilla couldn't control the weather, she had lucked out there too. A cloudless, blue sky blanketed her side of Nornö.

I attributed that to the unfair law of the universe: the less you need, the more you receive. Camilla had been blessed with an extra sprinkling of fairy dust, from her modeling days to her present-day life. When she'd asked for good weather, Mother Nature had delivered. Still, I couldn't criticize Camilla's generous hospitality or her desire to be welcomed into the Nornö community. We were a far cry from her glamorous New York life, but she had opened her home to the eccentric characters that made up our little island. And *everyone*—except Agnes—seemed to be in attendance. Crusty old locals, who had unearthed their outdated finery, hobnobbed with the bourgeois summer crowd that favored red chinos and floaty sundresses. It was the most luxurious gathering Nornö had ever seen, and guests exuded an air of contentment, scarcely masking their glee at being invited.

It wasn't lost on me that the people who had criticized Camilla the most were the same ones who were now sipping her alcohol and slurping her oysters. Beyond the house's lofty peak, I could sense that an unspoken reality was taking root: the Eastons' arrival signaled a shift in power on the island. Despite her down-to-earth demeanor, Camilla had barreled into Nornö like a storm, and I wasn't sure the island was ready for it.

I stopped studying the crowd and realized I was still holding the bag with our housewarming gift.

"My goodness! I forgot to hand over the candles," I said to Zoë. "Would you mind getting me some rosé while I find Camilla or one of the staff?"

"Sure, no problem," Zoë replied, heading in the direction of the bar set up at the edge of the yard.

I reentered the house and found Camilla and a man in the kitchen. Their backs were turned, bent over food trays on the island countertop.

"Excuse me, Camilla," I said, lightly touching her shoulder.

They both turned. I froze.

"Oh, honey!" Camilla exclaimed. "This is the nice woman with the beautiful daughter I was telling you about. Their family has been in Nornö for generations, and they own the store down in the village." She set her sapphire eyes on me and said, her voice laced with warmth, "Linn, this is my husband, Walter Easton, but everyone calls him—"

Wes.

7

ZOË

I loitered by the bar, a drink in each hand: a glass of rosé for my mother, and a Coke Zero for myself. I had spent the previous ten minutes jockeying my way through the crowd, greeting familiar faces *ooh*ing and *aah*ing over my dress and hair. They were accustomed to seeing me in a grayish-white polo and a top knot, so their effusive compliments were embarrassing. Linn would have loved the attention and flattery by association, but it was a party, and she already seemed to have forgotten about me. Maybe a guy had offered her a cocktail and she was engaged in an amusing conversation elsewhere. It had been silly of me to think we could come here together and party responsibly.

I looked around. The temptation was everywhere. Alcohol flowed, voices grew louder, and a few people already seemed weak at the knees. I prayed the next one wouldn't be my mother; I would disown her if she lost control at Camilla's party. I was a pro at putting on a front, and as far as the Eastons were concerned, the Holmgrens were a respectable Nornö family.

Despite the festive atmosphere, I felt out of place. There were hardly any people my age, and truth be told, I wouldn't have minded hanging out with Camilla. Her life seemed so fascinating, and judging by this lavish bash, she had brought some of that luster to Nornö.

Irritated, I sipped my Coke, shifting my attention to the

lawn chess set where Douglas—who was clad in black metalhead garb, even though it was high summer—moved a piece from one square to another. Another guy, taller and decidedly more clean-cut, watched. I was sure he was Gunnar Easton and experienced an inexplicable urge to go over there and make myself seen. But then I saw Linn rushing toward me, a crazed expression on her face.

"Zoë, we have to go home now," she said.

"Home?" I scoffed. "I've been standing here for over ten minutes with our drinks, waiting for you. What's the matter?"

"Nothing. It's too crowded, and I don't feel like seeing all these people. Even dressed up, they're still annoying."

"Um, that was harsh."

"I was joking."

"Well, I don't want to go. This is a fabulous party, and we should stay."

"Yeah, it's great, but I've seen enough. Mormor's at the store without us, and I feel bad about that."

"She was invited and didn't want to come!"

"Still—"

"It'd be rude to leave now. Camilla was so happy to see us."

"I've seen enough," she insisted. "It's time for us to go."

"Seriously, Mamma, stop being so dramatic."

"I'm not being dramatic! I just want to leave. But you're welcome to stay here without me."

"I will," I said, holding my ground.

Linn turned on her heel and strode off, taking it down a notch as she dodged the other guests, smiling and waving as though she hadn't had a meltdown, and everything was perfectly fine. She veered left, and I lost sight of her as she disappeared behind the Eastons' house.

Fuming, I walked back to the bar and slammed the drinks

on the counter. This sudden about-face made no sense yet was so typical—Linn flipping out and making the afternoon all about her. I sighed, struggling to understand the source of her mood swing. The day had started so nicely, and Linn had seemed like she clicked with Camilla.

Seemed.

Maybe that was the problem. Maybe Linn felt inferior and even envious next to Camilla. It was no secret that my mother's life hadn't lived up to her original plans. In contrast, Camilla had fulfilled many of the ambitions Linn had dreamed of—world travel, living abroad, and meeting new people. Or could it be something as simple as Linn feeling threatened by having another good-looking woman on the island? My mother could be superficial like that. She was prone to harping on about how plain and boring the people in Nornö were but probably secretly enjoyed being the resident beauty queen.

I knew I sounded bitchy, but my mother's irrational behavior spawned these evil thoughts. If she couldn't act like a normal person, then I would be forced to dig for an explanation.

My hypotheses were interrupted when Camilla, her husband, and Gunnar gathered in front of the house and asked for everyone's attention. All eyes focused on the photogenic trio, each holding a glass of champagne. Gunnar stood taller than his parents and wore chinos and an untucked linen shirt like his father, who reminded me of Dr. McDreamy in *Grey's Anatomy*. Gunnar's longish, dark blond hair fell over his forehead, but his skin was pale, as though he hadn't been out in the sun since arriving in Nornö. Camilla spoke once the guests quieted down, welcoming everyone in Swedish to wild applause before changing to English for her husband and son's benefit.

"Thank you so much for coming today. I know it was short notice, but Wes, Gunnar, and I are so touched by this turnout," Camilla said.

The crowd chuckled knowingly. As if we would miss this party!

"Nornö is a place filled with beauty and mystery, a place my cousin Karin loved so much and called home for most of her life. She always told me I had to come back to Sweden, but I never found a place that felt right after so many years abroad. As many of you have told me today, Karin was a strong, wise woman who did things her way. And she always looked out for me—even from a distance. By giving me this property, she gave me a chance to come back to Sweden, and for that, I will always be grateful. I can't imagine a more fitting place to create new memories and honor all the things about Nornö that Karin held so dear."

At that moment, Karin's spirit seemed to flow through the gathering, and everyone grew solemn. Camilla sensed the change and raised the volume of her voice, sounding like a perky cheerleader.

"We look forward to taking morning dips in the sea and eating *runebullar* buns from the bakery. Most of all, we can't wait to get to know all of you better, so *Skål!*" She lifted her champagne glass, and everyone followed suit, cheering for the Eastons and their new home.

Afterward, the crowd returned to their previous clusters, and I was alone again, silently cursing my mother for disappearing. Douglas hadn't budged from the chess set, so I walked over to him in desperation.

"*Hej!*" I called out, straining to sound cheerful. "Having fun?"

"*Tjaaa,*" Douglas muttered, barely lifting his chin.

I pointed to a chess piece and asked, "Are those things heavy?" Each one reached Douglas's waist.

He waited a few seconds longer than necessary before responding. "The heavier the piece, the better the quality." A whiff of superiority spiked his comment: *Like, duh, Zoë.*

"So . . . can I play with you?" I asked, feeling like a five-year-old at recess again, begging for Douglas's attention. Morfar had taught me to play chess, and we had waged many friendly battles when he was alive.

"I'm actually in the middle of a round with Gunnar. He's just getting us some beers."

"Oh." Swallowing my pride, I added, "Can I watch?"

Douglas shrugged, noncommittal. "I guess."

I pulled down my minidress as much as possible and sat on the stone bench. It took me less than a minute to figure out Douglas was a chess novice. His rooks were scattered in the middle of the board and not protecting each other, meaning he must have played a weak opening game for them to be so dispersed. Morfar had warned me about rooks going on an "adventure" too early. *Leave them exposed,* he would say, *and they could quickly be surrounded. Connect them to avoid diagonal attacks.* How things looked now, Gunnar's bishops and knights could ambush Douglas's rooks and chase them around the board.

I weighed whether I should share my tips or sit, watch, and let him get outplayed, but my competitive instinct forced me to speak up. "You should get a pawn out of the way and make an open file for your rooks."

He guffawed. "Since when did you become a chess prodigy?"

Why did I even bother with him? Shrugging, I said, "Just

some friendly advice."

Gunnar finally returned and gave Douglas a bottle of Corona.

"Thanks, man," he said, sucking down nearly half the bottle. He turned back to the board without introducing me to Gunnar. Only after Gunnar raked his floppy hair from his eyes did he seem to notice me, acknowledging my presence with a passing nod. Pissed off at being cast aside by both guys, I walked over to Gunnar and extended my arm in greeting. "Hi, I'm Zoë. I also grew up in Nornö, just like Douglas."

My hand hung like a question mark in the space between us. He finally reached out and offered a limp handshake. "Gunnar," he mumbled, scarcely looking me in the eye.

"Congratulations on your new house. It's incredible."

"It's okay."

I couldn't tell if that was a humblebrag or if Gunnar was genuinely ungrateful. Nevertheless, I plowed on. "Have you been to Sweden before?"

"Stockholm, when I was younger."

"Coming from Manhattan, Nornö must be a huge change for you."

"Yup."

"Do you understand any Swedish?"

"Not reablly."

"I hear you're going to college in a few months."

"Yup."

"Where to?"

He narrowed his eyes. "You know American schools?"

"Sure. Harvard, Stanford, Columbia . . ."

He gulped his beer and replied, "None of the above."

Gunnar's rudeness threw me for a loop. Not that I demanded his undivided attention, but a little courtesy would have been appreciated. After all, he was one of the hosts and a newbie on my home turf. Was Douglas, who was now prowling the chessboard like an ominous bat, that much more interesting? There were few people my age in Nornö, so a part of me had hoped to make a new friend, but sadly, another loathsome upper-class idiot had landed on the island. I didn't have time for Gunnar's bad behavior and wanted to bring our "conversation" to a close.

"Well, enjoy your stay in Nornö," I said. Totally lame, but I couldn't think of anything better to say.

He finally looked me in the eye. "I don't even want to be here, so I doubt it."

Did he just diss Nornö? And me as well—indirectly? I couldn't reconcile Gunnar's stank attitude with Camilla's graciousness. At least Douglas was as slippery as his parents; I had no illusions about him. But I had given Gunnar more credit, mistaking his preppy good looks and glossy upbringing for some semblance of class.

Crossing my arms over my chest, I hissed, "It's a shame your first complete sentence had to be so obnoxious."

That line may have come from one of *The Real Housewives,* but it expressed my disgust perfectly.

I didn't wait to see his reaction and stomped from the chess corner to the center of the lawn with more grit than I felt, and I kept walking until I reached the back of the house. My heart pounded. It always quickened whenever I stood up for myself and struck back, but it happened so rarely, leaving me on the verge of tears. After prying my bike loose from a pile of other bicycles that had fallen over like dominoes, I checked the time. It was only four thirty, but the garden party was gradually becoming a barbecue. I saw a chef stacking spareribs on the stone grill, and the pungent smell of garlic and charred smoke wafted through the air.

In the background, I heard a group of people hoot with laughter. It sounded like the new arrivals had won over Nornö. So why was I the one who felt like an outsider?

8

LINN

I hunkered down in the deck chair, nursing my second glass of Pinot Noir and a guilty conscience. My goal was to feel numb enough to forget the deceit I had unwittingly partaken in—on a woman who seemed kind and open, with a man who could be a sociopath.

Everything had stopped when I saw Wes's face. It had taken every ounce of self-control not to hike up my eyebrows and stare open-mouthed. But Camilla's bubbly introduction had overpowered my shock, and I'd been able to eke out, "Nice to meet you."

"Likewise!" Wes had responded, friendly as ever, reaching out to enshroud my small hand with his large one. Had I imagined a slight squeeze at the end—extra pressure to scare me into silence?

Unflappable, he'd prattled on, asking a few questions about the store, wondering when it was best to book a tennis court, nodding when Camilla said Zoë had to show their son, Gunnar, "the lay of the land." One of the caterers had interrupted the niceties, and I'd been able to make what was hopefully a graceful exit. But my heart had thudded; my breath coming in short spurts of panic. I'd only wanted to find Zoë and get out of there, but Zoë's confusion and hostility was understandable. Why leave the party of the summer so suddenly? Especially when the hostess had received us so graciously. Zoë hadn't known I was fighting for my sanity, so

I'd accepted her rebuke, the presumption that I was an unstable social misfit, because the truth was so much worse.

Wes's neighborly reaction had been so convincing, I automatically began to doubt whether he was the man who had treated Alicia and me to drinks at Grand Hotel. Or belted out sloppy verses of "Helan går" before downing shots. Or, most flagrantly, taken me to bed. He may have looked like the blue-eyed, dark-haired American I had met in Stockholm, but the man with whom I'd exchanged pleasantries in the kitchen was, in actuality, a loving husband and father, welcoming me to his wife's dream house. His talent of gaslighting with only a few courteous phrases lobbed in my direction made me come undone. Staying for the remainder of the garden party had been out of the question.

The gullible, somewhat ethical part of me refused to accept he would have screwed around the minute he stepped onto Swedish soil, operating without guilt or fear of consequences. I must have been delusional when I saw the face resembling the man I had been intimate with. Didn't they say everyone had a double? A doppelgänger? The Wes at Grand Hotel and the Wes with Camilla may have shared the same first name, but they couldn't be one and the same, living on the other side of Nornö. Such a brutal coincidence was impossible.

I reexamined the photo I had taken on my iPhone before leaving the room at Grand Hotel, when Wes was sleeping and seemingly harmless. I zoomed in on his face, concentrating on his lips and the tiny scar by his eyebrow, and knew, with absolute certainty, that he was Camilla's husband.

I had been trying to talk myself out of this obscene fact, but the photographic evidence knifed through me, deflating my shaky sense of self-worth and skewering my habit of making one bad choice after another. I hated how easily I devoured the crumbs of attention men paid me. I hated myself for craving emotional connection, no matter how superficial or toxic. What were the odds this one would come back to haunt me? He'd supposedly been a visiting American on a business trip. There hadn't been a wedding band on his finger or any indications of having a wife or son, not even a slip of the tongue. It had been meaningless fun. We were never supposed to see each other again.

I let go of the phone and covered my face. How could a girls' night out go so terribly wrong?

I refilled my wineglass. Things had started to go wrong a long, long time ago. I had been putting myself in questionable, potentially dangerous situations from a far younger age than Zoë's eighteen years. The summer between eighth and ninth grade had been a turning point—the season I was desperate to grow up and distance myself from everything connected to Nornö.

The confirmation/sailing camp on an island a half hour away had been filled with well-to-do kids from all over the country. Stockholm proper was heavily represented, along with sentimental expat Swedes from around the world. My family wasn't overly religious, but this camp had been a tradition in the Holmgren family, and since I already knew how to sail, it had been a natural decision to go. While my parents considered confirmation camp a time for reflection and moral contemplation, every fifteen-year-old boy and girl secluded on that island for three weeks—without their parents or any means of external communication—saw it as a gateway to freedom and experimentation. During confessional twilight conversations on a cliff, boys and girls held hands under blankets. Or they snuck out from their beds in the middle of the night to steal kisses in the woods. Innocent enough.

But I'd had my eye on one of the instructors, Nicolas, who was going into his last year of high school. For nearly three weeks, I was tireless, teasing and flirting, batting my eyes in his direction and walking by him in my bikini. I eventually was alone with him near the outdoor bathroom on the night of the camp's final event, a disco-themed party where everyone dressed up in vintage sequins, raggedy bell-bottoms, and tattered boas from the costume trunk. I'd asked Nicolas point-blank if he liked me, and when he finally admitted it, we'd shared a chaste kiss that progressed to full-on smooching. When we were both gone long enough for the priest to come looking and he caught us almost topless—a fifteen-year-old confirmand and an eighteen-year-old counselor—he'd had no choice but to send us home, two days before the confirmation ceremony.

The news had spread like wildfire among the kids and their parents, crossing the camp's borders, a cautionary tale to others who might have entertained similar thoughts. I'd felt humiliated, partly because I'd gotten caught and fled the island with everyone watching but also because Nicolas had refused to look or speak to me afterward. I could tell he was shocked and ashamed, as if I had tempted him into committing a cardinal sin. My mother was hysterical, furious at me for depriving the family of this important rite of passage. The priest had later contacted Agnes and Thomas, informing them I could still get confirmed in a private service, but I'd refused. It wouldn't be the same without the rest of the group, and the white eyelet dress purchased at NK during one of my family's rare trips to Stockholm—which I'd envisioned myself in for months—would remain in my closet, gathering mothballs.

On top of everything else, Agnes and Thomas had punished me: leaving Nornö and hanging out with my new friends was now forbidden. But the worst punishment was intangible. I feared being out-of-sight would mean being out-of-mind.

That was when the clandestine drinking began. Those three weeks at confirmation camp had opened up a whole new world of relationships and opportunities, but instead of moving forward, I had regressed and remained trapped in Nornö. The local kids I had played with my whole life were country bumpkins by comparison. I couldn't care less about the topics my neighbors talked about—building permits, the sea's dwindling fish supply, or, most boring of all, the groundwater level. I wanted to recapture that first sense of freedom I had experienced at confirmation camp. Sequestered at home, the only outlet I had to test limits and forget my punishment and isolation was alcohol.

Although the legal drinking age was eighteen, my parents had let me taste wine during the holidays and special dinners to "diminish" the allure of alcohol, but it had had the opposite effect. I found it electrifying: the color and smell of the liquid, the elegant feel of the stemmed glass in my hand, the way it fueled my passion for make-believe. I found sneaky ways to satisfy my curiosity, like offering to get my father's nightly tumbler of whiskey from the cabinet, pouring a few milliliters for myself into an old jam jar, and stowing it in my underwear drawer for a later date. When I finally took that first sip of Bushmills after dark on the small terrace attached to my second-floor bedroom, the smoky, spicy taste had made me wince, but as the syrupy liquid coursed down my throat, I felt warm all over, which tempered my mood. My father didn't drink much vodka, so replacing the missing quantities with water became another form of deception. I started throwing back shots secretly, alternating between cloudy bottles of Absolut and Smirnoff. My parents had remained ignorant; they worked from morning to night at Holmgren's and were grateful I stayed in my room without making a fuss. It had become a game, testing how much I could fool them, seeing how much I could get away with under their noses.

But the final straw came when I got careless and made the mistake of bringing a water bottle containing a mixture of rosé and Fanta to school. One of my enemies, Sara, who had once accused me of thinking I was better than everybody else, stole it from my book bag and ratted me out to our teacher. Yet again, Agnes and Thomas were called in and alerted that I was showing signs of "serious emotional and behavioral problems." Ironically, this only confirmed my self-perception that I was misunderstood; I had always felt things more acutely than everyone else. The gloomy conditions on Nornö discouraged unnecessary enthusiasm, and the locals' emotional state seemed to be frozen on neutral, personifying the Swedish concept of *lagom*—not too much, not too little, just the right amount of feeling and sensitivity. But I was a free spirit and didn't conform to the school's norms and expectations, their attempts to socialize me into a good citizen who never colored outside the lines. My parents, especially Agnes, saw the school's assessment as a sign of failure, an inability to raise me into a secure, well-adjusted individual.

Still, there was a potential solution to the problem. Agnes had done her research and suggested boarding school at Sigtuna to instill more discipline and self-control. Neither of my parents had a connection to Sigtuna, but the king had gone there. The school's stated values of providing a "high-quality, rigorous education" based on "humanistic, holistic principles" to foster every student's "unique talents and potential" spoke to my parents' increasing sense of desperation.

Sigtuna was supposed to be a course correction, a quasi-reform school to fix my wayward self, but it was the answer to all my prayers: a means of escaping Nornö. It was easy for me to adapt to life on the mainland. My reputation from the incident at the confirmation camp preceded me, giving me a bit of notoriety in Sigtuna's social scene. I'd already been labeled fun and flighty, so there was no reason to contradict that image. The student body reminded me of the types I had met at camp—a mix of Stockholmers, kids who had grown up on rural estates, and a handful of international Swedes. I was the only one from a remote island in the archipelago, but the school uniform (a gray pleated skirt or pants, white shirt, navy blazer, and diagonally striped tie) fostered cohesion and a sense of community. Plus, I was a quick study, learning the style and affectations of my worldly boarding-school peers (Fjällraven jackets, Converse high tops, cigarettes). And even though we had the option to go home every other weekend, I'd preferred staying on campus or exploring Stockholm, hanging out at malls and coffee shops with my new friends. Nornö became more and more of a metaphoric second home, as though I were one of the tourists who only took up residence in the summer.

Clouds had obscured the sun, and a whiff of cool air descended upon the dock. I rubbed my arms to warm up but didn't want to return to the house. I shuffled to the sauna and found my father's old yellow Tenson jacket. It was sun-bleached and stained, but neither my mother nor I had the heart to get rid of it. He had worn it year-round, on biting winter days while shoveling snow and chilly summer nights while driving his Bertram. My father had been tall and burly, so the jacket now swaddled me like a quilt.

"Pappa, I messed up again," I said aloud, slumping in the chair and closing my eyes. My father had tolerated my mischief, giving me the impression I could weasel my way out of any situation: fake IDs, overdrawn bank accounts, Zoë. Even the punishments he meted out had worked to my advantage, warping my concept of what was permissible and what could be forgiven. But I wasn't a kid anymore, and this misstep had come home to roost.

A thought suddenly dawned on me. I opened my eyes and sat up. What if I was overreacting? What if Wes hadn't placed me as the woman from Grand Hotel? I had given him a fake name and false information about where I lived, carefully maintaining the illusion that I was just another lighthearted party girl. Camilla's Wes would have never been so friendly if he had recognized me in the kitchen. I was a petite blonde and could easily pass for someone else.

Still, I couldn't shake the stinging sensation I had brought this humiliation upon myself by playing a childish game when I should have been honest about my details. If I had mentioned Nornö, Wes would have associated it with his wife and backed off. But "Linn from Nornö" had never been enough for me. Inventing a fantasy world and getting recklessly drunk and wrapped up in the moment had always been my downfall.

By now, I should have known better.

9

ZOË

During the bike ride home, my disappointment had mushroomed into determination.

"Hello?" I called out upon entering the hallway, but I only heard Simba's heavy breathing as he came to greet me. I went to the glass veranda and saw Linn's figure on the dock, sitting in one of the sun chairs, the silhouette of a wine bottle conspicuous on the side table. Mormor was probably still at Holmgren's; it wouldn't close until seven. I had the house to myself, which suited me perfectly, since I was in no mood for small talk or my mother's unnecessary drama. But my stomach growled; I hadn't eaten anything at the Eastons', which annoyed me because the food had looked delicious. I whipped up a bowl of vanilla yogurt, berries, and muesli and clambered up to the attic with Simba. Between my spoonfuls of yogurt, I changed from the halter dress into sweats and bunched my hair into a high ponytail.

Instantly, I felt like Zoë again. Today's experiment with the flowy outfit and neat hair had been for other people's benefit. Although I was ashamed to admit it, I had wanted to impress Camilla and her son, to show them that the people of Nornö weren't hicks. But Gunnar's shady vibe only confirmed he was a snob. Maybe it was a guy thing—he and Douglas could bond over beers—but I had irritated him, for whatever reason. A thought crossed my mind, one I usually took pains to repress: Could Gunnar be a closet racist? Had my brownness surprised him?

On days like this, when my mother's erratic behavior was in full swing and Mormor was preoccupied with the store, I felt so alone, adrift in hostile waters. Long ago, a good cry or climbing into one of my grandparents' laps would have comforted me, but that time had passed. As the only child in an unconventional family, I'd been given a silent ultimatum: grow up quickly or get left behind. I'd chosen the former, vowing to stay strong no matter what. That perseverance, through thick or thin, was part of the Holmgren character, but no matter how hard I tried, I could never outrun my mother's struggles. I had done everything my grandparents and teachers expected to compensate for her volatility, but I was tired of being strong and accepting my life as it was, rather than striving for what it could be. I did believe my mother had no idea who my father was, where he lived, or if he was still alive. Whoever or wherever he was, he didn't know I existed.

Today, one of those things was going to change.

The search for my father had begun anew last year, after I'd come across an article in *Aftonbladet* promoting a documentary about the Hultsfred Festival. The story had been buried in the back of the paper with the other television listings and I could have easily missed it, but I often read the tabloid from cover to cover when things were slow at Holmgren's.

The word *Hultsfred* had been engraved in my mind from the moment I'd forced Mamma to confess the true circumstances of my birth. After that, she'd refused to discuss anything about that fateful weekend in June 2000, balking whenever I mentioned it. I had to patch information together on my own, so I googled "Hultsfred Festival" regularly, keeping tabs on its checkered history, from cancellation and bankruptcy in 2010 to its rebirth in 2013. From the scant details I had extracted about my father, I learned he was originally from North Carolina and went by the nickname "J.G." He had worked as part of Kelis's road crew before going into the Army. I'd researched Kelis online, hoping to find a link to my father, but no J.G. ever appeared in any accounts of her musical career. I also googled my father's initials plus "U.S. military," but endless listings with the words *Lieutenant (junior grade)* came up, discouraging me from searching further.

But that *Aftonbladet* article—only a few paragraphs long—had profiled a Hultsfred fan who happened to be a videographer and had spent years shooting footage. He'd finally edited the material into a documentary celebrating youth culture at the annual music festival. Nothing significant about Hultsfred had surfaced in a long time, and this documentary would touch on an aspect of the festival that hadn't been extensively covered: the festivalgoers themselves. The organizers and performers were usually at the center of Hultsfred's reportage, but the participants were the ones who'd kept the festival going despite setbacks.

I debated whether to tell Linn about the documentary. Perhaps we could watch it together? But a territorial impulse gripped me, stemming from her history of half-truths and evasiveness. She hadn't earned my trust, so I would watch it alone. Deep down, I didn't want to lift my hopes either. My father had vanished after Hultsfred, and despite my Google search superpowers, I had never been able to find him. Why would this time be different?

❦

The night the documentary aired, my mother and Mormor sat in the den, engrossed in a *Wallander* detective movie. I went to my room with Simba and locked the door. Propping pillows behind me, I rested my laptop on a tray and prepared to enter the exhilarating world of the Hultsfred Festival.

The retro footage was grainy, showing old-school boom boxes and grunge and hip-hop fashion enjoying a comeback. My introduction to festival culture had been through Instagram posts from models, actors, and influencers at Coachella and Burning Man. I was used to social media images of outrageous designer duds, pimped-out RVs, and shameless product placements. But Hultsfred was folksy, portraying a bygone purity and innocence, a lack of pretension and commercialism, that was reminiscent of the hippies in the sixties and seventies. The narrator explained that from the beginning, the festival had been a platform for music lovers to join a collective and push boundaries. For three days, enthusiasts fled the conformity of their everyday lives for an alternative, freer existence. People both changed and became changed by the festival.

Watching them sing, whirl, and mosh onscreen, *I got it.* I finally understood what had drawn my mother there in the first place. She was a restless soul with a rebellious streak and had found her people at Hultsfred.

The film charted how easy it had been for festivalgoers to interact with folks they didn't know. There were interviews with individuals who had become best friends or lovers overnight, giving me a ray of hope my mother and father might turn up. I searched past the faces in the foreground with each reel, looking for a young Black man moving equipment on a sound stage or wandering among the masses, but the documentary ended, and no such figure appeared. Crushed, tears welled in my eyes, and I stared, zombielike, at the closing credits rolling on the computer screen, feeling helpless and hopeless. When the credits stopped, I moved the cursor to close the tab, but another scratchy clip appeared, inviting me to watch.

It was a blooper reel where the filmmaker had asked a pair of Swedish sound technicians the same question multiple times, but they doubled over in laughter whenever the microphone came in their direction. In Southern-drawl English, a male voice shouted off-camera, "Y'all so stupid!" The video then panned to a brown-skinned guy, who was laughing and wearing a yellow trucker hat.

I jerked up, wiping away my tears.

The filmmaker approached him, asking in English, "What do you think of the Hultsfred Festival?" His Swedish accent was strong, and the question came out in a staccato.

The young man made a show of rearranging his facial expression to look more serious. "I've met some nice people, seen some great artists, so yeah, man, it's been a dope experience," he said in a deep voice.

Swedish subtitles translated his response—right above his name. His full name. Jean-Gabriel "J.G." Latour.

Jean-Gabriel. It was a unique name I could've never cobbled together on my own. It sounded fancy and French, but I knew my father came from humble origins, based on Linn's vague descriptions.

There was no misinterpreting what I'd just seen and heard. Nineteen years later, my father seemed to be grinning at me, encased in my laptop like a photograph.

My hands trembled as I toggled back to the Google home page and typed out his full name. Just like that, professional photos of him in a white lab coat appeared: "Jean-Gabriel

Latour, MD, Brickell Medical Group."

He had the same handsome face, though more fully developed; I guessed he was around forty years old, forty-two max. His skin lacked wrinkles, his smile was confident and friendly, and his eyes possessed the same playful glint I had witnessed in the video clip.

My father was alive—living and working as a primary care physician in Florida. The last piece of the puzzle was so simple and straightforward that it almost felt like a letdown, a statement on how incompetent my previous attempts to find him had been. Why hadn't Linn tried to track him down? My father wasn't hiding. He was living a normal life; unaware he may have fathered a child in Sweden.

I zoomed in on his features, analyzing the angles and planes for similarities. Maybe our eyes? His were dark and almond-shaped like mine. I also owed my bow-shaped lips to him. My father didn't have a long digital trail—the entries I found were all professional—but I saved the few pictures to my phone, moving them to a new album I labeled "Brickell" to browse in private.

Almost as exciting was learning his parents—my paternal grandparents—were from Haiti, a detail captioned in a photo of when he had volunteered at a medical facility on the island. Ethnically, this made me half Haitian, an extra dimension to my racial identity I had never imagined. By the lilt in my father's voice, I had assumed his roots were in the American South, but the Latours were immigrants, and he was a first-generation American.

I dove into this new aspect of my cultural heritage: Haiti's history of slavery, the revolt against the French in 1804 that had formed the first Black republic, Duvalier's brutal dictatorship, and the catastrophic earthquake of 2010.

Pictures of Haitians in jazzy costumes dancing at Mardi Gras and images of children playing soccer in impoverished streets touched a chord, and I felt an instant connection. *That could have been me.* Although Haitians had been fighting oppression and poverty for centuries, they were resilient, finding joy in difficult circumstances—not unlike my ancestors in Nornö.

My father's professional success and charity work were impressive. He was an American success story, based on his accomplishments. What if he and Linn had kept in touch? How would he have reacted if he'd known about her pregnancy? Would he have urged her to come to the United States? Would we have become a family? Would he still have pursued his goals if he had known about me? Or would he have lingered in a state of limbo, like my mother?

I avoided analyzing those questions. Sowing more seeds of doubt and ambiguity wouldn't help. Still, knowing I had another parent halfway around the world and understanding I was part of a community outside the borders of Nornö and Sweden gave me strength. Mormor and Morfar had showered me with love and support, but my mother had shown me time and again how irresponsible and flaky she could be. Finding my father would give me other options.

Since half of my identity had always been a big question mark, I'd walked around Nornö feeling separate and apart, disjointed. The idea of my father in the flesh began to fill the void, but I decided to keep the facts of his existence to myself. Linn's unpredictable nature was too risky. What if she contacted J.G. and exploded, blaming him for getting her pregnant? No, letting her in on the secret could sabotage my plans and destroy the only shred of hope that was keeping me going.

Taking the laptop and yogurt to my desk, I sat. After

graduating high school, I had no official obligations in Sweden, at least not on paper. The emotional attachment to Mormor and Holmgren's had held me back, but today's strange letdown at the Eastons' proved I needed to pursue my own path. I had to follow the road leading to my father.

The chess pieces had been in place for some time. The moment had come for me to make the first move.

I clicked on the Draft folder in my Gmail. The email had been sitting there for months. I had painstakingly chosen photos of nineteen-year-old Linn from albums and photographed them with my phone, adding them to the document as attachments, and I'd already included pictures of myself at various stages, culminating with my graduation portrait in a white dress and cap. The final piece of evidence was the Hultsfred documentary outtake I downloaded from the channel's website.

The subject line and body of the message, however, remained empty. Since I'd be sending it to the email address displayed on his business website, I finally titled it, "Greetings from Sweden." It was general but would still catch his attention, hopefully bringing back memories of nineteen years ago.

I agonized over how to notify J.G. from North Carolina— now a respected doctor in Florida—that he'd fathered a daughter with a woman he'd barely known at a crazy music festival, but there was no perfect way of announcing something so earth-shattering. Better to keep it short and sweet.

July 6, 2019

Dear J.G.,

You met my mother, Linn, at the Hultsfred Music Festival in mid-June 2000. Nine months later, she had a daughter, and I think you're my father. Please see the attachments. I hope to hear from you soon!

Sincerely,

Zoë Holmgren

I pressed Send before I could overthink it, and the email whooshed off into cyberspace.

Interlude

Linn

June 15, 2000

After the bathroom incident, Alicia, J.G., and I ate lunch at one of the Max Burger kiosks.

"This is the best hamburger I've ever had!" he declared. "That pink sauce is the bomb!"

"Yummier than McDonald's," I agreed.

"It's even better with a hangover," Alicia laughed, dipping a seasoned fry in ketchup.

"I read somewhere we should be eating a *Smålandsrulle*," I said.

"What's that?" Alicia asked.

"Some Hultsfred specialty. A vegetarian wrap with chickpeas, sprouts, and cheese," I explained.

Alicia scowled. "Sounds gross."

J.G. shrugged. "I don't know, I might try one. You know what they say—'when in Rome . . .'"

"How'd you end up touring with Kelis?" I asked. My embarrassment over the porta-potty incident had faded as my curiosity about him grew.

"My cousin went to high school with her in New York. It was a performing arts school, the one the movie *Fame* is based on," he said.

"Love that movie!" Alicia squealed.

"He was supposed to tour with her as a roadie but broke his foot shooting hoops and asked if I wanted to take his place," J.G. explained.

"Lucky you," I said.

"No doubt. I report for basic training in September, so this is the last good time I'll be having in a long time," he said.

We all laughed, but I had no clue what he was talking about. "Basic training?"

"I joined the Army. Uncle Sam has a piece of me now, so there'll be none of this"—he pointed to the burger—"at boot camp. More like push-ups, running, and learning how to shoot."

That was a lot for me to take in. Sweden had compulsory military service for males, but we were a neutral, nonthreatening country and hadn't gone to war in a hundred years. My Swedish guy friends regarded the military as an extension of their general education, a lesson in toughening up. But the American military was hardcore, and I found the concept much scarier.

"Interesting," I said.

"I think your life as a roadie sounds way more interesting," Alicia interrupted. "Tell us more about that."

If J.G. objected to our cross-examination, he didn't show it. He grinned and answered, "Most of my job is packing and unpacking equipment, acting as security, and getting food and drinks. There's a lot of sitting and waiting, hanging out with the crew and the rest of the band."

"C'mon," Alicia prodded. "There must be a lot of partying between shows?"

"I did party hard the first week, but then I had to get up early every morning, so that got old pretty quick," he admitted.

"Where have you guys been so far?" I asked.

"Last week, it was a town in Germany I can barely pronounce, *Nur-burg-ring*—"

"Never heard of it," Alicia said.

"If you've never heard of it, what about me?!" he quipped. "But the festival was huge, and it took place on a racetrack, so that was dope. This week we're here, then it's Glastonbury the week after. I'm looking forward to that one—I've always wanted to go to England. And then we go to Denmark for Roskilde at the end of June."

"I've always wanted to go to Roskilde," I said. "Aren't Pearl Jam and the Cure playing this year?"

"They'll be there, but Kelis will be adding some much-needed flavor to the festivities," he said, winking.

"Meaning there aren't that many other Black artists performing?" Alicia asked, picking up on J.G.'s subtle reference.

I had always admired how Alicia's years living in Kenya and Washington, D.C., had heightened her awareness of racial issues. She had brought that broader viewpoint to classroom discussions at Sigtuna, where most Swedes—me included—had little direct experience, though I wasn't completely clueless. My parents had raised me to accept and respect everyone, regardless of race or religion. Martin Luther King, Jr. was a hero in our family; my grandparents had saved newspaper and magazine clippings from when he'd received the Nobel Peace Prize. My parents and I had watched the live CNN broadcast when Nelson Mandela was released from prison in South Africa. I believed Swedes were liberal and didn't tolerate prejudice—at least, that was how I saw myself—but there was no denying I didn't interact with the Black population in my own country. Based on my daily activities and social circle, our paths rarely, if ever, crossed. My exposure to Black people was more cultural through entertainment and history, not in the laid-back way I was talking to J.G. now.

"Ziggy Marley and the Melody Makers and Youssou N'Dour, but no hip-hop," he replied.

"At least Hultsfred had Wu-Tang a couple of years back," I pointed out.

"Indeed," J.G. agreed. "Didn't they ask for, like, four hundred and fifty condoms?"

"That's what legend says," I answered, a little embarrassed.

"That shit's crazy! You can't go through that many. Not even on a good weekend!" he joked. We burst into laughter again. "But much respect to you guys in Europe. You're showing Kelis's music way more love than she's getting in the US, so it's all good."

"Why do you say that?" I asked.

"Her album came out last November, but her music's hard to define—is it funk, R and B, rock, or hip-hop? So American radio stations haven't been giving it the proper airtime," he explained. "You know her debut single, 'Caught Out There'?"

"Well, duh!" Alicia said.

J.G. grinned. "My bad. Just checking. Anyway, this is how it works in the American music business. Execs want to pigeonhole you because it's easier to sell records that way. A Black woman with a rainbow Afro and an alternative sound, screaming about how much she hates her man, doesn't fit into a neat category."

"That's so messed up," I said.

"Sad but true," J.G. said.

"But that's what makes Kelis so cool—she does her own thing," I said. "Who cares what other people think?"

J.G. sighed. "I hear you. But Europeans are more chill about stuff like that. We have a long way to go in the US."

"Her single did really well here, so you have nothing to worry about," I assured him.

He made a prayer sign with his hands. "Thank you. Appreciate the love. You guys gotta come to the show tomorrow night."

"We'll definitely be there!" Alicia said. "Can you get us backstage passes?"

Chuckling, J.G. shook his head. "But I might be able to get you into an after party."

"Good enough!" Alicia said.

He wiped his mouth and threw the napkin on the table. "Which act are you guys seeing tonight?"

"Oasis!" Alicia and I said at the same time.

"Everyone's been talking about them. What's up with that?" J.G. asked, knitting his brows.

"The two brothers who are the frontmen, Noel and Liam Gallagher, are fighting, and Noel, the lead guitarist, dropped out and isn't performing," I said.

"People are wondering if the band will still be as good without him," Alicia added.

Stroking his chin, J.G. asked, "Isn't that kind of a rude thing to do to their fans?"

"Yeah, but they're rock stars, so I guess they can get away with it," I said.

J.G. looked like he was about to say more but stopped himself. Instead, he knocked back his Coke and glanced at his watch. "Linn, Alicia, it's been nice, but I gotta get back to work." Standing, he adjusted his trucker hat and added, "If we don't see each other beforehand, let's meet by the zebra bus after Kelis's set tomorrow night."

"Zebra bus?" I asked.

"Ask around. Everybody knows where it is. Catch ya later!" J.G. said, tipping his hat to us.

My eyes followed his slim figure as he trotted toward the

main performance stage, which was weirdly named "Hawaii". He was unlike anyone I had ever met before. His music cred was impressive, but for all his jokes, there was a wholesomeness that softened my jaded view of the world. He had the guts to take a job as a roadie with no experience whatsoever, and I was charmed by his wide-eyed enthusiasm at being in Europe for the first time. I couldn't imagine him in camouflage holding a rifle, but he seemed solid and loyal.

Alicia noticed me watching him and said, "See? I told you he was cool."

With J.G. gone, Alicia and I soon realized a large part of festival life involved roaming the grounds between sets, drinking beer and gabbing with strangers in varying states of intoxication. Although everyone was super friendly, their perspectives didn't diverge significantly from mine, and I found myself less engaged in what they had to say. It was nothing personal, but I would have rather talked to J.G. I wanted to pick his brain about music and ask him what the acronym on his trucker hat stood for and why he had joined the Army. But it was impossible to find him again in the crowd. He was at Hultsfred to work and couldn't wander around like us.

When the temperature dropped further, Alicia and I returned to the campground for warmer clothes. At first, we had trouble finding our tent. More people had put down stakes, and it was beginning to look like a land invasion.

"We should have hitched a flag to our tent like these other people!" Alicia complained, pointing to the pieces of fabric poking out.

"Sorry! Another rookie mistake. Next year, we'll know better," I said, trying to appease her.

After changing into jeans and thick sweaters, we trekked

back to the Hawaii stage with a few minutes to spare until Sahara Hotnights came on. It was unseasonably cold and I shivered throughout the performance, wishing I had worn a pair of long johns under my jeans. When Oasis finally appeared onstage, the crowd screamed and jumped uncontrollably, but I couldn't move. The chill had entered my bones, and I hunched my shoulders to stay warm. Blue-and-white lights flashed in the darkness, the crowd swung back and forth, and people bumped into me haphazardly. Oasis opened with "Go Let It Out" from their first album, *Definitely Maybe,* and Alicia sang along, entranced by Liam Gallagher's nonchalance, raspy voice, and rocker style; he wore round sunglasses and a zipped-up leather jacket. The band followed up with "Who Feels Love?" and "Supersonic," but the screechy guitar riffs grated on my ears.

Alicia jabbed me in the stomach and screamed, "Isn't this amazing?!"

I nodded but noted how Liam mainly stood still, banging on a tambourine. I wondered if he was tired or upset because his brother had ditched the gig and he had to carry the show by himself. Maybe J.G.'s comment about the family drama being unfair to their fans had colored my perception. I stayed passive for most of the set, but once the guitarist strummed the first few chords of "Wonderwall"—my favorite song ever—I was overwhelmed with joy mixed with sadness. The lyrics about winding roads and blinding lights seemed especially poignant that night. I was living my dream at Hultsfred but scared about what lay ahead, my life once the music stopped and the crowd disappeared. The emptiness within me that I'd been trying to hide.

I rocked to Liam's vocals and sobbed quietly, afraid I would never find that thing to save me.

It was freezing inside our tent when I woke up around 9:00 Saturday morning. My back was damp; moisture from the wet ground had seeped through the thin floor mat into my sleeping bag. I had slept with wool socks to warm my feet, but an eye mask to block the light would have also been nice. Hearing Alicia snore regularly told me my friend was in serious sleep mode. I wished I could go back to bed, but my body ached, and it was difficult to swallow. Shit! The last thing I needed was to get sick again, especially not on our first full day at Hultsfred, with the Kelis concert and a private after party on our schedule.

My thoughts turned to J.G., and I wondered if I was developing an obsession. I was prone to mild crushes, especially if the guy in question inhabited the same geographical space, walking and breathing alongside me. J.G. was the coolest person I had ever met, but he was probably only being friendly. Hultsfred was the ideal place to form ad hoc friendships, so I wouldn't read too much into our conversation.

I squirmed out of the sleeping bag and stretched my arm to wake Alicia. "Rise and shine. Time to get up."

She moaned, rolling away.

"I don't feel well," I said, trying another tack. "I want to go to the pharmacy and get some medicine."

"I don't feel well either," Alicia replied hoarsely.

"That's from singing. But I might be coming down with something again."

"Just give me ten or fifteen more minutes."

"Fine—forget it!" I huffed, walking in a crouch. "I'll go to the pharmacy by myself."

"Can you buy me some cough drops?" Alicia mumbled.

I pulled on my clothes and unzipped our tent, but the

stench of urine and vomit assailed me. Debris and remnants of food and drink were flung in every direction. In the archipelago, camping was always done on pristine islands— open spaces, pure air, and sacred soil, not this pigsty. And we still had two more nights! How would I deal with the filth and flimsy tent if I got sick?

Tramping to the special toilets with running water and showers, I braved the long line to brush my teeth and check my appearance. The scratched mirror above the sink reflected my matted hair and smeared makeup. I tried to touch up the damage with wet wipes but soon gave up. It was hygienically impossible to look cute at Hultsfred, so I gave in to the messy, boho aesthetic and braided my hair into pigtails. I helped myself to a free takeout cup of tea and took the shuttle train to the town center. At the pharmacy, I bought Alvedon paracetamol tablets for myself and Halls cough drops for Alicia. But the store had sold out of bottled water.

I passed a pizzeria a few doors down and went inside to buy water. Although it was only eleven in the morning, the place was noisy and jammed with people remedying their hangovers with margheritas and capricciosas.

When I got the water and swallowed two Alvedons, I noticed J.G. sitting with a group of guys. I debated whether I should go over and say hello but hesitated. *What's the big deal?* It wasn't a big deal. We were sort of friends now, so I began walking toward his table. I must have entered his field of vision because he smiled, waving me over. After introducing me to the others, he asked about the Oasis concert.

"It was good but really cold, so I think I'm getting sick," I said, holding up my plastic bag from the pharmacy.

Everyone at the table laughed. "The weather always sucks here," an older man with tattoos and a beer belly said. "How was Oasis without Noel?"

"Not bad, but they're better together," I said.

"You should have seen their performance in '94, the first time they came to Hultsfred," he continued. "They were greenhorns, not rock stars. Now that was something."

"I bet," I said, impressed.

"Where's Alicia?" J.G. asked.

"Back in our tent, sleeping. I got some cough drops for her, so I should be heading back there now. I—I guess I'll see you later." That last sentence sounded more like a question than a statement, and I felt silly.

"No doubt," J.G. said.

That could mean various things: *No doubt, we'll meet up later as planned,* or *No doubt, we're bound to run into each other someplace.*

I nodded and said goodbye, leaving so quickly that I only heard their voices in response behind me. Outside on the sidewalk, it had begun to rain. It seemed I was destined to get sick, but I flipped over the hood of my jacket and dashed toward the shuttle. When I heard the stomping of feet behind me, I spun around.

"Hey, is it okay if I join you?" J.G. asked. "I need to get back to the festival grounds too."

Shrugging, I said, "Sure."

We walked in companionable silence for a little while, and then he said, "I hope you feel better for Kelis's concert tonight because I promise you, it's gonna be off da hook!"

His enthusiasm was infectious, and I laughed. "Don't worry. I'll be there."

"Good." He paused. "How's life in the tent village?"

"You want to know the truth?"

"Hit me."

"I hate it. I'm not trying to sound spoiled, but there's garbage everywhere, and it's gotten stinky and gross."

"Damn. That sounds nasty!"

"It is! The tent is so lightweight, it'll collapse if there's a downpour. And it's too cold!"

"Word. Where's summer at?" he joked.

"This is Sweden. Summer might come—or it might not. You just never know," I said.

"I can't stand the cold. My parents are from the Caribbean, so it's not in my blood."

"Well, I was born here, and I'm not sure it's in my blood either."

He laughed. "Have you ever been to the States?"

I shook my head.

"But I'd like to visit one day. You know—New York, LA, Miami . . ."

"Those are all the fun places, but there's more to the U.S. than that."

I shrugged. "You have to start somewhere."

The shuttle arrived, and J.G. motioned for me to get on first. I took a window seat, and he plopped down next to me. Once the train had whistled from the station, I pulled back my hood and spoke again. "Can I ask you a question?"

"Sure."

"Why'd you join the Army?"

"I guess I don't exactly look like the type, huh?"

"Aren't you afraid of signing over years of your life?"

"It's only between two and six years."

"No offense, but that would still hold you back, and you seem to have such a zest for life."

"Are you implying that I'm gonna die in the Army?"

"Not literally. But the military's so controlling. It's like going to school all over again, but worse."

He gazed out the window for a few moments, lost in thought. "I'm joining the Army because I want to go to school," he said. "Right now, I'm in Europe, listening to great music, meeting a pretty girl like you—"

"Nice try," I interrupted. "I haven't even showered."

"Whatever. You know you look good."

Guys had called me cute and pretty, but "look good" was low-key enough to sound more genuine. I might have blushed and wished I had kept the hood to cover my cheeks. "Anyway, continue."

"I think you get my drift. But this isn't my reality. My parents are working-class, doing double-shift jobs. They couldn't afford to send me to some big university. Even with financial aid, it would've been a stretch. I have three other siblings; I couldn't do that to them. I did some odd jobs and went to a community college for two years, but if I want to go to med school, the Army's the best way for me to reach that goal."

I was taken aback by his honesty. No one I knew dared to expose themselves so fully. Most were intent on maintaining a façade where money, status, and opportunities abounded. It never felt like anyone struggled because no one talked about it.

"What if there's a war, and you get called to go? Aren't you scared?"

"I could also get shot by a stray bullet walking down the street back home, so I'm kinda like, 'Same, same,' " he said.

"That sounds so depressing."

"You get used to it," he said, a brief, faraway expression clouding his gaze. "But enough about me," he said, bouncing back. "What's your story?"

"I graduated from high school a few weeks ago."

He narrowed his eyes, evaluating me. "Are you seventeen, eighteen . . .?"

"I'm nineteen. We start school a year later here. How old are you?"

"Twenty-one."

"I figured you were a few years older than me."

"What are you planning on doing?"

"What do you mean?"

"Your life. After school."

"Oh!" I said, cursing how ditzy I must have sounded. "Working, and then Alicia and I will travel around Asia."

"That's so European—traveling the world. You guys don't seem pressed."

"I guess it's because we're socialists. Everything's taken care of."

"Even college?"

"Yeah. But our taxes are high, so it's not exactly a free lunch."

"Still, you're lucky. College is 'free,' but you're not gonna go?"

"My grades weren't that great. Besides, I'm not sure a college degree is necessary to get ahead."

He chuckled. "Spoken like a white woman of privilege."

My eyes widened in astonishment.

"Sorry! Hope I didn't offend," he added quickly.

"Trust me, I'm not that privileged," I retorted, thinking back to some of my cushy Sigtuna classmates. "I come from a small town. Only about a hundred people live there. My parents own one of the businesses and work all the time."

"Alicia told me you guys met at boarding school?"

I nodded.

"I rest my case," he said, chuckling again.

"Whatever. It's all relative. Life here isn't a utopia either."

"Maybe, but it's not as unequal as the US. The haves and have-nots—all that shit."

"It *is* more of an even playing field in Sweden, I'll give you that."

"At the same time, I can't deny my parents came to the US with nothing, and by working their butts off, they managed to buy a house and raise four kids. We may not have a lot, but it's better than where they came from." He paused. "I guess I kind of still believe in the American dream. Hence my willingness to join the Army."

"I can't figure you out. One minute, you sound like a rapper, and the next, Shakespeare."

"Shakespeare was kind of a rapper, no?"

"Hmm . . . I guess you could say that."

"You remember that older dude from the pizzeria?"

"The chatty one?"

J.G. nodded. "He's been a sound technician since Hultsfred started and said something very interesting about it."

"What was that?"

J.G. stopped staring ahead and faced me. "'At Hultsfred, you're free to be anything you want, and everyone's the same.'" He paused. "I thought that was pretty cool. Don't you?"

Smiling, I nodded. "Yeah, that is pretty cool."

We parted ways when the train stopped at the festival grounds, and this time, J.G. made a specific reference to meeting up by the zebra bus after the concert. I felt better walking back to the tent village. The Alvedon had done the trick, but meeting J.G. again had also revived me, especially since our conversation had been refreshingly free of the superficial topics—drunken escapades and bad-mouthing other people—I usually discussed with guys.

I was still thinking about our conversation when I returned to the tent village. Alicia was miraculously feeling better, sitting on a lawn chair and drinking beers with a few other people.

"What took you so long?" she asked.

"There were long lines everywhere," I fibbed for no reason. I could have easily mentioned running into J.G., but an inexplicable need for privacy kept me quiet. "Here are your cough drops," I said, handing them over.

"And here's a beer to get you back in party form," Alicia said, offering me one from the cooler on the lawn.

I stared at it, waffling. "You know what? I'm okay." I noticed a bag of Polar bread and a package of presliced Herrgårds cheese. "But I will have one of those sandwiches. Then we can get out of this shithole!"

Stomachs fortified, we meandered through the festival grounds for the second day in a row, saying hello to friendly faces and listening to bands play on the other stages. Songs by the Wannadies or Thåström were unfamiliar, but the manic energy in the audience rubbed off on us. It was easier to go with the flow and accept the beers and cigarettes shoved in my face than resist. Being buzzed also heightened my appreciation of the absurd—I tripped on one of the floor cushions in the Löfbergs Lila coffee tent and exploded into giggles. Decorated in a starry, purple *Arabian Nights* theme, I drank an Americano and pretended to read people's palms, making one outlandish prediction after another. After bumming around there for a while, Alicia and I moved on to the ZTV marquee, which broadcasted the concerts live. We lingered and gossiped about the various acts until it was time to revisit our tent for an outfit change. Midway, we stumbled upon a bus painted with black-and-white zebra stripes and shrieked in anticipation of the night ahead.

Later, our joy was cut short when a power outage killed the Hawaii stage's lights and sound.

"Oh no!" Alicia said. "What's going on?"

"I hope this place doesn't become a mob scene," I said, glancing at the screaming crowd. People were cursing, demanding to know the problem. "Luckily, it's still light outside."

"Should we stay or go?" Alicia asked.

"We have to stay! Kelis is up next."

"What if it takes hours?"

"If we leave, J.G. will be disappointed. He said the show would be 'off da hook,' " I said, making air quotes.

"When did he say that?" she asked. "I don't remember."

Damn Alicia for picking up on my white lie. "Oh, um, today. I ran into him in the town center this morning."

"What?! And you're just telling me this now?"

"It's not a big deal. I didn't think it was important."

"I think *you* think it was too important to tell me."

"That's crazy!"

"You like him, don't you?" Alicia teased me.

"Who wouldn't? He's funny and cute."

"I mean you *like* him, as in you're attracted to him. I should have guessed something was up when you put on that camisole and your leather jacket, even though you've been complaining about how cold it is."

"Listen, can we drop it? Even if I like him a little, it's crazy because we barely know each other."

"But it doesn't matter at a place like this!" she hooted. "*Leva livet.* Live in the here and now." Canvassing the crowd, she added, "I wouldn't have minded a weekend fling myself, but I'm just not into these slobbering guys."

"This is our weekend together! We don't need any guys!" I said, hugging my friend.

The stage lights and sound hummed back to life about an hour later, and the public roared its approval, jumping up and down. But a few lamps dimmed again, and a drummer assumed his position at the back of the stage. He was accompanied by an all-female cast—guitarist, bassist, and three backup singers—bedazzled in belly-grazing tops, flared pants, stacks of jewelry, scarves, and an array of braids, Afros, and twists. Then Kelis made her entrance, her brown complexion popping against a fitted white bustier and vinyl bell-bottoms with side vents. She had styled her technicolor curls in a high, voluminous ponytail and strutted confidently as the guitar's first notes played.

"This is a song for y'all out there who've been lied to by your men—and we know you've been lied to," Kelis purred into the mic. Lowering her voice a few octaves, Kelis crooned the opening lines to her hit single, "Caught Out There." Her anger about a love gone bad intensified, so when she screamed the angry refrain, trashing a cheating boyfriend—"I hate you so much right now!"—we chimed in at the top of our lungs, a fist-thumping, hip-thrusting validation of her pain. I worked up a sweat keeping up with the fierce women onstage, whose moves and attitude said *Fuck you* to the cheaters and naysayers. Their presence, fearless and unconstrained, pushed boundaries, and I didn't care if I sang or moved out of tune. I was enraptured by the funk fusion, girl power, and sexual force; I was carried aloft on a metaphoric high, bouncing and flailing with the crowd for half an hour. Kelis and her band were tireless, and just when I thought it couldn't get any better, they closed with an earsplitting rendition of Nirvana's "Smells Like Teen Spirit."

United in song, I was sure this was what heaven felt like.

I levitated to the zebra bus, a flurry of pent-up emotions needing release. As Alicia and I smoked cigarettes with another group waiting to rendezvous with friends, I kept watch for J.G. After thirty minutes with no sign of him, I questioned whether he would show up at all.

"Should we just move on?" Alicia asked, as though she could hear my doubts.

"I don't know . . ." I said, feeling increasingly ridiculous. How long should we wait? The others had already reunited with their buddies, leaving Alicia and me alone.

"We'll stay. I'm sure he'll turn up," Alicia said.

And a few minutes later, he did, wearing a black sweatshirt printed with the word CREW and his ever-present trucker hat. Panting, he apologized for being late.

"It took longer than I thought to break down the equipment," he explained, his face dewy from exertion.

Swooning from adrenaline, Kelis's empowering anthems, and a spiraling physical attraction, I marched over, cupped J.G.'s face, and kissed him on the lips. It was chaste, but his body twitched, startled by my forwardness. I drew back but couldn't stop grinning like an idiot.

"Whoa, I didn't expect that!" he exclaimed.

"That was the best concert I've ever been to," I gushed, unsure if I had come on too strong—and, at the same instant, not caring if I did. It felt great in the moment, and impulse control had never been my strong suit.

"Told ya it was gonna be good. Are you guys ready to go?" he asked,

I smile-nodded, and Alicia, who had been hanging back discreetly, fell in step with us. She plied J.G. with questions about the cause of the power outage and the girls in Kelis's band. I began to worry if I had made a fool of myself, but Alicia's constant babbling rescued the situation. J.G. shared what he knew, as though nothing strange had just occurred. We rode the shuttle train to the shopping center and trooped several blocks to a boxy brick house that rented rooms to the traveling road crew. Red lightbulbs created a spacy, psychedelic vibe, and the smoke made everything hazy, but I saw a few faces from the pizzeria. The crowd included a motley crew of diehard fans, girlfriends, and hangers-on. J.G. pointed to some musicians in the room, but they were no one I recognized. Beer, wine, and whiskey poured freely, shadowed by the musky fragrance of pot. Classic rock, like the guitar-laden tunes my father played whenever he cleaned his boat, blared in the background. I squeezed into an empty space at the end of a brown leather sofa, leaving J.G. to balance on the armrest. It became apparent Alicia didn't want to disturb us. She remained standing and let a skinny, goateed guy light her cigarette, murmuring to him between puffs.

"Do you want anything?" J.G. asked.

"What are you having?" I asked.

"A Jack Daniels to unwind."

"I'll have the same."

He raised an eyebrow but left to get our drinks. Soon after, he returned with two clear plastic cups of mahogany liquid. As he brought the rim to his lips, I touched his arm.

"Wait. Wanna see how we toast in Sweden?" I asked.

"You bet. Show me how it's done."

"We don't click our glasses together like you do in the US," I told him. "First, hold your cup in front of your chest." J.G. did as I instructed.

"Then make eye contact with the person you're toasting—in this case, me."

He peered into my eyes but sealed his lips together, struggling to keep a straight face.

"Try not to laugh!" I admonished.

"This is crazy," he muttered.

"Then we bow our heads slightly—"

Eyes locked, we lowered our chins.

"—and take a sip," I said, tasting the whiskey. "Then our eyes meet again, and we give each other a friendly nod."

We both nodded, completing the custom in a fit of laughter.

J.G. bent and said, "Thank you, Miss Sweden, for that cultural lesson."

"*Varsågod.* That's Swedish for 'you're welcome.'"

"Will you keep speaking more Swedish as the night goes on?"

"Depends how long we stay up."

The banter continued until our glasses emptied and the liquor had the desired effect on me. It warmed my insides, thawing my jittery nerves.

After discarding our cups on the side table, J.G. said, "Sorry this party is so mellow. I thought it was gonna be livelier."

"I'm having fun."

"Are you sure?" he asked, awkwardly leaning forward so I could hear him.

I nodded. "But I think you would have more fun if you weren't sitting in such an uncomfortable position."

"You have a better one in mind?"

I rose from my seat and took his hand. "I think you should move," I suggested, guiding him to my vacated spot. "And I'll sit here," I finished, sinking into his lap.

He let out that evasive laugh again. I wasn't sure if he liked having me in his face or if he was too polite to push me away. I could smell the whiskey on his breath, masculine and sexy, and my insides tingled again. In biology class, I'd learned those stomach butterflies were a chemical reaction associated with the body's fight-or-flight response. The brain reacted to a potential threat by raising the heartbeat and breathing rate while the stomach muscles became extra sensitive, causing that swirling feeling of vulnerability.

But the threat had nothing to do with J.G. I'd done enough naughty, stupid things to know I was my own worst enemy. Deciding how far I wanted to go with this flirtation both frightened and exhilarated me.

"What are you thinking?" I asked.

"You're a very funny girl, with much more going on than meets the eye."

"And you're a total nerd," I said, taking off his hat. I'd sent J.G. signals all night, but he'd refused to take the bait. "What does *N.E.R.D* stand for, anyway?"

"No One Ever Really Dies."

"Mm-hmm . . . I thought it was some secret science society or something."

"It's a side band formed by the producers of Kelis's album. Their sound is dope. You should listen to them."

"Listen to you! You're so into music. I'm sorry, but I think that's what you should do with your life."

"I don't have the talent or the luxury. Okay, let me ask you something—who would you rather date? A musician or a doctor?"

"Hmm."

"Forget I asked," he chuckled. "I think I know the answer."

"How about a musician now and a doctor much, much later?"

He shook his head in exasperation. Backing off a few inches, I assessed his face. I had never been this close to a Black guy before—and then I chided myself for making that reflection. Then again, he had probably never experienced a Swedish girl curled up in his lap either. Was that part of the attraction? Would we say something about it? Or was it overplayed? Too predictable?

"I think you look older without your hat," I said, trying it on. "How do I look?" I struck a few poses, watching as he stared at me.

Finally, JG cleared his throat. "Very, um . . . hot."

I threw back my head and laughed, hair loose and swinging, leather jacket skating off my shoulders. His gaze was steady and less guarded when I met his eyes again. He thumbed my cheek, guiding my face toward his, finally kissing me.

His lips were soft, and it lasted for several seconds. Then, our mouths opened at the same time, as though the slow buildup had been excruciating—which, for me, it had—and our kissing became hungrier and more eager. I shifted my angle, gently straddling him, and the hat fell off. I was keenly aware of others in the room but lacked any inhibition about making out in front of strangers. I didn't care if we were being watched. In fact, that added to the seduction. Years later, when I had the presence of mind to analyze why the evening progressed as it had, I understood that the feeling of being outside of myself, of submitting to the slightly seedy environment, was a powerful aphrodisiac. Lusting after a hot, intriguing American at a music festival after party seemed so cool, so adult, *so rock 'n' roll.*

Suddenly, J.G. stopped.

Confused, I caught my breath, but could feel my heart pounding in my chest.

"We push out tomorrow morning," he said.

"Oh." I frowned, unsure of what to say. I had assumed J.G. would stay for the entire festival, but his early departure was logical. Kelis's set was over. There was no need to stay in Sweden.

"If we only have a few hours . . ." He paused. "Do you wanna go someplace more private?"

That option hadn't occurred to me, mainly because I didn't think it was possible. But I nodded without hesitation when J.G. suggested it, following him up the stairs to a small room with two twin beds.

"Is this where you've been staying?" I asked, sitting beside him at the edge of the mattress.

He nodded. "Some perks of the job."

"I should have been a roadie."

"I see you more as a groupie."

"You're probably right," I said, kissing him again.

Making out moved in phases—sitting up, lying down, and finally, feeling each other up more as pieces of clothing came off. J.G. wasn't as skinny as he seemed in the loose hoodie and jeans; his arms were defined and strong, and his torso ended in a smooth *V* above the waist. We explored each other's bodies slowly, and though it was left unspoken, I could tell we were trying to draw out our time together. When our desire peaked, he asked if I wanted him to continue.

I whispered, "Yes," waiting with my eyes closed, listening to the rustling sound of the condom's foil packaging. Once he slipped it on, we found a rhythm, and I caressed his back, licking the groove in his neck and nibbling his earlobe. He moved faster with each flick of my tongue and eventually convulsed on my chest, our breathing rising and falling in unison.

While cuddling afterward, we laughed about how we'd met only a day before, but there was no judgment on how fast things had progressed. It was a byproduct of festival life—the intense connections, the urgency to act on intuition. We dozed off for a bit, and then he asked me to teach him a few words of Swedish slang.

"*Rocka fett,*" I said.

"*Rock fat?*" he repeated.

"It's like, 'You rock!' You say it when something's amazing. You know, like *dope.*"

"Aha. Got it."

"Here's another one: *dunderskön.*"

"*Thunder shine?*" he guessed.

I swatted his arm, laughing at how wacky that sounded. "It means something's nice. Like you."

There was plenty of kissing and caressing in between, and our desire took on a strange desperation as time ticked by and more light permeated the room. When we reached the precipice of sex once more, J.G. realized he didn't have another condom.

In a nanosecond, I made a decision that would irrevocably change the course of my life. I told him I was on the pill—which was true—and he, in turn, swore he never engaged in unprotected sex. Thus, on that dusky, tempestuous night in Hultsfred, we felt naively safe with each other, ignoring common sense and whatever sex ed had taught us, consummating our burning infatuation a second pivotal time.

When Alicia knocked gently on the door and the hour of goodbye arrived, we uncoupled with tenderness, an appreciation for having met but also a mutual understanding that it would end there. Our lives—our plans—were like night and day. The chances of intersecting ever again were minuscule; it was futile to promise otherwise. For my part, choosing to close this door was deliberate. I wanted to preserve the mystique, to safeguard memories untouched by the minutiae of everyday life. Every girl deserved an unscripted, compulsive romantic encounter, and I would never forget the passion in that room. Still, it would be a vignette, a memorable set piece in my evolving narrative—a precursor to traveling the world, testing various careers, and eventually settling down. I envisioned sitting with Alicia years later, reminiscing about all the Hultsfred Festivals we'd attended— and the charismatic American who had transformed our very first one.

Little did I know it would become *the* experience to define me.

10

ZOË

Camilla emailed Holmgren's before I could thank her for the party, and I felt guilty. Etiquette dictated that I send a word of thanks, but I wasn't sure if it should come from Linn or me. We hadn't discussed the party, even though it had left us with a strange aftertaste. But after a few days' perspective, I started having second thoughts about my interaction with Gunnar. I always did this—doubting my original interpretation of a situation, overanalyzing it, and seeing it from multiple angles until it mutated from offensive to something totally benign. Maybe I had been a horrible guest by stomping out of the party like that. Worse yet, what if Gunnar told his mother about it, and Camilla questioned her favorable first impression? That issue raised why I cared about the Eastons' opinion in the first place. But boredom on a remote island made me attach more significance to small things.

Camilla's email the Monday after was friendly, thanking us for the trio of scented candles, but her true purpose was to ask if Holmgren's could special-order gluten-free items. She had found a series of products from the Semper brand and would be "so grateful" if the store could bring them to the island. The Eastons' party food didn't seem gluten-free, but maybe Camilla hadn't eaten any of it. Former models like her possessed superior willpower and superhuman skills in abstinence.

I relayed Camilla's request to Mormor. She responded with

a skeptical, "Hmph."

"Can we place the order?" I asked impatiently, holding a printout of the email.

"Since when did so many people become gluten-free?" Mormor asked.

"It's not a choice. It's a legitimate condition! People can't help it if—"

"In my day," Mormor interrupted, "you ate whatever you were served. No complaints. No allergies. During World War II, my grandparents recycled cooking oil and made meals from anything available."

I had heard these wartime stories before, but they'd become less effective as the years passed. "I think it would be a good idea for us to stock gluten-free food. A lot of people ask for it." Mostly American tourists, but I didn't want to feed Mormor's skepticism.

"Let me see that list," she said, extending her hand.

I obliged, wishing I could have placed the order without involving Mormor.

"Gluten-free crackers, lasagna, and waffle mix!" Mormor exclaimed, ticking off the list. "And that's just half of it. What's next? That Holmgren's should go all-organic?"

"Well," I began, "since you asked—"

Gluten-free. Organic food. Niche specialty products. Those were the current grocery trends—and they were here to stay. But Mormor had worked at Holmgren's forever, and her perspective was outdated. She had become blind to the flaws at the store. Arthritis prevented her from spending more time on the floor, but I stocked shelves and operated the register, coming into direct contact with customers, and I had heard their criticisms. They grumbled about our high prices and limited selection but shopped at Holmgren's anyway because it was convenient to have a supermarket on the island. The locals knew we were providing a community service, but the tourists were brazen, asking flat-out why they paid more for dented apples in Nornö than for perfect ones in Stockholm. *Take a two-hour boat ride into the city and shop there,* Mormor would say in private. But times had changed. Customers had become pickier and had no consideration for how difficult it was to run a grocery store in the archipelago, with the pressures of pricing and the demand for bulk orders. FoodDirekt was nipping at our heels and stocked more gourmet cheeses, specialty meats, and condiments than we did. I frequently trolled their website to see what we were up against and didn't see how we could compete unless we made major changes.

However, I was afraid Mormor didn't have the energy or desire to do so. If I had planned on staying at Holmgren's, I would have redone the store completely, building an extension and curating the assortment to keep up with contemporary tastes, moving it from a scrappy mom-and-pop operation into a charming seaside food hall. I would commission a new website with online shopping and offer moped delivery. Modern but still retro, like the classic British milkman who delivered milk to the doorstep. With her creative eye, Linn could design an eco-friendly, reusable tote bag with Holmgren's logo. But even as I scoured photos on Instagram and Pinterest, conceptualizing this new direction, I knew Mormor would snicker and say, *You young people and your ideas! Where's this money to revamp Holmgren's going to come from?*

And there was no money. It was easier to stick to a proven—albeit dying—formula, complaints and all.

"Just get her what she wants," Mormor said, handing the

printout back to me like it was contaminated.

"Okie dokie," I said, backing off. I placed the order and was tempted to tell Mormor it had totaled over a thousand kronor—a nice little sum—but figured it was best to drop the subject.

I texted Camilla when her order arrived two days later, but Gunnar showed up at the store for the pickup. I hadn't seen him since the garden party and was vaguely curious about what he'd been doing. Not much, I concluded after one glance. He looked like he had just rolled out of bed with straggly hair, varsity shorts, a ratty Putnam Prep t-shirt, and a pair of beat-up Nikes—the preppy slacker, down to a T.

Going straight to the checkout line, where I sat behind the register, he asked, "My mom says there's a delivery for us?" No hello, no chitchat.

I took a deep breath and replied, "Yeah, the stuff's downstairs. I'll get them for you."

I ran down to the cellar to collect four bags, and when I returned, Gunnar was standing right where I had left him. He didn't offer to lighten my load.

"We also need some milk," he said. "Lactose-free."

I dropped the bags and pointed to the dairy refrigerator. Shaking my head, I went back to the checkout station.

Gunnar returned, holding two white cartons with green stripes. "Is this it?" he asked, thrusting one in front of the register.

Glancing at it, I replied, "*Lactose-free* is basically spelled the same way in Swedish, so yeah, that's the one." *Idiot.* I rang up the purchases. "That's 1,119 kronor total."

"Oh, my mom wondered if we could set up an account?"

"Sure, that'd be fine. We bill on a weekly basis."

"Can you email her that? I might forget."

Are you capable of anything? Smiling tightly, I said, "Sure."

"Great," he said, also smiling a little.

"Don't forget the other bags."

He turned around and scratched his head as though seeing them for the first time. "Right, thanks."

Adding the milk cartons to the haul, Gunnar grabbed two bags in each hand and shuffled out the door. Again, no goodbye or chitchat. I watched him arrange the bags on the flatbed of a brand-spanking-new carrier moped and speed away. He was driving too fast in the middle of the village, and I sincerely hoped one of the cranky old-timers would tell him off for it.

Dumbfounded, I tried to narrow down what made Gunnar a little off. Aside from being socially awkward, he seemed like a fish out of water in Nornö, behaving like he'd been sentenced to prison—or disinherited. What was wrong with him? Had he just been sheltered? Was he one of those spoiled kids raised by nannies, servants, and tutors, cut off from hands-on experience with the real world? Is that what wealth and privilege produced? An empty shell with a warped sense of entitlement?

Whatever, I thought. Gunnar wouldn't give me the time of day, so why waste my time and effort psychoanalyzing his personality? Lowering my gaze, I spotted a squashed beet leaf on the conveyor belt. I scraped it away with my index finger, but the green-and-magenta residue stained my skin. I held out my hand, examining all five fingers. Earlier in the day, I had sifted through a shipment of new potatoes, and soil was trapped underneath my fingernails. The pungent odor of ripe strawberries, coffee, and citrusy detergent wafted above my register. It was a combination so ingrained in my sensory bank that I swore I sometimes smelled it beyond the store's range.

Gunnar might have seemed like another laid-back local to an outsider, but we were poles apart. His people dialed in their orders, dropping in when it was time for pickup, while my daily life consisted of mopping, dusting, and unloading boxes. Mormor had instilled the Holmgren Work Ethic in me, and having dirty hands was considered a badge of honor. It was funny that I'd never contemplated how those hands might look to someone else.

After work and a quick bite to eat, I headed up to my room with Simba, trying not to think about how I hadn't heard from my father. It sounded insane to think the thought, let alone say the word aloud. *Father.* I was 95 percent sure I had solved the mystery of his identity, but the remaining 5 percent dreaded that I'd made a colossal mistake. It had almost been too easy once I found out his full name. What if Linn had been lying to me the whole time? What if J.G. had been a convenient cover, and my birth father was really some sleazy, nameless stranger she had drunkenly hooked up with at Hultsfred but was too ashamed to admit it?

Maybe a nurse or secretary might check his emails first, and he hadn't seen it. Or worse—what if someone forwarded it to him, and the revelation put him in an embarrassing situation, potentially damaging his reputation? I snorted in exasperation, my resentment brewing. It had been directed solely at my mother for so long, and now I suddenly had another villain, someone else with the potential to inflict hurt. But it was too late. I had to stop thinking about other people and the adverse effect my existence would have on their lives. I'd been robbed of my birthright for eighteen years, the chance to know both sides of my origin. The truth was long overdue, no apologies necessary.

My phone dinged during an episode of *RuPaul's Drag*

Race. A message from Douglas Bohlander. What did he want? We hadn't texted each other since graduation. After six years of sharing the boat to school, our regular messaging about homework or transportation to events on the mainland had ended after the last party. There had been a huge misunderstanding, and while I had put it behind me, Douglas's hostility made it clear he still harbored a grudge. I clicked on the message with caution.

Douglas:
What r u doing?

Why did he care? I typed back: Watching a show.

Douglas:
A bunch of us are by the beach. Wanna
come?

I reread the last sentence. After weeks of giving me the cold shoulder, somehow, he'd decided to let things go tonight. And who was "a bunch of us"? It was still light outside, the evening comfortably balmy after another daytime hot spell. Linn always bugged me about being cooped up in my room, which always made me defensive. I wasn't always alone by choice. "Hanging out" necessitated people, and my options were limited.

Drumming my fingers on the laptop, I weighed the pros and cons. Should I finish the show and my pint of Ben & Jerry's Chocolate Caramel Cookie Dough? Or should I get dressed and subject myself to Douglas's obnoxiousness?

"What should I do, Simba? Should I stay, or should I go?"

Simba groaned and bared a few teeth, venting his

disapproval while flopped on the floor next to my bed. We were supposed to keep each other company. But as I scratched the top of his head, curiosity got the better of me. I was used to being on the margins, so Douglas's text was a bit flattering—and I wouldn't be crashing whatever they were doing, since he had invited me. Staying home would only fuel my curiosity—obsessively checking Snapchat to see if anyone had posted what was happening. It was better to have a front-row seat than to watch the instant replay.

Convinced I had nothing to lose, I typed: Kk, be there in 15.

"Sorry, Simba," I said, patting his back. But I knew he and my beloved drag queens would be there later.

I ditched my pajamas for boyfriend jeans, a tank top, and a cable-knit sweater that had previously belonged to someone else in my family. Who knew how old it was—after moving from closet to closet, it had wound up in mine, and the oatmeal-colored wool still smelled of lanolin.

But the night air was still and windless, so I threw the sweater in the basket as I biked across the island to Brunnsbad Beach. As I parked my bike against a tree, I saw a small bonfire with several figures behind the orange flames and plumes of charcoal smoke. As I got closer, the images sharpened, explaining why Douglas had invited me. Gunnar was there, along with two guys from my high school class and two other Stockholm girls who summered in Nornö. Douglas flagged me down, and I approached them warily, unsure of my place in this group of familiar strangers.

"Hi, everyone," I said.

"*Tjaaa,*" a few of the Swedes called out.

Douglas touched the right side of his head in salute, as if I had begged him to come and he hadn't asked me to join them. Surprisingly, the other two guys from my graduating class,

William and Hugo, walked over, giving me stiff, one-armed hugs.

"Are you guys staying in Nornö?" I asked. William and Hugo had occupied the middle rung of the social ladder at DG. Translation: they were insecure, and I wasn't considered cool enough, so they looked away whenever I passed them in the halls. But freed from peer pressure, they could cut me some slack. Next to them, Douglas was a kingpin—loud, bossy, and always willing to goof off.

"We live in Ekerö, and Douglas said a few people would be chilling at the beach," William explained.

"So we drove our jet skis over," Hugo added.

"Nice," I said. William and Hugo tried to sound casual about it, but I could tell they were happy to be there. Maybe I was, too, despite Douglas's bad manners.

I glanced at the spread Douglas had put together. Beers and cider were sweating in a cooler. Packs of Camel Activate and Lyft *snus* were scattered on an oversized quilt. Music was blaring from a portable speaker. Girls were prettying up the beach. I was certain it was all done for Gunnar's benefit.

One of the girls, Tilde, and I had gone to the same sailing and confirmation camps but drifted apart after her parents' divorce. For the past few years, she'd only spent a couple of weeks in Nornö, working at the coffee and ice cream bar by the harbor. Tilde had styled her strawberry-blonde hair in the same cutesy style with bangs since we were little, but now it looked edgy instead of babyish. What I secretly envied were her skinny legs and thigh gap. She could wear the shortest cutoffs—like now—without looking slutty, since the denim hanging from her hips scarcely touched her skin. Next to Tilde, I always became self-conscious about my dimensions— I was busty, with a flat abdomen, round booty, and muscular thighs. "Slim thick" was how I once saw it described in a magazine, next to pictures of Rihanna. I tried channeling RiRi's self-confidence, but it was hard to stay body positive when Mormor had to take in the waist of my jeans, since I always had to buy a larger size to accommodate my thighs. Whenever the girls at school repeated the lewd comments boys made about my butt, they assumed I would be pleased, grateful for the "compliment." Instead, they made me feel like an exotic specimen. Linn and Mormor had characteristic Swedish builds, a straight line from top to bottom, so the curves must have come from my father's side.

I was sick of sticking out. I longed for an environment where my skin tone and body type were better represented.

"Zoë!" Tilde exclaimed, leaning in for a gentle squeeze. "I haven't seen you in forever!"

"I've been at my usual spot," I said, "working at the store."

"Me too. I never have any free time when I'm at the café. But at least we don't have to go back to school after the summer."

"Thank God. What are your plans this fall?" I asked.

"My mom fixed me up with an internship at SWEA in London."

"Sounds serious."

Tilde giggled. "I don't think I'll be able to bullshit my way through it. How about you?"

"Haven't decided yet," I lied.

"Will you stay in Nornö and work at the store?" Tilde gave me a sour-lemon expression, puckering her eyebrows and nose, making the question sound like a fate worse than death.

I shrugged and smiled. I didn't owe her an explanation. I peeked at Gunnar, who was standing at the water's edge with Molly, a snobby Stockholmer and wannabe influencer. She loved posting her Euro travel highlights and designer bags to her public Instagram account, as though she were an it-girl like Olympia of Greece or Talita von Furstenberg. Beers in hand, Gunnar and Molly were shoeless, water pooling at their feet. She only wore a bandeau top and sweatpants jacked up to her knees.

Tilde followed my gaze and remarked, "Molly's such a flirt. She made a play for him as soon as he came down to the beach."

"Mm."

"She barely has any clothes on," Tilde continued.

I almost burst out laughing. Tilde hardly had any clothes on either. Gunnar and Molly began walking back to the rest of the group. "Wonder what the attraction is?" I asked, almost to myself.

"Him or her?"

What was I doing, chatting so freely with Tilde? We barely knew each other anymore.

"Forget it," I said, laughing it off.

Tilde held up her Somersby apple cider. "Want one?"

I glanced at Douglas, who was hunched next to the cooler like a bodyguard, and that never-ending fear of outsiderness gripped me again. *I have to try harder. I have to stop acting like a freak.* "Sure, I'll have something," I said, reaching for a beer.

"*Ojojoj,* Zoë!" Douglas crowed, uncapping the bottle of Norrlands Guld with an opener from his keychain. "You never drink. What's the occasion?"

Taking the beer, I gave him the stink eye. He, of all people, knew why I didn't.

My mother's vices were well-known among Nornö's locals. They had been whispering about them since her high school days, but Linn wasn't the only one who struggled with alcohol.

Half the island lived at the little pub in the wintertime. Linn's mistake was fighting her demons in public, and as a Holmgren, she was an easy target for the gossipmongers. Her drinking had also become my burden, and I carried it obsessively, denying myself even a drop of the substance that haunted her. In a place where kids experimented with alcohol as young as thirteen, I deserved a fucking gold medal for my self-discipline. I had put up with so much—the teasing, the joking-but-serious jabs that I was boring, the loneliness of being excluded from get-togethers. But how long should I make up for my mother's poor judgment? This was the second time I had accepted a drink in my entire life; the first had been at my graduation a month earlier. After sprinting out of my high school building, I'd indulged in champagne toasts and ridden in the beer-soaked caravan like all the other kids. I wouldn't say I enjoyed the taste, but I'd wanted to be part of the crowd for a change. Tonight, was no different.

When Molly and Gunnar rejoined the rest of the gang, he mumbled, "Hi," while she gave me a hug that was too big for our level of friendship.

"Oh my God, Zoë, you're so lucky to have your skin color!" Molly said, looking at me up and down. "I'm so pale. Have to use fake tanner all the time!"

I couldn't tell if that was a sincere compliment or if Molly wanted to single me out for not looking like the rest of them. Regardless, I spotted the telltale line bordering her orangy chin and pasty neck and remarked, "I can tell."

Gunnar plopped down on the towel, and Molly sat next to him, close enough for their knees to touch. William and Hugo annexed the towel side near the cigarettes, leaving Tilde and me in the space opposite Gunnar and Molly. I sipped the beer and almost burped from the fizzy bubbles. It tasted bitter and yeasty, and I wished I had taken the low-ABV cider. After a mental headcount, I realized the boy-to-girl ratio was off, but no one seemed to care in the waning light, stoked by alcohol and the swishing echo of waves lapping the shore.

William helped himself to a cigarette and asked Douglas if he had a light. I purposely avoided looking directly at Gunnar, fixing my gaze past his shoulder. Douglas changed the music to A$AP Rocky, and the conversation turned to the fight that had happened the previous month between the African American rapper's crew and an immigrant from Afghanistan on a Stockholm street. Douglas, William, and Hugo thought it was justifiable self-defense. Tilde criticized A$AP's bodyguards for kicking the Afghan while he was down. Gunnar was shocked A$AP was still in jail because Sweden didn't have a bail system. Unsurprisingly, Molly was excited by all the international attention Sweden was getting. I'd been following the *#FreeRocky* hashtag on social media and told them Sweden was coming across as racist for keeping A$AP in custody. I waited for someone to voice an opinion for or against it, but the R-word hopscotched through the air like a pebble they were too skittish to touch. Douglas changed the subject after a long, awkward minute by asking Gunnar about his "secret stash."

Gunnar dug in his pocket, removing a Ziploc bag and a small silver canister.

"Oh shit!" Hugo said. "Where'd you get that?"

From Hugo's reaction, I got the sense Gunnar wasn't holding a bag of broccoli.

"From my boy in the city," Gunnar said with a cocky grin.

"Stockholm?" Hugo asked.

"Uh, no. New York City," Gunnar answered.

William's mouth hung open. "How'd you fly with it?"

Gunnar unzipped the bag and took out a chunk of marijuana. "In my carry-on, hidden in an empty bottle of Tylenol."

Douglas whistled, impressed. They all seemed in awe of Gunnar's smart-ass attitude. He was literally about to roll and smoke a joint in the middle of Nornö's public beach. I was sure many others had done the same thing before, but I had never witnessed it. What was most nerve-wracking was that I'd soon be guilty by association since cannabis was illegal in Sweden. But Gunnar didn't seem to care. He broke the chunk apart, placing smaller pieces inside the cannister.

"New York pot—I'm sure it's stronger than what we have here," Molly said, and there was more ingratiating laughter for the stupidest comment I had ever heard. I wondered if Molly had ever actually smoked Swedish pot or if she was trying to impress Gunnar.

Nevertheless, I couldn't take my eyes off what he was doing and hated myself for it. "What's that?" I asked, pointing to the cannister.

"It's a weed grinder," Gunnar said.

His tone was very matter-of-fact, but Molly rolled her eyes in exasperation. Her condescension was infuriating. What the hell? Was I stupid for not knowing what a weed grinder was? Was it one of those life hacks everyone should know by eighteen? I'd never even seen marijuana in real life until now. *No, Zoë, you're not stupid. Stop second-guessing yourself.*

"Gluten-free, but you take drugs?" I quipped, but it came out more like a reprimand than an attempt at humor.

"Weed's not a drug," Gunnar retorted without missing a beat. The lid was back on the canister, and he rotated it like a pepper mill. "It's an herb. Au naturel."

His explanation provoked another round of overblown

laughter. They all sounded fake, behaving as though they were already high. Gunnar withdrew a sheet of rolling paper from the Ziploc bag and tapped the ground marijuana onto it. I stopped watching once he began rolling the joint and took out my phone, pretending to be transfixed by my Instagram feed, but it got boring quickly, so I switched to my email.

Wedged between a Facebook birthday notification and my SoundCloud Weekly playlist was a message from J.G. Latour, MD. The phone nearly slipped from my hand.

"I have to go," I said, leaping to my feet.

"Are you okay?" Tilde asked. "You look like you've seen a ghost."

I think I have.

I left without saying goodbye but heard the words *weird* and *stiff* and *Goody Two-shoes* behind my back, and for the first time, I didn't care what they thought of me.

I had never cycled home so quickly. I practically broke down the front door, racing up to my room as fear and hope jostled in the pit of my stomach. The suspense was almost unbearable, but I didn't want to read the message on my phone. Laptop in hand, I burrowed in the corner of my bed under the eaves, where the ceiling sloped the lowest. The tight space made me feel safe, and I needed cover from the unknown. I clicked on the unread message, and my father's words came to life.

July 9, 2019

Dear Zoë,

I'm sorry it's taken me a few days to respond to your email. I wrote several responses that I was close to sending but scrapped each one at the last minute. I didn't think they expressed what I wanted to say or how I wanted to say it, and I'm still not sure if what you're going to read right now is the best one, but here goes.

I have very vivid memories from the summer of 2000. It was probably my last taste of freedom right before entering the military. Sweden and Hultsfred always stood out, since that's where I met your mother, Linn. She was straightforward, outgoing, and beautiful, but our time together was destined to be short. I guess we both had that youthful arrogance, that feeling of being invincible, so getting to know each other properly with details like last names, hometowns, parents, etc., didn't seem necessary. Even though I often wondered how things had turned out for her over the years, I could never follow up.

In other words, Zoë, I never forgot your mother. This brings me to your life-changing email. I read it many times, coming to terms with what you said, but I wasn't completely surprised. I always felt like something was left unfinished between Linn and me, and now I know what that was: you.

I looked through the pictures you sent and didn't need further proof that you're my daughter. Genetics don't lie; you look like so many of my—your—relatives. Your sudden appearance has opened a range of happy emotions I wasn't even sure I had, but I can imagine the shock and confusion Linn must have felt when she got this unexpected news nineteen years ago. We were so young, and nothing could have prepared her for that. I'm so sorry she had to go through it alone. Please believe me when I tell you that I had no idea you existed. I would have never walked away from my responsibility to you. But I'm full of admiration and gratitude to Linn and your grandparents for raising you into the lovely, poised, mature young woman I saw in those photographs.

Zoë, I wish I could have been a part of your life growing up. I apologize for not being there with every fiber of my being; I hope that can change. I'm in complete awe over how you could track me down, and maybe I'm getting ahead of myself, but I think you're signaling a willingness to let me into your life? If the answer is yes, nothing would please me more. As I'm sure you do, I have so many questions and things to tell you and would like to make up for lost time. Please let me know how you want to move forward.

Sincerely,

J.G.

P.S. I've also attached some photographs to give you a fuller picture of myself and the other side of your family. Please be kind when judging the ones from my youth 😊!

I chuckled at his postscript, tasting the salty tears that had wound their way down my face. I wanted to print out the letter and hug it against my skin. I wanted to feel my father's words in my hands and unpeel their meaning. Clues about himself and how I'd come into being were buried in each line, delivering the affirmation I had sought my entire life.

Since Douglas had introduced the phrase *one-night stand* into my vocabulary, I'd been plagued by shame, the unspoken stigma of being an accident, illegitimate, unwanted. The sleazy connotations always lurked beneath, and I struggled to blot them from my mind. I'd been skeptical of the man who would show himself in that email. Would he deny it? Call me a troublemaker? Defend being a deadbeat dad? Although my plans hinged on J.G.'s reaction, I had steeled myself for rejection as a defense mechanism. His unconditional acceptance was more than I had dared to hope for, but at the same time, his response confused me. J.G.'s recollections of my mother's former self, and his concern over how she'd had to parent on her own, suggested Linn was also a victim of circumstance. What if my father knew the real toll Linn's pregnancy had taken—her lies, the fallout of her bad choices, her refusal to ever search for him? Would he still be so sympathetic?

Reflexively, my whole body shook, banishing the thought. What was I thinking? I could never rat out my mother and tell him the entire story.

Wiping my cheeks with the bedsheet, I downloaded each file and double-clicked on the first one. A mustard-hued '70s-style wedding photograph appeared. The white-bordered image showed a couple standing at a church altar, the bride in a high-necked lace gown and layered bubble veil; I assumed they were my paternal grandparents on their wedding day. J.G. must have attached the photos in chronological order, since the next picture was of an adorable toddler dressed in shorts and suspenders, standing against a speckled, light blue backdrop. It had to be J.G. Maybe a professional portrait for his first birthday? There was another photo with four kids, three girls, and one boy sitting on a front door stoop. His siblings? They were slightly different versions of each other, and I wondered where he was in the birth order. A class picture of boys, clad in identical plaid ties and gray pants, with a big cross to the right, followed. Catholic school? Were the Latours religious? Then came the teen years—staged poses in various basketball jerseys, J.G.'s hair styled in a hi-top fade. Another in a hoodie and backward baseball hat, à la Will Smith circa *The Fresh Prince of Bel-Air.*

The goofy shots made me laugh, leaving me unprepared for

the next photo: a solemn headshot of J.G. in his Army uniform, framed by the American flag. I paused on the unnerving image. His eyes were stony, as though something had sapped his joy. Then the chronology skipped to happier times just as abruptly: J.G., clad in a black robe and a funny circular cap with a tassel, surrounded by his parents and siblings. Grinning, he held a diploma. Medical school graduation? His parents were older and rounder, but their smiles beamed with pride. I knew J.G.'s family was not as well-off or established as Linn's, yet they looked more dignified, stricter in their behavior and expectations. The Latours seemed to have flourished, while I often felt we Holmgrens were in decline. It would probably blow J.G.'s parents' minds when they learned of a long-lost granddaughter in Sweden. The last photo of J.G. was taken on a boardwalk and seemed more recent. In jeans, a T-shirt, and sunglasses, he gripped the handlebars of a bike. I lingered on that one, curious about the person behind the camera. It was the kind of picture a woman would take.

I closed my eyes, deconstructing each photo again—this time, through a mental split-screen, comparing the brown-skinned images on my father's side with the blonde, blue-eyed members of my mother's, the family who'd raised me. The contrast was startling. Swedish. Haitian. American. Black and white.

Sometimes I was wracked by resentment and anger because Linn and Mormor treated my biracial identity as an afterthought. *Nothing to dwell on,* they said. *You're a Holmgren. You're Zoë.* Even though they had tried to brush aside the racial differences within our family, it was still inescapable, manifesting in things as seemingly minor as the Sankta Lucia assembly at school. My teachers always cast me as the *pepparkasgumma*—never Lucia—because my "gingerbread" skin tone was "perfect" for the brown-skinned character in the procession. At first, I'd felt special in the brown costume decorated with white trim, but as the Decembers accumulated, I became increasingly envious of the celebration's star: the blonde, fair-skinned Lucia in her white gown and red sash, a majestic crown of candles on her head.

Why hadn't Linn or Mormor said anything to my teachers? Didn't they see how patently stereotypical this was? Why hadn't my teachers opened their minds and seen I could also be Lucia? But Linn and Mormor had no context, no language to express what they didn't know or understand. As I got older, it had become clearer that my sparse education on the subject would be inadequate. I'd started schooling myself, relying on Black, brown, and biracial personalities, YouTube videos, and online articles for guidance to process things I had experienced but couldn't articulate.

Would J.G. fill in the blanks? Were the photographs my blueprint for piecing together those missing fragments of my identity?

I closed the pictures and reread his email. I wanted to know more.

11

LINN

My cell phone rang soon after I gave a guest a facial at the Nornö Hotel. I couldn't place the number, but unlike others who wouldn't swipe right unless they recognized the name or digits, I couldn't afford to be picky. Every call could be a potential client, so I responded without hesitation.

"Linn Holmgren," I said in my best professional voice.

"*Hej!* It's Camilla Easton. How are you?"

My entire body tensed as my mind raced to predict the purpose of Camilla's call. *She knows. She knows. Wes confessed, and she's going to tell me off.* It didn't matter that the liaison had been mutual; husbands always blamed it on the other woman. Camilla's cheery tone could be a ploy, adding to my nervousness. I chose the easiest option: playing dumb.

"Camilla! So nice to hear from you. You beat me to it—I was about to send you a note," I fibbed. "Thank you so much for the loveliest summer party Nornö has ever seen."

"Happy you enjoyed yourself! It got so crowded. I'm sorry we didn't get a chance to chat again."

Apparently, Camilla hadn't noticed my hasty retreat. "No need to apologize. That's just the sign of a great party."

"Well, I'm calling for another reason," she began.

I steeled myself for a smackdown. "Yes?"

"I suffer from acute lower back pain, and I hear you're the best masseuse on the island."

I was still wary, but the tautness in my chest receded.

"That's nice of you to say, but I'm the *only* masseuse on the island."

"Which is why I was wondering if you have time today. Apologies for the late notice, but I must have thrown out my back lifting some things after the party, and I'm in pretty bad shape . . ."

"Have you been able to move around at all?"

"With difficulty. Evalina Bohlander suggested I give you a call. Says you have magic hands," Camilla chuckled.

I was glad I could hide my disdain over the phone. Evalina's flattery was nothing more than a power play. I had given her a massage once, many years ago. She'd never paid me for it, and after several reminders, I finally let it go. We weren't friends, so the recommendation was a move on Evalina's part to win over Camilla.

"So, do you have an opening today?" Camilla asked.

I realized I had waited a tad too long to respond, and she'd put me on the spot. To compensate, I said a little too quickly, "Yes, as a matter of fact, I do."

I hadn't analyzed the serious implications of what I had agreed to—seeing Camilla again in an intimate treatment setting—but the woman was in pain, and I did believe I could help. I was small but strong, with dozens of testimonials from grateful clients who said I'd alleviated their stubborn aches. My skills as a masseuse made me doubly proud since it was the first professional goal I had achieved. The educational requirements had been within my reach, the training program manageable for a single mother. I'd also been drawn to the profession's low overhead cost and relatively high earning potential per session. I could set my hours— an asset with a child—and, with a portable table, practice anywhere. I'd then studied skin care; the plan had been to build a client base in

Stockholm, but fifteen years later, that part of the equation hadn't come to fruition. Nevertheless, it gave me confidence, helping others feel better.

"I can come to you around four o'clock. Does that work?" I asked, giving myself half an hour to organize my mobile massage kit.

"It's perfect! Meet me at the shed in the back of the house," Camilla said, and after some closing remarks, we hung up.

I left the hotel and got on my bike, wondering if I was making a big mistake. What if I ran into Wes again? But it would have looked even more suspicious if I had snubbed Camilla. Nornö was so small, we would eventually run into each other. Saying no would only prolong the inevitable. I would pretend that whatever happened with Wes that night in Stockholm *did not* happen. It already seemed like ages ago, an act of foolishness performed while under the influence. I wanted nothing more than to wipe it from my memory.

Back home, I gathered my collapsible massage table and a duffel bag containing the towels and an assortment of oils and arranged everything onto our old flatbed moped, the preferred mode of transport on Nornö. My grandfather Lars had bought the Crescent three-wheeler in the 1960s. It was weather-beaten; the once-gleaming emerald paint had disintegrated to a dull moss shade. The engine was temperamental but still kicking, shuttling me to my at-home massage appointments. The three-wheeler was a rare piece of nostalgia I had difficulty consigning to oblivion. There were too many joyful childhood memories attached to it—mainly my father driving me around Nornö at high speeds—while I sat on the platform, bumping up and down, laughing uncontrollably.

I mounted the Crescent's seat, inserted the key, and

pressed hard on the pedals. Once the whirring sound of the motor accelerated, I cruised out of my property and, ten minutes later, reached the Eastons. In the back, I stationed the moped in front of a building the size of a guest cottage. Hoisting the duffel bag onto my shoulders, I gripped the handles of the thirty-pound massage table and tottered toward the "shed."

"Hello? Hello?" I called out when I reached the front door.

I heard some pitter-patter, and then Camilla stuck her head out. "Oh my gosh, Linn, let me help you with that!" she cried, widening the entryway to take the table from my hands.

"That's okay—your bad back!" I said, stepping inside. I struggled not to gape. Of course, the Eastons had built themselves a private gym. "Wow!" I remarked, giving the room a once-over. Oak wood flooring, mirrored walls, a flatscreen TV, a barre, a dumbbell set, a cross-trainer, and the pièce de résistance: a Peloton bike, which was impossible to find in Sweden. "This is amazing!"

"My husband insisted—it was either this or a man cave. You're a saint for coming on such short notice," Camilla said, pointing to the mat at one end of the room. "I was doing some stretches, but they haven't helped."

"Where would you like me to set up?" I asked.

"I can move the mat so you can put the table in the space between the wall and the bench. Will that give you enough room to move around?"

"More than enough," I said, gently lowering the massage table and duffel to the floor. Camilla rolled the mat away, and I couldn't help spying on her, catching how she winced while bending down. Black tights sculpted her narrow hips and long, toned legs; a purple sports bra evened out her breasts to perfection. Camilla's stomach was flat but had a little overhanging skin over her waistband, though you would never be able to tell when she was fully clothed. She exuded that ageless quality a select few possessed, which no amount of plastic surgery could buy. Was Camilla aware that regular women studied her? That we subconsciously compared our looks and bodies to hers?

The gym also had a bathroom, and while Camilla changed out of her workout clothes, I prepared the massage table, molding the fitted towels around the corners and headrest. I placed an extra-large bath sheet on the bed for coverage and retrieved the wooden storage box with therapeutic oils.

Camilla returned, wearing a white bathrobe. "Ready to go," she said, smiling modestly.

"Before we get started, I just have a few questions to understand better how to treat your pain," I said.

"Sure, go ahead."

"How often do you normally get massages?"

"Once a week. More often if we go skiing or I'm on vacation."

Why am I not surprised? The thought crossed my mind before I could stop it, but I wasn't contemptuous of Camilla's wealth. Alicia had also led a posh life with Jonas, and my best friend's soon-to-be-ex flaunted his money, expecting undying gratitude for his self-aggrandizing largess. But he was still nouveau riche, a wannabe who wasn't in the same league as the Eastons. Jonas moved in little, insular Stockholm, while the Eastons had a larger platform. Their New York currency and connections gave them international prestige and access to exclusive experiences and services. Camilla's privileged status was so intrinsic that she could be blunt about her lifestyle, ditching the false modesty that I found considerably more off-putting.

"How often do you get lower back pain?"

"Almost every day."

"That's tough," I sympathized. "You have to stretch once or twice a day to loosen your muscles and strengthen your lower back. But I'm sure you know that already."

"I do, but sometimes I'm not in the mood, and it's easier to take a pill."

"I know it can be boring, but stretching is an important complement to massages—and pills."

"That's why we built this gym, so I'd have no excuse!"

I chuckled. "Where are your other areas of discomfort?"

"My neck and shoulders."

"Upper body tension is common. It comes from tightening our shoulders when we work sitting down or feel stressed. I honestly think the neck pain comes from staring at our phones too much."

"I try not to bend my head when I use my phone, but it feels unnatural."

"Do you have any other conditions? Previous injuries or areas I should avoid?"

"I have endometriosis," Camilla replied. "Do you know what that is?"

I turned the word over in my head. "I think I do . . . bad period cramps?"

"Hmph," Camilla said scathingly. "If it were only that minor. It's when the tissues inside your uterus move to other parts of your body, leading to severe cramps and heavy bleeding, among other things."

"Oh my. Like lower back pain?"

She nodded. "But I'm not menstruating now, so I think I just did something stupid and threw out my back."

I unfolded the bath sheet and held it in front of Camilla.

"Let's get started so you can feel better."

She disrobed and lay facedown on the bed, audibly sighing as she relaxed her shoulders. "This feels better already."

"Let yourself go and take a few slow, deep breaths. Do you mind if I play some calming music?"

"Not at all."

I rested my wireless speaker and iPhone on a window ledge and put on my go-to massage track, Brian Eno's "Thursday Afternoon." Sixty-one minutes long, the trancelike composition was perfect for an hour-long session.

Back at the massage table, I tucked the towel into Camilla's waist. "What kind of oil would you prefer? I have coconut, jojoba, almond, grapeseed . . ."

"Almond oil, please. I like the mild scent."

"And it's nice to work with, so that's a good choice." I dropped a teaspoon of almond oil in my palm and rubbed my hands together to warm it. I began at Camilla's lower back, moving upward at both sides of her spine to the shoulders. I repeated these gliding movements—long, even strokes— several times, gradually increasing the intensity to loosen up the back muscles, mindful to also concentrate on her shoulders and neck. "Is the pressure okay?" I asked.

"Mm-hmm."

I switched to a kneading technique, using shorter, circular strokes to enhance deeper circulation. I knuckled my hands up and down in the lumbar region, triggering a grunt from Camilla. I stopped. "Does that hurt?"

"In a good way," Camilla murmured. "That's where the pain is."

I continued massaging her, squeezing tension points and running my hands across her legs, arms, and buttocks. Her flesh was smooth and unblemished—a sign of good genes and a rigorous skin-care regimen. Early on, I discovered that massages gave me a rare glimpse into a client's physical and mental state. The condition of their bodies alluded to their stressors and priorities, vanity, and insecurities. A masseuse had to create trust with clients; intimacies were shared without having to say a word. It was a forced closeness, where I had to desexualize the touch experience. Good draping and frequent communication were crucial, but even I could see how there could be a sensual component to the interaction.

Under normal circumstances, I stayed focused on finding those knots in my clients' bodies, detached from awkward undertones. But today, with *this* client and Brian Eno's meditative acoustics droning in the background, my attention strayed. Whenever my hands melted into Camilla's skin or dug into her muscles, I thought of Wes. I pictured his fingers traveling the same route, somewhere along Camilla's shoulder blades or over her thighs. Coming in such personal—though different—physical contact with both husband and wife was perverse. Agreeing to give Camilla a massage had been pure madness. The ramifications of my stupidity closed in on me, and the room suddenly felt warm and oppressive.

Mercifully, the music stopped a few minutes later.

"Camilla, that's our session for today," I whispered in a strained, soothing tone. "I hope you feel better."

"Mmm . . ."

"I'm going to leave the room, but when you're ready, wiggle your fingers and toes to revitalize your body," I advised. "Get up carefully and knock on the door when you're ready for me to come back in. You also need to hydrate. Would you like me to get you a glass of water from the house?"

"We have water bottles in that little fridge near the hand towels," Camilla mumbled.

"Perfect."

I brought her an Evian and went outside. Folding my arms across my chest, I wished I had a cigarette or a glass of wine to settle my nerves. The massage had felt like another betrayal. Worse yet, Camilla had surrendered to it. Justice would have been served if she'd been a rude, demanding client, but she was friendly and unassuming. Fidgety, I watched for Wes out of the corner of my eye, rehearsing what I would say if I saw him.

Soon after, Camilla opened the door. She was back in her workout tights, but a stretchy jacket covered her torso.

"Evalina was right," she said, smiling. "I feel like a ton of bricks have been lifted from my back."

"Happy to hear that," I said, reentering the gym to gather my things. "Remember to stretch and eat. Take a warm bath and relax for the rest of the day."

"Are you in a rush?" Camilla asked. "Do you want to stay for a predinner snack?"

Every minute in Camilla's company stressed me out. The specter of Wes hung over me like a bomb that could go off at any time, and I was desperate to leave. Clearing my throat, I said, "Thank you for asking, but I don't want to impose on you and Wes."

"Wes is on a business trip in London, so it'd be no imposition."

I kept my head down and stripped the fitted towel from the massage table. *More like a business trip with benefits*, I thought. Silent outrage coursed through me as I imagined Wes in a hotel bar, telling lies, ordering drinks for an impressionable young woman, or hitting on a tipsy good-time girl. I had fallen for it, and someone else would too.

Meanwhile, his wife stayed home alone, coping with a bad back and begging for company. Wes's conceit, self-importance, and disrespect for Camilla tempted me to shake her and shout, *Do you know what your husband is doing? The games he plays when you're not around?* But confronting Camilla would reveal my complicity, and a megaphone blasted inside my head: *Stay out of it. Don't get involved.*

But a distorted sense of female solidarity outweighed the warning signals, and I said, "Sure, that would be great."

After disassembling my equipment and packing everything in the moped, I joined Camilla at the front of the house. She had arranged a crudité platter and a cheese and charcuterie board on the dining table. Beside them, a pitcher of iced tea and a bottle of white wine was cooling in a bucket. Camilla couldn't have prepared that spread in ten minutes; she must have anticipated I would say yes and join her. The Eastons were persuasive, and I scolded myself for being so susceptible to their charms.

Camilla was seated in a chair facing the sea, and I pulled out the one next to her. "What a view!" I exclaimed, sitting down.

"I want to pinch myself. Can't believe what I've been missing out on all these years." Camilla pointed to the drinks. "What should we have?"

"Sorry, but alcohol after a massage is a no-no. It'll slow down your body's recovery, so I'd suggest the iced tea."

"I was afraid you'd say that!" Camilla said, laughing.

She poured us each a glass, and after a mock Swedish toast, we sipped our iced teas, quietly contemplating the scenery. In a strange paradox, Camilla's paradise commandeered the choppiest chunk of Nornö. Only a portion of the land was visible from the forest, and most hikers assumed that part of the woods led to nowhere special. Although the ground had been flattened to construct the new house, the cliff's chiseled, rocky contours couldn't be tamed. A southwesterly wind cooled the air, and the current could be rough, cresting with pointed white peaks. Wooden stairs built into the hilltop offered a steep descent from the headland to a private beach. The terrain unraveled slowly, like a thorny fairy tale, before crescendoing to a happy ending. Nornö—the beautiful and the bleak—ran through my veins, but I was unsure an outsider could appreciate its contradictions.

"Is Nornö what you expected?" I asked Camilla, sticking a carrot in the hummus dip.

"You guys are nicer than I expected," Camilla said.

"*You're* nicer than we expected!"

"Ha! It's been both easier and tougher than I imagined."

"How so?"

"The slower pace of life suits where I'm at in life right now. I love the solitude, I have a backlog of books to read and charity work to catch up on, but it takes planning to be here. Shopping for food"—she winked at me—"transportation to and off the island . . . those small creature comforts you take for granted, like getting a manicure or dyeing your hair, are more complicated. But I think it's healthy not to have everything served up so easily. Forces you to adapt and be more creative."

"Hmm. That's probably the best description I've heard for surviving Nornö."

"What was it like for you growing up here?"

"It was cute. The island felt so free when I was little but became claustrophobic as a teenager."

"I can relate. Ljusdal was like that for me," Camilla said, munching on a nugget of Parmesan cheese.

"Luckily, you had your modeling. You could escape."

Camilla laughed sardonically. "Yes and no."

Arching an eyebrow, I asked, "What do you mean? It must have been a dream job."

"Don't get me wrong—I feel fortunate an agent scouted me and it gave me many opportunities, but it's super competitive. No matter how hard you work, there's always someone new around the corner who's younger, prettier, skinnier." She paused. "Not to mention all the sleazeballs."

"I see what you're saying. It looks glamorous from the outside, but I'm sure there are drawbacks."

Camilla nodded ruefully. "Back in the '90s, I was a teenager, roaming the world alone. Nobody talked about the sexual harassment or abuse models faced. It was like, 'You're beautiful! Traveling! Getting free clothes and bags! Going to star-studded parties! What are you complaining about?!' The agency sent girls like me on casting calls and photo shoots with an understanding we were lucky to be there—especially if it was for a famous photographer. So, what was the big deal if he asked you to take off your bra or if he wanted to see you in your underwear? 'Don't make a fuss if he follows you to the bathroom. You should be thrilled if he asks you to do a private session.' Agents expected us to do what it took to book the job or get that perfect shot." She shrugged slightly, palms up. "We were trained to put up with the bad behavior and putting up meant . . . shutting up."

Camilla's revelation was jarring. First Wes, and now this: another crack in the veneer of her supposedly perfect life. I searched for an empathetic response, but the words seemed insufficient. Finally, I said, "Thank God things are changing with *#MeToo* and people speaking up. Society and companies are taking those issues much more seriously now. It's long overdue."

Ignoring my no-alcohol advice, Camilla took a goblet and

filled it with the Sancerre. I didn't have the heart to reproach her. Hell, she needed something more potent than iced tea after that outpouring of emotion. After a deep swallow, she asked, "But what if the damage has already been done?"

Her question, which was loaded with unsettling connotations, erased my previous apprehension, justifying why I had agreed to meet her again. Pain was more than a physical sensation. After a heavy silence, I spoke again. "I'm so sorry. I feel terrible about bringing it up. Let's not talk about it anymore."

"Oh, it's okay. It was so long ago. I'm a big girl now. I try to be a stoic Swede and not dwell on the past."

I touched her arm. "You know, massages can make people very emotional, both positively and negatively, so don't feel like you need to play it down."

"Seriously, I've moved on. I married Wes and became a mother, but people still see me as a former model. I've done so much more with my life since then."

"When did you stop modeling?" I asked.

"I was twenty-eight. After Wes and I got engaged."

"Did he ask you to quit?"

She shook her head. "Quitting was my decision. Wes liked my modeling in theory, but in practice, I had a very unpredictable schedule and traveled a lot. My endometriosis also worsened, and I thought it was from all the running around. I wanted to settle down and start a family."

My inquiring mind spun, and I knew where it was headed. Despite my dismal performance history, I decided one glass of white wine wouldn't break me, and I needed a nerve quencher for my next question. "How did you and Wes meet?" I asked.

Camilla let out a throaty laugh. "It's so cliché—at a party in the Hamptons. I had a share in a house with some other

Swedish models, but it was so expensive that I could only afford five weekends. I met Wes at a Memorial Day party in 1997—my first weekend out there—and we've been together ever since."

"I guess you had no problem filling in those other weekends?" I said, attempting a half-witted joke.

"Yes, he had a house there"—Camilla laughed—"so I was covered."

"Well, Wes is a lucky guy," I said—and meant it. "I hope he knows that."

Gazing into the distance, she replied, "Men are complicated. You have to remind them how lucky they are every so often, but Wes came through with this place, so he's on my good side at the moment."

"He didn't want you to keep Karin's gift?!"

"Look, he's a business guy—"

"Real estate, right?" I asked and then realized I had slipped up. Wes had mentioned his line of work to me that night at Grand Hotel.

"Mm . . . kind of. Easton Carpet Mills is one of America's leading residential and commercial carpet companies, so Wes deals with many new builds and development projects. He likes to dabble in real estate, and he didn't see the upside in spending a ton of money on building a house in the middle of nowhere—oops. I didn't mean it that way!"

I chuckled. "Nornö *is* the middle of nowhere."

"He said we'd only visit for a month out of the year at best," she finished.

"How'd you get him to come around?"

"Well, I told him I was having a midlife crisis, and building the house would be cheaper than getting a divorce!"

Camilla's flippant comment puzzled me. Was there a

subtext? An awareness her husband was unfaithful? But I remembered the togetherness they had projected in the kitchen at their garden party. Surely, Camilla wouldn't have been so affectionate if she knew about Wes's cheating? I decided her barefaced candor was another Americanism, an acquired habit of oversharing. For many Swedes— conditioned to be reserved and detached—this tendency seemed artificial, but I found it to be the opposite: refreshing and authentic. Camilla was brave enough to speak her truth, unlike many Swedes who preferred to talk about the weather rather than broach a topic that carried any depth or controversy. It was something we called *integritet.* Swedes wore this personal trait with pride, respecting privacy and personal space, separating the exterior and interior lives. But I thought it was a cop-out, born out of fear and insecurity. It closed people off from each other, preventing them from confronting pain or doubt and finding common ground.

"Sounds to me like you deserved it," I remarked. "Tell Wes your house is a good investment. You've already raised the property values for the rest of us in Nornö, so thank you!"

Camilla held up her wineglass. "No, thank *you* for the excellent massage and for listening to me. I think there was some truth serum in that almond oil."

I grinned. "You're welcome."

"Maybe we could set up a weekly massage appointment? Can you fit me into your schedule?" Camilla asked.

I sipped my wine, stalling for time and wishing I had met Camilla first. We could have developed a friendship untainted by Wes and my gnawing guilt. Maybe this was my chance to make amends.

"I'm sure something could be arranged," I said, ignoring the beeping alarm bells: *Stay out of it. Don't get involved.*

12

ZOË

Following the lunchtime rush the next day, I went home and collected Simba for his daily walk in the forest. Since I was usually strapped for time in the early morning, I took the easy way out, opening the back door so he could relieve himself and get a boost of fresh air. But afternoon exercise was doable, and Simba could run free among the trees. I also got a breather from the midday witching hour, when the customers' comments began to irk me, asking as they did for things that were sold out and bitching about how slow the line was.

I carried Simba's leash and doggie bag, letting him dash ahead. We had a routine: I allowed him to play around the woods as much as he liked, but I'd trained him to stop and wait for me where the trail split in three directions.

Strolling behind him, I became lost in thought. Establishing contact with my father hadn't solved all my problems. I still had to ask him about coming to Florida— along with the small detail of telling Linn I had found him in the first place. Almost as daunting was the prospect of informing Mormor I wanted to leave Nornö and Holmgren's.

As I got deeper into the forest, the houses peeking from behind tree branches disappeared, and the invigorating smell of pure, damp earth quieted the chaos in my head. But my solitude was interrupted by a dog's high-pitched *woof*ing in the backwoods, followed by Simba's screechy, rapid-fire barks. I bolted in the direction of the commotion and found Simba hunched on his forelegs, growling at a small dog on a leash.

"Simba!" I scolded.

He snarled at the jumpy Cavalier King Charles Spaniel again and then backed off.

I knelt and patted Simba's back to calm him. "Sorry about that—" I began saying to the other dog's owner but cut myself off when I saw who it was.

"You should keep her on a leash," Gunnar said, peering down at me.

"There usually aren't any other dogs around this time of day," I retorted. "And it's a 'he,' by the way."

"Maybe Leia did lunge at him first," he allowed. "But only because she was scared."

"Leia? As in Princess Leia?" I asked, clipping on Simba's leash.

He gave a sheepish smile. "What can I say? I'm a *Star Wars* fanatic."

"How sweet," I said sarcastically. "I would have never guessed." Back on my feet, I wrapped Simba's leash firmly around my fist and kept walking.

"It feels like you and I got off on the wrong foot," Gunnar said, tagging along.

"That's all right. Your mother makes up for it."

"No, seriously. I was a douchebag at our house. I'm sorry."

As we walked side-by-side, our dogs began sniffing each other and seemed to reach a truce.

"I know Nornö sucks. You don't have to rub it in."

"Okay, I never said it sucked. I just said I didn't want to be here."

Raising an eyebrow, I said, "You didn't seem to mind last night. At the beach."

Open-mouthed, he was speechless for a second and then

let out a booming laugh. "Point taken."

I smirked, enjoying his discomfort. "Forget about it. We can turn over a new leaf."

"Fair enough." He gave me his hand. "Hi, I'm Gunnar."

I narrowed my eyes but offered my own hand. "Zoë."

Handshakes out of the way, we let the dogs lead, watching their tails wag in the distance.

"How old's Simba?" he asked.

"Nine. And Leia?"

"She's only three."

I gazed at Leia's short legs, working double-time to keep up with Simba. "Such a cute little thing. Feisty but cute."

"You can say that again. She's my mom's baby. We had an English bulldog before. When he died, Mom got to choose our next breed."

"I thought it was an unspoken rule that kids got to pick the dog?"

"Yeah, but Winston drooled and shed all over our apartment, so Mom wasn't down with that. Since she's also going to take care of the new dog after I go to college, she won the argument, and we got Leia. At least I got to name her."

"Ah, college. Still a sore topic?" I asked, giving him another chance to elaborate.

"For a variety of reasons," he said evasively. Sighing, he added, "I just wanted to spend this summer with my friends before we all head off in different directions. But I'm stuck here, all by myself."

"I get it. I'd be pissed too."

"You graduated with Douglas, right?" I nodded. "Are you gonna stay in Nornö like him and work with your family?"

I shook my head. "I'm going to spend a few months with my father in the US." The words slid from my tongue, smooth as silk, no big deal. Saying them made the possibility more real.

"Cool. Where?"

"Florida."

"Are your parents divorced?"

"No. My mom had me young, so he wasn't involved, but he wants to change that now." Despite fudging the details, I felt no embarrassment in disclosing my family situation. It gave me some status, a distinctive birthmark that separated me from the other, more ordinary folks in Nornö.

"Lucky you. My dad's *too* involved. I call him Black Hawk Dad."

"'Black Hawk Dad'?"

"You know, like that movie *Black Hawk Down,* about attack helicopters?"

"I don't, sorry."

"Anyway, he's like a chopper, hovering, waiting to strike if something doesn't go my way. Or, more accurately, if something doesn't go the way *he* thinks it should."

"Oh, we have a Swedish word for that too: *curling.* Sweeping the ice so your kid doesn't get hurt." I paused. "My mom isn't like that, though." *For better or worse.*

"I guess it'll be good to get away from it all."

"Mm-hmm." It would be good. But I wasn't so sure I could pull it off.

We passed a colony of uprooted trunks lying on the ground, as if a punch had knocked them out.

"Why are there so many overturned trees?" Gunnar asked.

"We had some bad windstorms this year. We lost a tree on our property."

"Must have been a killer storm to rip them out like that."

"It was," I said, remembering the whipping gusts of air, the sudden, cracking thump, and then the sight of a crippled birch tree over Mormor's raspberry bush. "But storms on this island have a strange beauty to them. I actually think the sound of thunder and rain is comforting. The wind and water are almost violent, but it's hypnotic. There's nothing to do except watch and wait." I paused, startled by my effusiveness. I hadn't meant to go into such detail. "I probably sound like a psycho."

"No, just kind of trippy," he said, smiling. "I know what you mean, though. I've gone to the beach before a hurricane and had the same feeling watching these giant waves roll in and out. You become in awe of Mother Nature."

"Exactly!" I said, relieved he hadn't mocked me. "How long are you guys staying in Nornö?"

"Until mid-August. I want to go back to New York for a few weeks before I leave for school."

We reached a tract in the woods where the twigs and moss on the forest floor thinned out, tapering off into sand and sea. "Well, this is where Simba and I head back home," I told him.

"You don't let him run on the beach?" Gunnar asked, surprised.

"It's too messy. Simba gets all wet and sandy, and I have to go back to work."

"Right." He paused. "Well, see you around."

I gave him a toothless smile. "Yeah. See you around."

I tried not to think about Gunnar when I returned to Holmgren's, but our walk—and first genuine conversation— had been a pleasant diversion. It put me in a better mood for the rest of my shift, and I kept Linn company after dinner instead of fleeing to my room.

"How was the beach last night?" she asked, wiping down the kitchen counter with a Wettex dishcloth. We had made pizza out of a kit, and the dough had stuck to the surface.

"Okay. How'd you know?" It bewildered me how fast news spread in Nornö.

"Tilde came in the store at lunchtime looking for you and said you'd been with a bunch of kids at the beach."

She'd probably come to check why I'd freaked out and left so dramatically. "We weren't a big group. It was only, like, six people."

"Well, I think it's nice you're meeting friends on the island," Mamma said, turning and smiling at me. "I always thought Tilde was a nice girl."

Her veiled criticism about my being antisocial did not go unnoticed, but I ignored it. All things considered, I was starting to feel sorry for my mother. She didn't have the slightest idea of what was *really* going on. The beach was insignificant compared to what had happened afterward in the privacy of my room. How would my mother react if she knew that right now, on the same phone sitting on the kitchen table, I had solved the mystery about my father? His name. His whereabouts. His email address. What would my mother say if she knew we had begun corresponding? Would she be so quick to judge my social skills?

"Yeah, Tilde's adorbs," I said, continuing the charade.

Linn threw the dishcloth in the sink and asked, "What's Gunnar like?"

"He's nicer than I thought," I replied, our lunchtime walk—not his propensity for pot—still fresh in my mind.

"Ha. That's exactly my opinion of Camilla! I gave her a massage yesterday, and then we had an aperitif."

"Was his dad there?"

Linn coughed, covering her mouth. "Why do you ask?"

"No reason. Gunnar mentioned him, and I wondered if you had met him and maybe formed an opinion."

She sat at the edge of a chair and shook her head. "No, he wasn't there. Camilla said he was in London." Leaning closer, she asked, "What did Gunnar say about him?"

"Nothing specific, but I got the sense he's bossy. Likes to be the one in control."

Linn stared at me for a few seconds and then chuckled softly, swatting my comment away with her hand. "Oh, honey, he's just one of those high-powered businessmen. I'm sure he's fine."

Gunnar had tried to sound casual, but I knew what it was like to have a parent who meddled in all the wrong areas of your life. His offhand statements were probably a way of masking his irritation.

"Yeah, you're probably right," I said.

I caught sight of Gunnar again the next day, soon after my shift at Holmgren's ended. He was sitting on a bench outside the small café that made takeout sandwiches and pasta salads. Leia was sprawled by his feet, sunbathing. The chestnut splotches on her pearly-white fur were nearly the same shade as Gunnar's hair. Their size difference was comical, but Gunnar's sporty physique made him look like the dog's protector, and they made an adorable pair.

I contemplated going over and starting another conversation. Our spontaneous walk-and-talk in the forest had made Gunnar seem more approachable and less angry. There was still so much I was curious about, despite his elusiveness. But what mood would he be in now? What if he behaved like a douchebag again, humiliating me yet again?

But wouldn't I look extra foolish walking past him without saying hello? There was no safe bet, so I strode ahead. At the café, I hunched down to tickle Leia's back.

"Hi, cutie," I said as the dog sniffed my sneakers.

"Are you only this nice to four-legged creatures?" Gunnar asked.

"Some humans make the cut. Not many. Just a few."

"Are you done working?"

I nodded. "What have you been up to today?"

He lifted his shoulders. "Not much. I got up before noon, which was good."

I refrained from asking if he had been getting high or hanging out with Douglas and Molly. Yet, he seemed relaxed, so I took a chance and sat beside him, watching the summertime tableau unfold like one of my great-grandfather's Axel Sjöberg paintings. People in the open-air tavern munched on early dinners or sipped cocktails. Kids in orange life vests ran barefoot in all directions. Further down by the harbor, tourists milled around kiosks selling Nornö sweatshirts, mugs, and place mats.

"If you're gonna survive Nornö for the next month, you've gotta follow the rhythm of the island," I told him.

"Rhythm? This island has a rhythm?" he asked.

"Mm-hmm. People do things differently here. Think of this place as a detox."

"Detox? Are you trying to tell me something?" The inflection in his tone could be amusement or exasperation. It was difficult for me to read, as were his eyes, which were shielded behind a pair of aviator sunglasses.

"At least I didn't say *rehab*, if that makes you feel better!" I exclaimed.

"I'm not a druggie because I occasionally smoke a jay. It's practically legal in New York."

"Well, it's not legal in Sweden, and you smuggled it in your carry-on!"

"If I'd gotten caught, I would've told them it was for medical purposes," he said with a smirk.

Gunnar's nonchalance about breaking the law on both sides of the Atlantic astounded me, hinting at his ability to talk himself out of tricky situations. How condescending, to go through life thinking you were above the rules. "Well, Swedish police are no joke about that stuff, so watch out."

"Yes, ma'am."

"Whatever. Back to my original point: there's a flow to the days here. Get up early, take a dip in the sea, run in the forest, play tennis, or go kayaking. Then have lunch, sunbathe, read a book, and maybe go swimming again. *Fika* with a *runebulle*. Mix cocktails before dinner. Then fire up the grill, go in the sauna, and call it a night with a movie or TV series. If you do that, day in and day out, the month will fly by."

"You've got to be kidding! Listening to you made me tired. Is that how you spend your days?"

"I live here and work all day! I'm just telling you how the other half—people like you—live. Swedes aren't good at sitting still. There's always something to fix or build, an archipelago triathlon to train for—my grandfather spent one vacation painting our house."

"Maybe that's the problem."

"What?"

"Too much running around and not enough leisure."

Shrugging, I said, "Sorry. I'm just trying to save you from getting antsy."

He turned to me, tilting his head, and I saw my reflection in the mirrored lenses. "Do you know how I spent the last three summers?"

"I couldn't possibly imagine."

"SAT prep, college enrichment programs, being a lacrosse camp counselor, an internship at a tech start-up, a service trip to Haiti—"

"Wait, wait, wait. You've been to Haiti?"

He nodded. "Last summer."

"My dad's parents are from Haiti! What was it like?"

"Beautiful country and people, but the poverty's intense."

"What were you doing there?"

"I was part of a group that went around villages picking up garbage."

"Are you serious?" I couldn't see Gunnar—lily-white, lazy Gunnar—picking up scraps and debris from the streets of Port-au-Prince.

"Yeah, Styrofoam boxes, plastic bags, soda bottles. There were mountains of it on the side of the road, at the beach . . ."

"We're starting to get a garbage problem here too. I don't get why it's so hard for people to throw their shit in a trash can."

"Except in Haiti, they barely have trash cans," Gunnar explained. "Most garbage is burned or ends up in the ocean."

I was acutely aware of this problem, living next to the Baltic Sea; plastic containers floating in our waters and marine animals found with microparticles in their stomachs. "That's so sad."

"It is, but it felt like we were making a difference, as corny as that sounds."

"It's not corny at all. How long were you there for?"

"Three weeks."

"I'd like to go someday."

"You should. I want to go back and scale up our project."

By the conviction in his voice, his volunteer work sounded legit, and I felt guilty for doubting his commitment to the cause. By trying to figure out what made him tick, I wanted to put him in a box, I realized. It was much easier to deal with a caricature than a three-dimensional person, especially when he went off-script, forcing me to push the reset button.

I was also a bit jealous. It was unfair that Gunnar had visited Haiti while I had only recently discovered that aspect of my family history. No matter how irrational, spoiled, or misguided my emotions were, I felt like a piece of my heritage had been appropriated. I had more right to go to Haiti than he did.

"Wow. Impressive," I said, trying to sound neutral.

"But you get my point, right?" he continued. "I was trying to chill this summer and get away from all the stress and obligations."

Now he sounded a little bit annoyed, almost pleading. What was my problem, lecturing him like his mother? Even Camilla was too cool to nag him about banal stuff like sleeping until noon.

"I guess I'd do the same if I had the choice. Anyway, I need to get home," I said, standing. After a slight pause, I added our standard, "See you around."

Gunnar got to his feet. "I can walk home with you—if you don't mind?" he asked.

"Um—yeah, sure, not at all," I stammered, surprised my boatload of unsolicited advice hadn't turned him off and equally confused by how much I welcomed his attention.

I guided him from the café to the wide footpath bridging the Midsummer meadow and the small beach where families with small kids liked to splash around and where the elderly took their morning swims. The maypole stuck out like a scorched stick figure. Its cascading leaves had gone from kale green to burnt ember. It made the meadow, which was already otherworldly with the imposing Nornir runestones, downright spooky.

"I wish somebody would take that maypole out of its misery," I said.

"It does look pretty sad," Gunnar agreed. "When I was younger, my mother threw these huge Midsummer parties in the Hamptons. We had a much smaller maypole, but we danced around it, and they let me stay up all night."

"That sounds wonderful," I said. Although I had mixed feelings about Midsummer, celebrating it abroad, Easton-style, sounded charming.

"Then it got too big and crazy, and she switched to a Lucia cocktail."

I could visualize the pre-Christmas tradition under Camilla's creative control—glimmering candles, a professional Sankta Lucia choir, mulled wine served in delicate crystal mugs, gluten-free saffron buns, and pepper cookies. "It's nice she wanted to keep that Swedish connection."

"Yeah," he mused, "but in kind of a superficial way. She never wanted to go back to Ljusdal, where she's from."

"Does anyone ever want to go back to where they came from? Even I'm planning my getaway."

He grinned. "True. Though I doubt I'll ever leave New York for good."

"If I lived in New York, I don't think I'd ever leave either."

"My mom bent over backward, adapting to my dad's life. I'm glad she has this place now."

"It's your place, too, as much as you try to forget it."

"How can I, when you keep reminding me?" He pointed to the runestones. "Can we go over there? I haven't seen them up close yet."

"Are you sure you're ready?" I asked.

"Why?"

"They're possessed," I said in an exaggerated stage whisper.

"Possessed? Sounds like an old wives' tale."

"Tsk, tsk—that's sexist, and the Norns don't like that."

"Okay, fine. A myth. A story this island has cooked up to get tourists."

"You just got here and already think you're an expert! Do you even know what a norn is?"

Now he looked like I had insulted him. "They're frost giants. They live in Jotunheim, one of the Nine Realms, where Loki was born. I've seen *Thor*."

I rolled my eyes. "Where would Norse mythology be without those Marvel movies?"

"Are you a superhero fan?"

"Well, duh."

"Who's your favorite?"

"Kind of cringe," I warned, "but I love Captain America."

"Do you love Captain America, or do you love Chris Evans?"

"Is there a difference?" I shot back. "How tragic is it that Steve never got to take Peggy dancing?!"

"Not tragic. Cringe."

"Okay, fine," I said, chuckling. "Who's your favorite?"

Gunnar stroked his chin. "Depends. In the Marvel Universe, Iron Man. In the DC Universe, the Flash."

"Well, in the Nornö Universe, three female giants traveled mysteriously from Jotunheim to Asgard," I said, segueing into the saga of the Norns.

"Home of the gods," Gunnar added smugly.

"Exactly. But on Asgard, they live in a hall by the Well of Fate near Yggdrasil, the World Tree."

"O-kay," he said slowly. "This is getting confusing."

"A little but stay with me. The three main Norns water this tree every day because it holds the Nine Realms in its branches and roots. These roots connect the universe and protect all creation. So, you see why the Norns are so important? Without them, the World Tree would dry up and die."

We came to the clearing, a barren plot of land save for the three runestones. Gunnar dropped Leia's leash, gawking at the first stone from the left. I said nothing and let him absorb the magic of the Norns. Being in their presence weakened one's defenses. Even if you didn't believe in the myth, the sensory experience of these centuries-old, twelve-foot-tall blocks of rock arranged in an eerie formation stunned you into silence.

"Incredible. Which one is this?" Gunnar asked.

"That one is named after Urd, the oldest norn," I said, walking to the third runestone. "And this is Skuld, the youngest. The second stone represents the middle sister, Verdandi. Together"—I inserted a theatrical pause—"they decide the fate of mortals and gods."

"Three sisters, like the Fates in Greek mythology. Past, present, and future."

"Exactly!"

"My private school education wasn't a total waste," he joked.

"Think of the Greater Norns as badass women, weaving the threads of life on cloth or carving someone's fate in runes."

Gunnar wandered to Skuld and sat back on his haunches, inspecting the markings. "And the runes are symbols like the ones on this stone?"

I nodded, crouching beside him. "It's the Viking alphabet system."

"Something about the shape of those letters seems familiar," he commented.

"You're probably thinking of the Bluetooth symbol. It's a combination of the rune letters *H* and *B*."

"Aha! No wonder." He took off his sunglasses and googled it on his iPhone. "Named after Harald Bluetooth," he read, "tenth century, second king of Denmark. Pretty cool."

"This is also where things get a little creepy," I said.

"How?"

"The inscription. It's pretty freaky."

He exhaled, making a *brrr* sound with his lips. "Okay. Shoot."

Even though I knew the text and English translation by heart, I stared at the engraving. "'The Norns did both good and evil. Few escape what the Nornir decide.'"

Neither of us moved. Finally, Leia barked and broke the spell.

"Holy shit," Gunnar said. "That gave me the chills."

"There's more," I said, gesturing to the bottom of the stone. "You see the smaller rune symbols over there?" He nodded. "They stand for 'Prophecy of Destruction.'"

"Meaning?"

"Whoever messes with the stones is in deep shit."

"Like death?"

"Or doom, or something terrible happening to you. I don't know, and I don't care. I leave those stones alone."

"Has anyone ever messed with them?"

"Legend has it there was a farmer back in the 1800s who wanted to extend his potato field and tried to remove one of the stones."

"How? These things are cemented to the ground!"

"He heated the stone with fire and thought it would crack by pouring cold water over it, but a poisonous snake, a *huggorm,* came out of nowhere and bit him."

"Wait—there are poisonous snakes on this island?"

"Some vipers, so you have to be careful, especially with Leia. You rarely die if they bite you, but this poor guy was unlucky. Died alone and in agony."

Gunnar squinted suspiciously at the stone. "You actually believe in this curse?"

"I see no reason not to believe it." I shrugged. "Better safe than sorry."

"How the hell do you know this stuff?"

I straightened, unsure whether his question was a compliment or a criticism of my nerdiness. The runestones hadn't just rescued Nornö from insignificance; they'd also saved me. My childhood had been lonely and confusing, but the runestones were bigger than my daily woes. Commanding a far-fetched space in the archipelago, they were enchanted objects that had captured my imagination. Generations of Holmgrens had revered the Three Norns; our house had at least a dozen old books in their honor. I'd spent countless hours going through them, examining the pictures when I couldn't read the complicated text. I'd drawn them with my coloring pencils and concocted fairy tales about Skuld, my favorite Norn. As I got older and the kids around me focused on drinking, sex, and going out, my fascination with the Norns began to feel childish. Until this moment with Gunnar, I hadn't spoken freely about them for years.

"We learned about it in school," I told him, revealing only a portion of the truth. "I used to charge fifty kronor to give guided tours when I was younger."

Rising, he took hold of Leia's leash. "Profiting from the Norns! Isn't that, like, blasphemy?"

"The whole island profits from these stones! I made a lot of money. Nobody can say no to a kid."

"I think they had trouble saying no to you," he said with a smile.

I was suddenly at a loss for words. Gunnar went from indifferent to friendly to charming faster than I could process.

"But these runestones aren't all doom and gloom," I explained, dodging his comment. "If you rub Skuld, it's supposed to bring good luck."

"What if I messed with the stones and then rubbed Skuld? Would that mean I'm saved?"

I threw up my arms in frustration. "I have no idea because I never tried it. But I do know rubbing Skuld can't hurt." Turning to him, I asked, "Are you in?"

Gunnar locked eyes with mine and nodded. Together, we reached out and rubbed the runestone at the same time.

13

LINN

Camilla texted me to say Wes had booked a standing tennis game every Tuesday afternoon from four to six. Could we schedule a weekly one-hour massage around the same time?

Although I'd said more massages were possible, I'd been preparing excuses about why I wouldn't be able to follow through with them. Extra duties at Holmgren's. Increased demand for my services at the Nornö Hotel. Going to Camilla's every week was riddled with snags, potential threats smoldering in every crevice of that perfect house. Had Wes deliberately made himself unavailable so Camilla could have her massage? Or—might he still believe I wasn't the woman from Grand Hotel?

There were just too many variables, and the back of my neck felt hot, flushed with worry. Continuing this arrangement was stupid; I should have nipped it in the bud. But Camilla was counting on me now. It would be strange— and unprofessional—not to uphold the agreement. The weekly fee of nine hundred and fifty kronor for an hour-long session would supplement my summer income. Some customers thought my rate was too high, but Camilla didn't bat an eyelid, clearly used to Manhattan prices. I would be in and out, strictly adhering to the time slot when Wes was away. He would never see me. The mental contortions were exhausting, so I finally sent Camilla a thumbs-up emoji, adding the recurring appointment to my schedule.

Post-massage on the assigned Tuesday, I sat on Camilla's terrace for a second time, enjoying a fresh glass of rosé and the late-afternoon sunshine. Even though I'd lived on Nornö since birth, Camilla's vantage point gave me new and improved sights of the island, as though my perception had been rebooted. I'd always taken the hardy fields of purple heather carpeting the unforgiving soil for granted, but Camilla had transferred flowering stems from her garden to bud vases. She scattered them on the tables, and I felt pedestrian for never having thought to do the same. Flora and fauna seemed to prefer Camilla's corner of the island, too—birds perched in secret enclaves, and a flock of black guillemot had overtaken the small, rocky reef near Camilla's private beach. I felt a kinship with these stray animals; maybe that explained why I'd been reluctant to cancel the massages. Aside from the beauty and order of Karintorp, I had fallen prey to the magnetic pull and paradoxes of Camilla's life, nurturing a female bond I'd never had on Nornö. I wasn't ready to walk away from this blossoming friendship.

When Camilla invited me to stay for cocktails again, I understood that this hunger for companionship might be mutual.

"Do you always fix such amazing happy hour appetizers?" I asked, grabbing one of the tomato, mozzarella, and basil sticks she had artfully arranged on a white serving dish.

Camilla smiled. "I try to. It's nice to head into the evening with a little ritual. And I enjoy fixing platters and boards—real food is the issue!"

"Well, you're a pro," I said, admiring the variety of tastes, colors, and textures. "Do you and Wes usually do cocktail hour together?" I knew that by mentioning his name, I was entering dangerous territory, but my curiosity about the terms of their marriage increased with every visit.

"Sometimes, if he's not on a business call. It's hard with the six-hour time difference. When it's five o'clock for us, the New York office hasn't even had lunch yet!" She took a swig of wine. "Gunnar's usually my date. He gets a kick out of being able to have a beer legally here."

"Was that your argument to convince him to come?" I said, vividly remembering my excitement once I could stop sneaking around and drink legally. But that right came with responsibility, and I'd been too young and arrogant to understand the concept of limits. I needed to look no further than my wild, alcohol-fueled night with Wes to see that I still lacked sound judgment.

Camilla chuckled. "One of them."

"How's Gunnar coping with Nornö?" I asked. Zoë hadn't spoken of him again since that beach outing. I was about to mention it in passing but stopped myself. What if that information got back to Zoë? She'd kill me for talking about her business; the last thing I wanted was to incur her wrath.

"Eh—I think he's still finding his footing. Hangs out with Douglas and some other kids from the neighboring islands." She paused. "Even if he thinks it's boring, I don't care. He needed to get out of that whole New York scene. The change of pace will be good for him."

"You sound very in tune with his needs," I observed.

"Wes works a lot, so I try to be. Are you and Zoë close?"

I mulled over her question with some nervous laughter. "Oh, you know—mothers and daughters. I think we've gotten better over time."

"Like fathers and sons! I think it's easier when you're the opposite-sex parent. It makes you less judgmental. You can't make comparisons to yourself."

But I could never compare myself to Zoë. My leverage in our mother-daughter relationship was lightweight—mostly advice on beauty and socializing. But in the spheres that mattered, the assets that groomed someone for a respectable life—duty, common sense, smarts—Zoë had bested me a long time ago. Any points I scored as a mother were a stroke of luck. Miraculously, the apple had fallen very, very far from the tree. But Camilla didn't need to know this. "Gunnar and Wes have issues?" I asked.

"Wes has such high expectations. He always wants Gunnar to be the best. That puts a lot of pressure on him."

"Like to take over the family business?"

"The business, sports, school . . . To equal—or surpass—Wes's accomplishments. That's why it's better for Gunnar to be here this summer. He can recharge before college. I feel sorry for the kids today. So much stress!"

"I would have never managed that stress in my day, but Zoë's pretty grounded. I think it comes from growing up here, away from all the noise," I said, thinking my laissez-faire approach might have had certain benefits. Right or wrong, my imperfections were laid bare, but Wes hid under the hypocrisy of excellence, demanding standards of his son that he eschewed for himself. Poor Gunnar was chasing the approval of a fraud.

"You're so lucky. She's lovely," Camilla said. "I wish I had a girl too. One of each would have been perfect, but it was hard for me to conceive with my endo."

"I saw that after doing some research on endometriosis," I confessed, embarrassed I had delved into Camilla's medical condition.

"Poor you," Camilla said, but she didn't seem to mind the intrusion. "Wish I knew less about it."

"Then you must've heard some doctors think massaging the regions near the ovaries and uterus can reduce the pain. Have you tried it?"

Camilla nodded. "I've tried massages, yoga, acupuncture, heat therapy, giving up red meat, going gluten-free and caffeine-free. I drew the line at going alcohol-free, though!"

I gave a forced smile. Glib jokes about giving up alcohol always hit a nerve. Did a problem drinker ever joke about it? Maybe if you were several years sober, but what if you were still hanging by a thread? Someone with my checkered history shouldn't be swilling a glass of rosé at five o'clock on a Tuesday afternoon, but abstaining would have pried open a Pandora's box of faults and mistakes I had no desire to revisit. Easing into the evening, surrounded by the ebbing streams of heat and sunlight, was too glorious to resist. I had coaxed myself into thinking I deserved it after a long day.

"I'm not trained to work on those parts of the body. Otherwise, I would have tried that with you."

"I appreciate the thought, but your massages help with my back pain, and I've been stretching. Before I knew what was wrong with me, I couldn't even get out of bed some days. The cramping and the bleeding—Wes thought I had cancer! At least I can manage my endo now."

"How'd you figure out you had endo?"

"We'd been trying to conceive, but nothing was happening. It wasn't until we went to a fertility specialist that my endo was finally diagnosed. I was worried I might be infertile, but I had surgery to remove scar tissue and got pregnant with Gunnar after one round of IVF."

"Wow. How wonderful that it worked out!"

Camilla swirled the rosé in her goblet, pensive. "I wish more kids had been in the cards, but I feel blessed we have

Gunnar. How about you? What was it like for you with Zoë?"

I broke into another performative smile to disguise my—what? Shame? Inferiority complex? "Your average single-mom story. Zoë's dad wasn't in the picture." I had discovered that statement always made people understanding at best, uncomfortable at worst. Predictably, Camilla's brows and lips crinkled in that universal expression of sympathy.

"I have so much admiration for women doing it on their own," she said.

Camilla must be thinking of celebrity single moms, those with the money, nannies, Academy Awards, and the self-assurance to do whatever they wanted. Sandra Bullock. Charlize Theron. Halle Berry. Even Kylie Jenner. Adoption. Surrogacy. Dumping the baby daddy. These women had ushered single-motherhood-by-choice into a trend, a statement of female liberation. But society excluded the less-glamorous, morally suspect solo moms. Women like me—who were themselves sometimes kids—were thrust into motherhood before we had a chance to become adults. Our situation was considered pathetic, not praiseworthy.

"Well, I just hope I didn't screw up too badly," I said.

Camilla chuckled. "Don't we all."

At that moment, my phone alarm went off. I had set it for a quarter to six to ensure I left Camilla's house before Wes returned. "My goodness! I better get going. I have another massage appointment to get to," I lied.

Camilla's shoulders drooped almost imperceptibly, but I caught it. "I understand," she said. "See you next week?"

"Yes, see you next week, and thank you for the aperitif!" I trilled.

I got on the Crescent and drove home at medium speed, digesting why my emotions had fluctuated so much. Oddly,

Wes wasn't a factor—it was Camilla. She had been so curious, disarming me with her candor and questions. Yet this was how friendships developed. In a normal conversation, people shared experiences, exchanged confidences, and showed empathy. Aside from Alicia, I never let anyone in—male or female.

Things usually started cordially, but once my caginess and superficial responses wore out, these would-be friends expected someone honest and accessible. If they only knew how those shallow interactions depleted me. I lacked the bandwidth to engage fully, so that outward persona eventually morphed into the totality of my being, the only one I could conjure up. Inevitably, would-be friends turned away, wondering who I was without that plastered smile or a drink in my hand.

If I had to sequence my emotional genome, I could pinpoint exactly when my openness, trust, and self-confidence began to deteriorate. Some would say it was time to get over it and move on, but my accidental pregnancy had affected every one of my relationships. Nearly two decades had passed, but the aftershocks remained.

Interlude

Linn

June 30, 2000

J.G. still lingered in my mind after Hultsfred. Two weeks later, on June 30, a stampede during the Pearl Jam concert at the Roskilde Festival in neighboring Denmark killed nine people. Nine music-loving young men were crushed to death in the mosh pit. Alicia and I were grief-stricken by the news, knowing we could have easily been among the crowd of fifty thousand people crammed together in a field at eleven o'clock that night, waiting to hear one of the world's hottest bands. The news was sketchy in the immediate aftermath; the victims' names weren't publicized, but nothing indicated Americans were among the dead. That calmed me, but I wished I had a full name or telephone number to reach J.G. or a contact person in Hultsfred who might have more information about his whereabouts. Although the Danish authorities began an investigation immediately, the festival continued the next evening with Youssou N'Dour taking the somber stage, consoled by candles and flowers in a nearby memorial. Oasis and the Pet Shop Boys called off their appearances out of respect for the dead, and a devastated Pearl Jam canceled the rest of their tour.

Roskilde hit too close to home and weighed heavily on my mind. The impermanence of life had touched members of my generation—one of the victims was a twenty-year-old Swede—and I had nightmares about being trapped in large crowds. I wanted to erase those gruesome images, to blank out the injustice that had struck an unsuspecting soul, snuffing out his life. I accompanied Alicia to Sainte-Maxime and tried to live in the present. Alicia's parents' villa had been in the family since the '70s, and it was a throwback, decorated with palm-patterned wallpaper and salmon-pink furniture. But the campy decor set the right tone for luxuriating in the decadent Mediterranean milieu. The jet-set playground of Saint-Tropez was only a fifteen-minute water-taxi ride away, and we whizzed across the azure bay with the Green Boats shuttle as often as Alicia's parents allowed.

Alicia's dad had warned us about gangsters and predators, and we promised to keep our guards up, categorically avoiding any men who looked to be over twenty-five. But we still attracted attention, walking along the quay or people-watching at the legendary Café Sénéquier. We befriended a group of permatanned playboys from Paris who took us dancing at Les Caves du Roy inside the Byblos Hotel. By some process of natural selection, Alicia and I had paired off with two of them. My suitor was a hairy political science major, and after some serious dirty dancing, he put his hand under my dress. His palm was rough and sticky, like the scales of a frisky fish. I shoved him away, and he toppled over a circular drinks table, knocking down bottles and glasses. Soggy with sweat and alcohol, he began cursing in French. Frightened, I ran out of the nightclub in tears.

Alicia found me outside and asked what had happened, but I could barely choke out an explanation. I should have been in seventh heaven; the glitzy scene and male attention satisfied my hunger for adventure and validation. Yes, the Frenchman's moves were vulgar and degrading, but I'd been subject to advances like that before—had even encouraged and responded to them. But his glazed, beady eyes as he'd sidled up to me—his presumption that I would sleep with him—had provoked a self-disgust I had never experienced before. Though I may have romanticized my one-night stand with J.G., the memory still maintained a sweetness, whereas the incident at the nightclub made me feel dirty. But I didn't want to ruin Alicia's vacation or seem ungrateful, so I returned to the villa, snapped out of my funk, and partied on.

I'd returned to Nornö feeling more like my old self—brownish from too much sunbathing and sluggish from too many late nights. My parents had no sympathy and said I had to work overtime to finance my Southeast Asian road trip with Alicia. After hours, I kept company with the island's summer help, a boisterous clique always itching for beers, cigarettes, and impromptu dance parties on the dock. A fling with Max, a competitive sailor from Gotland, had been a welcome diversion and restored my sexual confidence, but I didn't miss him when he left for a race in Spain.

Nornö was mournfully quiet when September arrived, giving me the impression my graduation, Hultsfred, Sainte-Maxime, and all the other highlights characterizing that summer had occurred ages ago. For the first time in three years, I had nothing to do, and I missed the structure and community of boarding school. My former classmates were either in Stockholm or scattered around the globe at various universities and cultural excursions. Alicia was interning at a law firm until our December departure date. I spent a few weekends with her in the city, but early autumn was also a busy time in Nornö. Unlike the summer, there was no expectation of warm temperatures and no sullen expressions when light showers ruined picnics, so the clear, brisk days lured tourists only to see the Norns. On a good afternoon, shafts of brilliant sunlight collided with the Nornir runestones, illuminating them like saintly sculptures, and visitors lined up reverently for photographs. The trees had already shed most of their leaves, and the meadow reminded me of a tart layered in pumpkin, cinnamon, and butterscotch foliage—a riot of color before Nornö's misty, ashen hue took hold.

The transition to October signaled time was marching forward, each day bringing me closer to our Southeast Asia journey. That trip would be my launching pad from Nornö and Holmgren's to something hitherto undefined, but it would be new and different—that was all that mattered. I spent most of my spare time surfing the internet, creating a travel itinerary with more enthusiasm and focus than I had ever given my studies. I was pleased with how the program was taking shape:

Thailand: Bangkok (cheap, safe, and friendly), Phuket (with a special stop in Koh Phi Phi Leh Island, where *The Beach* was filmed), and Chiang Mai (markets, massage, and mediation).

Laos: Luang Prabang (for the temples and French-style cafés) and Nong Khiaw (hiking and dramatic limestone cliffs).

Vietnam: Hanoi (motorbikes, food, cheapest beer in Southeast Asia), Ha Long Bay (floating villages), and Ho Chi Minh (War Remnants Museum and Cu Chi Tunnels).

Cambodia: Phnom Penh (the tragic Killing Fields), Kep (fishing village and beach resort), and Siem Reap (Temples of Angkor).

The tour would come full circle in Bangkok for shopping and more massages.

I was in the middle of investigating youth hostels when I

began to feel unwell. Dizziness washed over me, and the computer monitor divided into shape-shifting halves. I rested my head on the table, attributing the condition to sitting and staring at the screen for too long. I avoided the computer the next day and decided to walk around the island to get my blood flowing. Halloween was just around the corner, and someone had decorated the naked tree branches near the runestones with hanging ghost decorations and fake cobwebs. Watching the figures sway back and forth made me nauseous. Why were they moving so much? I was on land but felt seasick. Despite leaning against a tree to regain my balance, the wooziness didn't disappear, so I walked back home with uneven steps.

"Mamma, I don't think you cooked the chicken long enough last night," I said to Agnes back at the house. She had cooked a stew for dinner, and I remembered seeing blood on one of the chicken thighs.

"It was in the oven for almost two hours, so it was more than cooked enough," Agnes replied.

"But parts were pink and bloody, and I feel nauseous now."

"That's because the chicken was young, and their bones were thin. The marrow leaked into the meat."

"But—"

Agnes laughed. "Trust me, I work with food for a living."

"Then why do I feel so queasy?"

"Maybe you're coming down with a stomach bug."

"It's only October. Isn't that a little too early in the season?" I asked.

My mother advanced toward me, and I thought she would check my forehead temperature. Instead, she stopped about an arm's length away and moved her head in painstakingly slow motion, inching her gaze from my feet to my midsection to my face.

"Linn, do you think," Agnes began, her voice low but emphatic, "you could be pregnant?"

I covered my mouth and snickered. "Nice try, Mamma. I'm on the pill, so I doubt it."

"When's the last time you had your period?"

I shrugged. "I don't know. It's been irregular for the past three years, ever since I went on the pill."

"But you've seen blood on your underwear?"

I nodded but was flabbergasted at having this conversation with my mother. We never discussed these things. She had explained sex and reproduction to me with the help of an illustrated book. I thought back to my menstrual cycle and the bleeding. These past few months, it had been fainter, but I had definitely seen red splotches.

Without warning, Agnes stuck out her arm and squeezed my right breast.

"*Vad fan!*" I shrieked. "What are you doing?"

"Did it feel tender when I did that?"

"It hurt when you did that!"

"Do your breasts feel swollen? Larger?"

"Mamma, you're scaring me!" I cried.

She took a deep breath and stroked the ends of my hair. "I'm sorry, *lilla gumman,* I didn't mean to hurt you. But to be sure, I'd like you to take a pregnancy test."

"Why? I told you; I can't be pregnant!"

"Wouldn't you feel better if you knew for sure?"

Confusion and clarity wrestled in my mind over what I had done the last few months. I backtracked, and my actions were irrefutable: two guys. I had slept with two guys the whole summer: J.G. and Max, using condoms on both occasions, except—except that second time with J.G., but I was on the pill, and more importantly, I didn't look pregnant! But a pregnancy test would end my mother's outrageous theory. Nodding meekly, I went to my room and tried to sleep off the chaos rocking my system.

Obtaining a pregnancy test wasn't so easy. No white strips or dipsticks were tucked away in Agnes's bathroom cabinet. Holmgren's carried medication for headaches, lice, and bug bites, but a pregnancy test kit had to be specially ordered and would take a day or two to reach the store. I slammed my mother over the stupidity of not stocking such an essential item, and for once, Agnes, who never liked to be criticized over the store's assortment, agreed with me. A doctor made weekly visits to Nornö, but his assigned day had already passed, and he wouldn't be back until the following week. However, my mother didn't want to wait. We took the ferry to Stavsnäs and visited a prenatal clinic near Nacka.

Gunilla, a midwife with silvery hair and red glasses, greeted us, and Agnes explained that I wanted to take a pregnancy test. After filling out the health declaration form, I wondered if Gunilla might widen her eyes in surprise at my date of birth and judge a nineteen-year-old girl in this precarious position. But Gunilla put my form in a file, displaying no emotion, and gave me a plastic cup to pee in. I disappeared into the bathroom and sat on the toilet, my heartbeat galloping. Nothing came.

Finally, I turned on the faucet and closed my eyes, filling the cup three-quarters of the way. Gunilla took the sample, and I rejoined my mother in the reception area. Neither of us knew what to do as we waited for the results. Every magazine focused on pregnant women, children, and families. We left them untouched by some tacit agreement and stared ahead without uttering a sound.

Gunilla came out with another poker face and asked me to follow her into the exam room. Agnes got up at the same time, but Gunilla told her she could only enter with my consent, since I was over eighteen.

"I want my mother with me!" I snapped. Gunilla was heartlessly drawing out the suspense at the most serious moment of my life. I needed my mother's support in that room to offset Gunilla's maddening inscrutability. Whatever friction Agnes and I may have had in the past, we had come this far together. From here on out, I sensed there would be a "before" and an "after" in our relationship.

We proceeded to the second door on the left. I grabbed the seat next to Gunilla's desk combo, and Agnes sat on the small sofa in the corner.

"Linn," Gunilla said, "the test result came back positive. You're pregnant."

Agnes gasped, but I eyeballed Gunilla, mouth agape, as if I'd heard but didn't hear. I zeroed in on the midwife's red glasses, an accessory that had seemed so cute a half hour ago but was now clownish and completely inappropriate for the magnitude of her claim.

"There must be some mistake," I whispered.

Gunilla shook her head. "The test is 99 percent accurate."

"But I'm on the pill and don't feel—or look—pregnant," I argued. Those words had become my mantra. By repeating them enough times, someone would finally believe me.

"When was the last time you had your period?" Gunilla asked.

"Last month." I paused. "I think."

"You're not sure?"

"I think I saw some blood on my panty liner, but it didn't last long. It's been irregular ever since I went on the pill."

"When was the last time you had sex?"

"Mid-June and then again in August," I replied, unaffected by my mother's presence in the room. The facts needed to get out. No more teenage lies, embarrassment, or cover-ups.

"So, you could have either conceived in mid-June or mid-August?" Gunilla pressed.

"This doesn't make sense. I'm on the pill!"

"Please listen to my daughter," Agnes said. "Can she take the test again?"

My mother was at her best in difficult situations, a never-cowering pillar of strength. I wanted to hug her for backing me up.

Gunilla steepled her fingers and said, "Since you're not sure about *when*, I'll perform an external ultrasound on your abdomen to confirm—"

"Or not confirm," I cut in.

"—the pregnancy."

"Then let's do it," I said.

Gunilla motioned to the exam table at the other side of the room. I took off my shoes and shuffled to it, reclining and baring my abdomen as she instructed. Agnes stood on the other side of the ultrasound machine and took my right hand, gently squeezing it.

Gunilla sat behind the ultrasound machine and held up a cord with a tip that resembled a doorknob. "I'm going to apply warm gel to your stomach and then move this probe around. It generates sound waves and will show images on the screen if there's a fetus in your uterus."

Shutting my eyes, I pressed my lips together, breathing through my nose and laying perfectly still, but tremors of fear shot through every molecule in my body. Gunilla coated my stomach and moved the probe back and forth. I registered how evenly it slid across. No bumps. No bulges. I heard staticky, gurgling sounds akin to tropical waves and then the movement of beats coming at regular intervals, like a pulsating wristwatch. I opened my eyes and stared at the ceiling.

"There's a fetus in there," Gunilla said, angling the monitor so I could see the image. "That's the head and arms. You can even see the little hands—"

The words landed like a thunderclap, but I refused to look. Blinking rapidly, my tears pooled and edged sideways.

"If you can make out those features, how old is the fetus?" Agnes asked. My mother's voice remained unshaken, her grip on my hand unwavering.

"Based on the measurements of the head, abdomen, and femur, I would say around eighteen weeks," Gunilla said.

A choking sound sputtered from my throat, and I finally turned to my mother, wailing. Agnes held my convulsing body against her own, alternately whispering, "Shhh" and brushing a hand through my hair. Eighteen weeks. Four and a half months. June. Hultsfred. I'd been reveling in the music and chill atmosphere, sleeping with a guy I'd just met. I'd been so sure of our precautions, but the situation had spun out of control like everything else I touched. What had seemed so cool and daring was, in fact, a grave error. The pregnancy verdict merely confirmed a hidden truth: I was a failure.

I'd always suspected this—I had spent my whole life running away from the label, but I felt a twisted sense of liberation, fully owning up to it. My parents had tried; the elite education and social connections were supposed to tame my darker impulses, but I knew that at my core, I was wild, tempted by the fire others avoided. A ticking time bomb waiting to explode. Pregnant at nineteen—was it such a surprise? Was that why my mother seemed so composed? Had she always been waiting for me to fuck up?

Gunilla finally softened and touched my back, offering me a box of tissues. I pulled out two and flattened them over my eyes, pressing deep into the sockets until starbursts flickered in the darkness.

Untangling myself from my mother, I folded the tissues together and blew my nose. Tears would not help. I had to start taking responsibility for my actions.

Shifting my body, I asked Gunilla, "When can I get an abortion?"

The midwife glanced at the ultrasound monitor. "You have the right to an abortion for any reason up to eighteen weeks of pregnancy." She paused. "But you're right at the cutoff point. Between the eighteenth and twenty-second weeks of pregnancy, permission for an abortion must be granted by *Socialstyrelsen.* Only the National Board of Health and Welfare can decide if there's a good reason for it—for example, if the health of the baby is at risk."

"The health of the baby is probably at risk!" I shrieked. "I had no idea I was pregnant. I was drinking and smoking, not taking good care of myself—"

"According to the scan and measurements, the baby's development is on track. There don't seem to be any detrimental effects unless—" Gunilla hesitated, adjusting her red glasses. "Unless *you* think there might be an ongoing substance abuse problem?"

"My daughter's habits are like most young people her age!" Agnes snapped. "Nothing unusual."

Gunilla stared at me. "Would you agree?"

I dipped my head and then looked up again, unsure if my arguments were helping or hurting my case. "What about mental issues? I cannot have a baby!" I screeched. "I'm only nineteen! I barely knew the father. He doesn't even live in Sweden."

"Mental health can be a legitimate claim, but it must be investigated. Would you like me to put you in touch with *Socialstyrelsen?*" Gunilla asked.

"I can't do this. I just can't," I sobbed, looking at my mother. I wanted her to speak for me. I wanted her to make it all go away.

"Would it be possible for us to see a doctor?" Agnes asked, businesslike again.

"Yes, that can be arranged." Gunilla went back to her desk and consulted a calendar on the computer. "Dr. Lindqvist can see you tomorrow at 10:00 a.m. Does that work?"

"We can make it," Agnes responded.

"But just so you know, after twenty-two weeks, abortions aren't allowed under any circumstances," Gunilla said. "By then, the fetus can survive outside the womb."

I left the clinic in a daze, drained of tears, and disembodied from the baby inside me. How could I be carrying another human being—a vital force growing and thriving without my knowledge—yet feel nothing, neither physically nor emotionally? My only thought was cruel and selfish: the baby's life was my death sentence.

Agnes said very little during the taxi ride back to Stavsnäs. She didn't ask about the who, where, or how. She told me to close my eyes, opening her arms so I could slump against her chest. But an hour later, as the ferryboat docked at the pier in Nornö, I posed the question that had tormented me since Gunilla's announcement: "What will we tell Pappa?"

Agnes smiled vacantly. "Let's wait until we've seen the doctor."

Dr. Shirin Lindqvist was in her thirties and very pretty,

with jet-black hair and perfectly curved eyebrows. She had been briefed on my situation and seemed human, not robotic like Gunilla, and offered us refreshments and cookies as soon as we sat in her office. Eighteen weeks pregnant and no visible symptoms. How was that possible?

Dr. Lindqvist offered a medical explanation: the fetus had produced a small amount of hCG, a hormone generated by the cells surrounding the growing embryo that built the placenta. The presence of hCG made home pregnancy tests turn positive, but it was also how the fetus communicated its needs. When the fetus didn't emit much of it, as in my case, there were few obvious signs of pregnancy in the initial stages—especially if the mother had little reason to expect them. No morning sickness. No cravings. Negligible weight gain. In the tug-of-war between the mother and the fetus, I was in the lead.

"But I was on the pill," I reminded Dr. Lindqvist.

"The pill isn't always foolproof. If you forget to take it or—" The doctor held up an index finger and skimmed my medical chart. "Mm . . . I see you were on antibiotics at the beginning of June." She looked back at me. "It hasn't been proven that accidental pregnancies can occur from taking birth control pills and antibiotics at the same time, but drug manufacturers have cautioned that certain antibiotics could decrease the effectiveness of birth control. They advise using an additional layer of birth control, just in case. Like a condom."

I had used double protection the first time with J.G. but thought we were safe that second time. I had had no reason to believe my birth control pills wouldn't work, and I was paying the ultimate price for my ignorance.

"Are you—are you saying the antibiotics made me get pregnant?" I asked.

"I don't know, Linn. It's a long shot, but it's the only theory that might explain why this happened."

"That must be a legitimate reason for a late-term abortion!" I persisted.

"Permission for an abortion after eighteen weeks demands special circumstances. For example, if the fetus isn't developing normally or the mother's life is at risk," Dr. Lindqvist said. "But if you're sure that's what you want, I can put in the request with *Socialstyrelsen,* and then you can make your case."

"Yes, that's what I want," I said. "Mamma, what do you think?"

Agnes crossed both arms over her rib cage. "I think we should discuss this further when we get home."

"What?!" I exclaimed, flinching at the steeliness of her voice. My mother had been a straight-backed, tight-lipped phantom, saying nothing except a polite greeting and accepting Dr. Lindqvist's coffee. But her silence was deceptive; she was now undermining me in front of the doctor.

Dr. Lindqvist seemed to pick up on the mounting tension between us and agreed that such a delicate issue had to be deliberated carefully, but time was "of the essence."

I didn't know what to make of my mother's unreasonable attitude. It was my life—my future—on the line, not hers. An invisible fissure had fractured our fledgling alliance, and we kept to our respective sides in the back seat of the taxi. The car dropped us off at Stavsnäs, but instead of turning onto the pier with the public ferry, she continued straight ahead toward the jetty reserved for private boats.

To my horror, I saw my father waiting for us in his Bertram. By the somber expression on his face, I could tell he knew. It was an ambush. My mother had planned everything in advance.

Stopping in my tracks, I confronted her. "You told him? You told him without my permission?" I shouted. "How could you? *How could you?*"

"Because I can't handle this by myself!" she barked. "Now shut up and get on the boat!"

Several passengers on the pier glared in our direction. I backed off, never having seen my mother so angry. The world as I knew it was collapsing, and it was all my fault. How could I have been so stupid? I ignored my parents on the boat, weeping silently and staring out the window as the Bertram bumped against choppy waters, wishing I could turn back time.

In Nornö, Agnes and Thomas ordered me to the kitchen table for a "no-holds-barred conversation."

"Tell us everything," my father said.

I had feared his reaction most. While Agnes seemed to guess everything about me before I could unscramble it myself, I wasn't as transparent to my father. He still had an image of me as his little girl, forgiving my blunders as natural acts of youthful mischief. But this—this would destroy every shred of my girlish innocence.

My father and I had always understood we could never compete with Holmgren's for Agnes's undivided attention. The store was her other child, her secret lover, her relentless taskmaster. She had a powerful sense of duty and shouldered responsibilities beyond our family, so we had to share her with the rest of Nornö. To make up for it, my father taught me everything he knew, from how to navigate a boat and ski cross-country to the differences between a Hans Wegner and an Alvar Aalto chair. He was my staunchest defender, always vouching for my essential goodness. He was also my conscience.

"Pappa, I'm sorry. So, so sorry," I stuttered, fiddling with my fingers.

"We're not angry," he said, encasing my hand with his. "We love you and want to help."

I held nothing back as Agnes filled and refilled our teacups from her hand-me-down blue-and-white Spode service. I explained meeting J.G. at Hultsfred, describing his kindness and decency. No, I didn't have details about who or where he was. But that didn't matter. I would deal with this problem on my own.

"But you're not alone," my mother said. "You have us."

"Both of us," my father added.

My eyes darted from one to the other. "You'll support my case with *Socialstyrelsen?*" I asked. Confiding in them had blunted my despair, like putting a Band-Aid on a bleeding wound, but the searing pain endured. Permanent treatment for what ailed me rested with a government agency.

"Linn, there's no easy way to tell you this"—Agnes inhaled and exhaled quickly—"but the likelihood of *Socialstyrelsen* allowing you to go through with a late-term abortion is very slim."

"How can you say that to me? Dr. Lindqvist was ready to submit my request."

"Because she has to, if that's what you want. But she doesn't make the final decision," Agnes said.

"I'm only nineteen, for God's sake!" I cried. "I'm only nineteen!"

"And let's say by some remote possibility the Board did agree—the fetus would be around twenty weeks old," my mother continued. "That's half-term, not some abstract concept anymore. You'd know if it's a boy or a girl by then! I'm afraid getting rid of it would be more traumatic than you think."

"What's done is done," my father said. "We have to talk about a way forward."

"What are you saying? That I should give it up for adoption?" As soon as I said it, the idea began to make sense. I could hide out in Nornö, give birth, present the baby to a loving, childless family, and then get on with the rest of my life.

A suspicious sideways glance passed between my parents. Agnes left her chair and crouched, facing me.

"*Älskling,* your father and I will help you raise the baby," she said.

"We'll welcome this baby and love it with all our hearts, the same way we love you," he added.

What were they suggesting? Bringing a baby into our unstable family dynamic? I was living proof things had gone awry. "And look how good that turned out!"

But they had already decided. My parents wanted to keep the baby. For a moment, I considered running away and giving it up for adoption, but how would I manage the next five months on my own? Where would I go?

Screaming, I banged the heel of my hand against my head. I bawled to the point of hyperventilation. My parents held me tight, whispering how much they loved me and that everything would be all right. The one thing I didn't do during my bout of self-hatred was aim those attacks at my stomach. Some emerging instinct held me back.

Those first few weeks afterward, when my belly finally ballooned, I became a recluse. I broke the news to Alicia over the phone, apologizing for having to bail on our trip to Asia. My best friend was distraught; she had introduced me to J.G.

and assumed responsibility for the turn of events.

"You didn't make me sleep with him," I told her.

"But I egged you on and let it happen," Alicia countered. Ignoring my protests, she came to Nornö, and we spent days locked up in my room, watching movies on the DVD player—*Notting Hill* was a favorite on repeat—and I sometimes forgot I was pregnant.

But I was reminded whenever I made the requisite visits to the midwife at the prenatal clinic, always accompanied by my mother and sometimes Alicia. Despite my psychological turmoil, the baby was developing normally. My parents took me to Babyland to shop for a crib, stroller, and other essential items. Agnes chose the tiny clothes and blankets; Thomas splurged on an all-terrain three-wheeler for walks around the island.

Being in Nornö shielded me from running into old friends, but word got around anyway. *How was it possible for Linn not to know she was pregnant? She must have been in denial or just plain crazy.* Some people called me a slut, and that hurt most of all. My neighbors in Nornö either avoided eye contact or were overly concerned and interested. I didn't trust any of them, convinced they were reveling in my misfortune.

While self-isolating, I had plenty of time to brood over the mystery of my pregnancy and reevaluated everything through that prism. I singled out clues, warning signs about my condition. My hypersensitivity after the Roskilde tragedy? Hormonal mood swings. Those hamburgers I had so greedily devoured all summer? Cravings. My jeans had felt tighter, but I'd blamed it on the burgers and my daily dose of ice cream. The blood from my "period"? Spotting from the embryo implanting to the uterus. I'd been foolish to place such blind trust in the pill and not reading up on—or asking the right questions—about the antibiotics. I'd been inexcusably lazy, seeing what I wanted to see, unwilling to examine the omens that meant nothing separately but together formed a coherent picture.

My due date was March 7, and Agnes started sleeping in my room as soon as the month began. When the early labor contractions came in the middle of the night, she tried to keep me comfortable and relaxed. We performed breathing exercises, and she ran a warm bath for me. My father put the private taxi boat company on standby, and once my water broke, we boarded it for the mainland. After almost three hours of labor at Södersjukhuset, I gave birth to a healthy baby girl on March 9, 2001.

She was paler than I had expected, with itty-bitty lips as thin as toothpicks, a smushed button nose, and spindly fingers and toes. But there was a serene aura about her, too, almost like a halo above her silky hair. The baby was innocent and trusting, latching onto me, unconscious of how defiant I had been about her existence—or that she would never know her father. I remembered a magazine article that described pregnancy as physical but motherhood as psychological, a state of mind. I did not become a mother overnight. The being I held in my arms felt like a little sister I'd delivered to my parents.

The most lighthearted part of my pregnancy had been pouring over lists of names with Alicia. It was the only area where I still had some agency, and I wanted something interesting and rare, hoping to give the baby an instant cool factor. In a subconscious nod to Hultsfred, I preferred rocker-inspired names. For a boy, I was a huge fan of Lenny Kravitz's music and style, but "Lenny Holmgren" sounded like a grouchy old uncle (and too much like my own moniker), so I leafed through my father's album collection. Bob Dylan, David Bowie, Pink Floyd—any of those last names would make hip first names in Sweden. But Lenny Kravitz was still in the running if I had a girl. He and actress Lisa Bonet had a daughter they'd named Zoë. I also learned "Zoë" meant "life" in Greek, enhancing its good karma.

As I stared at the baby—mine and J.G.'s creation—swathed like a burrito in the yellow hospital blanket, onesie, and beanie, I hoped the strange circumstances of her birth wouldn't haunt her future. My lips touched her squishy cheek, and I murmured, "Zoë Holmgren."

Inhaling her milky-sweet, powdery newborn smell, I had a feeling J.G. would approve.

14

ZOË

I awoke to another email from my father. Groggy, I rubbed the sleep out of my eyes and sat up to read it on my phone.

July 11, 2019

Dear Zoë,

I'm so happy you want to move forward! The photographs I sent you brought back many memories, and in my eagerness to connect, I realized there were so many things I left out, so many facts about myself I'd like to share. I guess a good place to start would be my life after Hultsfred. After spending three exciting months touring the European music festival circuit, I reported to Army basic training at Fort Jackson in Columbia, South Carolina, in September 2000. You can imagine how shocking it was to my system! I was a skinny, music-obsessed guy who had lived with my parents, eaten my mother's cooking, and had kind of been floating around with part-time jobs and studying at a community college. Boot camp lasted ten weeks, and it was a grueling physical and psychological experience. I hung in there by some force of will and can honestly say I became tougher, stronger, and more focused afterward. It amazes me how the military can create a sense of community and common purpose in such a short time. My reasons for enlisting had been mainly selfish, so I could earn money to continue my college education, but I became a believer by the time I left.

I then went on to Advanced Individual Training, where soldiers receive specific training in their chosen occupational specialty. Since I wanted to become a doctor, I chose the Medical Department Center and School in San Antonio, Texas. I was scheduled to stay there for one year, but everything changed on September 11, 2001. I'm sure you've studied the terrorist attacks at school and seen the pictures and videos, but nothing can describe the fear and sadness that those of us on American soil felt that day. Grief turned into action when my unit was deployed to Afghanistan toward the end of October. I won't elaborate on the death and destruction, but I will say that I was lucky—many times over.

Deployments became a part of my reality. After Afghanistan, I went back stateside before spending another fifteen months in Iraq. I transitioned to civilian life, completed my undergraduate degree, and returned to Afghanistan for another eleven months. By my third deployment, I had trained to become a combat medic, treating injuries and comforting the wounded. As gory as that sounds, it gave me excellent training for medical school. I eventually began at the University of South Carolina thanks to the Post-9/11 GI Bill when my tour of duty was over and got what I had aimed for: an Army-financed education. It came at a very high price, but it was the choice I made. I'd be lying if I said I didn't have some regrets—the largest one is not knowing of your existence—but I think I came out on the other side with a decent head on my shoulders.

In terms of my personal life, I never married. There was someone during the yo-yo years of my deployments and civilian life, and we talked about settling down once I left the Army. But I wanted to throw all my energy into med school, and in the end, we just wanted different things.

Work has been my outlet. I volunteer as a doctor at least once a year in high-risk areas affected by conflicts, epidemics, natural disasters, and healthcare shortages. It's rewarding and my way of saying thank you for surviving those war zones.

My parents are retired—they deserve some rest after all the hard work they put into raising me and my three sisters (two of whom are older than I am, and one is younger). Nicole and Laura have their own families, so you have seven cousins who keep your grandparents busy! I always felt like fatherhood was in the cards for me, but it began to seem less likely as the years passed. To think you were out there all this time, and I had no idea! I thought I was satisfied with my way of life, but you've opened a new world of possibilities. Although we're a tight-knit family, I haven't told my parents or sisters about you yet. I wanted to check with you first and see how you feel about involving other people at this stage. Have you discussed it with Linn?

Discovering I have a long-lost daughter who's eighteen years old has been wonderful but bittersweet. I can't stop thinking about all the things I've missed. Your surprise announcement has made me do quite a bit of soul-searching. While I have the material comfort I sought, there's also an emptiness. I hope I can gain your trust and earn the privilege of being your father in every sense of the word.

I feel like I've been rambling! Dads do that, right? Talk on and on ... Now I want to know everything about you. Can we set up a time to talk on the phone or via FaceTime? I'm so curious to hear your voice. Let me know what you think.

Sincerely,
J.G.

Tossing the sheets aside, I walked to the desk and opened my laptop. Where to begin? Who was I? That was the whole point of this quest to find my father. But finding him at eighteen, rather than ten, encouraged him to treat me like an adult. He had gone out of his way not to talk down to me or make flaky parental excuses. So different from my mother, who had perfected the art of giving vague answers to pointed questions or vanishing into a bottle of wine, barring me from accessing whatever was going on in her mind. J.G. seemed more real, less threatened by his emotions or his flaws.

I wanted to follow his example but feared my total honesty would scare him away. He had already slipped into the empty spaces with only two emails, filling the jagged cracks where questions about my paternity were inseparable from why everything felt so off-kilter—that ache of otherness, the fever of being misunderstood. Everything had hinged on his existence. If I'd had a father, maybe I'd have true friends and know how to act with boys. Perhaps my mother wouldn't have a drinking problem if I'd had a father.

My heart thumped frenetically. I was on the verge of disclosing everything but didn't know how to do it without seeming pathetic. Clamping my lips together, I waited for my pulse to normalize. J.G. needed a mentally stable daughter, not one who guilt-tripped him by replaying the complicated details of the last eighteen years. What purpose would it serve now? I had found him. It was better to look ahead. Time to construct a new storyline.

There was something else, too: I didn't want J.G. to think less of my mother. He had clung to a time-stamped, unblemished image of her that I didn't want to tarnish. I preferred his recollection of that weekend, imagining a bright-eyed and beautiful Linn without a care in the world. Despite the distortions and disappointments, she was still my mother, and I had pledged loyalty to that concept, even if it was detrimental to my well-being. I pictured her sleeping downstairs, a silk mask over her eyes, blocking the stubborn sunlight and whatever truths might leak out. Yet her presence circled my room, urging me not to betray her.

Wiggling my fingers above the keyboard, I wanted to whip out something safe so J.G. wouldn't think I was a total basket case. Gradually, words took shape, and I began typing.

July 12, 2019

Dear J.G.,

Thank you for filling in the blanks ❤. My mother was always afraid something had happened to you in the Army, since she'd assumed you were on the frontlines, fighting the War on Terror. It bothered her even more since she didn't know your full name or where you were from. I'm so glad you made it through, or else I would have never found you.

My showing up like this could have been a disaster, but I'm so happy you see me as a welcome addition! My upbringing has been boring yet unusual, if that makes any sense. I grew up on a very small island in the Swedish archipelago called Nornö, where my mother and her family have deep roots. It's so small, I'm not sure you would have remembered if Linn had told you. You probably wouldn't have been able to pronounce it either. That "o" with two dots confuses Americans. Nornö is a cute place with an interesting history, but the population is less than a hundred people, and you can only get here by boat. Right now, it's warm with the most amazing light.

Mom didn't love growing up here and always wanted to leave, but she stayed after I was born. My grandparents, Agnes and Thomas, did the bulk of raising me since Linn was so young. I call them Mormor ("mother's mother") and Morfar ("mother's father"). The three of us were super close, but Morfar died several years ago, so it's just me, Linn, Mormor, and my golden retriever, Simba. Mormor's family has owned Holmgren's, the village supermarket, for generations, and we all pitch in, but Linn's real job is as a massage therapist and esthetician. I'm taking a gap year (like many Swedish kids do) to work at the store and hopefully travel. I want to go to university, but I'm not sure what I want to study. I was an excellent all-around student; my best subjects were English and the social sciences. I enjoyed biology and chemistry, too, but not enough to go into medicine. Sorry!

Nornö is remote, but it's famous for its weird rock formations, so a fascinating mixture of people come and visit, especially this time of year. It's high season, so the store—and people-watching—keep me busy. When I'm not working, I like to go for walks in the forest (so Swedish!), read, watch movies, and bake. I loved to paint and make jewelry when I was younger, but that changed when I discovered social media.

I spend a lot of time on Instagram and Snapchat, but I've made peace with it. The advantages outweigh the disadvantages for someone like me who lives on a secluded island. Otherwise, I would feel completely disconnected from what's going on in the rest of the world. I convinced Mormor to start an Instagram account for Holmgren's, and it's fun creating artsy images inside the store and around the island.

I also have another hobby I haven't shared with anyone because I'm afraid people will think it's stupid: I love watching reality TV like documentaries, competitions, lifestyle programs, and self-improvement shows. Truth is so much stranger and more thrilling than fiction! Working behind the scenes as a producer or casting director for one of these shows would be my dream job. I'd love to come to the US one day and learn more about the business. New York or California would be ideal places to break into reality television.

I haven't told Linn or Mormor I've found you. Mamma has always been uncomfortable talking about what happened at Hultsfred, and I don't know how she would react. Can we keep this between the two of us? I love getting these emails from you, since I can save them and then go back and reread them whenever I feel like it. FaceTiming can sometimes feel awkward, and the six-hour time difference is hard.

When I was in fourth grade, we did a pen pal project with kids from a school in Chicago to practice our English and asked each other a bunch of getting-to-know-you-questions. It sounds corny now, but it broke the ice and took the pressure off to write these long, stimulating letters. If it's okay with you, maybe we can do the same? I think it would be nice for us to be secret (email) pen pals, too, for now 😊.

All the best,

Zoë

Did I use too many emojis? Was my English good enough? I was running late for work and didn't have time to reread and make edits. I finally hit the Send button, more concerned about how J.G. would react to the parameters I placed on our budding relationship. I hoped my hesitance wouldn't upset him, but now that my prayers had been answered, I suddenly had doubts, afraid I was getting cold feet. My desires had always been of the standard variety—a new pair of jeans (yes), the latest iPhone (usually not)—but my father had become an obsession. Nothing less than finding out who he was and what happened to him could lessen it. I had always assumed rejection would breed anxiety, but acceptance stirred the same emotion. Merging my old, familiar world in Nornö with this new foreign entity called J.G. twisted my stomach into knots. The two were on a collision course, and I could almost see Linn's reflection in the headlights. The longer I could keep her away from whatever lay ahead, the better.

Despite my anxiety, I did my job at Holmgren's as usual, stocking goods and ringing up customers. We received a delivery of summer toys: swim tubes; floaties; plastic buckets and shovels in red, yellow, and blue; and an inflatable flamingo that would look better in an aquamarine pool than the brownish Baltic. The summer was halfway over, and I was doubtful we would be able to sell them if the temperature cooled in August.

Mormor had shown little interest in choosing the store's novelty items once I'd stopped playing with toys and switched to playing with my phone. As a result, the games and gadgets crowding the shelves seemed arbitrary; I thought the knockoff Legos and walkie-talkies that broke after a few uses were beneath us. But on rainy days, parents bought them anyway, confirming Mormor's motto that anything sold if the pickings were slim. Was this what I was scared to leave? Cheap stuff that belonged at a garage sale? I had tried dropping hints, but whenever it came to Holmgren's, Mormor was inflexible. Sighing, I took a roomy display bin and began stacking the merchandise in size order, knowing some greedy kid would probably ransack the whole lot later.

When I was halfway through, my phone vibrated in my back pocket with a message from a +1917 number I didn't recognize:

> Hi, it's Gunnar. How long are you working today?

I stared at the words, more stunned that he had tracked down my number than the message itself. Where had he gotten it? Douglas? His mother? The Nornö telephone directory? It didn't matter; he had made the extra effort to reach out, even though he could have easily come into the store and purchased something, sending me into another incomprehensible tizzy. A text message from someone as contradictory as Gunnar seemed more meaningful.

> I get off at seven. Why?

> **Gunnar**:
> Great. Come by the Nornö Adventures store.

> Haha, okii

> **Gunnar**:
> 

Nornö Adventures offered guided seal safari tours and rented kayaks, bikes, and windsurfing equipment to tourists, a dizzying TripAdvisor-approved list of activities I never did. Biking only transported me around the island, and after eighteen years in Nornö, the archipelago sea outings and wildlife had become commonplace. I took them for granted, appreciating how they enhanced the scenery, but I could relate to those who lived in New York City but never visited the Empire State Building. Gunnar seemed like that type, so why would he want to meet up at Nornö Adventures?

Since I didn't take a brush or lipstick to work, I "borrowed" a cheap comb from the store after my shift and went down to the dingy bathroom in the cellar. I traced a center part in my hair, doused water on my hands, and flattened my tangled curls, slicking them back into a ponytail with the scrunchie I kept on my wrist. Someone had forgotten a pink-tinted lip gloss on the sink, so I squeezed a droplet onto my finger and dabbed it across my lips, instantly achieving a pouty shine. The change from scruffy to sleek (at least from the neck up) took only a few simple steps, yet the difference was glaringly obvious. I hoped it wouldn't look like I was trying too hard, but Gunnar had awakened something in me. I wasn't prepared to describe these conflicting emotions, but I knew I wanted to be a better-looking version of myself when I saw him.

On the way to Nornö Adventures, I spotted a FoodDirekt inflatable boat. I was tempted to give it the finger but changed my mind. Too crass. As I watched one of the guys unload, I grudgingly gave them credit for driving around the archipelago, delivering food while every other shop was about to close for the day. Holmgren's couldn't compete with that level of customer service.

The adventure store was the last building before the hotel, its square footage the size of three ordinary shops put together and packed with life vests, bikes, paddles, boards, and all manner of hale and hearty outdoorsy equipment. At first, I didn't see Gunnar amongst the other customers and gear, but I almost tripped down the aisle when I spotted him standing behind the checkout counter. He was wearing a rugby shirt and had swept his longish bangs to the side with hair wax. Scandinavian preppy—and far removed from the stoner who had been moping around the island.

"What are you doing?" I asked, silencing the laughter tickling my stomach.

"Ta-da!" Gunnar said, stretching out his arms. "I work here now. I took your advice and got myself a job!"

I couldn't hold it in any longer and started to laugh. "I don't remember saying you should get a job. You don't speak Swedish—or need the money!"

"But you were right. I need a daily routine, and what could be more constructive than working?"

"What are you *actually* doing? I hope they're not sending you out on any excursions."

He huffed in exasperation. "I can always count on a reality check from you. And no, I'm not taking anyone on boat rides and getting stranded somewhere without cell phone reception. They have me on risk-free tasks—booking trips and rentals, cleaning equipment, that kind of thing."

"Oh, okay. A lot safer than I expected."

"C'mon, give me some credit. I *have* worked before."

"If some trendy start-up counts as real work," I teased. "Anyways, what's up? Why'd you want me to stop by?"

Gunnar tilted his head a bit. "Um—uh—I wanted to tell you my news, and since I get off now, too, I was wondering if you wanted to walk home together?"

"Uh-huh." My bike was parked behind Holmgren's, but I'd pretend otherwise. "Um, sure."

"Great! Let me tell my boss I'm heading out."

I nodded. A jolt of excitement charged through me, an inkling that something interesting and undefined might be going on, but just as quickly, it disappeared. Gunnar was slippery and seemed to bounce from one person to another—Douglas, Molly. Now it was my turn. I wouldn't allow myself to be his flavor of the week. But watching him saunter from his manager toward me, a sheepish smile on his cute face, I couldn't help smiling back, filing those misgivings at the far end of my mind.

The air was warm, the sun a yellowish Day-Glo ball casting confusion over the precise time of day. *Kvällssolen,* the golden hour when disappointments evaporated in the forgiving light. A positive sign I had to get over my fear of rejection.

"By the way, I didn't mean to give you such a hard time about working," I said. "You surprised me, but I think it's great."

"It's okay. I'm getting used to your digs." Gunnar laughed. "For real, though, you did inspire me to get my shit together. Getting high every day is probably not the best way to spend my summer."

"It's not like I'm against smoking pot," I explained somewhat disingenuously. I wasn't sure where I stood, but I did know my mother's issues made me anti-anything that could become addictive. "It just caught me off-guard."

"I get that. Are you guys more into drinking than drugs here?" he asked. "Strange question, but you know what I mean."

"Our age group or in general?"

"Your friends, I guess. What are they like?"

"You know us Vikings—alcohol warms the winter," I joked and then got serious. "There's a lot of drinking at parties. I guess it's because Swedes are pretty shy and reserved. Alcohol loosens us up." It had never loosened me up. Twice I'd hoped it would unleash a more likable, fun-loving Zoë, so the other kids would realize they had misjudged me. I wasn't uptight and critical, and maybe with a few drinks, my chill side would come into full bloom. But I could never get past the taste—or my mother's bad behavior—and had accepted I would never be the life of the party. "Drugs are more common. I've heard that some people do coke at parties in town. But I mean, I don't get out much, so I wouldn't know personally."

"It's the same back home, just add the prescription drugs. So many of my friends who don't even have ADHD are popping Adderall." He shrugged. "I guess it doesn't matter what language you speak. We're all fucked up."

"Isn't that kinda sad, though?" I asked, conscious of how I could've also plummeted into the "fucked-up" category without Mormor and Morfar.

Another shrug from Gunnar. "That's just the way it is. But don't worry, I don't have any more pot left, and my dealer's halfway around the world, so . . ."

"Really?" I cut in. "Who'd you smoke it with? Molly?"

"Pfft. She wishes, but no. I finished it off on my own, on our dock at sunset."

"Sounds very picturesque."

"It was. The perfect farewell."

"Well, I'm happy to hear that. I prefer a Gunnar who isn't too stoned to look me in the eye."

"Good. 'Cause I like looking in your eyes."

It came out quickly, another stanza in our litany of wisecracks, but it landed differently on my body, arousing a fluttery feeling in my stomach.

"Oh, do you now?" I quipped, hoping my voice didn't betray the swooning sensation I was powerless to stop.

"Have you ever gone kayaking before?" he asked.

Gunnar had changed the subject so abruptly; I almost did

a double take.

"Uh, yeah, a few times when I was younger. Why?" I asked, trying to recover from misreading the conversation. Gunnar had an uncanny ability to lead me in a promising direction and then back off. Frustrating as it was, this unpredictability was part of his appeal. He kept me guessing, and I wondered if he did it on purpose.

"Well, I've never been, and we get a staff discount at Nornö Adventures if you ever want to try it again."

I stopped walking and asked coolly, "Are you offering me a coupon or asking me to go kayaking with you?"

He grimaced, hearing the annoyance in my voice. "I think it'd be fun if we went kayaking together."

I smiled, satisfied I'd forced him to be up-front. "I think it could be fun too."

We agreed to meet the day after tomorrow, early in the morning when the sea was calmer, but I deliberately didn't say anything to my mother or Mormor at dinner. Mormor would have remained blasé in any case; kayaking was nothing special to her, merely another island activity between friends. On the other hand, Linn would overdo it, bombarding me with questions. She might even mention it to Camilla Easton, with whom she had suddenly become chummy. I wished the two women in my life didn't represent such extremes. Their opposite reactions always canceled each other out, leaving me to fend for myself.

I had gotten in the habit of checking my emails before bedtime and again when I woke up; my father's messages usually appeared during those intervals. Sure enough, another one was waiting when my alarm went off the next day.

July 14, 2019

Dear Zoë,

This revelation has been quite a surprise for both of us, and I want you to process it all in a way that feels right. I understand your hesitation in telling Linn right now, and we don't have to call each other until you feel ready. I love getting your emails and "hearing" your voice, so I'm happy to continue our dialogue via email.

I googled Nornö and wish I had asked Linn more about her hometown because it looks beautiful! The beach seems so peaceful, in contrast to the craziness of South Florida ☺. I love the red houses, the sailboats in the harbor, and those amazing runestones. They're certainly a curiosity I'm eager to learn more about. I'll have to brush up on Swedish Viking history.

Holmgren's seems very charming based on your Instagram posts—good job! I'm sure Nornö was a very special place to grow up in, but it's natural to want a change of scenery at this stage of your life. The summer I traveled around Europe had a profound impact on me, and I got better at dealing with unfamiliar situations. I remember Linn telling me she wanted to travel the world. Given your American roots, the US would be a logical place for you to start. I'm your father, and you'd be welcome to stay with me whenever you want. Just say the word, and I'll make all the arrangements. We could also visit New York and California to give you a taste of both coasts.

You shouldn't be embarrassed about liking reality television! I've been known to linger on episodes (okay, maybe seasons) of *Master Chef*. It's the perfect show to watch while I'm making dinner. If that's what you're passionate about, we can investigate ways for you to take courses or get an internship. I did some research, and you're entitled to an American passport and dual citizenship, since you have an American father. Trust me, as the son of immigrants who were constantly worried about their legal status, not being dependent on a green card or an employer sponsoring you is a godsend. That's something we can take care of at the appropriate time.

Maybe I'm getting ahead of myself again, but I can't help but get excited about finally getting a chance to play an active role in your life. We should continue getting to know each other, so hit me with any questions you want!

Sincerely,

J.G.

My heart melted reading each sentence. Was this how it had been for my mother? Had she also been drawn to J.G.'s kindness and subtle humor? Or had their attraction to each other been purely physical? Heat spread across my forehead. Cringe. I didn't need to know. But I was finally beginning to grasp the perils of attraction—a creature unto itself—and how it propelled you to do things against your better judgment. I felt flighty and unmoored each time I met Gunnar, fearful I would lose my bearings just as my mother had.

I had to put thoughts of Gunnar aside. J.G. deserved my full attention, especially since he had now put it in writing: *I'm your father, and you'd be welcome to stay with me whenever you want. Just say the word, and I'll make all the arrangements.* His enthusiasm about meeting me and the plans he had laid out erased those second thoughts that had crept into my psyche. Although I'd tried to put the brakes on things, I couldn't stop our relationship from growing organically. We both wanted the same thing, but anxiety about my mother's reaction made me feel guilty.

Ultimately, I would have to take her out of the equation. Contacting J.G. had upended his peaceful life in Florida and keeping him at arm's length wouldn't be fair. I took my laptop from my bedside table and began typing, composing a list of questions.

July 15, 2019

Dear J.G.,

Thank you so much for your invitation to come to the United States! I've waited so long to visit because I always hoped that when I finally did, it would be to see you ♥. I won't be able to get away until September at the earliest, but here are a couple of things I've been wondering about:

What kind of music do you listen to?

Who's your favorite author?

What's your favorite movie?

Where's your favorite place to visit?

Do you collect anything?

What was the last show you binge-watched?

Which meal is your favorite: breakfast, lunch, or dinner?

Which phone app do you use the most?

Are you at all religious or spiritual?

Who do you admire most in the world?

What's your favorite sport to watch and/or play?

What would be your last "death row meal"?

Curiously yours,

Zoë

15

LINN

Camilla sent me a cryptic text before our next massage appointment:

> No need to bring a massage table or
> equipment! See you at 4!

The glibness of her tone annoyed me. Grabbing my tote bag in haste, I nearly tripped over a pair of Agnes's orthopedic sandals in the hallway. I didn't have time for this. Camilla treated these sessions like a book club meeting where they ate and gossiped instead of discussing the book. If she didn't want a massage, she should have canceled the appointment so I could find a replacement. Hanging out in Camilla's shadow, pretending I was also a lady of leisure, was idiotic. At the end of the day, it was *work*. Work to knead those knots out of Camilla's back. Work so I could make a living and not mooch off Agnes's overextended generosity. Finally, most exhaustingly, work to keep my head down and stay out of Wes's way. I was beginning to feel more and more like the hired help. I hadn't harbored any illusions about our relationship, but those cocktails blurred the lines. That text message reminded me I was at Camilla's beck and call.

But once I parked the moped outside Camille's exercise shed, I pulled myself together. I had to stay professional. It was the only way to survive this web of deception. I knocked on the door, feeling defenseless without my massage equipment. Setting up always gave me something to focus on, and the massage itself, in a freakish way, was the only time I ever felt superior to Camilla.

By the time Camilla opened the door, I was all smiles. "*Hej!*"

"Hi! Come in," she said, swinging the door open.

"Are you feeling sick?" I asked, stepping inside. "Is that why you don't want a—"

Just then, over Camilla's shoulder, I saw that a massage table had already been installed, equipped with thick beige towels and a small tray of oils.

"What's going on? Are you replacing me?" I asked half-jokingly.

Camilla shook her head. "No, of course not! But I figured since you're giving me these weekly massages, we might as well have our own table at the house. That way, you won't have to schlepp your stuff over here each time."

I wanted to point out—although I couldn't—that she wasn't my only client. I might have appointments before or after and would still have to "schlepp" my massage table around Nornö. But there was a catch to Camilla's voice, a longing for approval.

I walked over to inspect it. The upholstery was ecru-colored with adjustable arm and headrests, a solid steel base, and thermal heating. Not even Nornö Hotel possessed such high-quality equipment.

"This is what we call a deluxe model!" I said, genuinely impressed. "I've never given a treatment on something so high-tech."

"It's a German company," Camilla boasted. "They supply the best hotels and spas in the world."

"Well, I'm used to rinky-dink tables, so I hope I can do it justice."

Camilla shooed my comment away with her hand. "It's all about you, not the table. Besides, I bought it as an investment piece. It'll be good if Wes or Gunnar ever want a massage. You'll have to teach me your tricks!"

I tensed up at the mention of Wes's name. As I lifted the tray of oils from the massage bed, I flashed a tight smile and asked, "Shall we get started?"

Midmassage, dark clouds intruded through the expansive windows, casting a pall over the bright, state-of-the-art gym. When it started raining, I was relieved I wouldn't have to haul my equipment outside.

"Do you have time for a *fika?*" Camilla asked after the massage. "This weather has put me in the mood for something warm."

Rainy weather always made me sluggish, and a cup of coffee would be a welcome pick-me-up. I also still hadn't figured out how to politely say no, so I nodded. We dashed to the main house, entering through the same back door Zoë and I had snuck through on our first visit. Shaking off the rain, I realized I hadn't been inside since the housewarming party. The kitchen was still immaculate.

Camilla filled the Nespresso machine with water. "Do you want a *runebullar?* They're over there," she said, gesturing to a basket on the kitchen island.

"Sure, I haven't had one in a long time," I said. The buns, made of cardamom, almond paste, and dark chocolate, had been my favorite as a kid, gobbled daily in the summertime. But what adult over thirty-five could eat them so frequently? Even Camilla's enviable metabolism couldn't withstand the richness of *runebullar* every day. I took two buns out of the bag and reached into a glass cabinet for dessert plates.

At the same time, a young woman walked into the kitchen. I recognized her as one of the servers from the hotel, but at Camilla's, she wore yellow plastic gloves and carried a bucket with cleaning products, rags, and a rainbow duster.

"Oh, hi!" I said awkwardly.

"Hi! You're Linn, right?"

"Yes, I am," I replied, not bothering to ask how she knew. Everybody in Nornö seemed to keep tabs on the Holmgrens. "I'm sorry, but I didn't catch your name—"

"Raquel. I'm Raquel. I'd shake your hand, but—" She flapped a gloved palm in the air, and we both laughed.

Camilla appeared, bearing two mugs of Nespresso. "Raquel's boyfriend is the sous-chef at the hotel. She helps us out when she has extra time."

Raquel smiled. Her oversized, navy T-shirt and gray leggings couldn't obscure her prettiness; she was a freckly, lemony blonde with almost-translucent blue eyes. "Stefan works all the time, so keeping busy is nice."

"And we'll have the whole winter to rest," I quipped.

"Exactly!" After Raquel put the supplies in the cleaning closet, she said, "Camilla, I'm finished with the upstairs, so I'll see you on Thursday."

"Sure, that'd be great. Thank you for today."

Camilla and I set the table for our *lyxfika*—place mats, linen napkins, a glass creamer with oat milk, and a matching bowl with brown sugar cubes inside. She always brought out the good stuff, regardless of how small or casual the occasion was. I thought about Raquel, curious if she saw me as Camilla's friend or merely as her masseuse, another cog in Camilla's domestic arsenal. Sometimes it did feel like I had graduated from the hired help to confidante; I doubted

Camilla asked Raquel to *fika* with her. But I didn't think Raquel gave the matter a second thought. She was there to clean and go, no blurring of lines. Camilla seemed to collect people, amassing a Nornö working class dependent on her generous employment. I counted on this job like every other local, but seeing Raquel and Camilla side-by-side made me question my loyalty.

"I didn't realize you had a housekeeper," I said.

"She's not a housekeeper, unlike my full-time person in New York. Raquel only works twenty hours a week."

"How'd you find her?"

"I asked Erik at the hotel if anybody there might be interested in making extra money." She chuckled. "He seems to have a monopoly on the island employees."

"That's because no one in Nornö has help *inside* their homes. We all do everything ourselves," I said, and then, afraid I sounded too judgmental, I added, "That's the charm of country life, ha."

Camilla shrugged. "But why do it yourself when you can hire someone to help out? Raquel and Stefan are saving up to open a bed-and-breakfast, and I can't take care of this big house by myself, so it's a win-win."

What about getting your husband and son to help? I thought. Growing up, my parents had assigned me a list of household chores—vacuuming, laundry, and emptying the dishwasher, to name a few—and we expected Zoë to do the same. Camilla's explanation sounded like an elitist, rich-person comment Wes would make.

"I guess it is," I replied.

"I mean, she's okay. It's not like she does a great job. She never puts things back *exactly* the way I had them and I have to go around readjusting, but it's better than nothing."

I winced, troubled by the harshness of her thinking, and poured frothy milk into my coffee. Did Camilla say things like that about me behind my back? Complaining to whoever she could find, *The massage is okay, not like on Park Avenue, but it's better than nothing.* Had Camilla forgotten about her humble roots in Ljusdal?

"I'm sure she's doing her best," I said. "Or else Erik wouldn't have hired her."

"Speaking of Erik," Camilla said, switching topics. "Very much the big and brawny Viking."

I nearly snorted in surprise. "Uh-huh."

"Are you dating anyone now?"

I shook my head.

"What if I arranged an intimate dinner with me, Wes, you, and Erik?" she asked, dunking a piece of *runebulle* into her coffee. "I think you two would make such a cute couple."

The image of me, Camilla, Wes, and Erik on a double date made me want to spit out the morsels of *runebulle* in my mouth. There were limits to how far I would go to keep the peace. My lips began to twitch, so I raised the mug in front of my face to hide it. After taking a sip, I said, "Well, I've kind of already—"

"—been there, done that?" Camilla interjected.

"That's one way of putting it!" I gave her a fake, high-pitched laugh, silently questioning why Camilla was so interested in my private life.

"Mmm . . . that's too bad. The dating prospects in Nornö must be tough."

"They're not ideal, that's for sure. It'd be easier if I lived in Stockholm."

"Have you ever considered it? Moving to Stockholm?"

"I did, about seven years ago, when I was involved with a

guy who lived in town, but it didn't work out." I hadn't thought about Mattias Österholm in ages. We'd met at the thirtieth birthday party of a Sigtuna friend. Still embarrassed by my young-single-mother status, I hadn't wanted to go, but Alicia had convinced me it was better to show up, holding my head up high and looking fabulous, than hide out in humiliation. Mattias, a software programmer, had been the birthday girl's colleague, and we were seated next to each other during the formal dinner. He'd been funny and attentive, lampooning the same cheesy speeches as I did and gallantly topping off my wineglass. We'd danced with abandon on the dance floor—nothing more—and he'd asked for my number. I had told him about Zoë from the get-go, but he didn't seem fazed. We began dating; there'd been more wining and dining, movies in town, and parties at costly venues, some of which had required me to go away for the weekend. Zoë began to complain I was never home, and Agnes disapproved of Mattias's way of doing things, since he had shown little interest in coming to Nornö and getting to know my daughter.

When Zoë and Mattias finally met, I detected the suspicion in Zoë's eyes and began seeing his quirks in a new light. Mattias's head had been small in proportion to his body, reminding me of a turtle. The V-neck sweaters and button-downs he wore on rotation made him look older than his years. But most damning of all, Mattias cut Zoë off when she was in the middle of telling a story.

Admittedly, she had been a little long-winded, probably out of nerves and a desire to get the facts straight. But when he'd interrupted her, "joking" he would fall asleep if she didn't get to the point, I knew it was over. Zoë didn't crumble and cry; she scowled at him and refused to say another word for the rest of the evening. Mattias had apologized profusely, claiming he didn't know how to interact with kids. Before that incident, I had pondered what life would be like if Zoë and I moved in with Mattias. He could have learned how to connect with children and given Zoë the stability and home life she craved. But he had revealed his true colors, and I wouldn't subject Zoë to such insensitivity. I broke up with him and never regretted it. Staying with Zoë in Nornö, keeping our little circle tight—warts and all—had been the wisest decision.

"Because of Zoë?" Camilla asked, as if she could read my thoughts.

I nodded. "Zoë came first, and I could tell they wouldn't hit it off. Deep down, he wasn't really my type either."

"Nothing should come between our kids and us. You two probably weren't a good fit in the long run." She picked at the edges of a woven place mat. "Can I ask you something?"

My heart lurched, as it always did after one of Camilla's pronounced pauses. Why did I subject myself to this torture? Always on tenterhooks, afraid my moment of reckoning would come crashing down. "Ask away."

"Zoe's father. He's Black, right?"

"Yes," I answered, puzzled by the question. "Caribbean American, to be exact."

Camilla lifted her shoulder. "Maybe that's more your type. Not these super-Swedish guys."

I was speechless for a few seconds and then burst out laughing. "I don't have a 'type' per se. I like men who are kind, interesting, and easy to talk to. Black, Swedish, American—it doesn't matter."

"How did your parents react?"

"React to what?"

"To Zoë being half Black."

Camilla was straddling that danger zone between personal and prying, but I knew people wondered. She dared to voice what others whispered in secret. After all, I was a white woman who had given birth to a half Black baby with a guy my parents had never even met; surely, they must have been shocked. But Agnes and Thomas had already decided they would keep and love my child long before they knew her identity. She was a part of me, a part of *them.* That was all they needed to know.

"That was never an issue for them. My parents fell in love with Zoë from the moment I told them I was expecting. And when she was born, well, she was so cute and so good."

"I think mixed-race kids are the most beautiful," Camilla mused. "The best of both worlds."

I'd heard remarks to that effect from when Zoë could sit up in her stroller, her smiling face and big brown eyes on display for all to see. J.G. may not have been in the picture, but his fingerprint was unmistakable, enmeshed in Zoë's honeyed skin, thick, curly hair, and expressive mouth. Her distinctive looks seemed to give strangers the license to invade her space, touch her puffy ponytail, and ask intrusive questions—questions they never would've posed had I given birth to a blonde, blue-eyed baby. Because of my youth, people had assumed I was either the babysitter or a dizzy, loose girl who had gotten pregnant by a traveling rapper or basketball player, reducing my daughter and me to a cliché.

"You know, Zoë doesn't take that as a compliment anymore. She thinks it exoticizes multiracial people," I said.

Camilla groaned. "Kids are so sensitive these days!"

I shrank back in my chair, offended by her offhand comment. I may not have been as well-versed in these issues as I should have been, but I understood Zoë's frustration.

Camilla had glossed over my statement, missing the opportunity to learn from another point of view.

"Having a half Black child has opened my eyes to many things. It hasn't always been easy for her—or me," I said, struggling to keep my voice even.

"Here? In Sweden? Are you sure?" she said incredulously.

Why was Camilla patronizing me? I had empathized with the sexual harassment she'd experienced as a model, yet she was refusing to put herself in my or Zoë's shoes. "I can only speak from my personal experience," I said.

"But things are much more diverse now than when we grew up."

"Yes, but this part of the country is small and isolated. I don't know if being so secluded has done Zoë more harm than good. If we didn't have the runestones and tourists, Nornö would be a very homogenous place."

"So why didn't you ever leave?"

I bristled from the bull's-eye precision of Camilla's question, invalidating everything I had just explained. Her question implied, *If things were so bad, why did you stay?*

My stomach tightened, but I tried to stay calm. "My family was here, and so was our business."

A self-satisfied expression appeared on her face. "Trust me, I've traveled and lived in other countries, and things are much better here than in other places! I was one of the few white girls who hung with the Black models in my modeling days. The industry was so segregated, but I didn't care because we never considered skin color where I came from."

Really? I wanted to ask. *Never?*

"Maybe, but we've felt some strange vibes at times," I said. I wasn't sufficiently well-read or confident enough to continue the debate, and Camilla seemed to have made up her mind. I saw no point in pushing the issue. This exchange was our first heated discussion, which made me uneasy, like someone who had outstayed her welcome. Taking a last gulp of coffee, I glanced out the window. "The rain seems to have stopped for now. I better take advantage of that and get going." I helped Camilla clear the plates and steered the conversation to frivolity, specifically how great the new massage table was.

At the front door, Camilla called out, "Let's meet for dinner soon. We'd love to have you and Zoë over. I promise not to do any matchmaking!"

I offered a hearty wave but had no intention of going to the Eastons' for an intimate dinner. My only desire was to go home, talk to Zoë, and unpack the issues the *fika* had awakened. But the Crescent wouldn't rev up, and I was afraid water from the downpour had seeped into the engine. After several kick starts, it finally began moving at moderate speed, only to die again in the underbrush at the beginning of the forest. I put it in drive and kept pressing down on the pedals, but nothing. Switching to park, I got off and spotted a cyclist on the pathway. He noticed I was having problems and swerved in my direction. Hopefully, it was someone who tinkered with fifty-year-old mopeds as a hobby, but as he got closer, I realized it was Wes Easton.

He began walking his bike toward me, his eyes never leaving my face. There was a menacing quality to his gaze, and it was at that point I knew, with absolute certainty, that he remembered *exactly* who I was. I was trapped. My body vibrated with fear.

Wes stopped on the other side of the Crescent. "I want you to stay away from my wife," he snarled, nostrils flaring against his damp, ruddy face.

"*Now* you're playing the devoted husband?" I retorted,

surprised by my nerve.

"This is all your fault," he hissed. "If you had told the truth from the beginning and not lied about being 'Inga from Uppsala,' nothing would have happened."

"Whoa, whoa, whoa, this has nothing to do with me. I'm not the married one, and I only played you for the lying womanizer you truly are."

"You don't understand. Just leave Camilla alone."

"Leave Camilla alone?! She won't leave *me* alone! You abandon her with your tennis and business trips. She's lonely and needs a friend." I shook her head. "And quite frankly, I don't get it. Why?"

The irony was not lost on me. I was now defending the woman who had irritated me with her sense of entitlement and narrow-mindedness. But she wasn't a shameless snake like Wes—though I couldn't claim the moral high ground either, having knowingly entered into a friendship with Camilla after sleeping with her husband.

"I don't have to explain myself to you," he said, "but it's complicated. Camilla has some health issues."

"Do you mean her endometriosis? Give me a break. If she doesn't want to have sex, it's because she's in horrible pain. Have you bothered to consider that? It doesn't give you the right to fuck other women! You're revolting!"

He stared at me, dripping wet and fuming with rage, and I couldn't understand how I had ever found him attractive.

"Stay. Away. From. Us," Wes enunciated. "Camilla has worked so hard on that house. She wants nothing more than to be here, and there's no way I'll let you ruin it."

"The last thing I would do is hurt Camilla." That was the truth. Camilla was the innocent victim of this mess. Her only fault had been trying to strike up a friendship with me. "So, your dirty secret is safe."

"It'd better be. If not, you'll be very sorry."

"Don't you dare threaten me!" I screamed. "This isn't New York, and I'm not one of your dumb mistresses. You're an outsider here. Don't ever forget that."

"Do you think people would believe you over me?" he asked, laughing dismissively. "You're nothing but a whore! You don't even know who your daughter's father is!"

The words hit me like a slap in the face. Someone in Nornö had told him the truth about Zoë. I lunged at him, but he caught my wrist. After a few seconds, he brought the index finger of the same hand to his lips. *Shush.* A warning.

Coolly hopping on his bike, he cycled away.

Shaking, I rubbed my burning wrist and climbed aboard the moped again, pushing down on the pedals with all my might. The engine suddenly vroomed to life, and I sped home like a demon. Neither Zoë's bike nor Agnes's mobility scooter was parked in front of the house. I had planned to cook a family dinner of lemon-baked cod with cherry tomatoes and set a pretty table on the enclosed veranda, enabling us to catch the light but avoid the rain. Then we would sit and talk, partaking in that rare act of Holmgren togetherness.

Instead, I grabbed a bottle of red wine, a full-bodied Australian Shiraz I normally saved for the winter months and went upstairs to my room. Locking the door, I leaned against it, slithering to the floor. I unscrewed the cap and took a big gulp, ignoring the overflow that oozed down my chin and neck. Teardrops gliding down my face melded into the redness, but I didn't care. I wanted to sink into nothingness and zone out.

I wanted to silence the ugly words echoing inside my head: *You're nothing but a whore. You're nothing but a whore.*

16

ZOË

I'd had a fitful sleep, worried the stormy weather would make it too rough to kayak. But, by early morning, the clouds had passed, and the sky was a feathery cerulean blue. Mirrorlike, the sea rippled with faint horizontal stripes. I was supposed to meet Gunnar at six outside Nornö Adventures and had showered the night before to save time. After brushing my teeth and splashing water on my face, I plaited my hair into two French braids and dressed in a bikini, board shorts, and a long-sleeved rash guard. According to my weather app, the temperature had dropped by ten degrees, so I threw on a fleece jacket and biked down to the village without a minute to spare.

Gunnar was already there among the other adventurers preparing to hit the water. We greeted each other with a side hug, carefully keeping some distance, purposely avoiding full-frontal bodily contact.

"So, are you ready?" he asked.

"I guess so. I'm putting my life in your hands."

"Don't worry. I did a crash course yesterday with Christer, the owner," He rubbed his hands together. "But the water's only fifteen degrees, so we'll need wet suits."

Very few people looked good in a wet suit. Squeezing into one like a sausage had not figured in my mental image. Every inch of my body I self-scrutinized would be in full view, inviting comparisons to more delicate-boned Swedish body types. But I couldn't freeze for vanity's sake, so I smiled and said, "Good thinking."

Inside the store, Gunnar held a few wet suits against my frame and gave me a full-length version, a life vest, and a pair of water shoes. I undressed in the changing room and pulled it on, pausing to appraise myself. Better than I thought—curvy but tight and smooth.

Gunnar wore a short wet suit and looked like he belonged on a surfboard in Malibu with his muscular arms, solid abs, and tanned legs. His hotness was distracting, and the doubts crept in again. What was I doing here at the crack of dawn? I couldn't possibly be his type; he should be with his female equivalent, someone cool and confident like Molly. Inwardly, I cringed for getting carried away. I wasn't even sure if Gunnar considered me a friend, let alone anything else.

After putting my clothes and sneakers inside a numbered shelf behind the checkout counter, he chose two paddles and gave one to me.

"I'm impressed with your job performance so far. Very professional," I remarked as we walked to the sandy, shallow beach where the kayaks were parked in a row.

"Thanks. Christer seems pleased. Hey, I've got a joke for you." He paused. "What does a businessman wear to the beach?"

I shrugged.

"A wet suit," Gunnar deadpanned. "Get it? A wet suit."

"Ugh! That was so bad—"

"—it's actually kinda good?"

I laughed. "Kinda."

"Christer cracks corny jokes like that all day long. In English too. I think he hired me so he could practice."

"Christer?" I asked, surprised. "Didn't think he had it in

him. He's always so grumpy whenever he comes into Holmgren's."

"This place has so many characters. A couple of guys from the gas station come by every night to have beers with Christer and shoot the shit. It's supposedly some tradition. They might invite me to join them in a few weeks, but they say I have to earn it."

"Why are you getting all the special treatment?"

"I wouldn't get jealous about not getting to hang out with a bunch of old geezers!" Gunnar walked to a green kayak on the little beach and placed his paddle in a diagonal position under the web of ropes at the front. He directed me to the red kayak next to it, and I did the same.

"I was eight years old the last time I did this, so don't expect much," I said. "And it was in one of those double seaters with my grandfather, and I'm sure he did all the work."

"Don't worry. This will be kayaking for dummies." He pointed to the landmass directly across the shore. "We'll paddle to the back of that island. It should take about half an hour. I timed it with Christer."

"Okay," I said, taking a deep breath. "How do I get in this thing again?"

"Stand over the seat with one leg on each side," he said. "Then lower your butt down like you're straddling something."

I followed his instructions. "Then what?"

"Lift your legs and slide your feet into the cockpit. Scoot your butt into the seat and put your feet onto the foot pegs. Piece of cake."

Since I didn't have Gunnar's natural athleticism, I knew I would look clumsy attempting this—too many body parts moving in vaguely inappropriate positions—but luckily, I succeeded on the first try. Copying him, I eased the paddle away from the cordage and used it to move away from the shoreline. Suddenly, I was on the water, floating.

"Woo-hoo!" I shrieked, surprised by how weightless and buoyant I felt.

Gunnar turned to look at me. "Pretty cool, right?"

I let him go ahead of me, mimicking his strokes. Rotating my torso and the blades at the same time was strenuous, but the kayak sliced across the water like a razor on ice. The morning soundtrack was easy listening—birdsong, wings flapping in the air, and the occasional squawking of sea gulls. I watched them nose-dive for food from my eye-level position, marveling at their accuracy. Before Gunnar neared the shore of the neighboring island, I felt a tide of disappointment; our outing was halfway over. He paddled to the water's edge and swung his legs over the side, lifting himself into a standing position and pulling the kayak's bow onto the beach until it came to a full stop. I swayed gently in my kayak, unsure I could get out without flipping over or falling in. Gunnar gestured to a spot, and I maneuvered my paddle until our kayaks were adjacent. It skidded to a halt, and I boosted myself out of the seat, jumping, feet first, into the water. He applauded, and I couldn't stop smiling at my tiny triumph.

"That was awesome!" he exclaimed when I got to the beach. "What'd you think?"

"Amazing! One of the best mornings ever."

"Have you eaten breakfast?"

"No. Have you?"

Gunnar shook his head. "I have some sandwiches if you're hungry?"

"Sure. That would be great."

"Why don't you find a place where we can sit, and I'll be right there."

Treading lightly between the weeds, I scaled a gentle slope and found a flat slab of rock. I sat, unfastened my life vest, and finally exhaled, ecstatic the excursion was going better than expected. The setting was idyllic, with clear skies, a soft breeze, and the sun's sparkling reflection on the sea. As I watched Gunnar stride up the rocky hill, dressed in that black wet suit and holding a nylon sack, he reminded me of a James Bond character who had mysteriously surfaced from the water. He sat beside me and removed a demi baguette wrapped in wax paper and two bottles of Pago pear juice from the pouch.

"Did you make that?" I asked, pointing to the sandwich.

"I did."

"At home?"

"Okay, maybe not at home, but we provide picnics at Nornö Adventures. I wanted you to have the whole experience," he said, separating the precut sandwich down the middle. "I hope you like ham and cheese."

"I do."

"And the bread was baked this morning. Fresh from the bakery," Gunnar said, handing over my half.

"You're killing me with this platinum service," I said, unwrapping my sandwich. "I didn't think you had it in you."

"I'm killing myself! Not sure where the real Gunnar went."

My hand swept over the scenery. "Maybe this is the real Gunnar. Kayaking and becoming one with nature, ha."

"Hmph—you say that as a joke, but maybe you're right. The archipelago is growing on me, and I sometimes wonder if I'm meant to be somewhere else. Meant to do something else."

"You're only saying that because you're in the moment, and the archipelago is at its best. But trust me, it's not like this for the other three hundred days of the year. You'd go stir-crazy."

"Maybe. But I wish I could experience it anyway and decide for myself."

"Why can't you? Take a gap year."

Gunnar uncapped his Pago and chortled. "And not start college as planned? Wes would lose his shit."

I registered how Gunnar didn't call him "Dad." Another sign of their tense relationship?

"But you're an adult. It's your life. They can't decide over you," I said.

"Is that some liberal, Swedish, universal-rights-of-the-child thing? Because that sure won't fly at Casa Easton, not when Wes is the one footing all the bills."

"Have you asked him?"

"No."

"Then you don't know what he'll say. He might go for it."

"Have you told your mom you're going to Florida to see your father?" Gunnar countered, biting into his sandwich.

"No. But my mother *really* doesn't have a leg to stand on with that one. And she's not paying for anything either."

"I don't have a choice. I'm lucky I got a spot somewhere to begin with."

I sunk my teeth into Nornö Bakery's lauded crunchy-yet-soft sourdough, thinking back to the school photos of Gunnar I had seen online, where he looked like a model student. Why was he always so shady about college?

"What happened?" I asked after a few chews. "You never want to talk about it, but now you have to tell me. I told you about my father. No one else knows what I'm planning."

"Fair enough," he said. "Did you hear about that college admissions scandal a few months back?"

I nodded. When the story broke in the Swedish tabloids,

I'd been shocked by the qualifications beyond academics needed to get into an American school: extracurricular activities, sports, community service, *and* leadership positions. In Sweden, only your GPA mattered, and you filled out a simple form on the computer without needing essays or expensive counselors. "Oh my gosh, that was so crazy. Lynette from *Desperate Housewives,* I can see, but Aunt Becky from *Full House?!* Noooo!"

He chuckled sarcastically. "Well, you can add Wes Easton to that list."

"What?! Did he pay for someone to take your tests?"

"No!" Gunnar snapped. "I took my own damn tests."

"Sorry," I mumbled. "What happened?"

Gunnar sighed. "It came out that Wes had paid off the lacrosse coach at the university I was supposed to start at this fall. It was my first choice, so I applied early and got in as a lacrosse recruit. But when the administration discovered the scheme, they fired the coach and took back my acceptance to keep everything quiet and protect their reputation. It was either that or notify the FBI."

I groaned. "Oh, Gunnar. How did the school find out?"

"When everything went down, all these schools freaked out and had internal investigations. This lacrosse coach told my dad I'd be a shoo-in with a donation to his charitable foundation—basically, his personal bank account.

"But what I didn't know was that Wes donated fifty grand, and I got in, thinking I had done it all on my own. The university investigation found emails, payments, and phone records . . . . By the time the scandal broke, it was too late for me to apply to another school. So, instead of a top Division I school, I'll be at a third-rate college in the middle of bumfuck Massachusetts."

He paused. "I busted my ass all these years for nothing."

Gunnar's voice was loaded with bitterness and disappointment, and I finally understood why he often seemed angry and apathetic, escaping into a weed-filled fog.

"Oh, Gunnar, I'm so sorry! But it sounds like your father meant well. It's more the coach's fault than his."

"Not really. That's just how my dad rolls. He's a cheater. He'll do anything to get that extra edge. He says that's how he transformed his family's 'tired' carpet business into a 'leader in the industry.'"

"This other school might be better than you think."

"I doubt that. The worst part isn't that Wes paid off the coach, which is pretty horrendous in and of itself. It's that he had no faith in me. He didn't think I could get in on my own merits. He's always been that way. Whatever I do, it's never good enough."

"Well, prove him wrong."

"I've been doing that for the past eighteen years," he said. "I'm exhausted."

Wes had compromised not only Gunnar's future but also damaged their relationship. I wondered if Camilla had been aware of the plan. No one could ever know what flared beneath the surface, even in seemingly perfect families like the Eastons.

Turning to Gunnar, I said, "I have faith in you. I think you're pretty cool—and you're an awesome kayak instructor."

He smiled. "Thanks, Zoë. I think you're pretty cool too."

Our words were flippant. Maybe they had a deeper meaning or were applicable that minute, but I didn't care how Gunnar interpreted them.

If he suspected I "liked" him, so be it.

Afterward, we took a short walk around the little island,

posing for pictures (although not together) in the spectacular environment. The trip back to Nornö was uneventful until we got caught behind the wake of a thunderous speedboat. We managed to ride the big waves, but water entered our kayaks. Paddling frantically, we landed in Nornö wet and laughing, pumped up by the adrenaline rush.

"My arms are about to fall off, but that was worth it!" I cried. "I wish I didn't have to go to work after this."

"We could go kayaking again one night or when you have a day off," Gunnar suggested.

"I'd love to."

"Great. I'll text."

We parted with another hug. This one had a little more physical contact.

I felt the outbreak of chills and pedaled back home for a hot shower before reporting to Holmgren's. My mother appeared when she heard the front door slam shut.

"Where have you been so early in the morning?" she asked.

Linn's voice was deep and guttural, dripping with the unmistakable traces of a hangover. I'd been so hyped up about meeting Gunnar that I hadn't paid attention to her whereabouts the night before. Aside from a scratchy throat, her eyes were bloodshot.

"I went kayaking. With Gunnar."

I followed her to the kitchen, watching as she poured coffee from the pot into a large mug. She always liked it black and boiling the morning after; I figured the alcohol had deadened her taste buds. But each movement seemed labored, a performance in slow motion. Linn slouched to the kitchen table and sat, motioning for me to join her.

"I can't stay," I said. "I have to shower and go to work."

She nodded, inhaling steam from the coffee. "Maybe you

shouldn't be hanging around Gunnar."

"*What?* You're hanging around his mother all the time!"

"That's different. I don't want you to get hurt."

"What on earth are you talking about?"

"He's only here for a few more weeks. You can't take guys like that seriously. They only want one thing, and then poof, you're forgotten."

"I don't think Gunnar's like that."

My mother scoffed. "They're all like that."

Narrowing my eyes, I tilted my head and asked, "Why do you always have to ruin things for me?"

"I'm not ruining things for you! I only want to protect you. You've been so sheltered; you don't have much experience. I don't want things to end badly."

"How would you know how much experience I have? You know less about me than you think."

She put the mug down on the table and touched her forehead, acting as though our conversation and not the hangover was giving her a migraine.

"Just be careful. That's all I ask," she pleaded. "Think about what I said, and just be careful."

17

LINN

I stayed at the kitchen table long after Zoë left for Holmgren's, long enough to finish the pot of coffee that had gone cold and stale. The hollowness in my stomach disappeared after toast and orange juice, but my mental delirium remained, precipitated by something far more destructive than the red wine.

Wes's blistering attack had highlighted all my flaws—my promiscuity, my propensity to create elaborate fictions, and Zoë's inexplicable paternity. With that track record, it was no surprise she had rebuffed my advice about Gunnar. My lifetime of secrets and self-centered behavior had undermined my credibility. I had no influence over my daughter. I couldn't blame Zoë for basking in the novelty of Gunnar's attention either. I couldn't chastise her for thinking his niceties (a wholesome kayak date, for God's sake!) might sow the seeds of something deep and true. It was quite the reverse with his father, who had deployed the trashiest tactics to attract my attention at Grand Hotel.

In the beginning, my daughter had only wanted love and guidance. She had offered me unconditional loyalty, but I had shut her out, leaving Zoë with Agnes and Thomas to do the difficult work. In the years since Zoë learned the truth of her origins, I'd tried to win her back, but it was already too late. The scars of emotional abandonment, choosing fun and expedience over her security and happiness, infected every one of our interactions. Since the deceit had begun at birth, Zoë treated my latest attempts at honesty with suspicion. *And rightly so,* I thought ruefully.

Wes's threats also carried weight, since everyone in Nornö already thought I was slightly—if not seriously—unhinged. I had made some amends within the community through my professional behavior, but my past mistakes still dogged me. Nothing short of a public apology for a laundry list of perceived sins would satisfy them. But I was a Holmgren and would never pander to Evalina Bohlander or any other self-appointed member of the island's morality police. Without my family's contributions, Nornö would never be where it is today. How quickly these Nornö simpletons had forgotten!

But Wes Easton was a savvy New Yorker. He only had to ask a few strategic questions and they'd caved, divulging the most confidential information about my daughter. Their vile gossip and Wes's spiteful comment were nothing short of a personal violation, branding Zoë with a hot iron.

I shook my head in contempt. Nornö was *so* naïve. People here thought I was stupid, but partying had taught me a thing or two about human nature. Even Zoë underestimated my powers of perception, my ability to read the room and the people in it. I had no false hope; Nornö would sell me out to the Eastons in a heartbeat. I was damaged goods. They were shiny new objects.

I wished I could explain to Zoë the reasons behind my relapse, but doing so would expose my guilt. I had tried to warn her about Gunnar's family, implicating an innocent young man for his father's transgression. Without all the facts, it might seem like I was overreacting, shielding her from something that *might* happen, some hurt Gunnar *might* cause. Even I saw that it made no sense. Only I knew the true reason why they couldn't get to know each other better. If Zoë continued seeing Gunnar, Wes would come after me, stopping at nothing to protect his lies. But if I forbade Zoë from meeting Gunnar, it would push her further away from me and closer to him. I was in an untenable situation, suffering the consequences of my impulsive behavior.

I decided to send Zoë a text message as a peace offering: I know you can make good decisions. I'm sorry for doubting you.

I waited for ten minutes but didn't get a reply. Zoë and her phone were attached at the hip, so she was ignoring me on purpose. I imagined her glancing at the words, rolling her eyes, and stuffing the phone back in her pocket.

Sighing, I finally rose from the kitchen table. A full schedule of afternoon treatments at the hotel awaited me, and I couldn't fathom how I would get through them in my current state. I debated getting a few more hours' sleep or walking off my misery in the forest, but nausea while going up the stairs pushed away any thoughts of exercise. My mind was frazzled, and I felt so alone. The encounter with Wes had produced a feverish panic, an ill-fated awareness of being a passive bystander in the transcript of my life, of missing the deciding moment that could have altered the trajectory of events.

If I didn't unload my conscience, I would implode, and only one person had the dubious honor of always being present for my major screw-ups: Alicia. We had spoken a few times since that doomed girls' night out, but I never mentioned Wes. My silence had insinuated that he was a forgettable one-night stand, and Alicia never broached the topic. She was busy coping with her divorce and didn't have time to revisit that night's exploits.

Gripping my phone, I went to the little terrace outside my

bedroom and squatted on a fuchsia leather pouf. Luckily, Alicia answered after the second ring. Had it gone to voicemail, I might have lost the nerve to call her back.

"Hi, sweetie! You're calling bright and early today," she said.

"And you sound way too chipper."

"That's because I got a temp job at that PR and communications agency I told you about a few weeks ago! I'm going to be covering for one of the project coordinators who's taking a leave of absence until the New Year."

"Congratulations! That's wonderful."

"I think so too. It'll be a great way for me to get my feet wet. After ten years of unpaid labor, I need to build up my resume again."

"I know you'll do a great job."

"Hope so. I'm dying for something new to focus on."

"How are things going with Jonas?"

"The same. We just filed the joint divorce petition and will sell the apartment in September. It's not what I wanted, but I can't stop him if he's in love with someone else."

"Oh, Alicia, I'm so sorry." My heart ached for her. She had played by all the traditional rules, yet not only had Jonas cheated on her but he was also willing to split up their family and see his daughters part-time to cement his new relationship. How would Alicia react when I told her about Wes? Wouldn't she lump me in with all the other homewreckers? Suddenly, confiding in Alicia no longer seemed like a good idea.

"It's all right. I have no choice but to move on." She paused. "I'm sorry for being so depressing. How are things with you?"

I hesitated, but flashbacks from the previous evening, hiding in my bedroom with a bottle of red wine and guzzling it straight from the bottle like a drunk, assaulted me. I'd hit rock bottom. I couldn't continue this way.

"Do you remember that American guy from our night at Grand Hotel?" I asked.

"Ugh, don't remind me of that night! I'm lucky I made it to the bathroom in time. But yeah, sure, I remember him. He was so good-looking, very suave. Kind of a player, now that I think of it, but it may just be the angry divorcée in me talking. Why?"

"Well, it turns out he's married."

Alicia yelped. "Why am I not surprised?! But you could have never known that—it was one night. Don't beat yourself over it." She went quiet for a few seconds. "Wait. How did you find that out? Have you been seeing him?"

I gulped. "Not by choice. He's married to Nornö's newest resident. She's a former model, and they live in Manhattan. They're also rich and have built the biggest house on the island."

"Oh—thank God it's only that!"

"Meaning?"

"For a minute there, I was worried you were going to tell me you were—"

"Pregnant?"

"Yes."

"Alicia! Give me some credit."

"Sorry."

"There's more," I continued. "His wife, Camilla, and I have sort of—I don't even know what to call it. Become friendly? I give her weekly massages."

I heard Alicia gasp on the other end.

"What the hell? That's even worse than you accidentally sleeping with her husband! You have all the facts now. There's no excuse! Are you showing up and giving her a back rub as though nothing happened?"

Not mincing words, Alicia stated the obvious. But I balked at hearing them from the one person whose advice I valued the most.

"Yes," I whispered.

"Are you sure his wife doesn't know? This whole thing could be some weird marital game or sexual fetish they've got going on."

I had also considered that possibility, but Camilla seemed so straitlaced, more concerned with maintaining the perfect home than performing kinky sex or erotic role-playing.

"I don't think she's into that, and I don't think he's said anything to her either," I said.

"How can you be so sure? You never know what goes on behind closed doors."

"True, but it's just a feeling I have. I've tried to see Camilla as little as possible, but it's hard wiggling out of these massages without looking rude. On top of that, she's nice, and I've enjoyed her company."

"Who cares if she's nice? What about her husband? How often have you seen him?"

"I managed to avoid him for a while. At first, I didn't think he put two and two together since I had given him a fake name, but yesterday he confronted me in the woods, and I got scared, Alicia. Really, really scared."

"That sounds dangerous! Do you think he could get violent?"

"I don't know, but he's already got so much clout in Nornö. I can tell. People are awed by the Eastons' wealth and hospitality. Shit, even I even fell for it."

"Linn, you're playing with fire. No good can come of this."

"What am I supposed to do? How can I get out of it? The island is so small. I can't avoid them without it looking suspicious."

"Of course, you can. Cut off the massages and avoid them both—husband and wife! Invent excuses about why you're not available. Leave the island for the day if necessary. She'll eventually get the message, and it'll peter out. Her husband may be an asshole, but trust me, you don't want to get in the middle of their marital woes. That's not something you want on your conscience."

Alicia's advice was prudent—but also cowardly and spineless. As payback, I wanted to out Wes as a cheater. It would be so simple: I had proof of his indiscretion on my phone, and everyone in Nornö thought I was a bimbo anyway. I could take the heat. But what would happen if Zoë found out? She'd want nothing to do with me, and I couldn't blame her. Listening to Alicia—a scorned woman and soon-to-be ex-wife—I realized I had no choice. Evading the Eastons was the least disruptive and most face-saving option available.

I couldn't control Zoë, but I would put a mature end to this charade.

18

ZOË

The emails between my father and me flew at a rapid clip. They were no longer lengthy biographies or deep confessionals, just answers to friendly questions meant to ease the pressure of being sudden blood relations. J.G.'s favorite author was Colson Whitehead, whom I had never heard of, but I researched his books online and ordered *Sag Harbor*, a Black boy's coming-of-age story in the '80s, set in a Manhattan prep school and an African American enclave in the Hamptons. I was curious for cultural reasons, but the book also shared similarities with Gunnar's privileged background, and I wanted to know more about that world. *Breaking Bad* was the last series J.G. had binge-watched, and I suggested he fill the void with *Narcos*. He loved basketball (which was no surprise, judging from his childhood photos) and played a weekly game every Sunday in Wynwood. The phone app he used the most was Twitter. *It's addictive,* he wrote, *but I never tweet myself.* Like me, his favorite meal was breakfast, especially weekend brunch. But my favorite response was this: *I'm a little disturbed by your last "death row meal" question* 😮 *but if I had to choose, it'd be a traditional Haitian dish: my mother's pork griot, red beans and rice, and fried plantains. I think you'd love it!*

It was uncanny how my discovery of J.G. had coincided with the arrival of Gunnar in Nornö. I was in the middle of getting to know them both and liked the injection of male energy, since it blunted the tension with my mother. I was used to being angry with her, but never over the fact that I was going out and having fun. I had assumed she would be happy I was climbing out of my shell, but Linn had a talent for expressing the opposite of what I needed. Her apologetic text had come too late. She still hadn't learned that a sympathetic reaction in real time was more significant than a hastily scribbled expression of remorse later.

Gunnar and I had kept in touch since that early morning kayak trip, mostly sending Instagram memes and Nornö witticisms to each other. In late July, the weather fluctuated from sunny, halcyon days to windy, blustery nights, making it difficult to plan an evening trip when the sea was flat and visibility was good. I knew we could have met up someplace else—dinner at the tavern or over a game of tennis—but I preferred the beauty and privacy of the island across the harbor and sensed that Gunnar did too.

Nature finally worked in our favor a week later. Gunnar sent me a message, explaining the tidal current was mild, and finished off with: Let's suit up!

I sped down to Nornö Adventures, where Gunnar had already set aside our gear. We changed and got in the kayaks, paddles cutting through the water in tandem. We reached the neighboring island when the sky was bathed in a vaporous, whiteish blue, and the reeds rocked as gently as the waves. We settled in the same spot as before, and Gunnar took out a bag of Swedish mix-and-match candy, two plastic cups, and a bottle of white wine from his dry sack.

"Dessert?" I asked.

"It's already eight thirty. I figured you had already eaten."

"I'm pretty sure we're not supposed to be drinking and kayaking."

"But it's so much more cinematic. Only a few sips, I promise."

But he filled my cup to the rim, and we clinked the cheap plastic glasses together. The white wine was semicold, buttery, and not much to my liking, but it did amplify the experience, proving the clichés right. It was a mood enhancer that made me wonder if Gunnar would kiss me. The scene was tailor-made for a first kiss, and I debated taking the initiative. I could always blame my boldness on the wine. But Gunnar offered me the bag of loose candy, so I fished for the gummy pacifier rings. They would stick to my teeth and weren't exactly kiss-friendly, but he didn't seem like he was about to make any moves.

"I've been thinking about your dilemma," I said, switching gears from the romantic to practical.

"Which one?" he joked.

"Your college-slash-gap-year dilemma. I think you should do what you want. Your father can't guilt-trip you after what he did—practically ruining your life without your knowledge! I mean, what's he gonna say?"

"It's more like what he's gonna *do*."

"What can he do?"

"Cut me off financially."

I eyed him skeptically. "Your mother would never let that happen."

"She doesn't have her own money either. We're both dependent on Wes. The only thing that's 100 percent hers is that house in Nornö."

"I thought guys like you—"

"'Guys like you?' What's that supposed to mean?" he asked with a hint of a smile.

"I don't know. You might have a trust fund, savings

account, stock portfolio . . ."

He laughed. "Guilty as charged, but I can't access them until I turn twenty-three."

I took a large gulp and winced. I would have preferred a Coke Zero with the candy, but I liked how the drops of wine had loosened my tongue. "I still think you should look into it. Maybe you could take classes at Stockholm University or the Stockholm School of Economics. If you study here, your father can't say you're wasting time."

"That's a good point. I should do some research." He paused. "Will you help me? I won't understand the process since it's a different country."

"Of course! You should also have a defense ready for why you want to do this."

He groaned. "Sounds like my college essay all over again."

"It won't be as hard to explain why you'd want to stay in Sweden for a gap year."

"All right, here goes: exploring my Swedish roots, getting to know my mother's ancestry—"

"You can add in learning a new language."

"Getting work experience."

"The chance to travel around Europe."

"And meet new people," he added.

"Exactly! What about logistics? Where would you live?"

"I figure I could rent a room or sublet an apartment in Stockholm. But the house in Nornö would be my base."

I took that in, picturing what it would be like if Gunnar stayed past the summer. "Makes sense."

He took out some pieces of black licorice. "I don't like these. Do you?"

"I always thought they were overrated," I said, and we laughed. Then we grew silent, staring at the sea as though we were sidestepping the topics we genuinely wanted to discuss.

"What about you, then? Have you finalized your 'great escape' yet?" he asked finally.

"It's getting closer. My dad wants to send me a ticket, and we're shooting for a September visit."

"So, it doesn't sound like you'll be in Nornö that much this fall," he remarked.

"Well, I'm not sure. We'll see how things go. I can't stay away indefinitely." That had been my exact plan, but the possibility of Gunnar staying in Nornö was making me reconsider. I knew it was lame—and risky—to plan my schedule around a guy, especially one who had, so far, shown no interest outside of friendship, but my knee-jerk reaction didn't want to close any doors.

"What does your mom think?"

I dug out a pink-and-white marshmallow mushroom. "My mother doesn't know."

"Ha! How do you plan on pulling it off without telling her?"

I shrugged. "You're not the only one with secrets, Gunnar."

He creased his forehead together. "Details, please."

The wet suit began to feel constricting, or maybe my nerves were pressing down on my chest. Taking a deep breath, I began: "For the first ten years of my life, I thought my father was dead. But my mother had lied about him and how they met. They weren't a couple in love, like she claimed—he was a stranger, a one-night stand at a music festival and, well, here I am. I've been searching for him for years and finally found him about a month ago." I told Gunnar about the Hultsfred documentary that had unlocked my father's identity.

"Holy shit! That's a mind-blowing story!" he exclaimed at the end.

"Imagine living it."

"What's your dad like?"

I smiled. "He sounds like the nicest man. I can't wait to meet him."

Gunnar kept shaking his head. "Damn, Zoë."

"What?"

"That's the wildest story I've ever heard."

"I know! Please don't rub it in."

"Well, you're definitely not basic," he chuckled. "Living on this mysterious island with a long-lost father half a world away . . ."

"Is that what you thought when we first met? That I was basic?" I blurted out. "Is that why you were so rude to me?" Where had I gotten the nerve to say this?

"Ugh. I thought we'd forgotten about that."

"It hurt my feelings." The wine was talking now, but I didn't care anymore.

"Did it? I'm so sorry."

"So, what was it, then?"

He sighed. "My mom had mentioned meeting you at the store and said how nice and pretty you were. When you introduced yourself and were seriously, like, all those things, I was in a shitty mood—pissed at my dad, pissed about being in Nornö. You were so friendly, and it annoyed me because I wanted to wallow in my misery. So, I was a jerk instead of being nice back. Does that make any sense?"

"Sort of, in a roundabout way. But I appreciate your honesty," I said, seizing the compliments sprinkled in his convoluted explanation. "Maybe it was my fault. I was too forward and nosy. But I was just curious about you and your family."

"Now that you know the ugly truth about us, I hope you're

not too disappointed," he laughed.

"What about my truth? I'd say we're about even." *And you only know half of it.* My thoughts momentarily drifted to my mother's issues.

"Good. I couldn't handle it if you were too perfect."

We packed up and headed back to Nornö an hour later. The sun had technically set, but silvery streaks of light lingered between the ribbons of violet. It grew darker while we changed out of our wet suits, and Gunnar drove me home in his moped. I sat on the flatbed, feet dangling and bopping on the gravel pathway. The island was badly lit, but I knew my way around in the darkness, having memorized the shapes of trees and objects. Staring up at the star-drenched sky, I could identify the Big Dipper's glittering square pattern. I became so mesmerized by the sharp points of light and didn't realize Gunnar had taken a detour by the runestones until the moped stopped moving. I swiveled my head around and asked, "What's the matter? Are you lost?"

Shaking his head, he shut the motor, got off, and rounded the corner of the flatbed. "Can I sit next to you?"

"Sure," I said, scooting over. Gunnar's arm ended up behind my back.

"One of the things that got me thinking about making a change was your whole spiel about the legend of these Norns," he said.

I chuckled nervously. "The ladies didn't scare you away?"

"No, they clarified a couple of things. Maybe fate brought me to this place for a reason, and I can't ignore it. I need to see where it takes me."

The flatbed wasn't wide, and I had never been this close to Gunnar. I could smell his coconut sunscreen and the salty sea on his skin. The combination was heart-pumping, innocent, and sexy—which was also how I felt. I sensed what was coming and wanted it but became shy, holding my breath, afraid to look at him.

"Is it okay if I kiss you?" he asked.

I nodded, and he lifted my chin. Closing my eyes, our lips suddenly touched, and it felt lovely and romantic. My hands wrapped around his waist, our tongues twirled, and my stomach somersaulted. The darkness and the imposing runestones introduced an element of the forbidden that I found thrilling.

I didn't want it to end, but we were interrupted by a beam of light from the trail ahead all too soon. We separated hastily, but not before someone saw us.

"*Ojojojo!* What's going on here?" came a snarky voice.

It was Douglas Bohlander—and he was aiming his flashlight directly at our faces.

Gunnar raised his hand to shield himself from the glare. "Dude, chill. Don't flash that thing right at us."

Douglas sauntered over to the moped, his wiry body moving jerkily. "Hello, *Zoë*," he sneered.

After attending a handful of graduation parties together, I could tell when Douglas was plastered—and he wasn't a happy drunk either. Douglas got mean; the alcohol unleashed his worst instincts.

Cautious, I didn't respond.

"What's the matter?" he jeered. "Are you too good for me now?"

"Douglas, stop being silly," I said, springing to my feet. "You're a little drunk. Let us drive you home."

"Yeah. Sit up here, man, and I'll drop you off," Gunnar said.

"Pfft," Douglas replied. His flashlight fell to the ground,

and he hobbled over to Skuld, the runestone closest to the moped, the one said to represent the future. He undid his pants as though he were about to relieve himself. "Be careful, Gunnar," he howled, "she's a big tease."

Furious, I marched up to him.

"Shut up, you fucking idiot!" I shouted. "And don't pee so close to the stone!"

But I heard the words "Too late" above a trickling sound. I shoved Douglas back, but he lost his footing, tumbling sideways. The liquid he was in the middle of releasing squirted directly onto the runestone. I stood there, horrified.

Douglas had urinated on Skuld. He had defaced the stone.

And I was also to blame since I had pushed him.

"What the hell have you done?" I screamed. "You've jinxed us!"

Douglas was laughing, rolling in the dirt, soiling himself. "I can't believe you still—hic—believe that shit!"

"You're disgusting!" I screeched.

But he just kept shrieking with laughter.

Gunnar finally walked over to us and lifted Douglas from the ground, propping Douglas's arm around his shoulders. "All right, buddy, let me take you home," he said.

I followed behind them. Douglas wasn't fully upright, and his jeans were half open, but he let Gunnar drag him to the moped. Slumping down on the platform, Douglas coiled his body into a ball and closed his eyes.

Gunnar turned to me and asked, "Are you okay going home alone? He needs to get to bed." I nodded. "I'm sorry the night had to end this way."

"So am I."

I picked up Douglas's flashlight and walked toward my house, shaken and thoroughly spooked by what had happened.

19

LINN

July 29 was no ordinary day; it was Ingrid Agnes Sonja Holmgren's sixty-fifth birthday. Although it wasn't a dramatic entry into a new decade, halfway through was still a milestone. But it was peak season at Holmgren's, so it wasn't an opportune time to plan a big celebration. My father had also died in the summer, and we always felt his absence more acutely whenever Agnes celebrated another year of being alive without him. Swedish birthday tradition honored the person having a birthday first thing in the morning—ideal for a family like ours, who wouldn't have the day off.

I puttered about the kitchen with Zoë, preparing a tray with Agnes's favorite pastry, a miniature pink *prinsesstårta* from the village bakery. I didn't like the thick mound of whipped cream between layers of sponge cake and preferred to peel the marzipan top away and suck on it like candy. However, my mother, who was usually so sensible and unsentimental, expected a Princess cake every year and enjoyed the luxury of eating something so sweet and decadent before a proper breakfast.

Zoë moved furtively next to me, placing a bud vase with a single pink rose from Agnes's garden on the tray.

"That flower has opened up beautifully," I said.

"Mm," Zoë replied.

"Still not talking to me?" I asked, adding a wooden Swedish table flag to the composition.

"I'm talking to you now," she mumbled.

"Look, today's Mormor's sixty-fifth birthday, and I'd like us to try and get along. No arguing."

"You're right—it is Mormor's special day, so please, don't make it all about you for once."

I held my tongue. Our arguments had a way of bruising my flesh, leaving me swollen and raw. I'd barely seen Zoë the past few days and presumed she'd been spending her free time with Gunnar, ignoring whatever advice I'd tried to give her. The situation was rife with irony. I'd been so wild at the same age, but my parents had set very few restrictions, whereas Zoë was a responsible eighteen-year-old, and I wanted to squelch her first real crush.

Still, I knew Zoë had a good head on her shoulders. Possibly *too* good, and that was what frightened me most: someone could take advantage of her innocence. I poked one candle in the middle of the *prinsesstårta* and raised the tray to a carrying position. Fake smiling so broadly my cheeks pinched, I asked, "Ready?"

Zoë lit the candle, and we tiptoed up the stairs to Agnes's room, opening the door to sing the Swedish birthday song, "Ja må hon leva." Simba, who had followed behind us, stepped inside and began panting in excitement.

Agnes stirred under her comforter. We walked to the edge of her bed, and Zoë cheered, *"Grattis, Mormor!"*

Agnes finally sat up and gave us a sleepy-eyed smile. I always wondered if she had been asleep or just pretending, staying dutifully in her bedroom until the birthday ritual began. Once she blew out her candle, I put the tray down, and we took turns giving Agnes hugs while Simba tried climbing onto the bed. Agnes laughed but brushed him away, gently but firmly.

When Zoë began taking pictures with her iPhone, she exclaimed, "Zoë, please! Let me at least comb my hair."

"I wish I looked like that in the morning!" Zoë said, clicking away.

"You're beautiful, Mamma, just beautiful," I added.

Gazing at my mother, I imagined what I might look like in twenty-five years. Getting older in Nornö wasn't easy. Island life could be lonely and harsh; the cold, dry air hardened one's skin into a grayish pallor. But Agnes's cheeks remained rosy, and she carried a little extra weight, reducing the wrinkles. Once she'd stopped dyeing her hair, the texture had returned to its original thickness. Yes, my mother looked good. The only source of worry was her arthritis, but she insisted the limp looked worse than it felt.

We left Agnes to freshen up and resumed our breakfast preparations. Zoë scrambled eggs while I sliced strawberries, and with the bacon, yogurt, and freshly baked bread, the meal was more elaborate than what we ate on a regular weekday. But birthday breakfasts were supposed to be large and leisurely, a reminder to slow down and be thankful for another year around the sun. The only downside was the Nescafé instant coffee Agnes insisted on drinking. Despite my objections, she had consumed it by the gallon her whole life and refused to switch to a more premium brew.

It felt good to dote on Agnes. My parents had spoiled me on my birthday, showering me with presents from my wish list and baking a chocolate cake with vanilla frosting and rainbow sprinkles, since I'd said outright that I didn't want a *prinsesstårta* like everyone else. We'd continued the tradition with Zoë, but attendance at these birthday breakfasts had dwindled to three after my father died. I knew it was only a matter of time before it would only be Agnes and me, and we'd eventually decide these elaborate feasts required too much effort.

But my reservations dissipated when Agnes entered in her best morning robe, a frilly, turquoise velour concoction. She sat at one end of the table in the enclosed veranda, giving her a wide view of the sailboats crossing the inlet toward Nornö Harbor. Zoë set out the serving platters, and we all smiled at each other, three generations convening, momentarily forgetting our differences, old and new.

"So, Mormor, what are you going to do today?" Zoë asked. "I think you should give yourself a vacay."

"Britta Cederqvist is throwing me a ladies' lunch, so I'll only be working half the day."

"That is so cute!" Zoë said.

"That was very sweet of her to organize," I agreed. "You haven't been out properly in ages."

"I like solitude at my age," Agnes said. "Too much action at Holmgren's this time of year."

"Sixty-five is not old," Zoë said.

"And it sure won't be quiet with Britta and those other gossipy women!" I added.

Agnes chuckled. "Sixty-five may not be old in number, but I feel it in my bones. I guarantee we'll spend the entire first course discussing our aches and pains."

"But you feel good, right, Mormor?" Zoë asked.

"Yes, *sötnos*. I feel fine, so you have nothing to worry about," Agnes assured her.

"How are things going at the store?" I asked. My appointments at Nornö Hotel were on an upswing, leaving me fewer hours to help at Holmgren's. Truthfully, I preferred the calm and cleanliness of the treatment room, where I served one customer at a time, to the gritty chaos of Holmgren's.

"We're still getting lots of business with the day visitors, but earnings are down year-to-date." Agnes shrugged. "Oh well."

"You don't sound too worried," I said, alarmed by what this would mean for our finances in the off-season. Maybe it was time to cut back at the spa and help my mother steer Holmgren's in a more profitable direction.

"That's because I think we're doing our best. If people don't shop at Holmgren's, we cease to exist. This island will have to fend for itself. It's as simple as that."

"It's all FoodDirekt's fault!" Zoë cried. "We should lower our prices to compete."

"Then we won't be able to pay our bills," Agnes said brusquely. "But I don't want to discuss Holmgren's on my birthday. I need a mental break." She shaved off a thin piece of cheese and placed it on a slice of bread, topping it with cucumbers and peppers. "How are things working with that new family, the Eastons?"

I glanced at Zoë, but she was focused on spearing a strawberry with her fork.

"I think things are good," I replied. "I've been giving Camilla massages, and she seems to like being here."

Zoë finally looked up again and spoke directly to Agnes. "And Gunnar, their son, is working at Nornö Adventures. We've gone kayaking together a couple of times."

"Oh, that's so nice, Zoë. Are you guys da—"

"Mormor!" Zoë interjected. "No one dates anymore! We've just hung out a few times."

Agnes grinned. "In my day, we called that dating. What's he like?"

Smiling slightly, Zoë lifted one shoulder. "Well, he's smart and fun and very cute."

Agnes laughed, but I stayed silent, listening intently. Those few sentences were the most I had ever heard Zoë verbalize about her current situation with Gunnar, but she had always been more forthcoming with her grandmother. Agnes's offhand yet curious approach drew out Zoë's innermost thoughts and won her affection. Many moons ago, they would spend hours in a corner, reading picture books and chitchatting. These memories crossed my mind as I stared at them, envying the mutual warmth. The rift between Zoë and me seemed to grow with each passing year.

"Well, be careful when you're hanging out. There's been a theft on the island," Agnes said.

"What do you mean?" Zoë asked.

I raised an eyebrow. "I haven't heard anything."

"Kurt Bohlander called me last night to give us the heads-up."

I stifled an eye roll. Kurt thought he was the mayor of Nornö and treated Agnes like an honorary First Lady, but I appreciated how he kept an eye out for her. "What'd he say?"

"Someone stole the motor from Douglas's boat. Took it apart right on their dock!" Agnes said.

"That's crazy!" Zoë gasped. "When did it happen?"

"In the middle of the night, between Saturday and Sunday. It was gone when Kurt went down to his dock Sunday morning."

"Are you sure that's when it happened?" Zoë pressed.

"I don't know the exact details, *hjärtat*. But Kurt said the boat was definitely in one piece when they went to bed on Saturday."

"Oh," Zoë said.

"There have been similar thefts in the archipelago, and Kurt thinks there's a criminal gang behind them. Rumor has it they resell these motors in Estonia and Poland." Agnes shook her head in bewilderment. "Imagine going around taking people's motors? Other than houses, boats are probably our most prized possessions. Thomas would have flown into a rage if some thief had even *tried* to lay a hand on his Bertram. He would have chased him around the archipelago!"

I smiled. "The criminal would have never known what hit him."

"Talking about stolen boats on your birthday is a real buzzkill, Mormor," Zoë interjected and pointed to the little green box with a silk bow beside Agnes's plate. "Open your present."

I welcomed the change in topic. Mentions of my father still brought back memories of his shocking death. I knew he was never far from Agnes's mind—especially on a day like today when we should have celebrated her sixty-fifth as a complete family. Had Thomas still been alive, we would have been preparing for a large party on the lawn, with a tent, Agnes's favorite perch in white wine sauce, and the irresistible ABBA tunes she loved. His death had shattered Agnes's spirit; a little light had gone out, and she had retreated more and more into herself. Aside from the store, my mother played bridge and tended to her garden, but there had been no gentleman friends since Thomas. She rarely ventured beyond Nornö, remaining as physically close to her deceased husband as possible.

Agnes picked up the box and shook it to her ear. "You shouldn't have!"

"Mamma, don't say that. It's a big birthday!"

Agnes unwrapped the present carefully, rolling the bow into a ball and unsealing the tape on the edges like she might want to use the wrapping paper again. She finally got to the velvet box and lifted the lid. "Oh, my goodness!" she squealed. "It's too much!"

"It's not nearly enough for what you mean to us," Zoë said, rising from her chair to help her grandmother put on the delicate, white-gold necklace bejeweled with a small diamond-encrusted anchor.

"How do I look?" Agnes asked, elongating her neck to display the sparkly gem.

"It's perfect," I told her. Zoë had seen the necklace on a blog, and I had purchased it from a boutique in Stockholm on my way home from my night at Alicia's.

The breakfast cheer continued until Agnes left to prepare for her busy day. I knew she wanted to visit Thomas's grave beforehand—another ritual she observed on all our birthdays. I could picture my mother giving my father a full report on what he had missed.

As Zoë helped put the food away, I said, "Good job today. I think Mormor was happy."

Zoë smiled, and a pure, no attitude expression reached her eyes for a change. "Thanks. You too."

Later, I received welcome news from Camilla:

Hi Linn!

My apologies, but I have to cancel our massage tomorrow. Wes got us a table at Frantzén, and we'll spend the night at Ett Hem. I've been dying to try both—I hope you understand. See you next week!

Poor Camilla. It was no coincidence that Wes had snagged a coveted reservation at Sweden's first-ever three-Michelin-star restaurant on the day I usually gave her a massage. I felt horrible being entangled in this marital mess but shrugged the thought away. I would avoid seeing Camilla this week, invent another excuse the next week, and, just as Alicia said, the whole predicament would miraculously disappear.

20

ZOË

I couldn't stop thinking about the theft of Douglas's boat motor—or, more importantly, the time of the theft. Based on Kurt Bohlander's account, it had occurred a day after Douglas urinated on the runestone. That must have been his punishment! Douglas treasured that Ryds boat more than anything. He had gotten it as a confirmation present a few years back and taxied people between islands for a cheap fee. His stolen motor, the newest Mercury upgrade, had been a graduation gift from his parents. I felt sorry for Douglas, but it was a self-inflicted wound. He shouldn't have been near the Norns with his pants hanging down. I'd been walking on eggshells since that night, convinced the wrath of Skuld would bear down on me, too, but Douglas's punishment must have been a form of swift justice. Maybe I had immunity, since I had tried getting him away from the runestone.

Gunnar told me later that Douglas could barely stand when he tried to get him off the moped and into the Bohlander residence. After Gunnar carried him inside the house to his room, he panicked, afraid Douglas could choke on his vomit. He'd woken Kurt and Evalina up so they could watch their son. Awkward! And now, with the stolen motor, Douglas must have felt like the whole world was against him. I still shuddered when I thought about how the evening had disintegrated in such a shocking way. I wished I had kept my cool and not allowed Douglas to provoke me, but he'd called me a "big tease," alluding to a series of incidents I desperately wanted to forget.

My childhood memories were inextricably linked to Douglas Bohlander. Apart from being in the same classes in Nornö and then sharing the ferry to Djurö Gymnasium every morning, he was like an annoying brother, always needling me about being a goody-goody or badgering me for being the "teacher's pet." He called me Four-Eyes when I got glasses in third grade and told me I would look better with straight hair in eighth. I kept waiting for Douglas to grow up and leave me alone, but I gradually realized I was a convenient target for his insecurity. I put up with his bullying because we had known each other forever. Commiserating with him in Nornö was better than nothing.

Douglas suddenly turned a new leaf during our last year of high school and started being nicer. One time, he drove me back to Stavsnäs on his boat (free of charge!) when I'd forgotten an important textbook at school. He also helped me get invited to the most sought-after graduation parties— places my stuffy, non-drinking self would have never gotten asked to on my own. We'd texted and coordinated plans regularly, and although I would have never told him my deepest thoughts and dreams, I thought we had progressed to a more mature stage of friendship.

Everything changed when Douglas kissed me at Gustav Arwidson's graduation party. The kiss in and of itself was not the freaky part. *It was that I kissed him back.* I had never made out with anyone before.

Curious and eager, I began to think that maybe Douglas wasn't so bad after all. Even though I was inexperienced, he seemed like a decent kisser; there was no spatial awkwardness or unnecessary salivating. We locked lips for most of the night, including the taxi boat back to Nornö. He'd texted me for several days, and I'd allowed one more makeout session as a test, but it confirmed my gut feeling: *Meh.*

I wasn't attracted to Douglas. I didn't want to be his girlfriend. I never wanted to kiss him again. Without Nornö, we had very little in common, and saddest of all, he didn't seem particularly interested in life beyond its borders. Douglas represented a way of living, a way of thinking, that I wanted to leave behind.

I told him we should just be friends. Assured him he was practically my *best* friend, since I had known him longer than anybody else. Douglas had lashed out in retaliation, calling me a "tease." The texting stopped, and the taunts resumed.

His trash talking by the runestones in front of Gunnar had freaked me out. I was terrified he would tell Gunnar we had fooled around, jeopardizing my chances—however far-fetched—with him. I had only wanted Douglas to shut up and calm down, but his meanness had taken over. Ironically, Douglas had befriended Gunnar first, and now it seemed like I had come between them.

Still, I couldn't stop what I was feeling. Whenever I was with Gunnar, all the clichés applied—my heart *did* skip a beat. It was a nervous-but-excited intensity, a physical attraction that snowballed the more time I spent with him. I could never predict what he would say or the suggestions he would make. Take tonight, for example. His parents were staying in Stockholm overnight to eat a fifteen-course meal at some exclusive restaurant. Did I want to come over for burgers?

Of course I did.

What went unasked, however, was whether I would sleep over. I hadn't yet decided and had no intention of asking my mother's permission, but what was the point of a parent-free zone if you didn't at least entertain the possibility? Kissing Douglas had been an experiment—*Should I? Shouldn't I? Yes? No?* But with Gunnar, I felt absolute certainty; my body and mind were finally in sync. I fixed my hair in the same half-up, half-down style from the housewarming party and wore a tiered maxi skirt with a crop top. I added jeans and a sweater to my tote bag—along with a toothbrush, just in case.

I hadn't been to the Eastons' house again, and it seemed more seductive this time, knowing it would only be Gunnar and me. When I entered through the back door, he was sitting on one of the kitchen stools, scrolling through his phone in one hand and a bottle of Corona in the other.

"Hi," I called out. Leia trotted to me, barking.

Gunnar put his phone and beer down and came around, wearing a T-shirt and a pair of ripped, light-wash jeans. As I stood on tiptoe to hug him, his hand inadvertently touched the exposed part of my back, sending goose pimples over my bare skin.

"What's up?" he asked.

"Did you hear about Douglas's boat?"

"Yeah, he told me. Sucks for him."

"Did he say anything else?" I asked.

Gunnar walked to the refrigerator. "Just that he doesn't know how long it'll take to get a replacement. Do you want a Coke Zero?"

"Yes, please." I had told him it was my drink of choice and was happy he'd remembered and didn't suggest a beer. The taste hadn't grown on me, and I didn't want to blur tonight's memories with alcohol. I was looking for subtle changes in Gunnar's behavior, but he seemed to have forgotten Douglas's comment that had triggered the drama by the runestones. "I hope no more bad luck comes out of that night."

Gunnar wandered over, holding the little glass bottle of Coke Zero. "Oh, I don't know. I thought it was a pretty good night," he said, giving me the soda and a long kiss on the mouth.

My shoulders slacked. It felt like nothing had changed.

"Me too," I whispered.

I'd been leaning against a set of drawers, and Gunnar lifted me onto the counter, so our heights became more evenly matched. I put down the Coke, and our mouths smashed into each other again—deep, hungry kisses where I instinctively ran my hands through his hair. I arched my back as his lips trailed down my neck. The feel of him—solid muscle and soft tissue—was better than my wildest imagination. He stood between my legs, hiking the maxi skirt to my knees, and I moaned when his hand slid up my thigh. We resumed kissing, our tongues half in and half out like we couldn't get enough of each other. I wrapped my legs around his waist and could feel his erection. I hadn't expected it so soon, but it sent my blood surging, excited that I had this effect on him.

Then I remembered where we were. If something extraordinary was going to happen, I didn't want it to be here, wedged between the olive oil and balsamic vinegar.

I moved away and whispered, "We should make dinner."

He groaned a little, but we extricated ourselves from each other. It was hard to concentrate on food prep, but Gunnar had already seasoned and shaped the meat into patties. When he went outside to grill, I cut the lettuce, tomatoes, and onions for garnish. Rummaging around the Eastons' fridge and cabinets for condiments, plates, and utensils, I was struck by how systematic and uncluttered the layout was. Mormor got upset whenever Linn and I tried to organize her kitchen, returning a pan or tool to its original, nonsensical spot, so we gave up. Granted, there were decades' worth of objects at our house and the Eastons had only been in theirs for a few months, but I liked the idea of starting with a blank slate, of being able to fashion a space as one wished.

I set everything up on one of the smaller outdoor coffee tables, grouping the chair cushions on the flagstone for ground-level seating, hoping to create a more relaxed, youthful vibe. Gunnar returned with the platter of charred burgers, cheesy and plain. He'd toasted the buns for that "straight-off-the-grill" effect.

"Mmm. This looks so good," I said, reshuffling bottles and containers to make room for the serving dish.

"So does this table."

"Everything looks amazing here," I said. "You have the most Instagram-worthy house in the archipelago—not that I would ever take a picture or post anything—but it's a dream."

"Thanks. My mom did a good job with it," he said, sitting on a cushion at the other side of the table. Leia growled possessively at me and scuttled over to him. "I'm way more into this house than I thought I'd be."

"I thought you would've been back in New York by now," I teased.

"I'll have you know that I've been doing some research, and since I have a Swedish mother, I get automatic citizenship, so who's the hater now?"

I laughed. "Well, my dad told me I could get dual citizenship through him, so I guess we're even."

"Cool. I would still have to apply for it, but that's just a formality," Gunnar said. "And get this—as a Swedish citizen, I wouldn't have to pay university tuition! I'd be *saving* Wes money."

"That's much more generous than I thought. I figured

you'd have to pay something, since you're a foreign Swede."

"Nope."

"When are you gonna to tell them?"

"Our return ticket is on August 15, so sometime before then, I guess?"

Two weeks from now. I had only fifteen more days to hang out with Gunnar if his parents didn't give him their approval.

"And you're sure about this?" I asked.

"Yes. New student orientation is August 25, and I don't want to be there," he said, adamant. "I need another year to regroup."

"Okay, I just want to make sure you understand what you'd be getting yourself into. It's a new language and people. The cold and darkness, it's a big commitment—" I caught myself, thinking immediately, *Wrong word. Weird connotations.* "I mean, um, transition."

"How is that any different from you going to the US?"

I thought back to my latest email correspondence with J.G. We had finally agreed on a definitive date for me to visit. "I guess you're right," I said, shrugging. "But the US is more forgiving than Sweden. You guys are friendlier."

Gunnar leaned back and looked at me. "Not if you're gonna eat a burger with a knife and fork."

"What?" I asked, the fork inches from my mouth.

"You have to eat a burger whole. With both hands."

"It'll get messy and fall all over the place!"

Gunnar chuckled. "Remember what I said when you're at some dive and people look at you strangely."

"My dad lives in Miami. I'm sure they're much more sophisticated."

"Not where burgers are concerned!"

I threw my napkin at him. He caught it, and we continued

          A Norn in Bloom

the jokes before switching to more serious talk about our high school experiences. Gunnar described Putnam Prep as a place of faux-woke snobs ("climate activists who flew private"), but he was part of a pack that had known each other since kindergarten and was worried about how college would affect their friendship. Listening to him made me realize how much my fear of rejection had prevented me from making friends. Gunnar and I were much more open with each other now, but there were still things I kept hidden.

By the time dessert (strawberries with vanilla ice cream) was over, Leia was sleeping under the table, and I had taken her place on the cushion next to Gunnar, picking up where we had left off. A lot of rubbing and groping sweetened our kisses, but I wasn't ready to go further. We fell asleep on one of the chaise lounges, under the predawn, ombre sky, with two fleece blankets warming us in the cool air.

Hours later, the intensity of the new day's sun glowed like a heat lamp on my face. I opened my eyes and reached under the chaise lounge for my iPhone. 5:41—and three texts from my mother.

Where are you?

When are you coming home?

Please call me!

I disentangled my leg from Gunnar's and tried to roll off quietly, but he felt my body shift and woke up.

"Where are you going?" he mumbled.

"Home. Work," I said, reaching for my bra. "My mom's wondering where I am."

"You should have told her you were coming here. Our parents know each other. I'm sure she would have been cool with it."

"I didn't expect to be out all night," I lied, clasping my bra from the front and marveling at how Gunnar was so confident of his appropriateness. He would never understand why my mother was suspicious of his motives. Not so long ago, I hadn't been too impressed by him either. What a difference a few weeks made.

"Stay," Gunnar said, thumbing the small of my back.

I closed my eyes, isolating the swoony sensation in my stomach. I wanted to stay. I wanted to lay next to Gunnar and watch the sun dance across the sky. I wanted to hear the birds call and sing to each other, but my mother's text had tarnished the moment.

"You only want me to help you clean up," I teased, trying to demystify my emotions.

"A little longer . . . please," he said, wrapping his arm around my waist.

The flush of excitement spreading through my body was almost overpowering. But I couldn't get the sound of Linn's voice out of my head.

I took Gunnar's hand and kissed it. "Next time. I promise."

Linn was sitting in the kitchen again when I returned to the house. But this time, she was awake and alert, making me think she had never gone to bed.

"Were you at Gunnar's?" she asked.

"Yes," I replied. "Sorry I didn't say anything."

"Are you using protection?"

"Mamma!"

"I mean it. We haven't had this discussion before. But if you're having sex, use double or triple protection. Otherwise, you'll end up like—"

"Like what?" I shot back. "Like you? Stuck with a child like me? Why do you think I barely go out? Why do you think I barely drink? Why do you think I've never had sex?" My voice faltered, but I forced myself to continue. "Because I don't want to end up like you."

21

LINN

I made good on my plan and avoided Camilla for two consecutive weeks. She tried to reschedule her massages several times, but I told her I was fully booked. This past Tuesday hadn't been a lie either. I'd spent hours at Holmgren's, from open to close, intent on righting the mess of a ship the store had become. It was like a client who had waited too long to get a spa treatment; the place needed a makeover from top to bottom.

Zoë knew the procedures inside and out, but the rest of the staff—teenagers with no sense of urgency—tried my patience. It took them forever to unload boxes from a pallet delivery, and one kid didn't understand placing the "oldest" items—i.e., the ones that expired soonest—in the front. Another part-timer who worked the register fumbled to replace the receipt paper roll, and the affected customer had been on the brink of walking out the door before I came to the rescue.

Most bafflingly, Agnes seemed to have buried her head in the sand. When I asked to see the accounting statements from the last three months, she was noncommittal and switched to an unrelated topic. A part of me wondered if her cognitive ability had slowed, but I knew my mother was pin-sharp. She had been in top form at her birthday breakfast. No, Holmgren's had become unwieldy and overwhelming. My mother could no longer handle the store on her own.

I realized I'd have to intervene, or we would all be in dire straits. Reducing those private massages had suddenly become a necessity, not a lie. I made that decision after wrapping up my last appointment at Nornö Hotel a few days later. Once peak season was over, I'd have ample time to take a more active role at Holmgren's. Agnes had bridged those years when I'd been too selfish and immature to care for Zoë properly; it was my turn to look after her and preserve the Holmgren legacy. I'd been too distracted by Camilla, Wes, and Zoë's relationship with Gunnar.

The dirty towels I bundled and threw down the laundry chute underscored how far removed the Eastons were from my world. They lived in a bubble and couldn't relate to the duties and responsibilities of ordinary people. I had to distance myself from them and prioritize Holmgren's. And Zoë . . . Gunnar would leave soon, and I hoped she'd understand that I had only been trying to protect her.

Having committed to this new direction, I felt stronger and more focused. But on my way out, I came face-to-face with the last person I expected to see waiting in the spa wing at Nornö Hotel: Camilla.

"Oh, Camilla!" I said. "You startled me."

"I'm sorry," she answered with an embarrassed smile.

"Unfortunately, the spa's closed. You can call tomorrow morning at eight if you want to make an appointment—"

"That's not why I'm here. I wanted to talk to you."

She looked tired, dressed in a man's washed-out button-down, and had purplish half-moons under her eyes. Something was amiss, and my instinct for self-preservation went on high alert.

"Really? About what?" I asked, feigning ignorance.

"I know why you've been avoiding me," Camilla said.

"I haven't been avoiding you," I hedged.

"Yes, you have!" Camilla insisted. "And it's perfectly understandable."

"I don't understand what you're referring to—" Wild thoughts ran through my head, but I continued stonewalling.

"It's because of our kids. Gunnar and Zoë."

Her announcement startled me. Zoë's relationship with Gunnar was problematic, but I had expected Camilla to bring up Wes. "What about them?"

"They've been seeing each other."

"I think they've hung out a few times."

"It's been more than just a few times."

My pulse skyrocketed. Had Zoë done something indiscreet and put herself in a compromising situation? "Camilla, what are you getting at?"

Her eyes flickered around the room. "Can we talk in private?"

"Don't worry. There's no one else here."

"Zoë has convinced Gunnar to ditch college and stay in Sweden!" It came out high-pitched and hurried.

After a moment, I heaved a sigh of relief. "Is that it?"

Camilla threw up her hands in frustration. "What do you mean, 'is that it?' I think it's bad enough! This morning, he told us he wanted to spend a gap year in Stockholm or Nornö—I don't know! All I know is that he doesn't want to report to his college as scheduled, and Zoë put the idea in his head."

"How do you know that?"

"Because he told us she would help him sign up for classes at Stockholm University! He would have never come up with a crazy plan like that on his own, not when so much of his future is at stake!"

My God! What was Zoë doing by encouraging Gunnar to stay?

Under normal circumstances, I wouldn't think his gap year idea was foolish. He was an emerging adult, entitled to express his wants and explore other possibilities without fearing blowback from his parents. But I'd learned from observing the Eastons that wealthy Americans believed in micromanaging their kids. Ironically, on this point, Camilla and I were in agreement. I wanted Gunnar—and the Eastons—to leave Nornö. I needed time and space for the problem with Wes to fade and hopefully, we could all move on by next summer.

"Let's sit," I said, leading Camilla to the sofa. "Gunnar's probably just a little curious. I'm sure it'll blow over."

"He's only curious because your daughter's in the picture!"

"I understand your shock and disappointment, but I don't think Zoë could have influenced Gunnar if he wasn't already having doubts."

"He can't think straight because he's young and in lust!"

Camilla made it sound like Zoë—my innocent, level-headed Zoë—was some temptress who had trapped her son. Although I wanted him gone, I wouldn't let that comment go unanswered. "Gunnar is the one who pursued Zoë, not the reverse."

"She has to talk him out of it," Camilla pleaded. "Tell him he'd be making a big mistake." Wringing her hands in her lap, she added, "There's nothing for him here."

I arched an eyebrow. "What is that supposed to mean?"

"Look, Gunnar's had a different type of upbringing." Camilla's voice suddenly hardened. "Big things are expected of him."

Her anxious demeanor had turned into steely arrogance. In that instant, I saw the Eastons' true colors, asserting their Manhattan superiority against lowly Nornö.

"Here in Nornö, we expect 'big things' of our kids, too, as

long as they're happy, and Zoë has done fine."

"Even you said you weren't sure if staying here was right for her."

"For other reasons. Never her drive or ambition."

"Linn, let me repeat myself. Gunnar cannot take a gap year and stay here. Wes and I went to considerable lengths to get him where he is today. We won't let him throw it all away for a summer fling!"

"Stop talking about my daughter like that!" I said, stabbing the air with my index finger.

"C'mon, you must see they come from two completely different worlds!"

"Are you saying that because she's not blonde and blue-eyed?"

"What are you implying? That I'm racist?"

I shrugged. "Would you be saying these things if Zoë looked more like you and didn't come from a little island in—what was it you said again? 'The middle of nowhere?'"

"That has nothing to do with it, and you know it. I simply don't want Gunnar getting sidetracked. We're grooming him for the family business. We have properties and investments in New York. Social and philanthropic obligations. Gunnar is a part of all that, whether he likes it or not. Zoë wouldn't understand."

I listened to Camilla in complete stupefaction. She spoke like a haughty character from a Victorian period drama, declaring that Zoë wasn't good enough for her little prince.

She had gone too far. I stood, hands on my hips.

"Why do you and Wes think you're so much better than the rest of us? Is it your money? Your ability to build a mansion on a cliff? Pfft! I feel sorry for Gunnar. I don't blame him for wanting to get away from you both!"

"As though your daughter isn't trying to get away from you?" Camilla retorted. "She's planning on going to Florida to live with her father for a few months! How do you feel about that? That's what makes this whole thing so absurd. She's not even going to be here but is determined to keep Gunnar in her clutches for as long as possible!"

"That's ridiculous! Zoë's not in contact with her father!" *She doesn't even know who he is.*

"Are you sure about that?" Camilla asked.

I didn't know what to say. Florida? My mouth became paralyzed, a speechless oval.

Camilla caught the confusion on my face.

"Unlike you and your daughter, my son and I *do* talk to each other," she sneered. "Deep down, you know I'm right about them. I trust you'll speak to Zoë and tell her to leave Gunnar alone."

I watched Camilla stride out the frosted-glass door etched with a silhouette of the Nornir runestones. My head spun from her accusations; my heart ready to explode. After a few seconds, I stormed after her.

"Hey, Camilla!" I shouted down the passageway.

She was nearly at the other end of the hall but stopped and turned around.

"I wouldn't be so cocky if I were you." My voice boomed in the empty corridor. "Especially when it comes to your husband."

I ran back inside the spa and locked the door. Every atom in my body was on fire, so I poured myself a glass of water from the cooler. It was so cold, I got a brain freeze, but the pressure squeezing my temples roused me to action. I had to find Zoë. I had to get to the bottom of Camilla's startling claims. J.G. alive? How had that come about? Was it even true? Or had Zoë, who was perpetually ashamed of her birth story, manufactured this lie to save face with Gunnar?

To avoid running into Camilla again, I left the hotel from the employee exit and went directly to Nornö Adventures. I asked Christer if Gunnar was working or if he and Zoë had taken any kayaks for a tour. *No. No.* I checked every boutique and restaurant on the way home, but there was no sign of them. Zoë's bike wasn't in the yard, so I did something I swore I would never do.

I marched to the attic, opened the door to Zoë's room, and began snooping.

Her room was in a decent state of messiness—an unmade bed and empty cans of Coke Zero—but her laptop sat neatly on the desk. I flipped it open and pressed a few keys, but of course, it was password protected. Zoë was a pro; she would never use her birthday or an obvious combination of numbers, so there was no point in trying. I closed the computer and riffled through her papers. Old invitations to graduation parties. Her final grades. A notice to pick up a package at the Nornö post office. A printed flight itinerary to Miami, Florida, departing September 7.

I stared at the document, feeling like I had been punched in the gut. So, it was true. Camilla wasn't misinformed. Zoë *had* found her father.

What the hell was going on? How long had Zoë known of his existence? Why hadn't she told me? Did my daughter hate me so much that she was willing to flee and live, effectively, with a stranger?

Not if I had anything to say about it.

Pacing around the room, I tried putting myself in the mind of an eighteen-year-old, reconstructing the scene. Zoë had finished working a short time ago, so she couldn't have made it too far. Her Holmgren polo shirt and jeans were on the floor in front of an open drawer. The drawer where she kept her underwear, bras, and bathing suits.

The beach. Zoë was very likely at Brunnsbad Beach.

I hurried out of the house and grabbed one of the old bikes, pedaling furiously in the direction of Brunnsbad. Discarding it next to the access point, I took off my sneakers and started walking. At this time of the evening, the beach had emptied. Ferries took day visitors back to Stockholm, and Nornö families were home making dinner. Couples and campers were the only ones left. Clumps of dead eelgrass and broken mussel shells had collected at the water's edge, a latticework blackening the shoreline. I waded carefully through the beachfront debris with my bare feet until I found them cuddling underneath a huge blanket, Zoë's head on Gunnar's shoulder, her ringlets grazing his jawline. From a distance, they looked beautiful and flawless, oblivious to the consequences of their behavior.

"Zoë! Zoë!" I shouted, running as grains of sand pelted my legs.

She turned her head and leaped up.

I was astonished. My daughter, who remained impressionable and unspoiled in my mind, was clad in only a string bikini I had never seen before. I didn't want to think about what could have happened underneath that blanket.

"Mamma! What are you doing here?" she asked, horrified.

"It's time for you to go home," I told her.

"Mamma, please!" Zoë wailed.

"I want you to leave! And you, too, Gunnar. Your mother is looking for you."

"Mamma, are you drunk?"

I couldn't help releasing a loud cackle. When I finally

assumed the role of a responsible parent, she thought I was under the influence.

"I've never been soberer in my life," I said. "C'mon, let's go."

"You can't make me!" Zoë protested, trying desperately to sound like an adult but whining like a kid.

"Get your things and get going! I'm not leaving unless you come with me." I crossed my arms and began tapping my foot.

Gunnar, who had hung back like a schoolboy shipwrecked on a desert island, finally scrambled to his feet. "I don't know what's going on, Linn, but I'm sorry, whatever it is."

Shaking my head vehemently, I said, "Gunnar, I think you know *exactly* what's going on. Please go home to your parents and back to New York."

At least he had the decency not to respond. Instead, he folded the blanket and towels and gathered their garbage. I watched Zoë bite down on her lower lip—an old childhood habit to keep from breaking into sobs—but tears streamed down her face. She put on her shorts and T-shirt, avoiding my gaze. When they had packed up everything, Zoë and Gunnar shared a lingering hug and slowly walked off in opposite directions.

22

ZOË

I had never been so humiliated in my entire life. At first, the shock of seeing my mother so enraged infuriated me, but I became frightened when I realized she wasn't drunk and crazy. Something potent had set her off. And the way she had spoken to Gunnar—I wanted to jump down a hole and never come out. I almost lost my balance biking back to the house, my vision fuzzy with tears. But once inside, I noticed how Linn shielded herself with a shawl, sanctimoniously wrapping it around her shoulders like she bore no blame for the scene at the beach, and I wanted to vomit. Eighteen years of anger finally erupted from deep inside.

"You've ruined everything!" I screamed. "You can never act like a normal person, a normal *mother.* Your life is a mess, and you've done a pretty good job of fucking mine up too. You looked like a freak out there. And you know the weirdest part? I never told Gunnar the truth about you. I never told him you were a borderline alcoholic! I've never wanted to embarrass you. I've never wanted to be disloyal."

"I know I'm a mess, Zoë, but that has nothing to do with what just happened," she said.

I wasn't interested in her excuses anymore. They were just variations of the same old sob story and they'd lost their power. My mother acted on unchecked urges, suiting whatever emotional needs she had at that moment, rarely thinking of my feelings or desires.

"And what do you give me in return?" I continued. "Nothing but drama! You don't care about how your behavior affects me! I've just had to accept your bullshit." My breath came in shallow spurts, and I had to pause. "You know what, though? I'm done. Do you hear me? *Done.* I'm not taking it anymore!"

"Are you aware Gunnar used you as an excuse to tell his parents he wasn't going back to New York with them—or planning to start college?" she said, leapfrogging over everything I had communicated.

"Are you even listening to me?" I asked in disbelief.

"Camilla said you're screwing up her perfect son's life! 'Big things are expected of him,' she told me! That you and Gunnar come from 'different worlds,' and you're just a 'summer fling.' If you think I should have just let that go without defending you or getting you away from Gunnar, you're sorely mistaken about everything."

"Puh-leeze! Camilla and Wes should get off their high horses. They're fucked up too. His dad bought him a spot in college—without Gunnar's knowledge—and when it came out, the school dropped him. Why should they force him to go somewhere else? None of this is his fault. His parents refuse to admit they're the ones to blame. I can't help it if he likes it here—or if he likes me! He *sees* me! I'm here, but you don't see me!" I said, tearing up again.

Linn swooped in, wiping my face with her shawl. "But they're not good people. Even if Gunnar seems nice now, he's too much under the influence of his family. You'd never be able to trust him."

"But I like him so much!" I confessed. "He accepts me for who I am. I don't feel awkward with him like the other kids here. I've never had that before!"

"You don't need him or any of those stupid kids to feel good about yourself. You have so much going for you. Can't you see that?" she asked, massaging the crown of my head. It was a gesture that had soothed me as a kid, but I hadn't gotten physically close enough for her to do it in a long time.

I wanted to believe her, but the words were right out of a parenting handbook, advice that sounded good to the ear but had no real impact on a child's day-to-day life. They wouldn't stop the bullying or make the sting of inadequacy disappear. Gunnar had changed everything. What set me apart from everyone in Nornö had become something special. With him, I no longer felt self-conscious. I could finally be me.

My mother had caused the bulk of my hang-ups, yet she wanted to sabotage my newfound happiness. I closed my eyes, but the image of her tirade was imprinted in my mind. I saw Gunnar walking off and felt hot beads of fear multiplying above my lips. She would not escape blame for this the way she had gotten away with everything else.

I pushed her away from me. "This is all your fault! I will *never* forgive you for scaring him away."

She shrank back, stricken. "Zoë, that's not fair. I'm only trying to protect you."

"Give me a break! This thing with Gunnar is nothing compared to the shit you've put me through." I glared at her. "Are you satisfied? I have nothing now."

"Really?" she asked, narrowing her eyes to slits. "I thought you had your father. In Florida."

Suddenly, the room mutated like an exaggerated clip from one of my reality shows, with Linn standing stock-still and the camera panning to my open-mouthed face.

"My father?" I croaked out, unprepared for the direction this conversation was taking. I was supposed to be the one initiating *that* talk. My mother wasn't supposed to have the upper hand.

"Yes. *Your father.* When were you planning on telling me about him?"

"What—how—"

"Camilla. You told Gunnar, and Gunnar told her. That boy can't keep his mouth shut! It's inexcusable! How dare they know something this important before me and then throw it in my face? It's about my life, too—why didn't you tell me?" she raged.

"Because you've never cared!" I shouted back. "You made no effort whatsoever to figure out who he was, where he lived, or if he was still alive! Remember all those lies you told me when I was a kid? Well, you know what? It wasn't even that hard finding him. The clues were there if you were willing to look for them. But that would have taken precious time from your social life, partying, and whatever else you were doing while I was stuck here with Mormor and Morfar, wondering when you were coming home and why I didn't have a father. I didn't tell you because you didn't have the right to know!"

"How long have you known?" she asked.

"About a month."

"A month!"

"I learned how to lie and keep secrets from the best," I said triumphantly.

"I want to know everything. His name, address, telephone number—"

I shook my head.

"I forbid you to go to Florida and see him unless you give me that information. I want to talk to him."

"No! I don't have to give you anything. I'm eighteen and can do whatever I want without your permission."

"Not quite. This isn't your house—"

"It's not yours either," I said, turning my back on her and running upstairs to my room. I locked the door, securing it with the sliding latch and the skeleton key, and belly-flopped onto my bed. Soon after, I heard a knock on my door.

"Zoë, please let me in," my mother said. "I'm sorry. I only want to talk."

Bang, bang.

"Please, I promise not to interfere. I only want to talk to J.G.—"

How disrespectful it sounded when she finally said his name. I could attach a face, words, a personality I was beginning to know and love—but my mother could barely talk about one night at Hultsfred. His name did not belong on her lips.

"Leave me alone!" I shrieked.

"Zoë, I'm begging you!" she said, hysteria building.

"LEAVE. ME. ALONE."

The other side of the door remained quiet, but I heard my mother's footsteps walking away a few minutes later.

I screamed into my pillow. Here it was: Skuld's wrath. Total humiliation. My punishment for pushing Douglas so close to the stone. Rolling over, I stared at the ceiling, thinking about Gunnar. I couldn't comprehend why he would betray my trust and tell Camilla about J.G. He *knew* it was my most intimate secret. Pangs of doubt consumed me again, and I feared my mother might be right. Maybe I was nothing more than a disposable summer hookup.

Rationally, I knew it was too soon for me to be in love with Gunnar, but our compressed time together in Nornö had magnified every moment, convincing me it might be possible. It was all there—the sharing of uncomfortable truths we hadn't told anyone else, the discovery of similarities that shattered our preconceived notions of each other. To seal the connection, I had been thinking about losing my virginity to him. I had come close that night at his house, but he knew I had never been with anyone. There was no pressure, but our physical chemistry ignited temptations I was finding harder and harder to resist.

Even if Gunnar *had* slipped up, that didn't give my mother the right to ambush us at the beach and lash out at him. I suspected Wes and Camilla wouldn't let him stay in Sweden now, which meant we only had one more week together. Seven more days before they shipped him back to New York. Desperate, I banged out a deliberately casual text, trying to conceal my anxiety:

> I'm so sorry about what happened earlier!
> My mom went totally berserk. But she
> knows about my father. Your mother told
> her?? I hope we can see each other again
> soon. xx

I got under the comforter and closed my eyes. Maybe Camilla's revelation about J.G. was a blessing in disguise. I'd been planning to tell Linn but hadn't found the courage. Everything was out in the open now, and I would no longer have to hide my intentions. Linn's behavior had become increasingly irrational lately, as though she could sense I was pulling away from her. Today's events had only accelerated that process.

I was tired of being the dutiful daughter, enabling and making excuses for my mother's volatility. If this latest meltdown was a sign of things to come, I had to break free before she dragged us both down with her.

I would leave Nornö to see my father, and none of Linn's selfish arguments would stop me. Pulling the duvet to my chin, I curled into a fetal position. Sleep came within minutes, but a few hours later, I was awakened by a banging on my door and the simultaneous ringing of my phone.

"Zoë! Please open the door!" my mother cried. "There's been an accident."

23

LINN

I sat slumped in a metal-and-upholstered chair, staring vacantly at the walls inside Saint Göran Hospital's ICU waiting room. The chair was stained and uncomfortable, the hospital was short-staffed due to the summer holidays, and a little kid kept coughing without covering his mouth. But the true source of my anguish lay on a lonely cot in the labyrinth of rooms and hallways I wasn't allowed to enter.

Since it was easier to be mad at Agnes than to tackle the torturing uncertainty, I became angrier and angrier with my mother for being so hard-headed. If only Agnes had allowed me to declutter the kitchen properly. If only she had taken my advice and sold the antique kitchen cabinet (dating back to Nils Holmgren's day!), she might not have hit her head, stumbling on the stubborn edge of the area rug that kept curling up. While I agreed that Agnes's arthritic leg also had something to do with it—she limped, and it lagged—there was little margin for error in that kitchen, thanks to Agnes's hoarding of Holmgren family junk.

I had heard her yelp in surprise, followed by a loud *thud* on the floor. Rushing to the kitchen, I'd found my mother in a heap near the cabinet, her good leg splayed in front, her arthritic leg at a ninety-degree angle in the back. She'd dismissed the fall as nothing, but it was clear she couldn't get up alone. I'd tried lifting her, but my petite frame couldn't support Agnes from the kitchen to the couch. At that point, I'd rushed to the attic, begging Zoë to open the door.

It had taken a few attempts, but she'd come out dazed enough to have momentarily forgotten our fight earlier. We'd carried Agnes to the roomy but frayed Josef Frank sofa and given her an ice pack. I was paranoid when it came to head injuries. There were too many tragic stories, from babies who had rolled off changing tables (this had been my major fear when Zoë was an infant) to the sudden death of actress Natasha Richardson after a seemingly minor ski accident. I'd wanted to evaluate Agnes for signs of a concussion and asked Zoë to make a pot of tea under the guise of watching TV together. We became oddly riveted by a documentary about the classic *Tarzan* movies. It was the kind of random but educational late-night-in-the-archipelago movie my father and I would've watched to relax. After my heated confrontation with Zoë, I welcomed the diversion.

"When was this filmed?" Agnes asked when an image of the actress who played Jane, Maureen O'Sullivan, appeared onscreen.

"The 1930s, I think," Zoë replied.

"Really?" Agnes said. "Look at that outfit. Her hips are bare. Pretty racy for that era, don't you think?"

Zoë chuckled. "Mormor, you sound like such a prude."

"Are they swimming naked?" she asked.

Zoë squinted, leaning forward. "I think you might be right!"

"Hmph," Agnes said and watched the rest of the documentary in silence. When it was over, she said clearly, "It hurts my ears and heart to hear the two of you fight."

Zoë pointed to me. "She started it."

Ashamed, I said, "I'm sorry, Mamma. I wish it weren't so, but Zoë knows why."

"You gave us a lot more grief than Zoë—and that was before you got pregnant," Agnes reminded me.

"Yes, I know," I whispered.

"So, tell me, Zoë—what's your father like?" Agnes asked. Zoë gasped. "I may have a limp, but I'm not deaf. Did you think I didn't hear what you two were fighting about?"

"Um, he's very nice," Zoë said. "He's a doctor in Florida now, near Miami."

Agnes smiled. "Your mom always said he was a nice guy." She paused and then let out a deep sigh. "Zoë, what happened between them was a quirk of fate. As you get older, you'll understand that things can happen for no logical reason. Sometimes the craziest, most unbelievable situations are 100 percent real and honest. You were a blessed surprise. Don't punish your mother by not telling her where the father of her child is."

"I'm not trying to punish her!" Zoë protested.

"Yes, you are, and it's understandable. You think Linn abandoned you. You feel like she didn't mother you enough."

I cleared my throat, shocked by her bluntness and the spectacle of hearing my failings as a mother aired for the second time in one night. I knew Agnes and Zoë were right, but I needed room to absorb their condemnation. I needed time to repent.

"Mamma, I think you're getting tired. We can talk about this more tomorrow," I said.

She raised her chin, speaking directly to me. "It's my fault too. Mine and your father's. You always seemed to be searching for something—even as a child—and we felt like we had failed you somehow, so when you told us you were pregnant, we wanted to do the right thing. There was no question we would love the baby, but we also wanted to give Zoë the attention and discipline we hadn't given you. You never got the chance to be Zoë's mother because Thomas and I never let you assume that role. We took over and let you live your life as before. It must have been so confusing—I'm not surprised you thought alcohol would make you feel better." Agnes shrugged slightly. "That was another failure on our part. We saw what was happening and knew you had certain tendencies, but we turned a blind eye and hoped you'd grow out of it." Her voice cracked. "I'm so sorry, dear daughter. So, so sorry."

I moved to the couch, sitting on the edge near my mother. "It's okay, Mamma. I'm sorry, too—about so many things. But I want you to rest. Close your eyes and rest. Don't worry about Zoë and me. We'll work this out. Find a way to—"

"Shhh," Agnes interrupted. "I want to sleep."

Carrying Agnes one flight of stairs to her bed would have been too difficult, so Zoë and I covered her with a blanket and stayed in the living room, sleeping in individual armchairs. Simba also kept watch, parking himself at the foot of the sofa.

I woke up when the sun was aflame, a burning, orange bulb above the horizon. The summer light always played tricks on me; it looked like it was 8:00, but it was only around 4:00. I checked on Agnes and tried to wake her with a light nudge. No reaction. Her body seemed to have gone limp. Putting my ear to Agnes's nostrils, I heard the inhales and exhales of breath. I shook her again, this time with more force, but she was still unresponsive.

"Zoë!" I shrieked.

"Mmm," Zoë murmured, straightening her folded legs

from the armchair.

"Zoë, please call 112! I think Mormor has lost consciousness!"

Zoë's eyes popped open, and she fumbled for her phone. After dialing the emergency number, she gave it to me, and I explained what had happened to the operator. *My mother. She fell. Last night. No, she didn't vomit. She was lucid, talking. I don't think she seemed confused.*

Twenty minutes later, a helicopter whirred overhead, pinwheeling waves on the water's surface before landing on our lawn. Nine years earlier, another chopper had descended onto our property to recover my father's body. I almost couldn't bear watching them take Agnes away, but she was still alive. Every breath gave us time, but I refused to stay in Nornö and wait for the morning ferry. I demanded to ride in the helicopter and accompany her to the hospital.

Now, Agnes had been back there for five hours, but no doctor came out to give me a status report. I sat and waited, preparing for the worst.

As a kid, you thought your parents would live forever, but after losing my father, I knew Agnes was on loan and could be taken from me anytime. I had a daughter, but Zoë hated me and wanted to live with her father. Without Agnes, I would have no one.

Sobbing into my hands, I wondered how my life had come to this.

Soon after I wiped away my tears, I heard the word "Mamma" and looked up. Zoë stood there, flanked by Evalina and Kurt Bohlander. They had driven their boat from Nornö to Norr Mälarstrand in Stockholm so Zoë could be with Agnes and me. I had never been so happy to see the Bohlanders in my life. I gave them a sincere hug of gratitude.

"How is she?" Kurt asked.

"I don't know yet. The doctors are doing a CT scan," I said, holding back tears. "I should have called 112 right away. I waited too long. She seemed fine, but I should have known her condition could change on a dime. She just turned sixty-five, but I could tell she wasn't as strong as before—"

Zoë rubbed my shoulder. "I thought she was going to be fine too. We sat up with her, watching TV . . ." Her voice trailed off.

"Are you hungry?" Evalina asked. "We can go to the café and get coffee and sandwiches, if you'd like."

"Yes, please. I'm starving and can't see straight anymore," I said.

"Everyone in Nornö is thinking about Agnes and sending strength," Kurt said.

I gave him a weak smile. "I know you all love Agnes, and it means so much. Thank you."

When the Bohlanders left the waiting room, I sat again. Zoë grabbed the seat next to me and, after some hesitation, took out her iPhone.

"His name is Jean-Gabriel Latour," she said.

I turned to her, confused.

"My father. 'J.G.' stands for Jean-Gabriel. Isn't that a beautiful name?"

I nodded slowly.

"And he's a primary care physician, not a specialist. He likes being able to help as many people as possible with different medical issues."

"That's an admirable goal," I said.

"He went to med school after the Army. He did go to Afghanistan and Iraq—you weren't completely off about that—but he doesn't like going into detail about it."

I remembered my concerns about J.G. becoming a soldier. I couldn't imagine the carnage he must have experienced.

"What did he say when you told him you were his daughter?" I asked.

"We've only emailed each other and haven't spoken yet, but he was thrilled and excited—but also sad and sorry because he never knew I existed. He confirmed you guys never exchanged any info."

"In hindsight, I don't know why we didn't do that."

"Why didn't you ever try to find him?" Zoë asked.

I gave a half shrug. "I don't know. I guess I didn't think it would have made any difference. He was so far away." That was partly true, but I had to be honest with Zoë to move forward. "And I was scared."

Zoë knitted her brows. "Scared of what?"

"Aside from being pregnant at nineteen?" I asked wryly.

"Obviously you were scared about that. I get it. But what else? What's been stopping you all these years?"

Sighing, I rubbed the back of my neck. "Well, I was scared about how he would take the news. Suppose he blamed me for what happened?" I asked, recalling how hot-headed and impulsive I'd been that night. "We were both so young, and I barely knew him. What if he wasn't like I remembered? Maybe Hultsfred was a fluke, and the real J.G. was a disappointment. What if his life had no place for you? I thought it would be better to keep things within our family so you wouldn't get hurt."

"I'd say your strategy had the opposite effect."

"I know. That was the biggest mistake of my life."

"But you do believe that he had a right to know?"

"Yes, but as the years passed and things got messier with my personal life, I became ashamed. I was ashamed of what I had become—to you, to my parents. The partying—" I sighed heavily. "There was something fundamentally good about J.G. I didn't feel like I measured up, so what was the point of searching for him?"

"For *me*," Zoë said. "It would have been for me. Dead or alive, it would have given me—us—some closure."

I had robbed her of that. I'd been selfish and only thought about how finding J.G. would affect me.

"I know," I whispered. "Can you ever forgive me?"

"I'm trying, Mamma. I really, really am."

"I guess that's all I can ask for. But you were taking a huge risk, contacting him on your own. I wished we could have discussed it and done it together."

"I think it was better this way."

"Maybe. You *are* eighteen, and I probably couldn't have stopped you, even if I'd tried."

"I have half your genes. I can be stubborn when necessary."

Stroking Zoë's cheek, I said, "But if I had a chance to do it again, I would get his first and last name, address, and telephone number."

She laughed softly. "So, you would do it again?"

"For you? Absolutely."

"You don't think I've ruined your life?"

"Zoë, you *saved* me. Without you, who knows how I would have ended up? You've given my life purpose and shown me what love and responsibility means. I've learned so much from you, but I still have some issues I need to sort out."

"Mamma, maybe you should go talk to someone—a professional. They might be able to help you with the things you've been keeping inside."

I swallowed and felt the lump in my throat. "I know. I promise I'm going to keep trying to do better." Snuggling closer to her, I said, "I love you so much."

"I love you too."

How I'd longed to hear her say those words! No longer an impressionable child, Zoë saw my flaws but was still willing to give me a chance. I wouldn't gamble with our relationship again. We sat there, gently rocking sideways until I couldn't wait anymore.

"I'm dying of curiosity! Do you have any pictures of him?"

24

I tapped the album in my photos entitled "Brickell," presenting my mother with a visual narrative of the man she hadn't seen in nineteen years. Sliding through the images, I mixed my own observations with information J.G. had given me. Linn made all the right comments, fawning over his baby picture and remarking on how nice his family seemed, but it was difficult for me to read her emotions. It took the Army portrait for her to have a visceral reaction.

"His eyes look so sad!" she exclaimed. "That's not how I remember him." Pinching the screen, she zoomed in on the photograph. "He was so happy and funny when we met."

"I think those were difficult years, but keep going," I said. "They get better again."

When she came to the last photo of J.G., the one of him smiling on the boardwalk next to his bike, she lingered on it and smiled back, as though they were having a private conversation. "He's gotten so handsome. He was twenty-one and boyishly cute when we met. He had so much positive energy—it was refreshing. It looks like life turned out well in the end. Is he—"

"No, he's not married. Never been, and he didn't mention being in a relationship. No kids either. I'm his only child— that he knows of, ha."

"Zoë, that's not funny!"

"Sorry, I couldn't resist."

"But that does make things easier for you. You can step into his life without worrying about other people."

"I do feel like he's welcomed me with open arms."

She smiled feebly and ducked her head, but her eyes were shiny, fighting back the tears.

"Mamma, what is it?"

"Did he ask about me?" she asked.

"Yes, he did. He's mentioned you often and regrets that you guys never kept in touch." I debated showing my mother J.G.'s emails and the tender words he used to describe her but decided against it. I'd save them for another day. "He knows things were hard because you were so young, having this huge responsibility for the last eighteen years. It's a little unfair he gets to step in when the hardest part is over!"

"Right? So unfair," she replied, and we laughed, lightening the mood.

Kurt and Evalina returned with cups of coffee and sandwiches. We ate while the Bohlanders sat nearby for moral support. A doctor finally emerged at noon.

"Agnes Holmgren's family?" he asked.

Linn and I stood abruptly. Dressed in scrubs and navy Crocs, the doctor was medium height, with round glasses and a salt-and-pepper Caesar haircut.

"Sven Sibelius, chief physician in neurosurgery," he said.

The seniority of his title frightened me. Mormor's condition must have been serious to require his expertise.

"How is my mother?" Linn asked.

"A blood vessel near the surface of Agnes's brain burst, and she suffered something called an acute subdural hematoma," he explained. "Blood built up between the brain and the outer lining, causing pressure. This subdural bleeding compressed her brain, and that's why she lost consciousness."

"But we kept an eye on her, and she seemed better. She was talking, drinking tea—" Linn said.

"Fairly common falls—even at a low-level height—can lead to brain injuries in older people," Dr. Sibelius said.

"Is she awake?" I asked.

Dr. Sibelius shook his head. "She's sedated. We had to perform surgery right away to drain the hematoma and control the bleeding. The good news is that we didn't need to do a craniotomy, where we would have had to remove a portion of her skull—"

"I feel like I'm going to be sick," Linn muttered.

"—but Agnes's hematoma was smaller than one centimeter in diameter, so I was able to drill a small hole into her skull and insert a rubber tube to drain the blood," Dr. Sibelius continued.

Removing her skull. Draining a hole. Both procedures sounded macabre.

"What happens next?" I asked.

"She's still in recovery, and we put her on medication to prevent a seizure that could cause another subdural hematoma, so we'll keep monitoring her condition closely," Dr. Sibelius said.

"What—what's her prognosis?" Linn asked.

It was the question haunting the room like an evil norn, the one neither of us had dared to voice until now.

"Recovery times vary greatly between individuals," he said. "The speed depends on the damage to the brain, but since you got her to the hospital relatively fast and we were able to avoid a craniotomy, her odds are better than most."

"Oh, thank God!" Linn cried.

"But don't get your hopes up too high. The recovery process is unpredictable. We have to take it day by day. I might have to go in and repeat the procedure—"

Listening to Dr. Sibelius, I hoped my father wasn't this impersonal. "When can we see her?" I asked.

"You can see her for a few minutes now," Dr. Sibelius said.

We followed him through the glass doors to the ICU. Mormor was alone in a room alongside two other empty beds. Her skull was bandaged, and I wondered if the doctors had shaved her beautiful head of gray hair. Tubes and chords spiraled from machines and sockets, snaking out her arms and mouth. The equipment and fluorescent lighting transformed the space into a soulless mechanical chamber. Still, Mormor was in one of the beds opposite a window. Sunlight streamed in, and when she woke up, she could gaze at the trees and colorful apartment buildings outside.

Linn and I padded to either side of the bed, taking each of Agnes's hands in our own.

"Mamma, it's Linn and Zoë," my mother whispered. "You've had surgery, but everything will be fine."

I stroked Mormor's palm. Her hand was soft but cold. "You have the best doctor looking after you, Mormor. They'll take good care of you here."

"We love you so much," Linn said, her voice breaking.

"And we'll be right here with you," I added.

But Dr. Sibelius ushered us out after five minutes. Back in the waiting room, we decided Linn would stay at Alicia's place in the city, and I would go back to Nornö with the Bohlanders. Someone had to take care of the store, and I knew it would be what Mormor wanted. Things may have reached a standstill for our family, but life in Nornö continued uninterrupted.

Evalina and Kurt were sympathetic but kept the small talk to a minimum. However, their presence spoke volumes. At times like these, I appreciated Nornö's cool-headed character.

The brief but meaningful conversations. The respect for tradition and the community spirit rallying around my family. I promised to keep them updated, and Kurt offered to take me to Stockholm whenever needed. Their kindheartedness was a silver lining in this nightmare, but maybe they owed it to me.

I still believed their son, Douglas, had jinxed me. Whether I had pushed him or not, urinating on the Norns had set a chain of events in motion, resulting in devastating consequences. Nothing could convince me that a powerful force wasn't behind this tragedy. A hidden hand warned us of our hubris and inability to follow the basic rules of truth, love, and respect.

I walked through the sacred ground with the runestones and prayed for Mormor. I rubbed Skuld, asking her to watch out for the Holmgren family. Staring at the three Norns, I realized how gullible I'd been. I'd memorized the story of the doomed farmer, seen the Prophecy of Destruction on the runestone itself, but taken the warning literally. I'd assumed retribution would be bombastic, like getting struck by lightning or having your house burn down, but the Norns were wise, subtle entities, capable of both good and evil.

They seized upon that which mattered to you the most.

Simba lay on his doggie bed in the hallway when I returned home, listless and staring at the door. His favorite ball sat still in front of his nose.

"Hello there! Have you been sitting here the whole time?"

He looked up with sad eyes, and I bent to hug him. His golden coat, warm and soft, comforted me. But he whimpered in my arms, and I understood he was just as worried about

Mormor as I was.

The house was chillingly quiet without Mormor or Linn. Then again, we didn't do too many things together anymore, withdrawing as we did to our own private spaces after dinner. I had devalued real human connection, devouring trivial Instagram posts and Snapchat stories, unrealistic reality shows, or the latest must-see Netflix series. The pyramid of board games and rows of old DVDs in our living room sat untouched, gathering dust. Mormor wasn't one of those high-maintenance grandparents who demanded constant attention or asked tons of questions, so I could get by with casual hugs and hellos—and she was too easygoing to chastise me for it. Things would change. If Mormor got through this intact, I would give her the time and attention she deserved. I would stop being so preoccupied and self-centered.

"Come on, Simba. Let me fix you some food."

I poured a generous heap of dry kibble into Simba's bowl and thought of Morfar. Somehow, he'd known I would need the dog's company. Tears welled up in my eyes. Morfar was gone, and now Mormor was teetering between life and death.

I saw her before me, lying helpless in the hospital. We couldn't lose her. Mormor was the glue that held our chaotic, fragile world together.

Simba fell asleep after eating, and I took my laptop to the dock. I knew what I had to do but put it off a bit longer, watching the fleet of small Optimist dinghies drifting in the distance—kids at sailing camp, struggling with the tiller and mainsheet as I had. I vividly remembered the terrifying moment when my boat had capsized and the chilly water had splashed up my nose. My life vest had kept me afloat, but that initial jolt of fear and helplessness had invaded my dreams for months, and I would wake up gasping for air. I hadn't liked sailing camp, but now I felt only gratitude for how this Nornö tradition linked me to past and present generations.

I opened the laptop and clicked on my email. I had written to J.G. a few days ago, thanking him for the plane ticket. He'd responded enthusiastically, expressing how excited he was to meet me and catch up on all the years we had missed. Keen to create memories together, he had sent me a long list of sightseeing and restaurant options so I could plan our itinerary. His kind, fatherly treatment still astounded me, surpassing even my best-case scenario when I'd contacted him a month ago. I couldn't believe only a month had passed—a period bracketed by joy and sadness.

With a heavy heart, I sent J.G. another email:

August 9, 2019

Dear Dad,

There's been an accident in the family. Mormor fell in the kitchen and hurt her head. She was hospitalized, and they discovered she had swelling in the brain. The doctor was able to drain the fluid, but she's recovering, and we don't know how long it will take for her to get better.

Unfortunately, I won't be able to come to Florida next month and meet you. My mother, Mormor, and Holmgren's need me here. Based on what I've come to know about you, I'm sure you'll understand that my little family in Nornö has to come first right now. Thank you for everything ♥.

Love,

Your daughter Zoë

Gunnar texted me in the evening: I just heard about Agnes. I'm so sorry. Are you back in Nornö?

Hours had passed, and he never answered the message I'd sent him last night. I appreciated that he seemed to care about Agnes but was upset he hadn't addressed what happened on the beach, so I only replied: Yes.

Gunnar:
On my way home from work. Can I stop
by?

Mentally exhausted, I wrote back: Okay.

I let Gunnar in and took him up to the attic. I would be the only one in the house for the next few days, and it felt the least lonely in my room. He asked polite questions about Agnes, but I could tell something else was on his mind. He sat hunched over, hands clasped, not quite making eye contact.

"Are you mad at me?" he asked finally.

"I'm—I'm disappointed," I said, choosing the high road over drama.

"I'm sorry my mother told Linn about your father. She betrayed my confidence—and yours. I feel terrible about it."

I wondered how much detail he had given Camilla. My origin story was raw and personal, not something to be passed around carelessly.

"Why'd you tell her in the first place?" I asked, raising my voice. "It was confidential. I trusted you!"

"I know, I know!" Gunnar raised his hands in surrender. "But I only told her about your father when she asked about your future plans. I wanted to prove there were alternate paths, that not everyone had to be programmed a certain way, but she had no right using it against Linn—or you. I don't know what came over her." He grunted softly, gazing at me. "I told you my parents were fucked up."

"That's a lame excuse."

He sighed. "I know, but I hope you can forgive me."

His apology sounded sincere, and I could feel my disappointment in him weakening, evaporating like sea mist. I studied the guilty expression on his face and remembered how kissing him felt, how the touch of his lips lit up my skin. But then I felt ashamed. With Mormor in the hospital, fighting for her life, such thoughts were inappropriate, and I closed my eyes for a few seconds, trying to delete them.

"It is what it is," I said at last. "Now that my mother knows about him, maybe something good might come out of it."

"I hope so."

We sat on my bed in strained silence. The closeness that had evolved between us, casually forged on the islet across the harbor, had been stolen. I wanted it back.

"So, are you staying or going?" I asked. Whether I liked it or not, Gunnar's actions—his choices—affected me. I needed to know where things stood.

"Going—but not because of my parents. As much as I wanted to spend more time in Sweden, it felt like I was running *from* something instead of *to* something. I'll give this new school a try, and if I hate it, I can transfer."

"That makes sense. I think you'll be fine wherever you end up, Gunnar."

"And you?"

"Staying. I want to help Mormor and the store."

"That's probably the right decision, with everything that's happened."

"I think so, too, but I hope I can come to the US sometime this year."

"Massachusetts and Florida are both on the East Coast. We could meet up someplace in the middle if you wanted," Gunnar suggested. His hand grazed my knuckles, as though afraid I might push him away.

Instead, I interlocked our fingers and said, "I'd like that very much—and we'll always have Nornö."

25

LINN

October 2019

Agnes returned to Nornö in mid-September. Although the subdural hematoma had responded well to the burr hole surgery, her recovery was slow-going. She was prescribed medications to help reduce swelling around the brain and needed rehabilitation. A few times a week, we took a boat to the mainland for physical therapy to help with muscle weakness and poor coordination (which benefited her arthritic leg) and occupational therapy to help with everyday tasks. Agnes also received regular brain scans to check if the hematoma had returned. But Zoë and I were always on the lookout for longer-lasting problems: mood swings, failure to concentrate, memory loss, seizures, and speech impairment. I was terrified my strong, self-sufficient mother would suffer mental deterioration.

But it was early days, and apart from fatigue, Agnes still had a sharp tongue and curious mind. We did crossword puzzles as a brain exercise, and she always completed them before me. Whatever the outcome, I was grateful my mother had survived this terrible ordeal, which had brought the three of us closer.

Life would be easier once we finalized the sale of Holmgren's. The owner of FoodDirekt had heard of Agnes's accident, along with rumors our store was in financial trouble. Like any astute businessperson, he pounced. Zoë and I had tried to persuade Agnes to hold out; Holmgren's was our family legacy. We had fresh ideas and could take out a bank loan to reinvigorate the business. But my mother was classic Agnes again, stubborn and iron-willed (this was how I knew the brain damage wasn't as severe as we'd feared). She'd disregarded our opinions and advice.

Nevertheless, Agnes surprised me with her rationale, confessing she no longer had the energy or desire to run Holmgren's, lamenting how it had been a burden for the past ten years— ever since my father passed away. A sense of duty and attachment to Nornö had motivated her to keep it going, but it was time to move on. "Go and live your lives," she urged. Agnes believed the store was holding Zoë and me back, and our chance had finally come to cut the cord.

She succeeded in raising the asking price, and once the proceeds were divided in three, we'd have the financial security to pursue new interests. If Agnes's progress continued, I might buy an apartment on the mainland. Alicia joked that we should move in together, but it was time for me to stand on my own two feet.

Camilla Easton had sent my mother a "get well soon" card. As I read the formulaic note, written in Swedish on thick personal stationery with Camilla's slanting script, I contemplated why she went to the trouble. But it fit Camilla's pattern of behavior—it was elegant, superficial, and the "right" thing to do. No one could accuse her of being indifferent. My mind was too weary—and unmoved—to respond, inundated as it was with doctors, treatments, and uncertainty. But I pitied Camilla, especially since Wes continued to humiliate her. After they'd left for New York, talk spread around the island that he had made a pass at Raquel, their part-time housekeeper. I didn't doubt the story's validity; it was Wes's M.O. I wondered if Camilla would stay with him. Would they have the nerve to come back to Nornö? Gunnar and Zoë were still in touch, and it seemed like he would be the one to develop a lasting attachment to the island and their house.

I finally deleted the photos of Wes from my phone. I didn't need reminders of that fateful night, and it wouldn't have given me satisfaction to hurt Camilla with them. She appeared so confident on the surface, but I had witnessed her desperation. I had tasted how cruel she could be as soon as her well-ordered Easton life came under threat. I suspected Camilla was aware of Wes's transgressions; perhaps they had an agreement, and it was no one else's business. But Camilla's self-respect had withered from all the trade-offs, which was the saddest part.

Zoë had kept the store running for the past two months, in addition to helping coordinate Agnes's doctors' appointments. She also got lots of medical advice from her father. J.G. had FaceTimed Zoë after she told him about Agnes's accident, empathizing with our powerlessness and anxiety. He became very engaged, talking to Dr. Sibelius and sending us articles about effective courses of treatment.

When I finally heard his voice again after all these years—albeit more mature and professional—it was like I was nineteen again and teleported back to Hultsfred. We began talking without Zoë present, but the conversations dwelled heavily on our daughter's childhood—which I couldn't fully describe without disclosing my problem with drinking. I had been scared to tell him, but my new therapist said I needed to confront my past honestly and with humility, so I chose to be open.

J.G. was compassionate, revealing his struggles with PTSD after so many years in combat. We made a pact to listen to each other without judgment, and for the first time, I felt like I could forge ahead with less guilt.

Agnes's condition and the sale of Holmgren's postponed any long-term planning, but we hoped to return to some semblance of normalcy by December.

Zoë and I were expecting a special visitor from Florida.

Acknowledgments

This book emerged like a patch of sunlight after a rainy day in the Stockholm archipelago, where my future husband took me for the first time when I was nineteen years old. Despite various phases and moves, our home by the sea has been the one constant in our lives, where traditions and respect for those who came before are firmly rooted. From this backdrop, an idea about family, belonging, and secrets emerged, and I realized the story I wanted to tell was intertwined with the region's rocks, forests, and beaches. Therefore, I would first like to thank my beloved, Christian Dahlberg, for introducing me to the charms and contrasts of this unique landscape. Your unwavering love and encouragement have always given me the space and freedom to write, and it seems only fitting that the book finally came together in the place that has come to mean so much to me. I would also like to thank three people who are no longer with us: my father-in-law, Ove Dahlberg, and Christian's grandparents, Sven and Sonja Dahlberg, for creating a family retreat that generations of Dahlbergs have been able to enjoy, including a Haitian American girl from New York.

This novel, incorporating elements of Swedish music festival culture and Norse mythology, would have been all over the place without the thorough research of scholars Jonas Bjälesjö and Karen Bek-Pedersen. Bjälesjö in *Rock 'n' Roll i Hultsfred: Ungdomar, Festival och Lokal Gemenskap* presents a detailed account of the legendary festival, providing the factual and visual basis for many scenes I dramatized. His generosity and readiness to supply me with an authentic festival program from Hultsfred 2000 was a godsend, opening creative pathways to weave a story of being young, wild, and carefree. Bek-Pedersen's *The Norns in Old Norse Mythology* is another fascinating study, giving me the framework to imagine a fictional Nornö and explore the paradoxical nature of these female deities. The runestones themselves are inspired by the Björketorp Runestones in Blekinge.

I want to thank my Swedish editor, Jennifer Lindström, for having faith in my work and Heléne Jensen, for helping me refine the Swedish context. For the English-language edition, I am grateful to Larissa Melo Pientowski for her editorial expertise. Saul Bottcher outdid himself with the cover art, capturing the essence of a young woman coming into her own. Words cannot thank you enough for working with me again. Huge thank yous to my first readers, my sister Dominique Anglade Neblung and friend-like-family, Kristen Donovan. Your enthusiasm and willingness to see my messy pages enabled me to share them without fear. Many thanks to those who checked in on me, had patience when I was glued to my computer, listened to my doubts, and shared my joy. My wonderful parents, Serge and Fredline Anglade, showered me with unconditional love and provided me with a solid foundation from which I could dare to dream. You are always with me—from afar and above.

I am filled with gratitude to the Swedish readers who embraced this story, originally published as *Sommaren på Nornö* (Norstedts, 2021). Their posts, reviews, and comments meant the world to this nervous author. The theme of "otherness"—externally or internally—resonated with many, particularly those whose experiences have been underrepresented among fictional narratives set in Sweden.

Finally, this novel is, in many ways, an ode to youth and parenthood. I would be lost without my children, Yasmine and

James, and I want to thank them for being an endless source of wonder, inspiration, and information. Your feedback, quirks, and insights infiltrated these pages and elevated the story. I love you both infinity to infinity!

About Me

I grew up in suburban New York and graduated from Columbia University. I've lived in Sweden since 1997 and divide my time between an apartment in Stockholm and a cottage in the archipelago that inspired this novel.

To keep up with my writing and future books, please visit jenniferdahlberg.com and sign up for my (spam-free) mailing list. You can also follow me on Instagram @jennifer.anglade. dahlberg.

Also by Jennifer Anglade Dahlberg

Lagging Indicators

What happens when your career is your entire identity and it's suddenly taken away from you?

It's October 2009 and thirty-five year-old Mia Lewis is an independent woman at the top of her game. Sharp, attractive and the only senior female executive at Atlas Capital, she survived Wall Street during the worst financial crisis in modern history. Devoted to her job, Mia always fights for what she thinks is best for the firm—until one false move ushers her spectacular downfall.

Disgraced and broke, she escapes to a crumbling cottage in upstate New York to repair her reputation and plot her comeback. Alone and threatened by lasting unemployment, she risks becoming what she has always feared: a failure. But a chance encounter with a handsome single dad ignites feelings and a sense of longing that Mia had intentionally buried.

As she begins to consider a new life—one away from the stress and excess of Wall Street—the past comes calling, jeopardizing her whole future.

Uptown and Down

In her dynamic debut novel, Jennifer Anglade Dahlberg explores the headstrong ambitions and fragile dreams of a couple on top—and their drive for success, which tests the limits of privilege, love, and friendship in the most provocative of ways . . .

Nora Deschamps is an editor at a chic women's fashion magazine. Her husband Jeff Montgomery owns an independent record label that's edging into a mega-bucks hip-hop phenomenon. Tracked as one of New York Magazine's "25 Most Exciting Couples Under Forty," Nora and Jeff appear to have it all. But their future is about to be shaken, by Nora's on-the-rise career that's taking an intimate toll on their lives, by a crime that Jeff is powerless to prevent, and ultimately by the secret of a long-ago indiscretion and the revenge that now threatens all they've strived to achieve.

From the uptown high-life to the downside of love, betrayal, and long-standing lies, Nora and Jeff must now fight harder than ever to learn the meaning of trust.